William C. Hazlitt, William Hazlitt

Sketches and Essays

and Winterslow - essays written there

William C. Hazlitt, William Hazlitt

Sketches and Essays
and Winterslow - essays written there

ISBN/EAN: 9783337255435

Printed in Europe, USA, Canada, Australia, Japan

Cover: Foto ©Andreas Hilbeck / pixelio.de

More available books at **www.hansebooks.com**

SKETCHES AND ESSAYS;

AND

WINTERSLOW

(ESSAYS WRITTEN THERE.)

BY

WILLIAM HAZLITT

A NEW EDITION,

BY

W. CAREW HAZLITT.

LONDON:

BELL & DALDY, YORK STREET, COVENT GARDEN.

1872.

PREFACE.

THE Papers contained in the following pages were first collected by the Author's son, in two volumes, in the years 1839* and 1850† respectively. They are now reproduced without any alteration. I have introduced occasional notes, where they seemed to be necessary, and the names of persons, indicated only by initials in the former editions, have been printed in full.

W. C. H.

KENSINGTON, *September* 1, 1872.

---

* *Sketches and Essays.* By William Hazlitt. Now first Collected by his Son, 1839. A Second Edition called *Men and Manners, Essays by William Hazlitt*, appeared in 1852.

† *Winterslow; Essays and Characters written There.* By William Hazlitt. Collected by his Son, 1850.

ADVERTISEMENT TO THE EDITION OF 1839.

THE volume which the Editor has here the gratification of presenting to the public, consists of Essays contributed by their author to various periodicals. None of them have hitherto been published in a collective form, and it is confidently anticipated that they will be received as an acceptable Companion to *Table Talk* and the *Plain Speaker*.

CONTENTS.

1. SKETCHES AND ESSAYS.

2. WINTERSLOW.

SKETCHES AND ESSAYS.

On Reading New Books.[1]

"And what of this new book, that the whole world make such a rout about?"—STERNE.

I CANNOT understand the rage manifested by the greater part of the world for reading New Books. If the public had read all those that have gone before, I can conceive how they should not wish to read the same work twice over; but when I consider the countless volumes that lie unopened, unregarded, unread, and unthought-of, I cannot enter into the pathetic complaints that I hear made that Sir Walter writes no more—that the press is idle—that Lord Byron is dead. If I have not read a book before, it is, to all intents and purposes, new to me, whether it was printed yesterday or three hundred years ago. If it be urged that it has no modern, passing incidents, and is out of date and old-fashioned, then it is so much the newer; it is farther removed from other works that I have lately read, from the familiar routine of ordinary life and makes so much more addition to my knowledge. But many people would as soon think of putting on old armour as of taking up a book not published within the last month, or year at the utmost. There is a fashion in reading as well as in dress, which lasts only for the season. One would

[1] See *Memoirs of William Hazlitt*, 1867, ii, 154.—ED.

B

imagine that books were, like women, the worse for being old; [1] that they have a pleasure in being read for the first time; that they open their leaves more cordially; that the spirit of enjoyment wears out with the spirit of novelty; and that, after a certain age, it is high time to put them on the shelf. This conceit seems to be followed up in practice. What is it to me that another—that hundreds or thousands have in all ages read a work? Is it on this account the less likely to give me pleasure, because it has delighted so many others? Or can I taste this pleasure by proxy? Or am I in any degree the wiser for their knowledge? Yet this might appear to be the inference. *Their* having read the work may be said to act upon us by sympathy, and the knowledge which so many other persons have of its contents deadens our curiosity and interest altogether. We set aside the subject as one on which others have made up their minds for us (as if we really could have ideas in their heads), and are quite on the alert for the next new work, teeming hot from the press, which we shall be the first to read, criticise, and pass an opinion on. Oh, delightful! To cut open the leaves, to inhale the fragrance of the scarcely dry paper, to examine the type to see who is the printer (which is some clue to the value that is set upon the work), to launch out into regions of thought and invention never trod till now, and to explore characters that never met a human eye before—this is a luxury worth sacrificing a dinner-party, or a few hours of a spare morning to. Who, indeed, when the work is critical and full of expectation, would venture to dine out, or to face a coterie of blue-stockings in the evening, without having gone through this ordeal, or at least without hastily turning over a few of the first pages, while dressing, to be able to say that the be-

---

[1] " Laws are not like women, the worse for being o.d."—*The Duke of Buckingham's Speech in the House of Lords, in Charles the Second s time.*

ginning does not promise much, or to tell the name of the heroine?

A new work is something in our power: we mount the bench, and sit in judgment on it; we can damn or recommend it to others at pleasure, can decry or extol it to the skies, and can give an answer to those who have not yet read it and expect an account of it; and thus show our shrewdness and the independence of our taste before the world have had time to form an opinion. If we cannot write ourselves, we become, by busying ourselves about it, a kind of *accessories after the fact*. Though not the parent of the bantling that " has just come into this breathing world, scarce half made up," without the aid of criticism and puffing, yet we are the gossips and foster-nurses on the occasion, with all the mysterious significance and self-importance of the tribe. If we wait, we must take our report from others; if we make haste, we may dictate ours to them. It is not a race, then, for priority of information, but for precedence in tattling and dogmatising. The work last out is the first that people talk and inquire about. It is the subject on the *tapis*—the cause that is pending. It is the last candidate for success (other claims have been disposed of), and appeals for this success to us, and us alone. Our predecessors can have nothing to say to this question, however they may have anticipated us on others; future ages, in all probability, will not trouble their heads about it; we are the panel. How hard, then, not to avail ourselves of our immediate privilege to give sentence of life or death—to seem in ignorance of what every one else is full of—to be behind-hand with the polite, the knowing, and fashionable part of mankind—to be at a loss and dumb-founded, when all around us are in their glory, and figuring away, on no other ground than that of having read a work that we have not! Books that are to be written hereafter cannot be criticised by us; those that were written formerly have been criticised long ago : but a new book is the property, the prey of ephemeral criticism, which it darts triumphantly upon ; there is a raw thin air of ignorance and uncertainty about it, not filled up by any recorded opinion ; and curiosity, impertinence, and vanity, rush eagerly into the vacuum. A new book is the fair field for petulance and coxcombry to gather laurels in—the butt set up for roving opinion to aim at. Can we wonder, then, that the circulating libraries are besieged by literary dowagers and their grand-daughters, when a new novel is announced ? That Mail-Coach copies of the *Edinburgh Review* are or were coveted ? That the Manuscript of the *Waverley Romances* is sent abroad in time for the French, German, or even Italian translation to appear on the same day as the original work, so that the longing Continental public may not be kept waiting an instant longer than their fellow-readers in the English metropolis which would be, as tantilising and insupportable as a little girl being kept without her new frock, when her sister's is just come home and is the talk and admiration of every one in the house ? To be sure, there is something in the taste of the times ; a modern work is expressly adapted to modern readers. It appeals to our direct experience, and to well-known subjects ; it is part and parcel of the world around us, and is drawn from the same sources as our daily thoughts. There is, therefore, so far, a natural or habitual sympathy between us and the literature of the day, though this is a different consideration from the mere circumstance of novelty. An author now alive has a right to calculate upon the living public : he cannot count upon the dead, nor look forward with much confidence to those that are unborn. Neither, however, is it true that we are eager to read all new books alike : we turn from them with a certain feeling of distaste and distrust, unless they are recommended to us by some peculiar feature or obvious distinction. Only young ladies from the boarding-school, or milliners' girls read all the new novels that come out. It must be spoken of or against; the writer's name must be well known or a great secret; it must be a topic of discourse and a mark for criticism—that is, it must be likely to bring us into notice in some way—or we take no notice of it. There is a mutual and tacit understanding on this head. We can no more read all the new books that appear, than we can read all the old ones that have disappeared from time to time. A question may be started here and pursued as far as needful, whether, if an old and worm-eaten Manuscript were discovered at the present moment, it would be sought after with the same avidity as a new and hot-pressed poem, or other popular work? Not generally, certainly, though by a few with perhaps greater zeal. For it would not affect present interests, or amuse present fancies, or touch on present manners, or fall in with the public *egotism* in any way : it would be the work either of some obscure author—in which case it would want the principle of excitement ; or of some illustrious name, whose style and manner would be already familiar to those most versed in the subject, and his fame established—so that, as a matter of comment and controversy, it would only go to account on the old score : there would be no room for learned feuds and heart-burnings. Was there not a Manuscript of Cicero's talked of as having been discovered about a year ago? But we have heard no more of it. There have been several other cases, more or less in point, in our time or near it. A Noble Duke (which may serve to show at least the interest taken in books *not for being new*) some time ago gave 2,260*l.* for a copy of the first edition of the *Decameron :* but did he read it?[1] It has been a fashion also of late for noble and wealthy persons to go to

[1] It was the Duke of Marlborough, the grandfather of the present Duke, when Marquis of Blandford, who bought this volume against Lord Spencer at the Roxburghe sale, in 1812. At the White Knights sale, in 1819, however, Lord Spencer had the satisfaction of securing the book for less than 1000*l.*—ED.

a considerable expense in ordering reprints of the old Chronicles and black-letter works.   Does not this rather prove that the books did not circulate very rapidly or extensively, or such extraordinary patronage and liberality would not have been necessary?   Mr Thomas Taylor, at the instance, I believe, of the old Duke of Norfolk, printed fifty copies in quarto of a translation of the works of Plato and Aristotle.   He did not choose that a larger impression should be struck off, lest these authors should get into the hands of the vulgar.   There was no danger of a run in that way.   I tried to read some of the Dialogues in the translation of Plato, but, I confess, could make nothing of it: " the logic was so different from ours! " [1]

---

[1] An expression borrowed from a voluble German scholar, who gave this as an excuse for not translating the 'Critique of Pure Reason' into English.   He might as well have said seriously, that the *Rule of Three* in German was different from ours.   [See *Memoirs of William Hazlitt*, i, 35.]   Mr. Taylor (the Platonist, as he was called) was a singular instance of a person in our time believing in the heathen mythology.   He had a very beautiful wife.   An impudent Frenchman, who came over to London, and lodged in the same house, made love to her, by pretending to worship her as Venus, and so thought to turn the tables on our philosopher.   I once spent an evening with this gentleman at George Dyer's chambers, in Clifford's Inn, where there was no exclusion of persons or opinions.   I remember he showed with some triumph two of his fingers, which had been bent so that he had lost the use of them, in copying out the manuscripts of Proclus and Plotinus in a fine Greek hand.   Such are the trophies of human pride !   It would be well if our deep studies often produced no other crookedness and deformity !   I endeavoured (but in vain) to learn something from the heathen philosopher as to Plato's doctrine of abstract ideas being the foundation of particular ones, which I suspect has more truth in it than we moderns are willing to admit.   Another friend of mine [Leigh Hunt] once breakfasted with Mr. Dyer (the most amiable and absent of hosts), when there was no butter, no knife to cut the loaf with, and the tea-pot was without a spout.   My friend, after a few immaterial ceremonies, adjourned to Peele's coffee-house, close by, where he regaled himself on buttered toast, coffee, and the newspaper of the day (a newspaper possessed some interest when

A startling experiment was made on this sort of retrospective curiosity, in the case of Ireland's celebrated Shakspeare forgery. The public there certainly manifested no backwardness nor lukewarmness : the enthusism was equal to the folly. But then the spirit exhibited on this occasion was partly critical and polemical, and it is a problem whether an actual and undoubted play of Shakspeare's would have excited the same ferment ; and, on the other hand, Shakspeare is an essential modern. People read and go to see his real plays, as well as his pretended ones. The *fuss* made about Ossian is another test to refer to. It was its being the supposed revival of an old work (known only by scattered fragments or lingering tradition) which gave it its chief interest, though there was also a good deal of mystery and quackery concerned along with the din and stir of national jealousy and pretension. Who reads Ossian now ? It is one of the reproaches brought against Buonaparte that he was fond of it when young. I cannot for myself see the objection. There is no doubt an antiquarian spirit always at work, and opposed to the spirit of novelty-hunting ; but, though opposed, it is scarcely a match for it in a general and popular point of view. It is not long ago that I happened to be suggesting a new translation of *Don Quixote* to an enterprising bookseller ; and his answer was—" We want new Don Quixotes." I believe I deprived the same active-minded person of a night's rest, by telling him there was the beginning of another novel by Goldsmith in existence

---

we were young) ; and the only interruption to his satisfaction was the fear that his host might suddenly enter, and be shocked at his imperfect hospitality. He would probably forget the circumstance altogether. I am afraid that this veteran of the old school has not received many proofs of the *archaism* of the prevailing taste ; and that the corrections in his *History of the University of Cambridge* have cost him more than the public will ever repay him for. [This anecdote is worked up with capital effect in Hunt's *Men, Women, and Books*, 1846. It is the story of Jack Abbott's breakfast.]

This, if it could be procured, would satisfy both tastes for the new and the old at once. I fear it is but a fragment, and that we must wait till a new Goldsmith appears. We may observe of late a strong craving after 'Memoirs,' and 'Lives of the Dead.' [1] But these, it may be remarked, savour so much of the real and familiar, that the persons described differ from us only in being dead, which is a reflection to our advantage : or, if remote and romantic in their interest and adventures, they require to be bolstered up in some measure by the embellishments of modern style and criticism. The accounts of Petrarch and Laura, of Abelard and Eloise, have a lusciousness and warmth in the subject which contrast quaintly and pointedly with the coldness of the grave ; and, after all, we prefer Pope's *Eloise and Abelard*, with the modern dress and flourishes, to the sublime and affecting simplicity of the original Letters.

In some very just and agreeable reflections on the story of *Abelard and Eloise*, in a late number of a contemporary publication, there is a quotation of some lines from Lucan, which Eloise is said to have repeated in broken accents as she was advancing to the altar to receive the veil :

> " O maxime conjux !
> O thalamis indigne meis ! Hoc juris habebat
> In tantum fortuna caput ? Cur impia nupsi,
> Si miserum factura fui ? Nunc accipe pænas,
> Sed quas sponte luam." [2]

This speech, quoted by another person, on such an occasion, might seem cold and pedantic ; but from the mouth of the passionate and unaffected Eloise it cannot bear that interpretation. What sounding lines! What a

---

[1] I presume Landor's *Imaginary Conversations* is the work intended. There are also *Letters from the dead to the living*, and Fenelon's *Dialogues of the Dead.*—ED.

[2] *Pharsalia*, lib. 8.

pomp, and yet what a familiar boldness in their application—"proud as when blue Iris bends!" The reading this account brought forcibly to mind what has struck me often before—the unreasonableness of the complaint we constantly hear of the ignorance and barbarism of former ages, and the folly of restricting all refinement and literary elegance to our own. We are, indeed, indebted to the ages that have gone before us, and could not well do without them. But in all ages there will be found still others that have gone before with nearly equal lustre and advantage, though, by distance and the intervention of multiplied excellence, this lustre may be dimned or forgotten. Had it then no existence? We might, with the same reason, suppose that the horizon is the last boundary and verge of the round earth. Still, as we advance, it recedes from us; and so time from its storehouse pours out an endless succession of the productions of art and genius; and the farther we explore the obscurity, other trophies and other land-marks rise up. It is only our ignorance that fixes a limit—as the mist gathered round the mountain's brow makes us fancy we are treading the edge of the universe! Here was Eloise living at a period when monkish indolence and superstition were at their height—in one of those that are emphatically called the *dark ages;* and yet, as she is led to the altar to make her last fatal vow, expressing her feelings in language quite natural to her, but from which the most accomplished and heroic of our modern females would shrink back with pretty and affected wonder and affright. The glowing and impetuous lines which she murmured, as she passed on, with spontaneous and rising enthusiasm, were engraven on her heart, familiar to her as her daily thoughts; her mind must have been full of them to overflowing, and at the same time enriched with other stores and sources of knowledge equally elegant and impressive; and we persist, notwithstanding this and a

thousand similar circumstances, in indulging our surprise
how people could exist, and see, and feel, in those days,
without having access to our opportunities and acquirements, and how Shakspeare wrote long after, *in a
barbarous age !* The mystery in this case is of our own
making. We are struck with astonishment at finding
a fine moral sentiment or a noble image nervously
expressed in an author of the age of Queen Elizabeth ;
not considering that, independently of nature and feeling,
which are the same in all periods, the writers of that day,
who were generally men of education and learning, had
such models before them as the one that has been just
referred to—were thoroughly acquainted with those masters of classic thought and language, compared with
whom, in all that relates to the artificial graces of composition, the most studied of the moderns are little better
than Goths and Vandals. It is true, we have lost sight
of, and neglected the former, because the latter have, in a
great degree, superseded them, as the elevations nearest to
us intercept those farthest off ; but our not availing
ourselves of this vantage ground is no reason why our
forefathers should not (who had not our superfluity of
choice), and most assuredly they did study and cherish
the precious fragments of antiquity, collected together in
their time, " like sunken wreck and sumless treasuries ; "[1]
and while they did this, we need be at no loss to account
for any examples of grace, of force, or dignity in their
writings, if these must always be traced back to a previous source. One age cannot understand how another
could subsist without its lights, as one country thinks
every other must be poor for want of its physical productions. This is a narrow and superficial view of the
subject : we should by all means rise above it. I am not
for devoting the whole of our time to the study of the
classics, or of any other set of writers, to the exclusion and

[1] *Henry V.*, i, 2 [Dyce's edit. 1868, iv, 429].

neglect of nature; but I think we should turn our thoughts enough that way to convince us of the existence of genius and learning before our time, and to cure us of an over-weening conceit of ourselves, and of a contemptuous opinion of the world at large. Every civilised age and country (and of these there is not one, but a hundred) has its litera-ture, its arts, its comforts, large and ample, though we may know nothing of them; nor is it (except for our own sakes) important that we should.

Books have been so multiplied in our days (like the Vanity Fair of knowledge), and we have made such progress beyond ourselves in some points, that it seems at first glance as if we had monopolised every possible advantage, and the rest of the world must be left destitute and in darkness. This is the *cockneyism* (with leave be it spoken) of the nineteenth century. There is a tone of smartness and piquancy in modern writing, to which former examples may, in one sense, appear flat and pedantic. Our allusions are more pointed and personal: the ancients are, in this respect, formal and prosaic personages. Some one, not long ago, in this vulgar, shallow spirit of criticism (which sees everything from its own point of view), said that the tragedies of Sophocles and Æschylus were about as good as the pieces brought out at Sadler's Wells or the Adelphi Theatre. An oration of Demosthenes is thought dry and meagre, because it is not "full of wise saws and modern instances:" one of Cicero's is objected to as flimsy and extravagant, for the same reason. There is a style in one age which does not fall in with the taste of the public in another, as it requires greater effeminacy and softness, greater severity or simplicity, greater force or refinement. Guido was more admired than Raphael in his day, because the man-ners were grown softer without the strength: Sir Peter Lely was thought in his to have eclipsed Vandyke—an opinion that no one holds at present: Holbein's faces

must be allowed to be very different from Sir Thomas
Lawrence's—yet the one was the favourite painter of
Henry VIII., as the other is of George IV. What should
we say in our time to the *euphuism* of the age of Elizabeth,
when style was made a riddle and the court talked in
conundrums? This, as a novelty and a trial of the wits,
might take for a while: afterwards, it could only seem
absurd. We must always make some allowance for a
change of style, which those who are accustomed to read
none but works written within the last twenty years
neither can nor will make. When a whole generation
read, they will read none but contemporary productions.
The taste for literature becomes superficial, as it becomes
universal, and is spread over a larger space. When ten
thousand boarding-school girls, who have learnt to play
on the piano, are brought out in the same season, Rossini
will be preferred to Mozart, as the last new composer. I
remember a very genteel young couple in the boxes of
Drury Lane being very much scandalised some years ago
at the phrase in *A New Way to Pay Old Debts*—"an
insolent piece of paper"—applied to the contents of a
letter; it wanted the modern lightness and indifference.
Let an old book be ever so good, it treats (generally
speaking) of topics that are stale, in a style that has
grown " somewhat musty;" of manners that are exploded,
probably by the very ridicule thus cast upon them; of
persons that no longer figure on the stage; and of interests
that have long since given place to others in the infinite
fluctuations of human affairs. Longinus complains of the
want of interest in the *Odyssey*, because it does not, like
the *Iliad*, treat of war. The very complaint we make
against the latter is that it treats of nothing else; or that,
as Fuseli expresses it, everything is seen " through the
blaze of war." Books of devotion are no longer read
(if we read Irving's *Orations*, it is merely that we may go
as a *lounge* to see the man): even attacks on religion are

out of date and insipid. Voltaire's jests and the *Jew's Letters* in answer (equal in wit, and more than equal in learning), repose quietly on the shelf together. We want something in England about Rent and the Poor-Laws, and something in France about the Charter—or Lord Byron. With the attempts, however, to revive superstition and intolerance, a spirit of opposition has been excited, and Pascal's *Provincial Letters* have been once more enlisted into the service. In France you meet with no one who can read the *New Eloise*: the *Princess of Cleves* is not even mentioned in these degenerate days. Is it not provoking with us to see the *Beggars' Opera* cut down to two acts, because some of the allusions are too broad, and others not understood? And in America this sterling satire is hooted off the stage, because, fortunately, they have no such state of manners as it describes before their eyes; and because, unfortunately, they have no conception of anything but what they see. America is singularly and awkwardly situated in this respect. It is a new country with an old language; and while everything about them is of a day's growth, they are constantly applying to us to know what to think of it, and taking their opinions from our books and newspapers with a strange mixture of servility and of the spirit of contradiction. They are an independent state in politics: in literature they are still a colony from us—not out of their leading strings, and strangely puzzled how to determine between the *Edinburgh* and *Quarterly Reviews*. We have naturalised some of their writers, who had formed themselves upon us. This is at once a compliment to them and to ourselves. Amidst the scramble and lottery for fame in the present day, besides puffing, which may be regarded as the hot-bed of reputation, another mode has been attempted by *transplanting* it; and writers who are set down as drivellers at home, shoot up great authors on the other side of the water; pack up their all—a title-page and sufficient impudence; and a work, of which the *flocci-nauci-nihili-pili-fication*, in Shenstone's phrase, is well known to every competent judge, is *placarded* into eminence, and "flames in the forehead of the morning sky" on the walls of Paris or St. Petersburgh.   I dare not mention the instances, but so it is.   Some reputations last only while the possessors live, from which one might suppose that they gave themselves a character for genius : others are cried up by their gossiping acquaintances, as long as they give dinners, and make their houses places of polite resort; and, in general, in our time, a book may be considered to have passed the ordeal that is mentioned at all three months after it is printed.   Immortality is not even a dream—a boy's conceit; and posthumous fame is no more regarded by the author than by his bookseller.

This idle, dissipated turn seems to be a set-off to, or the obvious reaction of, the exclusive admiration of the ancients, which was formerly the fashion : as if the sun of human intellect rose and set at Rome and Athens, and the mind of man had never exerted itself to any purpose since. The ignorant, as well as the adept, were charmed only with what was obsolete and far-fetched, wrapped up in technical terms and in a learned tongue.   Those who spoke and wrote a language which hardly any one at present even understood, must of course be wiser than we. Time, that brings so many reputations to decay, had embalmed others and rendered them sacred.   From an implicit faith and over-strained homage paid to antiquity, we of the modern school have taken too strong a bias to what is new; and divide all wisdom and worth between ourselves and posterity—not a very formidable rival to our self-love, as we attribute all its advantages to ourselves, though we pretend to owe little or nothing to our predecessors.   About the time of the French Revolution, it was agreed that the world had hitherto been in its dotage or its infancy; and that Mr. Godwin, Condorcet, and others were to begin a new race of men—a new epoch in society. Everything up to that period was to be set aside as puerile or barbarous ; or, if there were any traces of thought and manliness now and then discoverable, they were to be regarded with wonder as prodigies—as irregular and fitful starts in that long sleep of reason and night of philosophy. In this liberal spirit Mr. Godwin composed an Essay to prove that, till the publication of *The Inquiry concerning Political Justice*,[1] no one knew how to write a word of common grammar, or a style that was not utterly uncouth, incongruous, and feeble. Addison, Swift, and Junius were included in this censure. The English language itself might be supposed to owe its stability and consistency, its roundness and polish, to the whirling motion of the French Revolution. Those who had gone before us were, like our grandfathers and grandmothers, decrepit, superannuated people, blind and dull; poor creatures, like flies in winter, without pith or marrow in them. The past was barren of interest—had neither thought nor object worthy to arrest our attention ; and the future would be equally a senseless void, except as we projected ourselves and our theories into it. There is nothing I hate more than I do this exclusive, upstart spirit.

> " By Heavens, I'd rather be
> A pagan suckled in a creed outworn,
> So might I, standing on some pleasant lea,
> Catch glimpses that might make me less forlorn,
> Have sight of Proteus coming from the sea,
> Or hear old Triton blow his wreathed horn."[2]

Neither do I see the good of it even in a personal and interested point of view. By despising all that has preceded us, we teach others to despise ourselves. Where

[1] *An Inquiry concerning Political Justice, and its Influence on General Virtue and Happiness.* London, 1793, 2 vols. 4to.—ED.

[2] Wordsworth's *Sonnets.*

there is no established scale nor rooted faith in excellence, all superiority—our own as well as that of others—soon comes to the ground. By applying the wrong end of the magnifying glass to all objects indiscriminately, the most respectable dwindle into insignificance, and the best are confounded with the worst. Learning, no longer supported by opinion, or genius by fame, is cast into the mire, and "trampled under the hoofs of a swinish multitude." I would rather endure the most blind and bigoted respect for great and illustrious names, than that pitiful, grovelling humour which has no pride in intellectual excellence, and no pleasure but in decrying those who have given proofs of it, and reducing them to its own level. If, with the diffusion of knowledge, we do not gain an enlargement and elevation of views, where is the benefit? If, by tearing asunder names from things, we do not leave even the name or shadow of excellence, it is better to let them remain as they were; for it is better to have something to admire than nothing—names, if not things—the shadow, if not the substance—the tinsel, if not the gold. All can now read and write equally; and, it is therefore presumed, equally well. Anything short of this sweeping conclusion is an invidious distinction; and those who claim it for themselves or others are *exclusionists* in letters. Every one at least can call names— can invent a falsehood, or repeat a story against those who have galled their pragmatical pretensions by really adding to the stock of general amusement or instruction. Every one in a crowd has the power to throw dirt: nine out of ten have the inclination. It is curious that, in an age when the most universally-admitted claim to public distinction is literary merit, the attaining this distinction is almost a sure title to public contempt and obloquy.[1] They cry you up, because you are unknown, and do not excite

---

[1] Is not this partly owing to the disappointment of the public at finding any defect in their idol?

their jealousy; and run you down, when they have thus distinguished you, out of envy and spleen at the very idol they have set up. A public favourite is "kept like an apple in the jaw of an ape—first mouthed to be afterwards swallowed. When they need what you have gleaned, it is but squeezing you, and sponge you shall be dry again." At first they think only of the pleasure or advantage they receive : but, on reflection, they are mortified at the superiority implied in this involuntary concession, and are determined to be even with you the very first opportunity. What is the prevailing spirit of modern literature? To defame men of letters. What are the publications that succeed? Those that pretend to teach the public that the persons they have been accustomed unwittingly to look up to as the lights of the earth are no better than themselves, or a set of vagabonds, miscreants that should be hunted out of society.[1] Hence men of letters, losing their self-

---

[1] An old friend of mine [the Rev. Joseph Fawcett] when he read the abuse and Billingsgate poured out in certain Tory publications, used to congratulate himself upon it as a favourable sign of the times, and of the progressive improvement of our manners. Where we now called names, we formerly burnt each other at a stake; and all the malice of the heart flew to the tongue and vented itself in scolding, instead of crusades and *auto da fés*—the nobler revenge of our ancestors for a difference of opinion. An author [Leigh Hunt, in the *Examiner*] now libels a prince; and, if he takes the law of him, or throws him into gaol, it is looked upon as a harsh and ungentlemanly proceeding. He, therefore, gets a dirty secretary to employ a dirty bookseller, to hire a set of dirty scribblers, to pelt him with dirt and cover him with blackguard epithets [this is probably levelled at Croker] till he is hardly in a condition to walk the streets. This is hard measure, no doubt, and base ingratitude on the part of the public, according to the imaginary dignity and natural precedence which authors take of kings; but the latter are men, and will have their revenge where they can get it. They have no longer their old summary appeal—their will may still be good—to the dungeon and the dagger. Those who "speak evil of dignities" may, therefore, think themselves well off in being merely *sent to Coventry;* and, besides, if they have *pluck,* they can make a Parthian retreat,

respect, become government tools, and prostitute their talents to the most infamous purposes, or turn *dandy scribblers*, and set up for gentlemen authors in their own defence. I like the Order of the Jesuits better than this; they made themselves respected by the laity, kept their own secret, and did not prey on one another. Resume then, oh! Learning, thy robe pontifical; clothe thyself in pride and purple; join the sacred to the profane; wield both worlds; instead of twopenny trash and mechanics' magazines, issue bulls and decretals; say not, let there be light, but darkness visible; draw a bandage over the eyes of the ignorant and unlettered; hang the terrors of superstition and despotism over them ;—and for thy pains they will bless thee; children will pull off their caps as thou dost pass; women will courtesy; the old will wipe their beards; and thou wilt rule once more over the base serving people, clowns, and nobles, with a rod of iron!

Florence, May, 1825.

On Cant and Hypocrisy.

" If to do were as easy as to teach others what were good to be done, chapels had been churches, and poor men's cottages princes' palaces."

Mr. Addison, it is said, was fond of tippling; and Curll, it is added, when he called on him in the morning, used to ask as a particular favour for a glass of Canary, by way of ingratiating himself, and that the other might have a pretence to join him and finish the bottle. He fell a martyr to this habit, and *yet* (some persons more nice than wise exclaim) he desired that the young Earl of

---

and shoot poisoned arrows behind them. The good people of Florence lift up their hands when they are shown the caricatures in the *Queen's Matrimonial Ladder* [by William Hone], and ask if they are really a likeness of the King?

Warwick might attend him on his death-bed, " to see how a Christian could die !" I see no inconsistency nor hypocrisy in this. A man may be a good Christian, a sound believer, and a sincere lover of virtue, and have, notwithstanding, one or more failings. If he had recommended it to others to get drunk, then I should have said he was a hypocrite, and that his pretended veneration for the Christian religion was a mere cloak put on to suit the purposes of fashion or convenience. His doing what it condemned was no proof of any such thing : "The spirit was willing, but the flesh was weak." He is a hypocrite who professes what he does not believe ; not he who does not practise all he wishes or approves. It might on the same ground be argued, that a man is a hypocrite who admires Raphael or Shakspeare, because he cannot paint like the one, or write like the other. If any one really despised what he affected outwardly to admire, this would be hypocrisy. If he affected to admire it a great deal more than he really did, this would be cant. Sincerity has to do with the connexion between our words and thoughts, and not between our belief and actions. The last constantly belie the strongest convictions and resolutions in the best of men ; it is only the base and dishonest who give themselves credit with their tongue, for sentiments and opinions which in their hearts they disown.

I do not therefore think that the old theological maxim —" The greater the sinner, the greater the saint "—is so utterly unfounded. There is some mixture of truth in it. For as long as man is composed of two parts, body and soul, and while these are allowed to pull different ways, I see no reason why, in proportion to the length the one goes, the opposition or reaction of the other should not be more violent. It is certain, for example, that no one makes such good resolutions as the sot and the gambler in their moments of repentance, or can be more impressed with the horrors of their situation ;—should this disposition, instead of a transient, idle pang, by chance become lasting, who can be supposed to feel the beauty of temperance and economy more, or to look back with greater gratitude to their escape from the trammels of vice and passion? Would the ingenious and elegant author of the *Spectator* feel less regard for the Scriptures, because they denounced in pointed terms the infirmity that "most easily beset him," that was the torment of his life, and the cause of his death? Such reasoning would be true, if man was a simple animal or a logical machine, and all his faculties and impulses were in strict unison; instead of which they are eternally at variance, and no one hates or takes part against himself more heartily or heroically than does the same individual. Does he not pass sentence on his own conduct? Is not his conscience both judge and accuser? What else is the meaning of all our resolutions against ourselves, as well as of our exhortations to others? *Video meliora proboque, deteriora sequor,* is not the language of hyprocrisy, but of human nature.

The hyprocrisy of priests has been a butt for ridicule in all ages; but I am not sure that there has not been more wit than philosophy in it. A priest, it is true, is obliged to affect a greater degree of sanctity than ordinary men, and probably more than he possesses; and this is so far, I am willing to allow, hypocrisy and solemn grimace. But I cannot admit, that though he may exaggerate or even make an ostentatious display of religion and virtue through habit and spiritual pride, that this is a proof he has not these sentiments in his heart, or that his whole behaviour is the mere acting of a part. His character, his motives, are not altogether pure and sincere: are they therefore all false and hollow? No such thing. It is contrary to all our observation and experience so to interpret it. We all wear some disguise—make some professions —use some artifice to set ourselves off as being better than we are; and yet it is not denied that we have some good intentions and praiseworthy qualities at bottom, though we may endeavour to keep some others that we think less to our credit as much as possible in the background :—why then should we not extend the same favourable construction to monks and priests, who may be sometimes caught tripping as well as other men—with less excuse, no doubt; but if it is also with greater remorse of conscience, which probably often happens, their pretensions are not all downright, barefaced imposture. Their sincerity, compared with that of other men, can only be judged of by the proportion between the degree of virtue they profess, and that which they practise, or at least carefully seek to realise. To conceive it otherwise is to insist that characters must be all perfect or all vicious —neither of which 'suppositions is even possible. If a clergyman is notoriously a drunkard, a debauchee, a glutton, or a scoffer, then for him to lay claim at the same time to extraordinary inspirations of faith or grace, is both scandalous and ridiculous. The scene between the Abbot and the poor brother in the *Duenna*, is an admirable exposure of this double-faced dealing. But because a parson has a relish for the good things of this life, or what is commonly called *a liquorish tooth in his head* (beyond what he would have it supposed by others, or even by himself), that he has therefore no fear or belief of the next, I hold for a crude and vulgar prejudice. If a poor half-starved parish priest pays his court to an *olla podrida*, or a venison pasty, with uncommon *gusto*, shall we say that he has no other sentiments in offering his devotions to a crucifix, or in counting his beads ? I see no more ground for such an inference, than for affirming that Handel was not in earnest when he sat down to compose a Symphony, because he had at the same time perhaps a bottle of cordials in his cupboard ; or that Raphael was not entitled to the epithet of *divine*, because he was attached to the Fornarina. Everything has its turn in

this chequered scene of things, unless we prevent it from
taking its turn by over-rigid conditions, or drive men to
despair or the most callous effrontery, by erecting a
standard of perfection, to which no one can conform in
reality. Thomson, in his *Castle of Indolence* (a subject on
which his pen ran riot), has indulged in rather a free
description of "a little round, fat, oily man of God,
who—

> " Shone all glistening with ungodly dew,
>   If a tight damsel chanced to trippen by;
>   Which when observed, he shrunk into his mew,
>   And straight would recollect his piety anew." [1]

Now, was the piety in this case the less real, because it
had been forgotten for a moment? Or even if this
motive should not prove the strongest in the end, would
this therefore show that it was none, which is necessary
to the argument here combated, or to make out our little
plump priest a very knave? A priest may be honest,
and yet err; as a woman may be modest, and yet half-
inclined to be a rake. So the virtue of prudes may be
suspected, though not their sincerity. The strength of
their passions may make them more conscious of their
weakness, and more cautious of exposing themselves; but
not more to blind others than as a guard upon themselves.
Again, suppose a clergyman hazards a jest upon sacred
subjects, does it follow that he does not believe a word of
the matter? Put the case that any one else, encouraged
by his example, takes up the banter or levity, and see
what effect it will have upon the reverend divine. He
will turn round like a serpent trod upon, with all the
vehemence and asperity of the most bigoted orthodoxy.
Is this dictatorial and exclusive spirit then put on merely
as a mask and to browbeat others? No; but he thinks
he is privileged to trifle with the subject safely himself,
from the store of evidence he has in reserve, and from the

[1] Canto I., st. 69, edit. 1841.

nature of his functions; but he is afraid of serious consequences being drawn from what others might say, or
from his seeming to countenance it; and the moment the
Church is in danger, or his own faith brought in question,
his attachment to each becomes as visible as his hatred
to those who dare to impugn either the one or the other.
A woman's attachment to her husband is not to be suspected, if she will allow no one to abuse him but herself. It
has been remarked, that with the spread of liberal opinions,
or a more general scepticism on articles of faith, the
clergy and religious persons in general have become more
squeamish and jealous of any objections to their favourite
doctrines: but this is what must follow in the natural
course of things—the resistance being always in proportion
to the danger; and arguments and books that were
formerly allowed to pass unheeded, because it was supposed
impossible they could do any mischief, are now denounced
or prohibited with the most zealous vigilance, from a
knowledge of the contagious nature of their influence and
contents. So in morals, it is obvious that the greatest
nicety of expression and allusion must be observed, where
the manners are the most corrupt, and the imagination
most easily excited, not out of mere affectation, but as a
dictate of common sense and decency.

One of the finest remarks that has been made in modern
times, is that of Lord Shaftesbury, that there is no such
thing as a perfect Theist, or an absolute Atheist; that
whatever may be the general conviction entertained on
the subject, the evidence is not and cannot be at all times
equally present to the mind; that even if it were, we are
not in the same humour to receive it: a fit of the gout, a
shower of rain shakes our best-established conclusions;
and according to circumstances and the frame of mind we
are in, our belief varies from the most sanguine enthusiasm
to lukewarm indifference, or the most gloomy despair
There is a point of conceivable faith which might prevent

any lapse from virtue, and reconcile all contrarieties between theory and practice; but this is not to be looked for in the ordinary course of nature, and is reserved for the abodes of the blest. Here, " upon this bank and shoal of time," the utmost we can hope to attain is, a strong habitual belief in the excellence of virtue, or the dispensations of Providence; and the conflict of the passions, and their occasional mastery over us, far from disproving or destroying this general, rational conviction, often fling us back more forcibly upon it, and like other infidelities and misunderstandings, produce all the alternate remorse and raptures of repentance and reconciliation.

It has been frequently remarked that the most obstinate heretic or confirmed sceptic, witnessing the service of the Roman Catholic church, the elevation of the host amidst the sounds of music, the pomp of ceremonies, the embellishments of art, feels himself spell-bound; and is almost persuaded to become a renegado to his reason or his religion. Even in hearing a vespers chanted on the stage, or in reading an account of a torch-light procession in a romance, a superstitious awe creeps over the frame, and we are momentarily charmed out of ourselves. When such is the obvious and involuntary influence of circumstances on the imagination, shall we say that a monkish recluse surrounded from his childhood by all this pomp, a stranger to any other faith, who has breathed no other atmosphere, and all whose meditations are bent on this one subject both by interest and habit and duty, is to be set down as a rank and heartless mountebank in the professions he makes of belief in it, because his thoughts may sometimes wander to forbidden subjects, or his feet stumble on forbidden ground ? Or shall not the deep shadows of the woods in Vallombrosa enhance the solemnity of this feeling, or the icy horrors of the Grand Chartreux add to its elevation and its purity? To argue otherwise is to misdeem of human nature, and to limit its capacities for

good or evil by some narrow-minded standard of our own.
Man is neither a God nor a brute; but there is a prosaic
and a poetical side to everything concerning him, and it
is as impossible absolutely and for a constancy to exclude
either one or the other from the mind, as to make him
live without air or food. The *ideal*, the empire of thought
and aspiration after truth and good, is inseparable from
the nature of an intellectual being—what right have we
then to catch at every strife which in the mortified professors of religion the spirit wages with the flesh as grossly
vicious? or at every doubt, the bare suggestion of which
fills them with consternation and despair, as a proof of
the most glaring hypocrisy? The grossnesses of religion
and its stickling for mere forms as its essence, have given
a handle, and a just one, to its impugners. At the feast
of Ramadan (says Voltaire) the Mussulmans wash and
pray five times a day, and then fall to cutting one
another's throats again with the greatest deliberation and
good-will. The two things, I grant, are sufficiently at
variance; but they are, I contend, equally sincere in both.
The Mahometans are savages, but they are not the less
true believers—they hate their enemies as heartily as
they revere the Koran. This, instead of showing the
fallacy of the *ideal* principle, shows its universality and
indestructible essence. Let a man be as bad as he will,
as little refined as possible, and indulge whatever hurtful
passions or gross vices he thinks proper, these cannot
occupy the whole of his time; and in the intervals
between one scroundrel action and another he may and
must have better thoughts, and may have recourse to those
of religion (true or false) among the number, without in
this being guilty of hypocrisy or of making a jest of what
is considered as sacred. This, I take it, is the whole
secret of Methodism, which is a sort of modern vent
for the ebullitions of the spirit through the gaps of
unrighteousness.

We often see that a person condemns in another the very thing he is guilty of himself. Is this hypocrisy? It may, or it may not. If he really feels none of the disgust and abhorrence he expresses, this is quackery and impudence. But if he really expresses what he feels (and he easily may, for it is the abstract idea he contemplates in the case of another, and the immediate temptation to which he yields in his own, so that he probably is not even conscious of the identity or connexion between the two), then this is not hypocrisy, but want of strength and keeping in the moral sense. All morality consists in squaring our actions and sentiments to our ideas of what is fit and proper; and it is the incessant struggle and alternate triumph of the two principles, the *ideal* and the physical, that keeps up this "mighty coil and pudder" about vice and virtue, and is one great source of all the good and evil in the world. The mind of man is like a clock that is always running down, and requires to be as constantly wound up. The *ideal* principle is the master-key that winds it up, and without which it would come to a stand: the sensual and selfish feelings are the dead weights that pull it down to the gross and grovelling. Till the intellectual faculty is destroyed (so that the mind sees nothing beyond itself, or the present moment), it is impossible to have all brutal depravity; till the material and physical are done away with (so that it shall contemplate everything from a purely spiritual and disinterested point of view), it is impossible to have all virtue. There must be a mixture of the two, as long as man is compounded of opposite materials, a contradiction and an eternal competition for the mastery. I by no means think a single bad action condemns a man, for he probably condemns it as much as you do; nor a single bad habit, for he is probably trying all his life to get rid of it. A man is only thoroughly profligate when he has lost the sense of right and wrong; or a thorough hypocrite, when he has not even the wish to be what he appears. The greatest offence against virtue is to speak ill of it. To recommend certain things is worse than to practise them. There may be an excuse for the last in the frailty of passion; but the former can arise from nothing but an utter depravity of disposition. Any one may yield to temptation, and yet feel a sincere love and aspiration after virtue: but he who maintains vice in theory, has not even the conception or capacity for virtue in his mind. Men err: fiends only make a mock at goodness.

We sometimes deceive ourselves, and think worse of human nature than it deserves, in consequence of judging of character from names, and classes, and modes of life. No one is simply and absolutely any one thing, though he may be branded with it as a name. Some persons have expected to see his crimes written in the face of a murderer, and have been disappointed because they did not, as if this impeached the distinction between virtue and vice. Not at all. The circumstance only showed that the man was other things, and had other feelings besides those of a murderer. If he had nothing else—if he had fed on nothing else—if he had dreamt of nothing else but schemes of murder, his features would have expressed nothing else: but this perfection in vice is not to be expected from the contradictory and mixed nature of our motives. Humanity is to be met with in a den of robbers; nay, modesty in a brothel. Even among the most abandoned of the other sex, there is not unfrequently found to exist (contrary to all that is generally supposed) one strong and individual attachment, which remains unshaken to the last. Virtue may be said to steal, like a guilty thing, into the secret haunts of vice and infamy; it clings to their devoted victim, and will not be driven quite away. Nothing can destroy the human heart. Again, there is a heroism in crime, as well as in virtue.

Vice and infamy have also their altars and their religion. This makes nothing in their favour, but is a proof of the heroical disinterestedness of man's nature, and that whatever he does, he must fling a dash of romance and sublimity into it: just as some grave biographer has said of Shakspeare, that "even when he killed a calf, he made a speech and did it in a great style."

It is then impossible to get rid of this original distinction and contradictory bias, and to reduce everything to the system of French levity and Epicurean indifference. Wherever there is a capacity of conceiving of things as different from what they are, there must be a principle of taste and selection—a disposition to make them better, and a power to make them worse. Ask a Parisian milliner if she does not think one bonnet more becoming than another—a Parisian dancing master if French grace is not better than English awkwardness—a French cook if all sauces are alike—a French *blacklegs* if all throws are equal on the dice? It is curious that the French nation restrict rigid rules and fixed principles to cookery and the drama, and maintain that the great drama of human life is entirely a matter of caprice and fancy. No one will assert that Raphael's histories, that Claude's landscapes are not better than a daub: but if the expression in one of Raphael's faces is better than the most mean and vulgar, how resist the consequence that the feeling so expressed is better also? It does not appear to me that all faces or all actions are alike. If goodness were only a theory, it were a pity it should be lost to the world. There are a number of things, the idea of which is a clear gain to the mind. Let people, for instance, rail at friendship, genius, freedom, as long as they will—the very names of these despised qualities are better than anything else that could be substituted for them, and embalm even the most envenomed satire against them. It is no small consideration that the mind is capable

even of feigning such things.   So I would contend against
that reasoning which would have it thought that if
religion is not true, there is no difference between
mankind and the beasts that perish ;—I should say, that
this distinction is equally proved, if religion is supposed
to be a mere fabrication of the human mind ; the capacity to conceive it makes the difference.   The idea alone
of an over-ruling Providence, or of a future state, is as
much a distinctive mark of a superiority of nature, as the
invention of the mathematics, which are true—or of
poetry, which is a fable.   Whatever the truth or falsehood
of our speculations, the power to make them is peculiar to
ourselves.

The contrariety and warfare of different faculties and
dispositions within us has not only given birth to the
Manichean and Gnostic heresies, and to other superstitions of the East, but will account for many of the
mummeries and dogmas both of Popery and Calvinism—
confession, absolution, justification by faith, &c. ; which,
in the hopelessness of attaining perfection, and our
dissatisfaction with ourselves for falling short of it, are
all substitutes for actual virtue, and an attempt to throw
the burthen of a task, to which we are unequal or only
half disposed, on the merits of others, or on outward
forms, ceremonies, and professions of faith.   Hence the
crowd of

> " Eremites and friars.
> White, black, and grey, with all their trumpery."

If we do not conform to the law, we at least acknowledge the jurisdiction of the court.   A person does
wrong ; he is sorry for it ; and as he still feels himself
liable to error, he is desirous to make atonement as well
as he can, by ablutions, by tithes, by penance, by sacrifices, or other voluntary demonstrations of obedience,
which are in his power, though his passions are not, and

which prove that his will is not refractory, and that his understanding is right towards God. The stricter tenets of Calvinism, which allow of no medium between grace and reprobation, and doom man to eternal punishment for every breach of the moral law, as an equal offence against infinite truth and justice, proceed (like the paradoxical doctrine of the Stoics) from taking a half-view of this subject, and considering man as amenable only to the dictates of his understanding and his conscience, and not excusable from the temptations and frailty of human ignorance and passion. The mixing up of religion and morality together, or the making us accountable for every word, thought, or action, under no less a responsibility than our everlasting future welfare or misery, has also added incalculably to the difficulties of self-knowledge, has superinduced a violent and spurious state of feeling, and made it almost impossible to distinguish the boundaries between the true and false, in judging of human conduct and motives. A religious man is afraid of looking into the state of his soul, lest at the same time he should reveal it to Heaven; and tries to persuade himself that by shutting his eyes to his true character and feelings, they will remain a profound secret both here and hereafter. This is a strong engine and irresistible inducement to self-deception; and the more zealous any one is in his convictions of the truth of religion, the more we may suspect the sincerity of his pretensions to piety and morality.

Thus, though I think there is very little downright hypocrisy in the world, I do think there is a great deal of *cant*—" cant religious, cant political, cant literary," &c., as Lord Byron said. Though few people have the face to set up for the very thing they in their hearts despise, we almost all want to be thought better than we are, and affect a greater admiration or abhorrence of certain things than we really feel. Indeed, some degree of affectation is as necessary to the mind as dress is to the body; we must overact our part in some measure, in order to produce any effect at all. There was formerly the two hours' sermon, the long-winded grace, the nasal drawl, the uplifted hands and eyes; all which though accompanied with some corresponding emotion, expressed more than was really felt, and were in fact intended to make up for the conscious deficiency. As our interest in anything wears out with time and habit, we exaggerate the outward symptoms of zeal as mechanical helps to devotion, dwell the longer on our words as they are less felt, and hence the very origin of the term, *cant*. The cant of sentimentality has succeeded to that of religion. There is a cant of humanity, of patriotism and loyalty—not that people do not feel these emotions, but they make too great a *fuss* about them, and drawl out the expression of them till they tire themselves and others. There is a cant about Shakspeare. There is a cant about *Political Economy* just now. In short, there is and must be a cant about everything that excites a considerable degree of attention and interest, and that people would be thought to know and care rather more about them than they actually do. Cant is the voluntary overcharging or prolongation of a real sentiment; hypocrisy is the setting up a pretension to a feeling you never had and have no wish for. There are people who are made up of *cant*, that is, of mawkish affectation and sensibility; but who have not sincerity enough to be *hypocrites*, that is, have not hearty dislike or contempt enough for anything, to give the lie to their puling professions of admiration and esteem for it.

Merry England.

"St. George for merry England!"

THIS old-fashioned epithet might be supposed to have been bestowed ironically, or on the old principle —*Ut lucus a non lucendo.* Yet there is something in the sound that hits the fancy, and a sort of truth beyond appearances.[1] To be sure, it is from a dull, homely ground that the gleams of mirth and jollity break out; but the streaks of light that tinge the evening sky are not the less striking on that account. The beams of the morning-sun shining on the lonely glades, or through the idle branches of the tangled forest, the leisure, the freedom, "the pleasure of going and coming without knowing where," the troops of wild deer, the sports of the chase, and other rustic gambols, were sufficient to justify the well-known appellation of "Merry Sherwood," and in like manner, we may apply the phrase to *Merry England.* The smile is not the less sincere because it does not always play upon the cheek; and the jest is not the less welcome, nor the laugh less hearty, because they happen to be a relief from care or leaden-eyed melancholy. The instances are the more precious as they are rare; and we look forward to them with the greater goodwill, or back upon them with the greater gratitude, as we drain the last drop in the cup with particular relish. If not always gay or in good spirits, we are glad when any occasion draws us out of our natural gloom, and disposed to make the most of it. We may say with *Silence* in the play, " I have been merry once ere now "—and this once was to serve him all his life; for he was a person of wonderful silence and gravity, though " he chirped over his cups," and announced with characteristic glee that " there were pippins and cheese to

---

[1] *Merry.* in its earlier acceptation, signified nothing more than *cheerful.*—ED.

come." *Silence* was in this sense a merry man, that is, he would be merry if he could, and a very great economy of wit, like very slender fare, was a banquet to him, from the simplicity of his taste and habits. "Continents," says Hobbes, "have most of what they contain"—and in this view it may be contended that the English are the merriest people in the world, since they only show it on high-days and holidays. They are then like a school-boy let loose from school, or like a dog that has slipped his collar. They are not gay like the French, who are one eternal smile of self-complacency, tortured into affectation, or spun out into languid indifference, nor are they voluptuous and immersed in sensual indolence, like the Italians; but they have that sort of intermittent, fitful, irregular gaiety, which is neither worn out by habit, nor deadened by passion, but is sought with avidity as it takes the mind by surprise, is startled by a sense of oddity and incongruity, indulges its wayward humours or lively impulses, with perfect freedom and lightness of heart, and seizes occasion by the forelock, that it may return to serious business with more cheerfulness, and have something to beguile the hours of thought or sadness. I do not see how there can be high spirits without low ones; and everything has its price according to circumstances. Perhaps we have to pay a heavier tax on pleasure, than some others: what skills it, so long as our good spirits and good hearts enable us to bear it?

"They" (the English), says Froissart, "amused themselves sadly after the fashion of their country"—*ils se rejouissoient tristement*[1] *selon la coutume de leur pays.* They have indeed a way of their own. Their mirth is a relaxation from gravity, a challenge to dull care to be gone; and one is not always clear at first, whether the appeal is successful. The cloud may still hang on the brow; the ice may not thaw at once. To help them out in their new

---

[1] It may be doubted, however, whether both the English word *sad* and the French word *triste* signify here more than *sober, grave.*—ED.

D

character is an act of charity. Anything short of hanging or drowning is something to begin with. They do not enter into their amusements the less doggedly because they may plague others. They like a thing the better for hitting them a rap on the knuckles, for making their blood tingle. They do not dance or sing, but they make good cheer—" eat, drink, and are merry." No people are fonder of field-sports, Christmas gambols, or practical jests. Blindman's-buff, hunt-the-slipper, hot-cockles, and snap-dragon, are all approved English games, full of laughable surprises and " hair-breadth 'scapes," and serve to amuse the winter fire-side after the roast-beef and plum-pudding, the spiced ale and roasted crab, thrown (hissing-hot) into the foaming tankard. Punch (not the liquor, but the puppet) is not, I fear, of English origin; but there is no place I take it, where he finds himself more at home or meets a more joyous welcome, where he collects greater crowds at the corners of streets, where he opens the eyes or distends the cheeks wider, or where the bangs and blows, the uncouth gestures, ridiculous anger, and screaming voice of the chief performer excite more boundless merriment or louder bursts of laughter among all ranks and sorts of people. An English theatre is the very throne of pantomime; nor do I believe that the gallery and boxes of Drury Lane or Covent Garden filled on the proper occasion with holiday folks (big or little) yield the palm for undisguised, tumultuous, inextinguishable laughter to any spot in Europe. I do not speak of the refinement of the mirth (this is no fastidious speculation) but of its cordiality, on the return of these long looked-for and licensed periods; and I may add here, by way of illustration, that the English common people are a sort of grown children, spoiled and sulky perhaps, but full of glee and merriment, when their attention is drawn off by some sudden and striking object. The May-pole is almost gone out of fashion among us: but May-day, besides its flowering hawthorns and its pearly dews, has still its boasted exhibition of painted chimney-sweepers and their Jack-o'-the-Green, whose tawdry finery, bedizened faces, unwonted gestures, and short-lived pleasures call forth good-humoured smiles and looks of sympathy in the spectators. There is no place where trap-ball, fives, prison-base, football, quoits, bowls are better understood or more successfully practised; and the very names of a cricket bat and ball make English fingers tingle. What happy days must "Long Robinson" have passed in getting ready his wickets and mending his bats, who, when two of the fingers of his right hand were struck off by the violence of a ball, had a screw fastened to it to hold the bat, and with the other hand still sent the ball thundering against the boards that bounded *Old Lord's cricket-ground!* What delightful hours must have been his in looking forward to the matches that were to come, in recounting the feats he had performed in those that were past! I have myself whiled away whole mornings in seeing him strike the ball (like a countryman mowing with a scythe) to the farthest extremity of the smooth, level, sun-burnt ground; and with long, awkward strides count the notches that made victory sure! Then again, cudgel-playing, quarter-staff, bull and badger-baiting, cock-fighting are almost the peculiar diversions of this island, and often objected to us as barbarous and cruel; horse-racing is the delight and the ruin of numbers; and the noble science of boxing is all our own. Foreigners can scarcely understand how we can squeeze pleasure out of this pastime; the luxury of hard blows given or received; the joy of the ring; the perseverance of the combatants.[1] The English also excel,

---

[1] "The gentle and free passage of arms at Ashby" was, we are told, so called by the chroniclers of the time, on account of the feats of horsemanship and the quantity of knightly blood that was shed. This last circumstance was perhaps necessary to qualify it with the epithet of "gentle," in the opinion of some of these historians.

or are not excelled in wiring a hare, in stalking a deer, in shooting, fishing, and hunting. England to this day boasts her Robin Hood and his merry men, that stout archer and outlaw and patron-saint of the sporting-calendar. What a cheerful sound is that of the hunters, issuing from the autumnal wood and sweeping over hill and dale!

> —" A cry more tuneable
> Was never halloo'd to by hound or horn."

What sparkling richness in the scarlet coats of the riders, what a glittering confusion in the pack, what spirit in the horses, what eagerness in the followers on foot, as they disperse over the plain, or force their way over hedge and ditch! Surely, the coloured prints and pictures of these, hung up in gentlemen's halls and village alehouses, how-

---

I think the reason why the English are the bravest nation on earth is, that the thought of blood or a delight in cruelty is not the chief excitement with them. Where it is, there is necessarily a *reaction ;* for though it may add to our eagerness and savage ferocity in inflicting wounds, it does not enable us to endure them with greater patience. The English are led to the attack or sustain it equally well, because they fight as they box, not out of malice, but to show *pluck* and manhood. *Fair play and old England for ever!* This is the only bravery that will stand the test. There is the same determination and spirit shown in resistance as in attack; but not the same pleasure in getting a cut with a sabre as in giving one. There is, therefore, always a certain degree of effeminacy mixed up with any approach to cruelty, since both have their source in the same principle, viz., an over-valuing of pain. (*a*) This was the reason the French (having the best cause and the best general in the world) ran away at Waterloo, because they were inflamed, furious, drunk with the blood of their enemies, but when it came to their turn, wanting the same stimulus, they were panic-struck, and their hearts and their senses failed them all at once.

(*a*) Vanity is the same half-witted principle, compared with pride. It leaves men in the lurch when it is most needed; is mortified at being reduced to stand on the defensive, and relinquishes the field to its more surly antagonist.

ever humble, as works of art, have more life and health and spirit in them, and mark the pith and nerve of the national character more creditably than the mawkish, sentimental, affected designs of Theseus and Pirithous, and Æneas and Dido, pasted on foreign *salons à manger*, and the interior of country-houses. If our tastes are not epic, nor our pretensions lofty, they are simple and our own ; and we may possibly enjoy our native rural sports and the rude remembrances of them, with the truer relish on this account, that they are suited to us and we to them. The English nation, too, are naturally " brothers of the angle." This pursuit implies just that mixture of patience and pastime, of vacancy and thoughtfulness, of idleness and business, of pleasure and of pain, which is suited to the genius of an Englishman, and as I suspect, of no one else in the same degree. He is eminently gifted to stand in the situation assigned by Dr. Johnson to the angler, " at one end of a rod with a worm at the other." I should suppose no other language than ours can show such a book as an often-mentioned one, Walton's *Complete·Angler*—so full of *naïveté*, of unaffected sprightliness, of busy trifling, of dainty songs, of refreshing brooks, of shady arbours, of happy thoughts and of the herb called *Heart's Ease !* Some persons can see neither the wit nor wisdom of this genuine volume, as if a book as well as a man might not have a personal character belonging to it, amiable, venerable from the spirit of joy and thorough goodness it manifests, independently of acute remarks or scientific discoveries ; others object to the cruelty of Walton's theory and practice of trout-fishing— for my part, I should as soon charge an infant with cruelty for killing a fly, and I feel the same sort of pleasure in reading his book as I should have done in the company of this happy, child-like old man, watching his ruddy cheek, his laughing eye, the kindness of his heart, and the dexterity of his hand in seizing his finny prey ! It must be confessed, there is often an odd sort of *materiality* in English sports and recreations. I have known several persons, whose existence consisted wholly in manual exercises, and all whose enjoyments lay at their finger-ends. Their greatest happiness was in cutting a stick, in mending a cabbage-net, in digging a hole in the ground, in hitting a mark, turning a lathe, or in something else of the same kind, at which they had a certain *knack*. Well is it when we can amuse ourselves with such trifles and without injury to others ! This class of character, which the Spectator has immortalised in the person of Will Wimble, is still common among younger brothers and retired gentlemen of small incomes in town or country. London is half suburbs. The suburbs of Paris are a desert, and you see nothing but crazy wind-mills, stone-walls, and a few straggling visitants, in spots where in England you would find a thousand villas, a thousand terraces, crowned with their own delights, or be stunned with the noise of bowling-greens and tea-gardens, or stifled with the fumes of tobacco mingling with fragrant shrubs, or the clouds of dust raised by half the population of the metropolis panting and toiling in search of a mouthful of fresh air. The Parisian is, perhaps, as well (or better) contented with himself wherever he is, stewed in his shop or his garret ; the Londoner is miserable in these circumstances, and glad to escape from them.[1] Let no one object to the gloomy appearance of a London Sunday, compared with a Parisian one. It is a part of our politics and our religion : we would not have James the First's *Book of Sports.*[2] thrust down our throats : and besides, it is a part of our character to do one thing at a time, and not to be dancing

---

[1] The English are fond of change of scene ; the French of change of posture ; the Italians like to sit still, and do nothing.

[2] *The King's Maiesties Declaration to his Subjects concerning lawfull Sports to be used*, published by James I. in 1618, and reissued by his son in 1633.—ED.

a jig and on our knees in the same breath. It is true the Englishman spends his Sunday evening at the ale-house —

> —————" And e'en on Sunday
> He drinks with Kirton Jean till Monday "—

but he only unbends and waxes mellow by degrees, and sits soaking till he can neither sit, stand, nor go : it is his vice, and a beastly one it is, but not a proof of any inherent distaste to mirth or good fellowship. Neither can foreigners throw the carnival in our teeth with any effect : those who have seen it (at Florence, for example), will say that it is duller than any thing in England. Our Bartholomew-Fair is Queen Mab herself to it ! What can be duller than a parcel of masks moving about the streets and looking as grave and monotonous as possible from day to day, and with the same lifeless formality in their limbs and gestures as in their features? One might as well expect variety and spirit in a procession of wax-work figures. We must be hard run indeed, when we have recourse to a pasteboard proxy to set off our mirth : a mask may be a very good cover for licentiousness (though of that I saw no signs), but it is a very bad exponent of wit and humour. I should suppose there is more drollery and unction in the caricatures in Fore's shop-window, than in all the masks in Italy, without exception.[1]

The humour of English writing and description has often been wondered at ; and it flows from the same source

[1] Bells are peculiar to England. They jangle them in Italy during the carnival as boys do with us at Shrovetide ; but they have no notion of ringing them. The sound of village bells never cheers you in travelling, nor have you the lute or cittern in their stead. The expression of " Merry Bells " is a favourite, and not one of the least appropriate in our language :

> " For him the merry bells had rung, I ween,
>   If in this nook of quiet bells had ever been."
>   *Castle of Indolence.*[1]

———————————

[1] Canto i., st. 62.

as the merry *traits* of our character. A degree of barbarism and rusticity seems necessary to the perfection of humour. The droll and laughable depend on peculiarity and incongruity of character. But with the progress of refinement, the peculiarities of individuals and of classes wear out or lose their sharp, abrupt edges; nay, a certain slowness and dulness of understanding is required to be struck with odd and unaccountable appearances, for which a greater facility of apprehension can sooner assign an explanation that breaks the force of the seeming absurdity, and to which a wider scope of imagination is more easily reconciled. Clowns and country people are more amused, are more disposed to laugh and make sport of the dress of strangers, because from their ignorance the surprise is greater, and they cannot conceive anything to be natural or proper to which they are unused. Without a given portion of hardness and repulsiveness of feeling the ludicrous cannot well exist. Wonder and curiosity, the attributes of inexperience, enter greatly into its composition. Now it appears to me that the English are (or were) just at that mean point between intelligence and obtuseness, which must produce the most abundant and happiest crop of humour. Absurdity and singularity glide over the French mind without jarring or jostling with it; or they evaporate in levity: with the Italians they are lost in indolence or pleasure. The ludicrous takes hold of the English imagination, and clings to it with all its ramifications. We resent any difference or peculiarity of appearance at first, and yet, having not much malice at our hearts, we are glad to turn it into a jest—we are liable to be offended, and as willing to be pleased—struck with oddity from not knowing what to make of it, we wonder and burst out a laughing at the eccentricity of others, while we follow our own bent from wilfulness or simplicity, and thus afford them, in our turn, matter for the indulgence of the comic vein. It is possible that a greater refinement

of manners may give birth to finer distinctions of satire
and a nicer tact for the ridiculous : but our insular
situation and character are, I should say, most likely to
foster, as they have in fact fostered, the greatest quantity
of natural and striking humour, in spite of our plodding
tenaciousness, and want both of gaiety and quickness of
perception. A set of raw recruits with their awkward
movements and unbending joints are laughable enough ;
but they cease to be so, when they have once been drilled
into discipline and uniformity   So it is with nations that
lose their angular points and grotesque qualities with education and intercourse : but it is in a mixed state of manners
that comic humour chiefly flourishes, for, in order that the
drollery may not be lost, we must have spectators of the
passing scene who are able to appreciate and embody its
most remarkable features—wits as well as *butts* for ridicule.
I shall mention two names in this department, which may
serve to redeem the national character from absolute dulness and solemn pretence—Fielding and Hogarth. These
were thorough specimens of true English humour; yet
both were grave men. In reality, too high a pitch of
animal spirits runs away with the imagination, instead of
helping it to reach the goal; is inclined to take the jest
for granted when it ought to work it out with patient and
marked touches, and it ends in vapid flippancy and impertinence. Among our neighbours on the Continent, Molière
and Rabelais carried the freedom of wit and humour to an
almost incredible height ; but they rather belonged to the
old French school, and even approach and exceed the
English licence and extravagance of conception. I do not
consider Congreve's wit (though he belongs to us) as
coming under the article here spoken of; for his genius
is anything but *merry*.   Lord Byron was in the habit of
railing at the spirit of our good old comedy, and of abusing
Shakspeare's Clowns and Fools, which he said the refinement of the French and Italian stage would not endure,

and which only our grossness and puerile taste could tolerate. In this I agree with him; and it is *pat* to my purpose. I flatter myself that we are almost the only people who understand and relish *nonsense.* We are not "merry and wise," but indulge our mirth to excess and folly. When we trifle, we trifle in good earnest; and having once relaxed our hold of the helm, drift idly down the stream, and, delighted with the change, are tossed about "by every little breath" of whim or caprice,

"That under Heaven is blown."

All we then want is to proclaim a truce with reason, and to be pleased with as little expense of thought or pretension to wisdom as possible. This licensed fooling is carried to its very utmost length in Shakspeare, and in some other of our elder dramatists, without, perhaps, sufficient warrant or the same excuse. Nothing can justify this extreme relaxation but extreme tension. Shakspeare's trifling does indeed tread upon the very borders of vacancy: his meaning often hangs by the very slenderest threads. For this he might be blamed if it did not take away our breath to follow his eagle flights, or if he did not at other times make the cordage of our hearts crack. After our heads ache with thinking, it is fair to play the fool. The clowns were as proper an appendage to the gravity of our antique literature, as fools and dwarfs were to the stately dignity of courts and noble houses in former days. Of all people, they have the best right to claim a total exemption from rules and rigid formality, who, when they have anything of importance to do, set about it with the greatest earnestness and perseverance, and are generally grave and sober to a proverb.[1] Swift, who wrote more idle or *nonsense* verses than any man, was the severest of moralists; and his feelings and observations morbidly acute. Did

---

[1] The strict formality of French serious writing is resorted to as a foil to the natural levity of their character.

not Lord Byron himself follow up his *Childe Harold* with his *Don Juan?*—not that I insist on what he did as an illustration of the English character. He was one of the English Nobility, not one of the English people; and his occasional ease and familiarity were in my mind equally constrained and affected, whether in relation to the pretensions of his rank or the efforts of his genius.

They ask you in France, how you pass your time in England without amusements; and can with difficulty believe that there are theatres in London, still less that they are larger and handsomer than those in Paris. That we should have comic actors, " they own surprises them." They judge of the English character in the lump as one great jolter-head, containing all the stupidity of the country, as the large ball at the top of the Dispensary in Warwick-lane, from its resemblance to a gilded pill, has been made to represent the whole pharmacopœia and professional quackery of the kingdom. They have no more notion, for instance, how we should have such an actor as Liston on our stage, than if we were to tell them we have parts performed by a sea-otter; nor, if they were to see him, would they be much the wiser, or know what to think of his unaccountable twitches of countenance or nondescript gestures, of his teeth chattering in his head, his eyes that seem dropping from their sockets, his nose that is tickled by a jest as by a feather, and shining with self-complacency as if oiled, his ignorant conceit, his gaping stupor, his lumpish vivacity in *Lubin Log* or *Tony Lumpkin;* for as our rivals do not wind up the machine to such a determined intensity of purpose, neither have they any idea of its running down to such degrees of imbecility and folly, or coming to an absolute *stand-still* and lack of meaning, nor can they enter into or be amused with the contrast. No people ever laugh heartily who can give a reason for their doing so: and I believe the English in general are not yet in this predicament. They are not metaphysical, but very much in a state of nature; and this is one main ground why I give them credit for being merry, notwithstanding appearances. Their mirth is not the mirth of vice or desperation, but of innocence and a native wildness. They do not cavil or boggle at niceties, or merely come to the edge of a joke, but break their necks over it with a wanton "Here goes," where others make a *pirouette* and stand upon decorum. The French cannot however, be persuaded of the excellence of our comic stage, nor of the store we set by it. When they ask what amuse-ments we have, it is plain they can never have heard of Mrs. Jordan, nor King, nor Bannister, nor Suett, nor Munden, nor Lewis, nor little Simmons, nor Dodd, and Parsons, and Emery, and Miss Pope, and Miss Farren, and all those who even in my time have gladdened a nation and " made life's business like a summer's dream." Can I think of them, and of their names that glittered in the play-bills when I was young, exciting all the flutter of hope and expectation of seeing them in their favourite parts of *Nell*, or *Little Pickle*, or *Touchstone*, or *Sir Peter Teazle*, or *Lenitive* in the ' Prize,' or *Lingo*, or *Crabtree*, or *Nipperkin*, or old *Dornton*, or *Ranger*, or the *Copper Cap-tain*, or *Lord Sands*, or *Filch*, or *Moses*, or *Sir Andrew Aguecheek*, or *Acres*, or *Elbow*, or *Hodge*, or *Flora*, or the *Duenna*, or *Lady Teazle*, or *Lady Grace*, or of the gaiety that sparkled in all eyes, and the delight that overflowed all hearts, as they glanced before us in these parts,

"Throwing a gaudy shadow upon life "—

and not feel my heart yearn within me, or couple the thoughts of England and the spleen together? Our cloud has at least its rainbow tints; ours is not one long polar night of cold and dulness, but we have the gleaming lights of fancy to amuse us, the household fires of truth and genius to warm us. We can go to a play and see Liston; or stay at home and read *Roderick Random*; or have Hogarth's prints of *Marriage à la Mode* hanging round our room. Tut! "there's livers" even in England, as well as "out of it." We are not quite the *forlorn hope* of humanity, the last of nations. The French look at us across the Channel, and seeing nothing but water and a cloudy mist, think that this is England. If they have any farther idea of us, it is of George III. and our Jack tars, the House of Lords and House of Commons; and this is no great addition to us. To go beyond this, to talk of arts and elegances as having taken up their abode here, or to say that Mrs. Abington was equal to Mademoiselle Mars, and that we at one time got up the *School for Scandal*, as they do the *Misanthrope*, is to persuade them that Iceland is a pleasant winter-retreat, or to recommend the whale-fishery as a classical amusement. The French are the *cockneys* of Europe, and have no idea how anyone can exist out of Paris, or be alive without incessant grimace and *jabber*. Yet what imports it? What! though the joyous train I have just enumerated were, perhaps, never heard of in the precincts of the Palais-Royal, is it not enough that they gave pleasure where they were, to those who saw and heard them? Must our laugh, to be sincere, have its echo on the other side of the water? Had not the French their favourites and their enjoyments at the time, that we knew nothing of? Why then should we not have ours (and boast of them too) without their leave? A monopoly of self-conceit is not a monopoly of all other advantages. The English, when they go abroad, do not take away the prejudice against them by their looks. We seem duller and sadder than we are. As I write this,[1] I am sitting in the open air in a beautiful valley, near Vevey: Clarens is on my left, the Dent de Jamant is behind me, the rocks of Meillerie opposite: under my feet is a green bank,

[1] The article was written, apparently, at Vevey in the summer of 1825. See *Memoirs of William Hazlitt*, 1867, chap. xv.—ED.

enamelled with white and purple flowers, in which a dew drop here and there still glitters with pearly light—

" And gaudy butterflies flutter around."

Intent upon the scene and upon the thoughts that stir within me, I conjure up the cheerful passages of my life, and a crowd of happy images appear before me. No one would see it in my looks—my eyes grow dull and fixed, and I seem rooted to the spot, as all this phantasmagoria passes in review before me, glancing a reflex lustre on the face of the world and nature. But the traces of pleasure, in my case, sink into an absorbent ground of thoughtful melancholy, and require to be brought out by time and circumstances, or (as the critics tell you) by the *varnish* of style !

The *comfort*, on which the English lay so much stress, is of the same character, and arises from the same source as their mirth. Both exist by contrast and a sort of contradiction. The English are certainly the most uncomfortable of all people in themselves, and therefore it is that they stand in need of every kind of comfort and accommodation. The least thing puts them out of their way, and therefore everything must be in its place. They are mightily offended at disagreeable tastes and smells, and therefore they exact the utmost neatness and nicety. They are sensible of heat and cold, and therefore they cannot exist, unless everything is snug and warm, or else open and airy, where they are. They must have " all appliances and means to boot." They are afraid of interruption and intrusion, and therefore they shut themselves up ·in in-door enjoyments and by their own firesides. It is not that they require luxuries (for that implies a high degree of epicurean indulgence and gratification), but they cannot do without *their comforts ;* that is, whatever tends to supply their physical wants, and ward off physical pain and annoyance. As they have not a fund of animal spirits and enjoyments in themselves, they cling to external objects for support, and derive solid satisfaction from the ideas of order, cleanliness, plenty, property, and domestic quiet, as they seek for diversion from odd accidents and grotesque surprises, and have the highest possible relish not of voluptuous softness, but of hard knocks and dry blows, as one means of ascertaining their personal identity.

On a Sun-dial.[1]

"To carve out dials quaintly, point by point."
SHAKSPEARE.[2]

Horas non numero nisi serenas—is the motto of a sun-dial near Venice. There is a softness and a harmony in the words and in the thought unparalleled. Of all conceits it is surely the most classical. "I count only the hours that are serene." What a bland and care-dispelling feeling! How the shadows seem to fade on the dial-plate as the sky lours, and time presents only a blank unless as its progress is marked by what is joyous, and all that is not happy sinks into oblivion! What a fine lesson is conveyed to the mind—to take no note of time but by its benefits, to watch only for the smiles and neglect the frowns of fate, to compose our lives of bright and gentle moments, turning always to the sunny side of things, and letting the rest slip from our imaginations, unheeded or forgotten! How different from the common art of self-tormenting! For myself, as I rode along the Brenta, while the sun shone hot upon its sluggish, slimy waves, my sensations were far from comfortable; but the reading this inscription on the side of a glaring wall in an instant restored me to myself; and still, whenever I think of or repeat it, it has the power of wafting me into the region of pure and blissful abstraction. I cannot

[1] Written in Italy, in 1825.—ED.
[2] *Henry VI.*, part 3, ii, 5. [Dyce's edit. 1868, v. 265.]

help fancying it to be a legend of Popish superstition. Some monk of the dark ages must have invented and bequeathed it to us, who, loitering in trim gardens and watching the silent march of time, as his fruits ripened in the sun or his flowers scented the balmy air, felt a mild languor pervade his senses, and having little to do or to care for, determined (in imitation of his sun-dial) to efface that little from his thoughts or draw a veil over it, making of his life one long dream of quiet! *Horas non numero nisi serenas*—he might repeat, when the heavens were overcast and the gathering storm scattered the falling leaves, and turn to his books and wrap himself in his golden studies! Out of some such mood of mind, indolent, elegant, thoughtful, this exquisite device (speaking volumes) must have originated.

Of the several modes of counting time, that by the sun-dial is perhaps the most apposite and striking, if not the most convenient or comprehensive. It does not obtrude its observations, though it " morals on the time," and, by its stationary character, forms a contrast to the most fleeting of all essences. It stands *sub dio*—under the marble air, and there is some connexion between the image of infinity and eternity. I should also like to have a sun-flower growing near it with bees fluttering round.[1] It should be of iron to denote duration, and have a dull, leaden look. I hate a sun-dial made of wood, which is rather calculated to show the variations of the seasons, than the progress of time, slow, silent, imperceptible, chequered with light and shade. If our hours were all serene, we might probably take almost as little note of them, as the dial does of those that are clouded. It is the shadow thrown across, that gives us warning of their flight. Otherwise, our impressions would take the

---

[1] Is this a verbal fallacy? Or in the close, retired, sheltered scene which I have imagined to myself, is not the sun-flower a natural accompaniment of the sun-dial?

same undistinguishable hue ; we should scarce be conscious of our existence. Those who have had none of the
cares of this life to harass and disturb them, have been
obliged to have recourse to the hopes and fears of the
next to vary the prospect before them. Most of the
methods for measuring the lapse of time have, I believe,
been the contrivance of monks and religious recluses, who,
finding time hang heavy on their hands, were at some
pains to see how they got rid of it. The hour-glass is, I
suspect, an older invention ; and it is certainly the most
defective of all. Its creeping sands are not indeed an
unapt emblem of the minute, countless portions of our
existence; and the manner in which they gradually slide
through the hollow glass and diminish in number till not
a single one is left, also illustrates the way in which our
years slip from us by stealth : but as a mechanical
invention, it is rather a hindrance than a help, for it
requires to have the time, of which it pretends to count
the precious moments, taken up in attention to itself, and
in seeing that when one end of the glass is empty, we
turn it round, in order that it may go on again, or else
all our labour is lost, and we must wait for some other
mode of ascertaining the time before we can recover our
reckoning and proceed as before. The philosopher in his
cell, the cottager at her spinning-wheel must, however,
find an invaluable acquisition in this "companion of the
lonely hour," as it has been called,[1] which not only serves
to tell how the time goes, but to fill up its vacancies.
What a treasure must not the little box seem to hold, as
if it were a sacred deposit of the very grains and fleeting
sands of life! What a business, in lieu of other more important avocations, to see it out to the last sand, and then
to renew the process again on the instant, that there may

---

[1] " Once more, companion of the lonely hour,
    I'll turn thee up again."
        Bloomfield's Poems— The Widow to her Hour-glass.

not be the least flaw or error in the account! What a
strong sense must be brought home to the mind of the
value and irrecoverable nature of the time that is fled;
what a thrilling, incessant consciousness of the slippery
tenure by which we hold what remains of it! Our very
existence must seem crumbling to atoms, and running
down (without a miraculous reprieve) to the last fragment.
" Dust to dust and ashes to ashes " is a text that might be
fairly inscribed on an hour-glass: it is ordinarily associated with the scythe of Time and a Death's-head, as a
memento mori; and has, no doubt, furnished many a tacit
hint to the apprehensive and visionary enthusiast in
favour of a resurrection to another life!

The French give a different turn to things, less *sombre*
and less edifying. A common and also a very pleasing
ornament to a clock, in Paris, is a figure of Time seated
in a boat which Cupid is rowing along, with the motto,
L'Amour fait passer le Temps—which the wits again have
travestied into *Le Temps fait passer L'Amour.* All this
is ingenious and well; but it wants sentiment. I like
a people who have something that they love and something
that they hate, and with whom everything is not alike a
matter of indifference or *pour passer le temps.* The French
attach no importance to anything, except for the moment;
they are only thinking how they shall get rid of one
sensation for another; all their ideas are *in transitu.*
Everything is detached, nothing is accumulated. It
would be a million of years before a Frenchman would
think of the *Horas non numero nisi serenas.* Its impassioned repose and *ideal* voluptuousness are as far from
their breasts as the poetry of that line in Shakspeare—
" How sweet the moonlight sleeps upon this bank!" [1]
They never arrive at the classical—or the romantic. They
blow the bubbles of vanity, fashion, and pleasure; but
they do not expand their perceptions into refinement, or

[1] *Merchant of Venice*, v, 1. [Dyce's edit. 1868, ii, 409.]

strengthen them into solidity. Where there is nothing fine in the groundwork of the imagination, nothing fine in the superstructure can be produced. They are light, airy, fanciful (to give them their due)—but when they attempt to be serious (beyond mere good sense) they are either dull or extravagant. When the volatile salt has flown off, nothing but a *caput mortuum* remains. They have infinite crotchets and caprices with their clocks and watches, which seem made for anything but to tell the hour—gold repeaters, watches with metal covers, clocks with hands to count the seconds. There is no escaping from quackery and impertinence, even in our attempts to calculate the waste of time. The years gallop fast enough for me, without remarking every moment as it flies ; and further, I must say I dislike a watch, (whether of French or English manufacture) that comes to me like a footpad with its face muffled, and does not present its clear, open aspect like a friend, and point with its finger to the time of day. All this opening and shutting of dull, heavy cases (under pretence that the glass-lid is liable to be broken, or lets in the dust or air and obstructs the movements of the watch), is not to husband time, but to give trouble. It is mere pomposity and self-importance, like consulting a mysterious oracle that one carries about with one in one's pocket, instead of asking a common question of an acquaintance or companion. There are two clocks which strike the hour in the room where I am. This I do not like. In the first place, I do not want to be reminded twice how the time goes (it is like the second tap of a saucy servant at your door when perhaps you have no wish to get up): in the next place, it is starting a difference of opinion on the subject, and I am averse to every appearance of wrangling and disputation. Time moves on the same, whatever disparity there may be in our mode of keeping count of it, like true fame in spite of the cavils and contradictions of the critics. I am no friend to repeating watches. The only pleasant association I have with them is the account given by Rousseau of some French lady, who sat up reading the *New Eloise* when it first came out, and ordering her maid to sound the repeater, found it was too late to go to bed, and continued reading on till morning. Yet how different is the interest excited by this story from the account which Rousseau somewhere else gives of his sitting up with his father reading romances, when a boy, till they were startled by the swallows twittering in their nests at daybreak, and the father cried out, half angry and ashamed—"*Allons, mon fils ; je suis plus enfant que toi !*" In general, I have heard repeating-watches sounded in stage-coaches at night, when some fellow-traveller suddenly awaking and wondering what was the hour, another has very deliberately taken out his watch, and pressing the spring, it has counted out the time ; each petty stroke acting like a sharp puncture on the ear, and informing me of the dreary hours I had already passed, and of the more dreary ones I had to wait till morning.

The great advantage, it is true, which clocks have over watches and other dumb reckoners of time is, that for the most part they strike the hour—that they are as it were the mouth-pieces of time; that they not only point it to the eye, but impress it on the ear ; that they " lend it both an understanding and a tongue." Time thus speaks to us in an audible and warning voice. Objects of sight are easily distinguished by the sense, and suggest useful reflections to the mind ; sounds, from their intermittent nature, and perhaps other causes, appeal more to the imagination, and strike upon the heart. But to do this, they must be unexpected and involuntary—there must be no trick in the case—they should not be squeezed out with a finger and a thumb; there should be nothing optional, personal in their occurrence; they should be like stern, inflexible monitors, that nothing can prevent from discharging their duty. Surely, if there is anything with which we should not mix up our vanity and self-consequence, it is with Time, the most independent of all things. All the sublimity, all the superstition that hang upon this palpable mode of announcing its flight, are chiefly attached to this circumstance. Time would lose its abstracted character, if we kept it like a curiosity or a jack-in-a-box : its prophetic warnings would have no effect, if it obviously spoke only at our prompting like a paltry ventriloquism. The clock that tells the coming, dreaded hour—the castle bell, that " with its brazen throat and iron tongue, sounds *one* unto the drowsy ear of night "—the curfew, " swinging slow with sullen roar " o'er wizard stream or fountain, are like a voice from other worlds, big with unknown events. The last sound, which is still kept up as an old custom in many parts of England, is a great favourite with me. I used to hear it when a boy. It tells a tale of other times The days that are past, the generations that are gone. the tangled forest glades and hamlets brown of my native country, the woodsman's art, the Norman warrior armed for the battle or in his festive hall, the conqueror's iron rule and peasant's lamp extinguished, all start up at the clamorous peal, and fill my mind with fear and wonder. I confess, nothing at present interests me but what has been—the recollection of the impressions of my early life, or events long past, of which only the dim traces remain in a mouldering ruin or half-obsolete custom. That *things should be that are now no more*, creates in my mind the most unfeigned astonishment. I cannot solve the mystery of the past, nor exhaust my pleasure in it. The years, the generations to come, are nothing to me. We care no more about the world in the year 2300 than we do about one of the planets. We might as well make a voyage to the moon as think of stealing a march upon

Time with impunity. *De non apparentibus et non ex-istentibus eadem est ratio.* Those who are to come after us and push us from the stage seem like upstarts and pretenders, that may be said to exist *in vacuo*, we know not upon what, except as they are blown up with vanity and self-conceit by their patrons among the moderns. But the ancients are true and *bonâ fide* people, to whom we are bound by aggregate knowledge and filial ties, and in whom, seen by the mellow light of history, we feel our own existence doubled and our pride consoled, as we ruminate on the vestiges of the past. The public in general, however, do not carry this speculative indifference about the future to what is to happen to themselves, or to the part they are to act in the busy scene. For my own part, I do ; and the only wish I can form, or that ever prompts the passing sigh, would be to live some of my years over again—they would be those in which I enjoyed and suffered most !

The ticking of a clock in the night has nothing very interesting nor very alarming in it, though superstition has magnified it into an omen. In a state of vigilance or debility, it preys upon the spirits like the persecution of a teazing, pertinacious insect ; and haunting the imagination after it has ceased in reality, is converted into the death-watch. Time is rendered vast by contemplating its minute portions thus repeatedly and painfully urged upon its attention, as the ocean in its immensity is composed of water-drops. A clock striking with a clear and silver sound is a great relief in such circumstances, breaks the spell, and resembles a sylph-like and friendly spirit in the room. Foreigners with all their tricks and contrivances upon clocks and time-pieces, are strangers to the sound of village-bells, though perhaps a people that can dance may dispense with them. They impart a pensive, wayward pleasure to the mind, and are a kind of chronology of happy events, often serious in the retrospect—births, marriages, and so forth. Coleridge calls them "the poor man's only music." A village-spire in England peeping from its cluster of trees, is always associated in imagination with this cheerful accompaniment, and may be expected to pour its joyous tidings on the gale. In Catholic countries, you are stunned with the everlasting tolling of bells to prayers or for the dead. In the Apennines, and other wild and mountainous districts of Italy, the little chapel-bell with its simple tinkling sound has a romantic and charming effect. The monks in former times appear to have taken a pride in the construction of bells as well as churches; and some of those of the great cathedrals abroad (as at Cologne and Rouen) may be fairly said to be hoarse with counting the flight of ages. The chimes in Holland are a nuisance. They dance in the hours and the quarters. They leave no respite to the imagination. Before one set has done ringing in your ears, another begins. You do not know whether the hours move or stand still, go backwards or forwards, so fantastical and perplexing are their accompaniments. Time is a more staid personage, and not so full of gambols. It puts you in mind of a tune with variations, or of an embroidered dress. Surely, nothing is more simple than time. His march is straightforward; but we should have leisure allowed us to look back upon the distance we have come, and not be counting his steps every moment. Time in Holland is a foolish old fellow with all the antics of a youth, who " goes to church in a coranto, and lights his pipe in a cinque-pace." The chimes with us, on the contrary, as they come in every three or four hours, are like stages in the journey of the day. They give a fillip to the lazy, creeping hours, and relieve the lassitude of country-places. At noon, their desultory, trivial song is diffused through the hamlet with the odour of rashers of bacon; at the close of day they send the toil-worn sleepers to their beds. Their discontinuance would be a great loss to the thinking or unthinking public. Mr. Wordsworth has painted their effect on the mind when he makes his friend Matthew, in a fit of inspired dotage,

> " Sing those witty rhymes
> About the crazy old church-clock
> And the bewilder'd chimes."

The tolling of the bell for deaths and executions is a fearful summons, though, as it announces, not the advance of time but the approach of fate, it happily makes no part of our subject. Otherwise, the "sound of the bell" for Macheath's execution in the *Beggars' Opera*, or for that of the Conspirators in *Venice Preserved*, with the roll of the drum at a soldier's funeral, and a digression to that of my Uncle Toby, as it is so finely described by Sterne, would furnish ample topics to descant upon. If I were a moralist, I might disapprove the ringing in the new and ringing out the old year.

> " Why dance ye, mortals, o'er the grave of Time ?"

St. Paul's bell tolls only for the death of our English kings, or a distinguished personage or two, with long intervals between.[1]

Those who have no artificial means of ascertaining the progress of time, are in general the most acute in discerning its immediate signs, and are most retentive of individual dates. The mechanical aids to knowledge are not sharpeners of the wits. The understanding of a savage is a kind of natural almanac, and more true in its prognostication of the future. In his mind's eye he sees what has happened or what is likely to happen to him, " as in a map the voyager his course." Those who read the times and seasons in the aspect of the heavens and the

[1] Rousseau has admirably described the effect of bells on the imagination in a passage in the *Confessions*, beginning " *Le son des cloches m'a toujours singulièrement affecté,*" &c.

configuration of the stars, who count by moons and know when the sun rises and sets, are by no means ignorant of their own affairs or of the common concatenation of events. People in such situations have not their faculties distracted by any multiplicity of inquiries beyond what befalls themselves, and the outward appearances that mark the change. There is, therefore, a simplicity and clearness in the knowledge they possess, which often puzzles the more learned. I am sometimes surprised at a shepherd-boy by the road-side, who sees nothing but the earth and sky, asking me the time of day—he ought to know so much better than any one how far the sun is above the horizon. I suppose he wants to ask a question of a passenger, or to see if he has a watch. Robinson Crusoe lost his reckoning in the monotony of his life and that bewildering dream of solitude, and was fain to have recourse to the notches in a piece of wood. What a diary was his! And how time must have spread its circuit round him, vast and pathless as the ocean!

For myself, I have never had a watch nor any other mode of keeping time in my possession, nor ever wish to learn how time goes. It is a sign I have had little to do, few avocations, few engagements. When I am in a town, I can hear the clock; and when I am in the country, I can listen to the silence. What I like best is to lie whole mornings on a sunny bank on Salisbury Plain, without any object before me, neither knowing nor caring how time passes, and thus "with light-winged toys of feathered Idleness" to melt down hours to moments. Perhaps some such thoughts as I have here set down float before me like motes before my half-shut eyes, or some vivid image of the past by forcible contrast rushes by me—" Diana and her fawn, and all the glories of the antique world;" then I start away to prevent the iron from entering my soul, and let fall some tears into that stream of time which separates me farther and farther from all I once loved!

At length I rouse myself from my reverie, and home to dinner, proud of killing time with thought, nay even without thinking. Somewhat of this idle humour I inherit from my father, though he had not the same freedom from *ennui*, for he was not a metaphysician; and there were stops and vacant intervals in his being which he did not know how to fill up. He used in these cases, and as an obvious resource, carefully to wind up his watch at night, and " with lack-lustre eye " more than once in the course of the day look to see what o'clock it was. Yet he had nothing else in his character in common with the elder Mr. Shandy. Were I to attempt a sketch of him, for my own or the reader's satisfaction, it would be after the following manner————But now I recollect I have done something of the kind once before,[1] and were I to resume the subject here, some bat or owl of a critic, with specta-cled gravity, might swear I had stolen the whole of this Essay from myself—or (what is worse) from him! So I had better let it go as it is.

————

On Prejudice.

PREJUDICE, in its ordinary and literal sense, is *prejudging* any question without having sufficiently examined it, and adhering to our opinion upon it through ignorance, malice, or perversity, in spite of every evidence to the contrary. The little that we know has a strong alloy of misgiving and uncertainty in it; the mass of things of which we have no means of judging, but of which we form a blind and confident opinion, as if we were thoroughly acquainted with them, is monstrous. Prejudice is the child of ignorance : for as our actual knowledge falls short of our desire to know, or curiosity and interest in the world about us,

[1] In the *Liberal*, 1823; but see *Memoirs of William Hazlitt*, 1867, i, 38 *et seq.*—ED.

so must we be tempted to decide upon a greater number of things at a venture ; and having no check from reason or inquiry, we shall grow more obstinate and bigoted in our conclusions, according as we have been rash and presump- tuous. The absence of proof, instead of suspending our judgment, only gives us an opportunity of making things out according to our wishes and fancies; mere ignorance is a blank canvas, on which we lay what colours we please, and paint objects black or white, as angels or devils, magnify or diminish them at our option; and in the *vacuum* either of facts or arguments, the weight of pre- judice and passion falls with double force, and bears down everything before it. If we enlarge the circle of our pre- vious knowledge ever so little, we may meet with some- thing to create doubt and difficulty; but as long as we remain confined to the cell of our native ignorance, while we know nothing beyond the routine of sense and custom, we shall refer everything to that standard, or make it out as we would have it to be, like spoiled children who have never been from home, and expect to find nothing in the world that does not accord with their wishes and notions. It is evident that the fewer things we know, the more ready we shall be to pronounce upon and condemn, what is new and strange us; that is, the less capable we shall be of varying our conceptions, and the more prone to mis- take a part for the whole. What we do not understand the meaning of, must necessarily appear to us ridiculous and contemptible; and we do not stop to inquire, till we have been taught by repeated experiments and warnings of our own fallibility, whether the absurdity is in our- selves, or in the object of our dislike and scorn. The most ignorant people are rude and insolent, as the most barbarous are cruel and ferocious. All our knowledge at first lying in a narrow compass (crowded by local and physical causes) whatever does not conform to this shocks us as out of reason and nature. The less we look abroad,

the more our ideas are introverted, and our habitual
impressions, from being made up of a few particulars
always repeated, grow together into a kind of concrete substance, which will not bear taking to pieces, and where the
smallest deviation destroys the whole feeling. Thus, the
difference of colour in a black man was thought to forfeit
his title to belong to the species, till books of voyages and
travels, and old Fuller's quaint expression of " God's image
carved in ebony," have brought the two ideas into a forced
union, and men of colour are no longer to be libelled with
impunity. The word *republic* has a harsh and incongruous
sound to ears bred under a constitutional monarchy; and
we strove hard for many years to overturn the French
republic, merely because we could not reconcile it to ourselves that such a thing should exist at all, notwithstanding the examples of Holland, Switzerland, and many others.
This term has hardly yet performed quarantine : to the
loyal and patriotic it has an ugly taint in it, and is
scarcely fit to be mentioned in good company. If, however, we are weaned by degrees from our prejudices against
certain words that shock opinion, this is not the case with
all : those that offend good manners grow more offensive
with the progress of refinement and civilization, so that
no writer now dares venture upon expressions that unwittingly disfigure the pages of our elder writers, and in this
respect, instead of becoming callous or indifferent, we
appear to become more fastidious every day. There is
then a real grossness which does not depend on familiarity
or custom. This account of the concrete nature of prejudice, or of the manner in which our ideas by habit and
the dearth of general information coalesce together into
one indissoluble form, will show (what otherwise seems
unaccountable) how such violent antipathies and animosities have been occasioned by the most ridiculous or
trifling differences of opinion, or outward symbols of it;
for by constant custom, and the want of reflection, the

most insignificant of these was as inseparably bound
up with the main principle as the most important, and
to give up any part was to give up the whole essence
and vital interests of religion, morals, and government.
Hence we see all sects and parties mutually insist
on their own technical distinctions as the essentials
and fundamentals of religion and politics, and, for the
slightest variation in any of these, unceremoniously attack
their opponents as atheists and blasphemers, traitors and
incendiaries.

In fact, these minor points are laid hold of in preference,
as being more obvious and tangible, and as leaving more
room for the exercise of prejudice and passion. Another
thing that makes our prejudices rancorous and inveterate
is, that as they are taken up without reason, they seem to
be self-evident; and we thence conclude, that they not
only are so to ourselves, but must be so to others, so that
their differing from us is wilful, hypocritical, and malicious. The Inquisition never pretended to punish its
victims for being heretics or infidels, but for avowing
opinions which with their eyes open they knew to be false.
That is, the whole of the Catholic faith, "that one entire
and perfect chrysolite," appeared to them so completely
without flaw and blameless, that they could not conceive
how any one else could imagine it to be otherwise, except
from stubborness and contumacy, and would rather admit
(to avoid so improbable a suggestion) that men went to
the stake for an opinion, not which they held, but counterfeited, and were content to be burnt alive for the pleasure
of playing the hypocrite. Nor is it wonderful that there
should be so much repugnance to admit the existence of a
serious doubt in matters of such vital and eternal interest,
and on which the whole fabric of the church hinged, since
the first doubt that was expressed on any single point drew
all the rest after it; and the first person who started a conscientious scruple, and claimed the *trial by reason*, threw

down, as if by a magic spell, the strongholds of bigotry
and superstition, and transferred the determination of the
issue from the blind tribunal of prejudice and implicit
faith to a totally different ground, the fair and open field
of argument and inquiry. On this ground a single
champion is a match for thousands. The decision of the
majority is not here enough: unanimity is absolutely
necessary to infallibility; for the only secure plea on
which such a preposterous pretension could be set up, is
by taking it for granted that there can be no possible
doubt entertained upon the subject, and by diverting men's
minds from ever asking themselves the question of the
truth of certain dogmas and mysteries, any more than
whether *two and two make four*. Prejudice, in short, is
egotism : we see a part, and substitute it for the whole ; a
thing strikes us casually and by halves, and we would
have the universe stand proxy for our decision, in order
to rivet it more firmly in our own belief ; however
insufficient or sinister the grounds of our opinions, we
would persuade ourselves that they arise out of the
strongest conviction, and are entitled to unqualified approbation ; slaves of our own prejudices, caprice, ignorance,
we would be lords of the understandings and reason of
others ; and (strange infatuation!) taking up an opinion
solely from our own narrow and partial point of view,
without consulting the feelings of others, or the reason of
things, we are still uneasy if all the world do not come
into our way of thinking.

The most dangerous enemies to established opinions
are those who, by always defending them, call attention to
their weak sides. The priests and politicians, in former
times, were therefore wise in preventing the first approaches of innovation and inquiry ; in preserving inviolate the smallest link in the adamantine chain with
which they had bound the souls and bodies of men ; in
closing up every avenue or pore through which a doubt

could creep in, for they knew that through the slightest crevice floods of irreligion and heresy would rush like a tide. Hence the constant alarm at free discussion and inquiry : hence the clamour against innovation and reform : hence our dread and detestation of those who differ with us in opinion, for this at once puts us on the necessity of defending ourselves, or of owning ourselves weak or in the wrong, if we cannot ; and converts that which was before a bed of roses, while we slept undisturbed upon it, into a cushion of thorns ; and hence our natural tenaciousness of those points which are most vulnerable, and of which we have no proof to offer ; for as reason fails us, we are more annoyed by the objections, and require to be soothed and supported by the concurrence of others. Bigotry and intolerance, which pass as synonymous, are, if rightly considered, a contradiction in terms ; for if, in drawing up the articles of our creed, we are blindly bigoted to our impressions and views, utterly disregarding all others, why should we afterwards be so haunted and disturbed by the last, as to wish to exterminate every difference of sentiment with fire and sword ? The difficulty is only solved by considering that unequal compound, the human mind, alternately swayed by individual biasses and abstract pretensions, and where reason so often panders to, or is made the puppet of the will. To show at once the danger and extent of prejudice, it may be sufficient to observe that all our convictions, however arrived at, and whether founded on strict demonstration or the merest delusion, are crusted over with the same varnish of confidence and conceit, and afford the same firm footing both to our theories and practice ; or if there be any difference, we are in general " most ignorant of what we are most assured," the strength of will and impatience of contradiction making up for the want of evidence. Mr. Burke says that we ought to " cherish our prejudices, because they are prejudices ;" but this view of the case will satisfy the demands of neither party, for prejudice is never easy unless it can pass itself off for reason, or abstract undeniable truth ; and again, in the eye of reason, if all prejudices are to be equally regarded as such, then the prejudices of others are right, and ours must in their turn be wrong. The great stumbling block to candour and liberality is the difficulty of being fully possessed of the excellence of any opinion or pursuits of our own, without proportionably condemning whatever is opposed to it, nor can we admit the possibility that when our side of the shield is black, the other should be white. The largest part of our judgments is prompted by habit and passion ; but because habit is like a second nature, and we necessarily approve what passion suggests, we will have it that they are founded entirely on reason and nature, and that all the world must be of the same opinion, unless they wilfully shut their eyes to the truth. Animals are free from prejudice, because they have no notion or care about anything beyond themselves, and have no wish to generalise or talk big on what does not concern them : man alone falls into absurdity and error by setting up a claim to superior wisdom and virtue, and to be a dictator and lawgiver to all around him, and on all things that he has the remotest conception of. If mere prejudice were dumb as well as deaf and blind, it would not so much signify ; but as it is, each sect, age, country, profession, individual, is ready to prove that they are exclusively in the right, and to go together by the ears for it. " Rings the earth with the vain stir." It is the trick for each party to raise an outcry against prejudice; as by .this they flatter themselves, and would have it supposed by others, that they are perfectly free from it, and have all the reason on their own side. It is easy indeed to call names, or to separate the word *prejudice* from the word *reason ;* but not so easy to separate the two things. Reason seems a very positive and palpable thing to those who have no notion of it, but as expressing their own views and feelings ; as prejudice is evidently a very gross and shocking absurdity (that no one can fall into who wishes to avoid it), as long as we continue to apply this term to the prejudices of other people. To suppose that we cannot make a mistake is the very way to run headlong into it ; for if the distinction were so broad and glaring as our self-conceit and dogmatism lead us to imagine it is, we could never, but by design, mistake truth for falsehood. Those, however, who think they can *make a clear stage of it*, and frame a set of opinions on all subjects by an appeal to reason alone, and without the smallest intermixture of custom, imagination or passion, know just as little of themselves as they do of human nature. The best way to prevent our running into the wildest excesses of prejudice and the most dangerous aberrations from reason, is, not to represent the two things as having a great gulf between them, which it is impossible to pass without a violent effort, but to show that we are constantly (even when we think ourselves most secure) treading on the brink of a precipice ; that custom, passion, imagination, insinuate themselves into and influence almost every judgment we pass or sentiment we indulge, and are a necessary help (as well as hindrance) to the human understanding ; and that to attempt to refer every question to abstract truth and precise definition, without allowing for the frailty of prejudice, which is the unavoidable consequence of the frailty and imperfection of reason, would be to unravel the whole web and texture of human understanding and society. Such daring anatomists of morals and philosophy think that the whole beauty of the mind consists in the skeleton ; cut away, without remorse, all sentiment, fancy, taste, as superfluous excrescences ; and in their own eager, unfeeling pursuit of scientific truth and elementary principles, they " murder to dissect."

It is a mistake, however, to suppose that all prejudices are false, though it is not an easy matter to distinguish between true and false prejudice. Prejudice is properly an opinion or feeling, not for which there is no reason, but of which we cannot render a satisfactory account on the spot. It is not always possible to assign a "reason for the faith that is in us," not even if we take time and summon up all our strength; but it does not therefore follow that our faith is hollow and unfounded. A false impression may be defined to be an effect without a cause, or without any adequate one; but the effect may remain and be true, though the cause is concealed or forgotten. The grounds of our opinions and tastes may be deep, and be scattered over a large surface; they may be various, remote and complicated; but the result will be sound and true, if they have existed at all, though we may not be able to analyse them into classes, or to recall the particular time, place, and circumstances of each individual case or branch of the evidence. The materials of thought and feeling, the body of facts and experience, are infinite, are constantly going on around us, and acting to produce an impression of good or evil, of assent or dissent to certain inferences; but to require that we should be prepared to retain the whole of this mass of experience in our memory, to resolve it into its component parts, and be able to quote chapter and verse for every conclusion we unavoidably draw from it, or else to discard the whole together as unworthy the attention of a rational being, is to betray an utter ignorance both of the limits and the several uses of the human capacity. The *feeling* of the truth of anything, or the soundness of the judgment formed upon it from repeated, actual impressions, is one thing; the power of vindicating and enforcing it, by distinctly appealing to or explaining those impressions, is another. The most fluent talkers or most plausible reasoners are not always the justest thinkers.

To deny that we can, in a certain sense, know and be justified in believing anything of which we cannot give the complete demonstration, or the exact *why* and *how*, would only be to deny that the clown, the mechanic (and not even the greatest philosopher), can know the commonest thing; for in this new and dogmatical process of reasoning, the greatest philosopher can trace nothing *above*, nor proceed a single step without taking something for granted;[1] and it is well if he does not take more things for granted than the most vulgar and illiterate, and what he knows a great deal less about. A common mechanic can tell how to work an engine better than the mathematician who invented it. A peasant is able to foretell rain from the appearance of the clouds, because (time out of mind) he has seen that appearance followed by that consequence; and shall a pedant catechise him out of a conviction which he has found true in innumerable instances, because he does not understand the composition of the elements, or cannot put his notions into a logical shape? There may also be some collateral circumstance (as the time of day), as well as the appearance of the clouds, which he may forget to state in accounting for his prediction; though, as it has been a part of his familiar experience, it has naturally guided him in forming it, whether he was aware of it or not. This comes under the head of the well-known principle of the *association of ideas;* by which certain impressions, from frequent recurrence, coalesce and act in unison truly and mechanically—that is, without our being conscious of anything but the general and settled result. On this principle it has been well

---

[1] Berkeley, in his *Minute Philosopher*, attacks Dr. Halley, who had objected to faith and mysteries in religion, on this score; and contends that the mathematician, no less than the theologian, is obliged to presume on certain *postulates*, or to resort, before he could establish a single theorem, to a formal definition of those undefinable and hypothetical existences, points, lines, and surfaces; and, according to the ingenious and learned Bishop of Cloyne, *solids* would fare no better than *superficials* in this war of words and captious contradiction.

said, that "there is nothing so true as habit;" but it is also blind : we feel and can produce a given effect from numberless repetitions of the same cause; but we neither inquire into the cause, nor advert to the mode. In learning any art or exercise, we are obliged to take lessons, to watch others, to proceed step by step, to attend to the details and means employed; but when we are masters of it, we take all this for granted, and do it without labour and without thought, by a kind of habitual instinct—that is, by the trains of our ideas and volitions having been directed uniformly, and at last flowing of themselves into the proper channel.

We never do anything well till we cease to think about the manner of doing it. This is the reason why it is so difficult for any but natives to speak a language correctly or idiomatically. They do not succeed in this from knowledge or reflection, but from inveterate custom, which is a cord that cannot be loosed. In fact, in all that we do, feel, or think, there is a leaven of *prejudice* (more or less extensive), viz. something implied, of which we do not know or have forgotten the grounds.

If I am required to prove the possibility, or demonstrate the mode of whatever I do before I attempt it, I can neither speak, walk, nor see ; nor have the use of my hands senses, or common understanding. I do not know what muscles I use in walking, nor what organs I employ in speech : those who do, cannot speak or walk better on that account ; nor can they tell how these organs and muscles themselves act. Can I not discover that one object is near, and another at a distance, from the *eye* alone, or from continual impressions of sense and custom concurring to make the distinction, without going through a course of perspective and optics?—or am I not to be allowed an opinion on the subject, or to act upon it, without being accused of being a very *prejudiced* and obstinate person? An artist knows that, to imitate an object in the horizon, he must use less colour ; and the naturalist knows that this effect is produced by the intervention of a greater quantity of air : but a country fellow, who knows nothing of either circumstance, must not only be ignorant but a blockhead, if he could be persuaded that a hill ten miles off was close before him, only because he could not state the grounds of his opinion scientifically. Not only must we (if restricted to reason and philosophy) distrust the notices of sense, but we must also dismiss all that mass of knowledge and perception which falls under the head of *common sense* and *natural feeling*, which is made up of the strong and urgent, but undefined impressions of things upon us, and lies between the two extremes of absolute proof and the grossest ignorance. Many of these pass for instinctive principles and *innate ideas;* but there is nothing in them " more than natural."

Without the aid of prejudice and custom, I should not be able to find my way across the room ; nor know how to conduct myself in any circumstances, nor what to feel in any relation of life. Reason may play the critic, and correct certain errors afterwards ; but if we were to wait for its formal and absolute decisions in the shifting and multifarious combinations of human affairs, the world would stand still. Even men of science, after they have gone over the proofs a number of times, abridge the process, and *jump at a conclusion :* is it therefore false, because they have always found it to be true ? Science after a certain time becomes presumption ; and learning reposes in ignorance. It has been observed, that women have more *tact* and insight into character than men, that they find out a pedant, a pretender, a blockhead, sooner. The explanation is, that they trust more to the first impressions and natural indications of things, without troubling themselves with a learned theory of them ; whereas men, affecting greater gravity, and thinking themselves bound to justify their opinions, are afraid to form any judgment at all, without the formality of proofs and definitions, and blunt the edge of their understandings, lest they should commit some mistake. They stay for facts, till it is too late to pronounce on the characters. Women are naturally physiognomists, and men phrenologists. The first judge by sensations; the last by rules. Prejudice is so far then an involuntary and stubborn *association of ideas,* of which we cannot assign the distinct grounds and origin; and the answer to the question, " How do we know whether the prejudice is true or false ?" depends chiefly on that other, whether the first connection between our ideas has been real or imaginary. This again resolves into the inquiry—Whether the subject in dispute falls under the province of our own experience, feeling, and observation, or is referable to the head of authority, tradition, and fanciful conjecture? Our practical conclusions are in this respect generally right; our speculative opinions are just as likely to be wrong. What we derive from our personal acquaintance with things (however narrow in its scope or imperfectly digested), is, for the most part, built on a solid foundation—that of Nature; it is in trusting to others (who give themselves out for guides and doctors) that we are *all abroad,* and at the mercy of quackery, impudence, and imposture. Any impression, however absurd, or however we may have imbibed it, by being repeated and indulged in, becomes an article of implicit and incorrigible belief. The point to consider is, how we have first taken it up, whether from ourselves or the arbitrary dictation of others. " Thus shall we try the doctrines, whether they be of nature or of man."

So far then from the charge lying against vulgar and illiterate prejudice as the bane of truth and common sense, the argument turns the other way; for the greatest, the most solemn, and mischievous absurdities that mankind have been the dupes of, they have imbibed from the dogmatism and vanity or hypocrisy of the self-styled wise and learned, who have imposed profitable fictions upon them for self-evident truths, and contrived to enlarge their power with their pretensions to knowledge. Every boor sees that the sun shines above his head ; that " the moon is made of green cheese," is a fable that has been taught him. Defoe says, that there were a hundred thousand stout country-fellows in his time ready to fight to the death against popery, without knowing whether popery was a man or a horse. This, then, was a prejudice that they did not fill up of their own heads. All the great points that men have founded a claim to superiority, wisdom, and illumination upon, that they have embroiled the world with, and made matters of the last importance, are what one age and country differ diametrically with each other about, have been successively and justly exploded, and have been the levers of opinion and the grounds of contention, precisely because, as their expounders and believers are equally in the dark about them, they rest wholly on the fluctuations of will and passion, and as they can neither be proved nor disproved, admit of the fiercest opposition or the most bigoted faith. In what " comes home to the business and bosoms of men," there is less of this uncertainty and presumption ; and there, in the little world of our own knowledge and experience, we can hardly do better than attend to the " still, small voice " of our own hearts and feelings, instead of being browbeat by the effrontery, or puzzled by the sneers and cavils of pedants and sophists, of whatever school or description.

If I take a prejudice against a person from his face, I shall very probably be in the right; if I take a prejudice against a person from hearsay, I shall quite as probably be in the wrong. We have a prejudice in favour of certain books, but it is hardly without knowledge, if we have read them with delight over and over again. Fame itself is a prejudice, though a fine one. Natural affection is a prejudice: for though we have cause to love our nearest connections better than others, we have no reason to think them better than others. The error here is, when that which is properly a dictate of the heart passes out of its sphere, and becomes an overweening decision of the understanding. So in like manner of the love of country; and there is a prejudice in favour of virtue, genius, liberty, which (though it were possible) it would be a pity to destroy. The passions, such as avarice, ambition, love, &c., are prejudices, that is amply exaggerated views of certain objects, made up of habit, and imagination beyond their real value; but if we ask what is the real value of any object, independently of its connection with the power of habit, or its affording natural scope for the imagination, we shall perhaps be puzzled for an answer. To reduce things to the scale of abstract reason would be to annihilate our interest in them, instead of raising our affections to a higher standard; and by striving to make man rational, we should leave him merely brutish.

Animals are without prejudice: they are not led away by authority or custom, but it is because they are gross, and incapable of being taught. It is, however, a mistake to imagine that only the vulgar and ignorant, who can give no account of their opinions, are the slaves of bigotry and prejudice; the noisiest declaimers, the most subtle casuists, and most irrefragable doctors, are as far ·removed from the character of true philosophers, while they strain and pervert all their powers to prove some unintelligible dogma, instilled into their minds by early education, interest, or self-importance; and if we say the peasant or artisan is a Mahometan because he is born in Turkey, or a papist because he is born in Italy, the mufti at Constantinople or the cardinal at Rome is so, for no better reason, in the midst of all his pride and learning.

Mr. Hobbes used to say, that if he had read as much as others, he should have been as ignorant as they.

After all, most of our opinions are a mixture of reason and prejudice, experience and authority. We can only judge for ourselves in what concerns ourselves, and in things about us : and even there we must trust continually to established opinion and current report; in higher and more abstruse points we must pin our faith still more on others. If we believe only what we know at first hand, without trusting to authority at all, we shall disbelieve a great many things that really exist; and the suspicious coxcomb is as void of judgment as the credulous fool. My habitual conviction of the existence of such a place as Rome is not strengthened by my having seen it; it might be almost said to be obscured and weakened, as the reality falls short of the imagination. I walk along the streets without fearing that the houses will fall on my head, though I have not examined their foundation; and I believe firmly in the Newtonian system, though I have never read the *Principia*. In the former case, I argue that if the houses were inclined to fall they would not wait for me; and in the latter, I acquiesce in what all who have studied the subject, and are capable of understanding it, agree in, having no reason to suspect the contrary. That *the earth turns round* is agreeable to my understanding, though it shocks my sense, which is however too weak to grapple with so vast a question.

Self-love and Benevolence.

A DIALOGUE.[1]

A. For my part, I think Helvetius has made it clear that self-love is at the bottom of all our actions, even

---

[1] I do not think that any exact account has been given of the history and date of this paper. But it seems probable that it was,

of those which are apparently he most generous and disinterested.

B. I do not know what you mean by saying that Helvetius has made this clear, nor what you mean by self-love.

A. Why, was not he the first who explained to the world that in gratifying others, we gratify ourselves; that though the result may be different, the motive is really the same, and a selfish one; and that if we had not more pleasure in performing what are called friendly or virtuous actions than the contrary, they would never enter our thoughts?

B. Certainly he is no more entitled to this discovery (if it be one) than you are. Hobbes and Mandeville long before him asserted the same thing in the most explicit and unequivocal manner;[1] and Butler, in the Notes and Preface to his Sermons, had also long before answered it in the most satisfactory way.

A. Ay, indeed! pray how so?

B. By giving the *common-sense* answer to the question which I have just asked of you.

A. And what is that? I do not exactly comprehend.

B. Why, that self-love means, both in common and philosophical speech, the love *of* self.

---

like the two preceding, written in Italy in 1825, and represents a conversation between the author (*A ?*), Landor (*B ?*), and Captain Medwin (*Captain C ?*). Compare the paper on *Self-love* in the *Literary Remains*, 1836, ii.—ED.

[1] " Il a manqué au plus grand philosophe qu'aient eu les Français, de vivre dans quelque solitude des Alpes, dans quelque sejour éloigné, et de lancer delà son livre dans Paris sans y venir jamais lui-même. Rousseau avait trop de sensibilité et trop peu de raison, Buffon trop d'hypocrisie à son jardin des plantes, Voltaire trop d'enfantillage dans la tête, pour pouvoir juger le principe d'Helvetius."—*De l'Amour*, tom. 2, p. 230.

My friend Mr. Beyle here lays too much stress on a borrowed verbal fallacy.

A. To be sure, *there needs no ghost to tell us that.*

B. And yet, simple as it is, both you and many great philosophers seem to have overlooked it.

A. You are pleased to be obscure—unriddle for the sake of the vulgar.

B. Well then, Bishop Butler's statement in the volume I have mentioned——

A. May I ask, is it the author of the *Analogy* you speak of?

B. The same, but an entirely different and much more valuable work. His position is, that the arguments of the opposite party go to prove that in all our motives and actions it is the individual indeed who loves or is interested in *something*, but not in the smallest degree (which yet seems necessary to make out the full import of the compound "sound significant," *self-love*) that that something is *himself*. By self-love is surely implied not only that it is I who feel a certain passion, desire, good-will, and so forth, but that I feel this good-will towards myself—in other words, that I am both the person feeling the attachment, and the object of it. In short, the controversy between self-love and benevolence relates not to the person who loves, but to the person beloved—otherwise, it is flat and puerile nonsense. There must always be some one to feel the love, that's certain, or else there could be no love of one thing or another—so far there can be no question that it is a given individual who feels, thinks, and acts, in all possible cases of feeling, thinking, and acting—"there needs," according to your own allusion, "no ghost come from the grave to tell us that" —but whether the said individual in so doing always thinks *of*, feels *for*, and acts *with a view to himself*, that is a very important question, and the only real one at issue; and the very statement of which, in a distinct and intelligible form, gives at once the proper and inevitable answer to it. Self-love, to mean anything, must have a double

mcaning, that is, must not merely signify love, but love
defined and directed in a particular manner, having *self*
for its object, reflecting and reacting upon *self*; but it is
downright and intolerable trifling to persist that the love
or concern which we feel for another still has self for its
object, because it is we who feel it. The same sort of
quibbling would lead to the conclusion that when I am
thinking of any other person, I am notwithstanding
thinking of myself, because it is *I* who have his image in
my mind.

A. I cannot, I confess, see the connection.

B. I wish you would point out the distinction. Or let
me ask you—Suppose you were to observe me looking
frequently and earnestly at myself in the glass, would you
not be inclined to laugh, and say that this was vanity?

A. I might be half-tempted to do so.

B. Well; and if you were to find me admiring a fine
picture, or speaking in terms of high praise of the person
or qualities of another, would you not set it down equally
to an excess of coxcombry and self-conceit?

A. How, in the name of common sense, should I do so?

B. Nay, how should you do otherwise upon your own
principles? For if sympathy with another is to be
construed into self-love because it is I who feel it, surely,
by the same rule, my admiration and praise of another
must be resolved into self-praise and self-admiration, and
I am the whole time delighted with myself, to wit, with
my own thoughts and feelings, while I pretend to be
delighted with another. Another's limbs are as much
mine, who contemplate them, as his feelings.

A. Now, my good friend, you go too far: I can't think
you serious.

B. Do I not tell you that I have a most grave Bishop
(equal to a whole Bench) on my side?

A. What! is this illustration of the looking-glass and picture his? I thought it was in your own far-fetched manner.

B. And why far-fetched ?

A. Because nobody can think of calling the praise of another self-conceit—the words have a different meaning in the language.

B. Nobody has thought of confounding them hitherto, and yet they sound to me as like as selfishness and generosity. If our vanity can be brought to admire others disinterestedly, I do not see but our good-nature may be taught to serve them as disinterestedly. Grant me but this, that self-love signifies not simply, "I love," but requires to have this further addition, "I love *myself*," understood in order to make sense or grammar of it; and I defy you to make one or the other of Helvetius's theory, if you will needs have it to be his. If, as Fielding says, all our passions are selfish merely because they are *ours*, then in hating another we must be said to hate ourselves, just as wisely as in loving another, we are said to be actuated by self-love. I have no patience with such foolery. I respect that fine old sturdy fellow Hobbes, or even the acute, pertinacious sophistry of Mandeville; but I do not like the flimsy, self-satisfied repetition of an absurdity, which with its originality has lost all its piquancy.

B. You have, I know, very little patience with others who differ from you, nor are you a very literal reporter of the arguments of those who happen to be on your side of the question. You were about to tell me the substance of Butler's answer to Helvetius's theory, if we can let the anachronism pass; and I have as yet only heard certain quaint and verbal distinctions of your own. I must still think that the most disinterested actions proceed from a selfish motive. A man feels distress at the sight of a beggar, and he parts with his money to remove this uneasiness. If he did not feel this distress in his own mind, he would take no steps to relieve the other's wants.

B. And pray, does he feel this distress in his own

mind out of love to himself, or solely that he may have the pleasure of getting rid of it? The first *move* in the game of mutual obligation is evidently a social, not a selfish impulse; and I might rest the dispute here and insist upon going no farther till 'this step is got over, but it is not necessary. I have already told you the substance of Butler's answer to this commonplace and plausible objection. He says, in his fine broad, manly and yet unpretending mode of stating a question, that a living being may be supposed to be actuated either by mere sensations, having no reference to any one else, or else that having an idea and foresight of the consequences to others, he is influenced by and interested in those consequences only in so far as they have a distinct connection with his own ultimate good, in both which cases, seeing that the motives and actions have both their origin and end in self, they may and must be properly denominated *selfish.* But where the motive is neither physically nor morally selfish, that is, where the impulse to act is neither excited by a physical sensation nor by a reflection on the consequence to accrue to the individual, it must be hard to say in what sense it can be called so, except in that sense already exploded, namely, that which would infer that an impulse of any kind is selfish merely because it acts upon some one, or that before we can entertain disinterested sympathy with another, we must feel no sympathy at all. Benevolence, generosity, compassion, friendship, &c., imply, says the Bishop, that we take an immediate and unfeigned interest in the welfare of others; that their pleasures give us pleasure; that their pains give us pain, barely to know of them, and from no thought about ourselves. But no! retort the advocates of self-love, this is not enough: before any person can pretend to the title of benevolent, generous, and so on, he must prove, that so far from taking the deepest and most heartfelt interest in the happiness of others, he has no

fceling on the subject, that he is perfectly indifferent to
their weal or woe ; and then taking infinite pains and
making unaccountable sacrifices for their good without
caring one farthing about them, he might pass for herioc
and disinterested. But if he lets it appear he has the
smallest good-will towards them, and acts upon it, he then
becomes a merely selfish agent ; so that to establish a
character for generosity, compassion, humanity, &c., in
any of his actions, he must first plainly prove that he
never felt the slightest twinge of any of these passions
thrilling in his bosom. This, according to my author, is
requiring men to act not from charitable motives, but
from no motives at all. Such reasoning has not an
appearance of philosophy, but rather of drivelling weakness or of tacit irony. For my part, I can conceive of no
higher strain of generosity than that which justly and
truly says, *Nihil humani à me alienum puto*—but, according
to your modern French friends and my old English ones,
there is no difference between this and the most sordid
selfishness ; for the instant a man takes an interest in
another's welfare, he makes it his own, and all the merit
and disinterestedness is gone. "Greater love than this
hath no man, that he should give his life for his friend."
It must be rather a fanciful sort of self-love that at any
time sacrifices its own acknowledged and obvious interests
for the sake of another.

A. Not in the least. The expression you have just
used explains the whole mystery, and I think you must
allow this yourself. The moment I sympathise with
another, I do in strictness make his interest my own.
The two things on this supposition become inseparable,
and my gratification is identified with his advantage.
Every one, in short, consults his particular taste and
inclination, whatever may be its bias, or acts from the
strongest motive. Regulus, as Helvetius has so ably
demonstrated, would not have returned to Carthage, but

that the idea of dishonour gave him more uneasiness than
the apprehension of a violent death.

B. That is, had he not preferred the honour of his
country to his own interest. Surely, when self-love by
all accounts takes so very wide a range and embraces
entirely new objects, of a character so utterly opposed
to its general circumscribed and paltry routine of action,
it would be as well to designate it by some new and
appropriate appellation, unless it were meant, by the
intervention of the old and ambiguous term, to confound
the important practical distinction which subsists between
the puny circle of a man's physical sensations and private
interests and the whole world of virtue and honour, and
thus to bring back the last gradually and disingenuously
within the verge of the former. Things without names
are unapt to take root in the human mind : we are prone
to reduce nature to the dimensions of language. If a
feeling of a refined and romantic character is expressed
by a gross and vulgar name, our habitual associations will
be sure to degrade the first to the level of the last, instead
of conforming to a forced and technical definition. But
I beg to deny, not only that the objects in this case are
the same, but that the principle is similar.

A. Do you then seriously pretend that the end of
sympathy is not to get rid of the momentary uneasiness
occasioned by the distress of another ?

B. And has that uneasiness, I again ask, its source
in self-love? If self-love were the only principle of
action, we ought to receive no uneasiness from the pains
of others, we ought to be wholly exempt from any such
weakness : or the least that can be required to give the
smallest shadow of excuse to this exclusive theory is,
that the instant the pain was communicated by our
foolish, indiscreet sympathy, we should think of nothing
but getting rid of it as fast as possible, by fair means
or foul, as a mechanical instinct. If the pain of sympathy,

as soon as it arose, was decompounded from the objects which gave it birth, and acted upon the brain or nerves solely as a detached, desultory feeling, or abstracted sense of uneasiness, from which the mind shrunk with its natural aversion to pain, then I would allow that the impulse in this case, having no reference to the good of another, and seeking only to remove a present inconvenience from the individual, would still be properly self-love : but no such process of abstraction takes place. The feeling of compassion as it first enters the mind, so it continues to act upon it in conjunction with the idea of what another suffers ; refers every wish it forms, or every effort it makes, to the removal of pain from a fellow-creature, and is only satisfied when it believes this end to be accomplished. It is not a blind, physical repugnance to pain, as affecting ourselves, but a rational or intelligible conception of it as existing out of ourselves, that prompts and sustains our exertions in behalf of humanity. Nor can it be otherwise, while man is the creature of imagination and reason, and has faculties that implicate him (whether he will or not) in the pleasures and pains of others, and bind up his fate with theirs. Why, then, when an action or feeling is neither in its commencement nor progress, nor ultimate objects, dictated by or subject to the control of self-love, bestow the name where everything but the name is wanting ?

A. I must give you fair warning, that in this last *tirade* you have more than once gone beyond my comprehension. Your distinctions are too fine-drawn, and there is a want of relief in the expression. Are you not getting back to what you describe as your *first manner?* Your present style is more amusing. See if you cannot throw a few high lights into that last argument !

B. Un peu plus à l'Anglaise—anything to oblige ! I say, then, it appears to me strange that self-love should be asserted by any impartial reasoner (not the dupe of a play upon words), to be absolute and undisputed master of the human mind, when compassion or uneasiness on account of others enters it without leave and in spite of this principle. What! to be instantly expelled by it without mercy, so that it may still assert its pre-eminence? No; but to linger there, to hold consultation with another principle, Imagination, which owes no allegiance to self-interest, and to march out only under condition and guarantee that the welfare of another is first provided for without any special clause in its own favour. This is much as if you were to say and swear, that though the bailiff and his man have taken possession of your house, you are still the rightful owner of it.

A. And so I am.

B. Why, then, not turn out such unwelcome intruders without standing upon ceremony?

A. You were too vague and abstracted before: now you are growing too figurative. Always in extremes.

B. Give me leave for a moment, as you will not let me spin mere metaphysical cobwebs.

A. I am patient.

B. Suppose that by sudden transformation your body were so contrived that it could feel the actual sensations of another body, as if your nerves had an immediate and physical communication; that you were assailed by a number of objects you saw and knew nothing of before, and felt desires and appetites springing up in your bosom for which you could not at all account—would you not say that this addition of another body made a material alteration in your former situation; that it called for a new set of precautions and instincts to provide for its wants and wishes? or would you persist in it that you were just where you were, that no change had taken place in your being and interests, and that your new body was in fact your old one, for no other reason than because it was yours? To my thinking the case would be quite altered by the supererogation of such a new sympathetic body, and I should be for dividing my care and time pretty equally between them.

Captain C. You mean that in that case you would have taken in partners to the concern, as well as No. I. ?

B. Yes; and my concern for No. II. would be something very distinct from, and quite independent of, my original and hitherto exclusive concern for No. I.

A. How very gross and vulgar! (whispering to D——, and then turning to me, added)—but why suppose an impossibility? I hate all such incongruous and far-fetched illustrations.

B. And yet this very miracle takes place every day in the human mind and heart, and you and your sophists would persuade us that it is nothing, and would slur over its existence by a shallow misnomer. Do I not by imaginary sympathy acquire a new interest (out of myself) in others, as much as I should on the former supposition by physical contact or animal magnetism? and am I not compelled by this new law of my nature (neither included in physical sensation nor a deliberate regard to my own individual welfare) to consult the feelings and wishes of the new social body of which I am become a member, often to the prejudice of my own? The parallel seems to me exact, and I think the inference from it unavoidable. I do not postpone a benevolent or friendly purpose to my own personal convenience or make it bend to it—

> "Letting *I dare not* wait upon *I would,*
> Like the poor cat i' the adage."

The will is amenable, not to our immediate sensibility, but to reason and imagination, which point out and enforce a line of duty very different from that prescribed by self-love. The operation of sympathy or social feeling, though it has its seat certainly in the mind of the in-

dividual, is neither for his immediate behalf nor to his
remote benefit, but is constantly a diversion from both,
and therefore, I contend, is not in any sense selfish.
The movements in my breast as much originate in, and
are regulated by, the *idea* of what another feels, as if they
were governed by a chord placed there vibrating to
another's pain. If these movements were mechanical,
they would be considered as directed to the good of
another : it is odd, that because my bosom takes part
and beats in unison with them, they should become of
a less generous character. In the passions of hatred,
resentment, sullenness, or even in low spirits, we voluntarily go through a great deal of pain, because *such is our
pleasure ;* or strictly, because certain objects have taken
hold of our imagination, and we cannot, or will not, get
rid of the impression : why should good-nature and
generosity be the only feelings in which we will not allow
a little forgetfulness of ourselves ? Once more. If self-
love, or each individual's sensibility, sympathy, what you
will, were like an animalcule, sensitive, quick, shrinking
instantly from whatever gave it pain, seeking instinctively
whatever gave it pleasure, and having no other obligation
or law of its existence, then I should be most ready to
acknowledge that this principle was in its nature, end,
and origin, selfish, slippery, treacherous. inert, inoperative
but as an instrument of some immediate stimulus, incapable of generous sacrifice or painful exertion, and
deserving a name and title accordingly, leading one to
bestow upon it its proper attributes. But the very reverse
of all this happens. The mind is tenacious of remote
purposes, indifferent to immediate feelings, which cannot
consist with the nature of a rational and voluntary agent.
Instead of the animalcule swimming in pleasure and
gliding from pain, the principle of self-love is incessantly
to the imagination or sense of duty what the fly is to the
spider—that fixes its stings into it, involves it in its web,

sucks its blood, and preys upon its vitals! Does the spider do all this to please the fly? Just as much as Regulus returned to Carthage, and was rolled down a hill in a barrel with iron spikes in it to please himself! The imagination or understanding is no less the enemy of our pleasure than of our interest. It will not let us be at ease till we have accomplished certain objects with which we have ourselves no concern but as melancholy truths.

A. But the spider you have so quaintly conjured up is a different animal from the fly. The imagination on which you lay so much stress is a part of one's-self.

B. I grant it: and for that very reason, self-love, or a principle tending exclusively to our own immediate gratification or future advantage, neither is nor can be the sole spring of action in the human mind.

A. I cannot see that at all.

D. Nay, I think he has made it out better than usual.

B. Imagination is another name for an interest in things out of ourselves, which must naturally run counter to our own. Self-love, for so fine and smooth-spoken a gentleman, leads his friends into odd scrapes. The situation of Regulus in a barrel with iron spikes in it was not a very easy one : but, say the advocates of refined self-love, their points were a succession of agreeable punctures in his sides, compared with the stings of dishonour, But what bound him to this dreadful alternative? Not self-love. When the pursuit of honour becomes troublesome, " throw honour to the dogs—I'll none of it ! " This seems the true Epicurean solution. Philosophical self-love seems neither a voluptuary nor an effeminate coward, but a cynic, and even a martyr ; so that I am afraid he will hardly dare show his face at Very's, and that, with this knowledge of his character, even the countenance of the Count Destutt de Tracy will not procure his admission to the saloons.

A. The Count Destutt de Tracy, did you say? Who is he? I never heard of him.

B. He is the author of the celebrated *Idéologie,* which
Buonaparte denounced to the Chamber of Peers as the cause
of his disasters in Russia. He is equally hated by the
Bourbons; and, what is more extraordinary still, he is
patronised by Ferdinand VII., who settled a pension of
two hundred crowns a year on the translator of his works.
He speaks of Condillac as having "*created* the science of
Ideology," and holds Helvetius for a true philosopher.

A. Which you do not! I think it a pity you should
affect singularity of opinion in such matters, when you
have all the most sensible and best-informed judges against
you.

B. I am sorry for it too; but I am afraid I can hardly
expect you with me, till I have all Europe on my side, of
which I see no chance while the Englishman, with his
notions of solid beef and pudding, holds fast by his substantial identity, and the Frenchman, with his lighter food
and air, mistakes every shadowy impulse for himself.

D. You deny, I think, that personal identity, in the
qualified way in which you think proper to admit it, is any
ground for the doctrine of self-interest?

B. Yes, in an exclusive and absolute sense, I do undoubtedly, that is, in the sense in which it is affirmed by
metaphysicians, and ordinarily believed in.

D. Could you not go over the ground briefly, without
entering into technicalities?

B. Not easily; but stop me when I entangle myself in
difficulties. A person fancies, or feels habitually, that he
has a positive, substantial interest in his own welfare
(generally speaking), just as much as he has in any actual
sensation that he feels, because he is always and necessarily
the same self. What is his interest at one time is therefore equally *his* interest at all other times. This is taken
for granted as a self-evident proposition. Say he does not
feel a particular benefit or injury at this present moment,
yet it is he who is to feel it, which comes to the same

thing. Where there is this continued identity of person, there must also be a correspondent identity of interest. I have an abstract, unavoidable interest in whatever can be-fall myself, which I can have or feel in no other person living, because I am always, under every possible circum-stance, the self-same individual, and not any other indi-vidual, whatsoever. In short, this word *self* (so closely do a number of associations cling round it and cement it together) is supposed to represent as it were a given con-crete substance, as much one thing as anything in nature can possibly be, and the centre or *substratum* in which the different impressions and ramifications of my being meet and are indissolutely knit together.

A. And you propose, then, seriously to take " this one entire and perfect chrysolite," this self, this " precious jewel of the soul," this rock on which mankind have built their faith for ages, and at one blow shatter it to pieces with the sledge-hammer, or displace it from its hold in the imagination with the wrenching-irons of metaphysics ?

B. I am willing to use my best endeavours for that purpose.

D. You really ought ; for you have the prejudices of the whole world against you.

B. I grant the prejudices are formidable ; and I should despair, did I not think my reasons even stronger. Besides, without altering the opinions of the whole world, I might be contented with the suffrages of one or two in-telligent people.

D. Nay, you will prevail by flattery, if not by argu-ment.

A. That is something newer than all the rest.

B. " Plain truth," dear A——, " needs no flowers of speech."

D. Let me rightly understand you. Do you mean to say that I am not C. D. and that you are not W. B., or that we shall not both of us remain so to the end of the chapter, without a possibility of ever changing places with each other?

B. I am afraid, if you go to that, there is very little chance that

"*I* shall be ever mistaken for *you*."

But with all this precise individuality and inviolable identity that you speak of, let me ask, Are you not a little changed (less so, it is true, than most people) from what you were twenty years ago? Or do you expect to appear the same that you are now twenty years hence?

D. "No more of that if thou lovest me." We know what we are, but we know not what we shall be.

B. A truce, then; but be assured that, whenever you happen to fling up your part, there will be no other person found to attempt it after you.

D. Pray, favour us with your paradox, without further preface.

B. I will try then to match my paradox against your prejudice, which, as it is armed all in proof, to make my impression on it I must, I suppose, take aim at the rivets; and if I can hit them, if I do not (round and smooth as it is) cut it into three pieces, and show that two parts in three are substance and the third and principal part shadow, never believe me again. Your real self ends exactly where your pretended self-interest begins; and in calculating upon this principle as a solid, permanent, absolute, self-evident truth, you are mocked with a name.

D. How so? I hear, but do not see.

B. You must allow that this identical, indivisible, ostensible self is at any rate distinguishable into three parts—the past, the present, and future?

D, I see no harm in that.

B. It is nearly all I ask. Well, then, I admit that you have a peculiar, emphatic, incommunicable and exclusive interest or fellow feeling in the two first of these selves; but I deny resolutely and unequivocally that you have any such natural, absolute, unavoidable, and mechanical interest in the last self, or in your future being, the interest you take in it being necessarily the offspring of understanding and imagination (aided by habit and circumstances), like that which you take in the welfare of others, and yet this last interest is the only one that is ever the object of rational and voluntary pursuit, or that ever comes into competition with the interests of others.

D. I am still to seek for the connecting clue.

B. I am almost ashamed to ask for your attention to a statement so very plain that it seems to border on a truism. I have an interest of a peculiar and limited nature in my present self, inasmuch as I feel my actual sensations not simply in a degree, but in a way and by means of faculties which afford me not the smallest intimation of the sensations of others. I cannot possibly feel the sensations of any one else, nor consequently take the slightest interest in them as such. I have no nerves communicating with another's brain, and transmitting to me either the glow of pleasure or the agony of pain which he may feel at the present moment by means of his senses. So far, therefore, namely, so far as my present self or immediate sensations are concerned, I am cut off from all sympathy with others. I stand alone in the world, a perfectly insulated individual, necessarily and in the most unqualified sense indifferent to all that passes around me, and that does not in the first instance affect myself, for otherwise I neither have nor can have the remotest consciousness of it as a matter of organic sensation, any more than the mole has of light or the deaf adder of sounds.

D. Spoken like an oracle.

B. Again, I have a similar peculiar, mechanical, and untransferable interest in my past self, because I remember, and can dwell upon my past sensations (even after the objects are removed) also in a way and by means of faculties which do not give me the smallest insight into or sympathy with the past feelings of others. I may conjecture and fancy what those feelings have been; and so I do. But I have no *memory* or continued consciousness of what either of good or evil may have found a place in their bosoms, no secret spring that, being touched, vibrates to the hopes and wishes that are no more, unlocks the chambers of the past with the same assurance of reality, or identifies my feelings with theirs in the same intimate manner as with those which I have already felt in my own person. Here again, then, there is a real, undoubted, original and positive foundation for the notion of self to rest upon; for in relation to my former self and past feelings, I do possess a faculty which serves to unite me more especially to my own being, and at the same time draws a distinct and impassable line around that being, separating it from every other. A door of communication stands always open between my present consciousness and my past feelings, which is locked and barred by the hand of Nature and the constitution of the human understanding against the intrusion of any straggling impressions from the minds of others. I can only see into their real history darkly and by reflection. To sympathise with their joys or sorrows, and place myself in their situation either now or formerly, I must proceed by guess work, and borrow the use of the common faculty of imagination. I am ready to acknowledge, then, that in what regards the past as well as the present, there is a strict metaphysical distinction between myself and others, and that my personal identity so far, or in the close, continued, inseparable connection between my past and present impressions, is firmly and irrevocably established.

D. You go on swimmingly. So far all is sufficiently clear.

B. But now comes the rub: for beyond that point I deny that the doctrine of personal identity or self-interest (as a consequence from it) has any foundation to rest upon but a confusion of names and ideas. It has none in the nature of things or of the human mind. For I have no faculty by which I can project myself into the future, or hold the same sort of palpable, tangible, immediate, and exclusive communication with my future feelings in the same manner as I am made to feel the present moment by means of the senses, or the past moment by means of memory. If I have any such faculty, expressly set apart for the purpose, name it. If I have no such faculty, I can have no such interest. In order that I may possess a proper personal identity so as to live, breathe, and feel along the whole line of my existence in the same intense and intimate mode, it is absolutely necessary to have some general medium or faculty by which my successive impressions are blended and amalgamated together, and to maintain and support this extraordinary interest. But so far from there being any foundation for this merging and incorporating of my future in my present self, there is no link of connection, no sympathy, no reaction, no mutual consciousness between them, nor even a possibility of anything of the kind, in a mechanical and personal sense. Up to the present point, the spot on which we stand, the doctrine of personal identity holds good; hitherto the proud and exclusive pretensions of self come, but no farther. The rest is air, is nothing, is a name, or but the common ground of reason and humanity. If I wish to pass beyond this point and look into my own future lot, or anticipate my future weal or woe before it has had an existence, I can do so by means of the same faculties by which I enter into and identify myself with the welfare, the being, and interests of others, but only by these. As I have already said, I have no particular organ or faculty of self-interest, in that case made and provided. I have no sensation of what is to happen to myself in future, no presentiment of it, no instinctive sympathy with it, nor consequently any abstract and unavoidable self-interest in it. Now mark : it is only in regard to my past and present being, that a broad and insurmountable barrier is placed between myself and others ; as to future objects there is no absolute and fundamental distinction whatever. But it is only these last that are the objects of any rational or practical interest. The idea of self properly attaches to objects of sense or memory, but these can never be the objects of action or of voluntary pursuit, which must, by the supposition, have an eye to future events. But with respect to these the chain of self interest is dissolved and falls in pieces by the very necessity of our nature, and our obligations to self as a blind, mechanical, unsociable principle are lost in the general law which binds us to the pursuit of good as it comes within our reach and knowledge.

A. A most lame and impotent conclusion, I must say. Do you mean to affirm ·that you have really the same interest in another's welfare that you have in your own ?

B. I do not wish to assert anything without proof. Will you tell me, if you have this particular interest in yourself, what faculty is it that gives it you—to what conjuration and mighty magic it is owing—or whether it is merely the name of self that is to be considered as a proof of all the absurdities and impossibilities that can be drawn from it ?

A. I do not see that you have hitherto pointed out any.

B. What! not the impossiblity that you should be another being, with whom you have not a particle of fellow-feeling ?

A. Another being! Yes, I know it is always impossible for me to be another being.

B. Ay, or yourself either, without such a fellow-feeling, for it is that which constitutes self. If not, explain to me

what you mean by self. But it is more convenient for
you to let that magical sound lie involved in the obscurity
of prejudice and language. You will please to take notice
that it is not I who commence these hairbreadth distinctions and special pleading. I take the old ground of
common sense and natural feeling, and maintain that though
in a popular, practical sense mankind are strongly swayed
by self-interest, yet in the same ordinary sense they are
also governed by motives of good-nature, compassion,
friendship, virtue, honour, &c. Now all this is denied by
your modern metaphysicians, who would reduce everything to abstract self-interest, and exclude every other
mixed motive or social tie in a strict philosophical sense.
They would drive me from my ground by scholastic sub-
tleties and newfangled phrases; am I to blame, then, if
I take them at their word, and try to foil them at their
own weapons? Either stick to the unpretending *jog-trot*
notions on the subject, or if you are determined to refine
in analysing words and arguments, do not be angry if I
follow the example set me, or even go a little farther to
arrive at the truth. Shall we proceed on this understanding.

A. As you please.

B. We have got so far, then (if I mistake not, and if
there is not some flaw in the argument which I am
unable to detect), that the past and present (which alone
can appeal to our selfish faculties) are not the objects of
action, and that the future (which can alone be the
object of practical pursuit) has no particular claim or
hold upon self. All action, all passion, all morality and
self-interest, is prospective.

A. You have not made that point quite clear. What,
then, is meant by a present interest, by the gratification of
the present moment, as opposed to a future one?

B. Nothing, in a strict sense; or rather, in common
speech, you mean a near one, the interest of the next

moment, the next hour, the next day, the next year, as it happens.

A. What! would you have me believe that I snatch my hand out of the flame of a candle from a calculation of future consequences?

D. (*laughing.*) A. had better not meddle with that question. B. is in his element there. It is his old and favourite illustration.

B. Do you not snatch your hand out of the fire to procure ease from pain?

A. No doubt, I do.

B. And is not this case subsequent to the act, and the act itself to the feeling of pain, which caused it?

A. It may be so; but the interval is so slight that we are not sensible of it.

B. Nature is nicer in her distinctions than we. Thus you could not lift the food to your mouth, but upon the same principle. The viands are indeed tempting, but if it were the sight or smell of these alone that attracted you, you would remain satisfied with them. But you use means to ends, neither of which exist till you employ or produce them, and which would never exist if the understanding which foresees them did not run on before the actual objects and purvey to appetite. If you say it is habit, it is partly so; but that habit would never have been formed were it not for the connection between cause and effect, which always takes place in the order of time, or of what Hume calls *antecedents* and *consequents.*

A. I confess I think this a mighty microscopic way of looking at the subject.

B. Yet you object equally to more vague and sweeping generalities. Let me, however, endeavour to draw the knot a little tighter, as it has a considerable weight to bear—no less, in my opinion, than the whole world of moral sentiments. All voluntary action must relate to the future: but the future can only exist or influence the mind as an object of imagination and forethought; therefore the motive to voluntary action, to all that we seek or shun, must be in all cases *ideal* and problematical. The thing itself which is an object of pursuit can never co-exist with the motives which make it an object of pursuit. No one will say that the past can be an object either of prevention or pursuit. It may be a subject of involuntary regrets, or may give rise to the starts and flaws of passion; but we cannot set about seriously recalling or altering it. Neither can that which at present exists, or is an object of sensation, be at the same time an object of action or of volition, since if it *is*, no volition or exertion of mine can for the instant make it to be other than it is. I can make it *cease* to be, indeed, but this relates to the future, to the supposed non-existence of the object, and not to its actual impression on me. For a thing to be *willed*, it must necessarily not be. Over my past and present impressions my will has no control: they are placed, according to the poet, beyond the reach of fate, much more of human means. In order that I may take an effectual and consistent interest in anything, that it may be an object of hope or fear, of desire or dread, it must be a thing still to come, a thing still in doubt, depending on circumstances and the means used to bring about or avert it. It is my will that determines its existence or the contrary (otherwise there would be no use in troubling one's-self about it); it does not itself lay its peremptory, inexorable mandates on my will. For it is as yet (and must be in order to be the rational object of a moment's deliberation) a non-entity, a possibility merely, and it is plain that nothing can be the cause of nothing. That which is not, cannot act, much less can it act mechanically, physically, all-powerfully. So far is it from being true that a real and practical interest in anything are convertible terms, that a practical interest can never by any possible chance be a real one, that is, excited by the presence of a real object or by mechanical sympathy.

I cannot assuredly be induced by a present object to take means to make it. exist—it can be no more than present to me—or if it is past, it is too late to think of recovering the occasion or preventing it now. But the future, the future is all our own; or rather it belongs equally to others. The world of action, then, of business or pleasure, of self-love or benevolence, is not made up of solid materials, moved by downright, solid springs; it is essentially a void, an unreal mockery, both in regard to ourselves and others, except as it is filled up, animated, and set in motion by human thoughts and purposes. The ingredients of passion, action, and properly of interest are never positive, palpable matters-of-fact, concrete existences, but symbolical representations of events lodged in the bosom of futurity, and teaching us, by timely anticipation and watchful zeal, to build up the fabric of our own or others' future weal.

A. Do we not sometimes plot their woe with at least equal good-will?

B. Not much oftener than we are accessory to our own.

A. I must say that savours more to me of an antithesis than of an answer.

B. For once, be it so.

A. But surely there is a difference between a real and an imaginary interest? A history is not a romance.

B. Yes; but in this sense the feelings and interests of others are in the end as real, as such matters of fact as mine or yours can be. The history of the world is not a romance, though you and I have had only a small share in it. You would turn everything into autobiography. The interests of others are no more chimerical, visionary, fantastic, than my own, being founded in truth, and both are brought home to my bosom in the same way by force of imagination and sympathy.

D. But in addition to all this sympathy that you make such a rout about, it is *I* who am to feel a real, downright interest in my own future good, and I shall feel no such interest in another person's. Does not this make a wide, nay a total difference in the case? Am I to have no more affection for my own flesh and blood than for another's?

B. This would indeed make an entire difference in the case, if your interest in your own good were founded in your affection for yourself, and not your affection for yourself in your attachment to your own good. If you were attached to your own good merely because it was *yours*, I do not see why you should not be equally attached to your own ill—both are equally yours! Your own person or that of others would, I take it, be alike indifferent to you, but for the degree of sympathy you have with the feelings of either. Take away the sense or apprehension of pleasure or pain, and you would care no more about yourself than you do about the hair of your head or the paring of your nails, the parting with which gives you no sensible uneasiness at the time or on after-reflection

D. But up to the present moment you allow that I have a particular interest in my proper self. Where, then, am I to stop, or how draw the line between my real and my imaginary identity?

B. The line is drawn for you by the nature of things. Or if the difference between reality and imagination is so small that you cannot perceive it, it only shows the strength of the latter. Certain it is that we can no more anticipate our future being than we can change places with another individual, except in an *ideal* and figurative sense. But it is just as impossible that I should have an actual sensation of and interest in my future feelings as that I should have an actual sensation of and interest in what another feels at the present instant. An essential and irreconcileable difference in our primary faculties forbids it. The future, were it the next moment, were it an object nearest and dearest to our hearts, is a dull blank, opaque, impervious to sense as an object close to the eye

of the blind, did not the ray of reason and reflection en-
lighten it. We can never say to its fleeting, painted
essence, " Come, let me clutch thee !" it is a thing of air,
a phantom that flies before us, and we follow it, and with
respect to all but our past and present sensations, which
are no longer anything to action, we totter on the brink of
nothing. That self which we project before us into it,
that we make our proxy or representative, and empower to
embody, and transmit back to us all our real, substantial
interests before they have had an existence, except in our
imaginations, is but a shadow of ourselves, a bundle of
habits, passions, and prejudices, a body that falls in pieces
at the touch of reason or the approach of inquiry. It is
true, we do build up such an imaginary self, and a proportionable interest in it ; we clothe it with the associations of the past and present, we disguise it in the drapery
of language, we add to it the strength of passion and the
warmth of affection, till we at length come to class our
whole existence under one head, and fancy our future
history a solid, permanent, and actual continuation of our
immediate being ; but all this only proves the force of
imagination and habit to build up such a structure on a
merely partial foundation, and does not alter the true
nature and distinction of things. On the same foundation
are built up nearly as high natural affection, friendship,
the love of country, of religion, &c. But of this presently.
What shows that the doctrine of self-interest, however
high it may rear its head, or however impregnable it may
seem to attack, is a mere contradiction,

" In terms a fallacy, in fact a fiction,"

is this single consideration, that we never know what is to
happen to us beforehand—no, not even for a moment—and
that we cannot so much as tell whether we shall be alive
a year, a month, or a day hence. We have no presentiment of what awaits us, making us feel the future in the
instant. Indeed such an insight into futurity would be

inconsistent with itself, or we must become mere passive instruments in the hands of fate. A house may fall on my head as I go from this, I may be crushed to pieces by a carriage running over me, or I may receive a piece of news that is death to my hopes, before another four-and-twenty hours are passed over, and yet I feel nothing of the blow that is thus to stagger and stun me. I laugh and am well. I have no warning given me either of the course or the consequence (in truth, if I had, I should, if possible, avoid it). This continued self-interest that watches over all my concerns alike, past, present, and future, and concentrates them all in one powerful and invariable principle of action, is useless here, leaves me at a loss at my greatest need, is torpid, silent, dead, and I have no more consciousness of what so nearly affects me, and no more care about it (till I find out my danger by other and natural means), than if no such thing were ever to happen, or were to happen to the Man in the Moon. It has been said that

"Coming events cast their shadows before;"

but this beautiful line is not verified in the ordinary prose of life. That it is not, is a staggering consideration for your fine practical, instinctive, abstracted, comprehensive, uniform principle of self-interest. Don't you think so, D——?

D. I shall not answer you. Am I to give up my existence for an idle sophism? You heap riddle upon riddle; but I am mystery-proof. I still feel my personal identity as I do the chair I sit on, though I am enveloped in a cloud of smoke and words. Let me have your answer to a plain question.—Suppose I were actually to see a coach coming along, and I was in danger of being run over, what I want to know, is, should I not try to save myself sooner than any other person?

B. No, you would first try to save a sister, if she were with you.

A. Surely that would be a very curious instance of *self,* though I do not deny it.

B. I do not think so. I believe there is hardly any one who does not prefer some one to themselves. For example, let us look into *Waverley.*

A. Ay, that is the way that you take your ideas of philosophy, from novels and romances, as if they were sound evidence.

B. If my conclusions are as true to nature as my premises, I shall be satisfied. Here is the passage I was going to quote: " I was only ganging to say, my lord," said Evan, in what he meant to be an insinuating manner, " that if your excellent honour and the honourable court would let Vich Ian Vohr go free just this once, and let him gae back to France and not trouble King George's government again, that any six o' the very best of his clan will be willing to be justified in his stead; and if you'll just let me gae down to Glennaquoich, I'll fetch them up to ye myself to head or hang, and you may begin with me the very first man."[1]

A. But such instances as this are the effect of habit and strong prejudice. We can hardly argue from so barbarous a state of society.

B. Excuse me there. I contend that our preference of ourselves is just as much the effect of habit, and very frequently a more unaccountable and unreasonable one than any other.

A. I should like to hear how you can possibly make that out.

B. If you will not condemn me before you hear what I have to say, I will try. You allow that D——, in the case we have been talking of, would perhaps run a little risk for you or me; but if it were a perfect stranger, he would get out of the way as fast as his legs would carry him, and leave the stranger to shift for himself.

[1] *Waverley,* vol. iii, p. 201.

A. Yes; and does not that overturn your whole theory ?

B. It would if my theory were as devoid of common sense as you are pleased to suppose ; that is, if because I deny an original and absolute distinction in nature (where there is no such thing), it followed that I must deny that circumstances, intimacy, habit, knowledge, or a variety of incidental causes could have any influence on our affections and actions. My inference is just the contrary. For would you not say that D—— cared little about the stranger, for this plain reason, that he knew nothing about him ?

A. No doubt.

B. And he would care rather more about you and me, because he knows more about us ?

A. Why yes, it would seem so.

B. And he would care still more about a sister (according to the same supposition), because he would be still better acquainted with her, and had been more constantly with her ?

A. I will not deny it.

B. And it is on the same principle (generally speaking) that a man cares most of all about himself, because he knows more about himself than about anybody else, that he is more in the secret of his own most intimate thoughts and feelings, and more in the habit of providing for his own wants and wishes, which he can anticipate with greater liveliness and certainty than those of others, from being more nearly "made and moulded of things past." The poetical fiction is rendered easier, and assisted by my acquaintance with myself, just as it is by the ties of kindred or habits of friendly intercourse. There is no farther approach made to the doctrines of self-love ,and personal identity.

D. E——, here is B—— trying to persuade me I am not myself.

E. Sometimes you are not.

D. But he says that I never am. Or is it only that I am not to be so?

B. Nay, I hope " thou art to continue, thou naughty varlet "—

" Here and hereafter, if the last may be ?"

You have been yourself (nobody like you) for the last forty years of your life : you would not prematurely stuff the next twenty into the account, till you have had them fairly out?

D. Not for the world, I have too great an affection for them.

B. Yet I think you would have less if you did not look forward to pass them among old books, old friends, old haunts. If you were cut off from all these, you would be less anxious about what was left of yourself.

D. I would rather be the *Wandering Jew* than not be at all.

B. Or you would not be the person I always took you for.

D. Does not this willingness to be the *Wandering Jew*, rather than nobody, seem to indicate that there is an abstract attachment to self, to the bare idea of existence, independently of circumstances or habit.

B. It must be a very loose and straggling one. You mix up some of your old recollections and favourite notions with your self-elect, and indulge them in your new character, or you would trouble yourself very little about it. If you do not come in in some shape or other, it is merely saying that you would be sorry if the *Wandering Jew* were to disappear from the earth, however strictly he may have hitherto maintained his *incognito*.

D. There is something in that; and as well as I remember, there is a curious but exceedingly mystical illustration of this point in an original Essay of yours which I have read and spoken to you about.

B. I believe there is ; but A—— is tired of making objections, and I of answering them to no purpose.

D. I have the book in the closet, and if you like, we will turn to the place. It is after that burst of enthusiastic recollection (the only one in the book) that Southey said at the time was something between the manner of Milton's prose-works and Jeremy Taylor.

B. Ah! I as little thought then that I should ever be set down as a florid prose-writer, as that he would become poet-laureate!

J. L. here took the volume from his brother, and read the following passage from it.

"I do not think I should illustrate the foregoing reasoning so well by anything I could add on the subject, as by relating the manner in which it first struck me. There are moments in the life of a solitary thinker which are to him what the evening of some great victory is to the conqueror and hero—milder triumphs, long remembered with truer and deeper delight. And though the shouts of multitudes do not hail his success—though gay trophies, though the sounds of music, the glittering of armour, and the neighing of steeds do not mingle with his joy, yet shall he not want monuments and witnesses of his glory—the deep forest, the willowy brook, the gathering clouds of winter, or the silent gloom of his own chamber, 'faithful remembrancers of his high endeavour, and his glad success,' that, as time passes by him with unreturning wing, still awaken the consciousness of a spirit patient, indefatigable in the search of truth, and the hope of surviving in the thoughts and minds of other men. I remember I had been reading a speech which Mirabaud (the author of the *System of Nature*) has put into the mouth of a supposed Atheist at the Last Judgment; and was afterwards led on by some means or other to consider the question, whether it could properly be said to be an act of virtue in any one to sacrifice his own final happiness to that of any other person or number of persons, if it were possible for the one ever to be made the price of the other ? Suppose it were my own case—that it were in my power to save twenty other persons by voluntarily consenting to suffer for them : Why should I not do a generous thing, and never trouble myself about what might be the consequence to myself the Lord knows when ?

" The reason why a man should prefer his own future welfare to that of others is, that he has a necessary, absolute interest in the one, which he cannot have in the other—and this, again, is a consequence of his being always the same individual, of his continued identity with himself. The difference, I thought, was this, that however insensible I may be to my own interest at any future period, yet when the time comes I shall feel differently about it. I shall then judge of it from the actual impression of the object, that is, truly and certainly ; and as I shall still be conscious of my past feelings, and shall bitterly regret my own folly and insensibility, I ought, as a rational agent, to be determined now by what I shall then wish I had done, when I shall feel the consequences of my actions most deeply and sensibly. It is this continued consciousness of my own feelings which gives me an immediate interest in whatever relates to my future welfare, and makes me at all times accountable to myself for my own conduct. As, therefore, this consciousness will be renewed in me after death, if I exist again at all—But stop—as I must be conscious of my past feelings to be myself, and as this conscious being will be myself, how if that consciousness should be transferred to some other being ? How am I to know that I am not imposed upon by a false claim of identity ? But that is ridiculous, because you will have no other self than that which arises from this very consciousness. Why, then, this self may be multiplied in as many different beings as the Deity may think proper to endue with the same consciousness; which, if it can be renewed at will in any one instance, may clearly be so in a hundred others. Am I to regard all these as equally myself? Am I equally interested in the fate of all? Or if I must fix upon some one ̖of them in particular as my, representative and other self, how am I to be determined in my choice? Here, then, I saw an end put to my speculations about absolute self-interest and personal identity. I saw plainly that the consciousness of my own feelings, which is made the foundation of my continued interest in them, could not extend to what had never been, and might never be; that my identity with myself must be confined to the connection between my past and present being; that with respect to my future feelings or interests, they could have no communication with, or influence over, my present feelings and interests, merely because they were future; that I shall be hereafter affected by the recollection of my past feelings and action; and my remorse be equally heightened by reflecting on my past folly and late-earned wisdom, whether I am really the same being, or have only the same consciousness renewed in me; but that to suppose that this remorse can react in the reverse order on my present feelings, or give me an immediate interest in my future feelings, before they exist, is an express contradiction in terms. It can only affect me as an imaginary idea, or an idea of truth. But so may the interests of others; and the question proposed was, whether I have not some real, necessary, absolute interest in whatever relates to my future being, in consequence of my immediate connection with myself—independently of the general impression which all positive ideas have on my mind. How, then, can this pretended unity of consciousness which it only reflected from the past—which makes me so little acquainted with the future that I cannot even tell for a moment how long it will be continued, whether it will be entirely interrupted by or renewed in me after death, and which might be multiplied in I don't know how many different beings, and prolonged by complicated sufferings, without my being any the wiser for it,—how, I say, can a principle of this sort identify my present with my future interests, and make me as much a participator in what does not at all affect me as if it were actually impressed on my senses? It is plain, as this conscious being may be decompounded, entirely destroyed, renewed again, or multiplied in a great number of beings, and as, whichever of these takes place, it cannot produce the least alteration in my present being—that what I am does not depend on what I am to be, and that there is no communication between my future interests, and the motives by which my present conduct must be governed. This can no more be influenced by what may be my future feelings with respect to it, than it will then be possible for me to alter my past conduct by wishing that I had acted differently. I cannot, therefore, have a principle of active self-interest arising out of the immediate connection between my present and future self, for no such connection exists, or is possible. I am what I am in spite of the future. My feelings, actions, and interests, must be determined by causes already existing and acting, and are absolutely independent of the future. Where there is not an intercommunity of feelings, there can be no identity of interests. My personal interest in anything must refer either to the interest excited by the actual impression of the object, which cannot be felt before it exists, and can last no longer than while the impression lasts; or it may refer to the particular manner in which I am mechanically affected by the idea of my own impressions in the absence of the object. I can, therefore, have no proper personal interest in my future impressions, since neither my ideas of future objects, nor my feelings with respect to them, can be excited either directly or indirectly by themselves, or by any ideas or feelings accompanying them, without a complete transposition of the order in which causes and effects follow one another in nature. The only reason for my preferring my future interest to that of others, must arise from my anticipating it with greater warmth of present imagination. It is this greater liveliness and force with which I can enter into my future feelings, that in a manner identifies them with my present being; and this notion of identity being once formed, the mind makes use of it to strengthen its habitual propensity, by giving to personal motives a reality and absolute truth which they can never have. Hence it has been inferred that my real, substantial interest in anything must be derived in some indirect manner from the impression of the object itself, as if that could have any sort of communication with my present feelings, or excite any interest in my mind but by means of the imagination, which is naturally affected in a certain manner by the prospect of future good or evil."[1]

J. L.[2] " This is the strangest tale that e'er I heard."

C. L. " It is the strangest fellow, brother John !"[3]

On Disagreeable People.

THOSE people who are uncomfortable in themselves are disagreeable to others. I do not here mean to speak of persons who offend intentionally, or are obnoxious to dislike from some palpable defect of mind or body, ugliness, pride, ill-humour, &c.; but of those who are disagreeable in spite of themselves, and, as it might appear, with almost every qualification to recommend

---

[1] *Principles of Human Action*, 2nd edit., p. 70.

[2] So in the original, on a folio leaf in my possession. In the edition of 1839, *J. L.* and *C. L.* are altered to *J. D.* and *C. D.* Lamb and his brother are evidently the persons intended. But the quotation is, of course, only borrowed from *Henry VI.* part 1. v, 4.—ED.

[3] In the reprint of *Sketches and Essays*, 1852, this article is omitted.—ED.

them to others. This want of success is owing chiefly to something in what is called their *manner;* and this again has its foundation in a certain cross-grained and unsociable state of feeling on their part, which influences us, perhaps, without our distinctly adverting to it. The mind is a finer instrument than we sometimes suppose it, and is not only swayed by overt acts and tangible proofs, but has an instinctive feeling of the air of truth. We find many individuals in whose company we pass our time, and have no particular fault to find with their understandings or character, and yet we are never thoroughly satisfied with them : the reason will turn out to be, upon examination, that they are never thoroughly satisfied with themselves, but uneasy and out of sorts all the time; and this makes us uneasy with them, without our reflecting on, or being able to discover the cause.

Thus, for instance, we meet with persons who do us a number of kindnesses, who show us every mark of respect and good-will, who are friendly and serviceable—and yet we do not feel grateful to them, after all. We reproach ourselves with this as caprice or insensibility, and try to get the better of it; but there is something in their way of doing things that prevents us from feeling cordial or sincerely obliged to them. We think them very worthy people, and would be glad of an opportunity to do them a good turn if it were in our power; but we cannot get beyond this : the utmost we can do is to save appearances, and not come to an open rupture with them. The truth is, in all such cases, we do not sympathise (as we ought) with them, because they do not sympathise (as they ought) with us. They have done what they did from a sense of duty in a cold dry manner, or from a meddlesome busy-body humour; or to show their superiority over us, or to patronise our infirmity; or they have dropped some hint by the way, or blundered upon some topic they should not, and have shown, by one means or other, that they were occupied with anything but the pleasure they were affording us, or a delicate attention to our feelings. Such persons may be styled *friendly grievances.* They are commonly people of low spirits and disappointed views, who see the discouraging side of human life, and, with the best intentions in the world, contrive to make everything they have to do with uncomfortable. They are alive to your distress, and take pains to remove it ; but they have no satisfaction in the gaiety and ease they have communicated, and are on the *look-out* for some new occasion of signalising their zeal; nor are they backward to insinuate that you will soon have need of their assistance, to guard you against running into fresh difficulties, or to extricate you from them. From large benevolence of soul and "discourse of reason, looking before and after," they are continually reminding you of something that has gone wrong in time past, or that may do so in that which is to come, and are surprised that their awkward hints, sly inuendos, blunt questions, and solemn features do not excite all the complacency and mutual good understanding in you which it is intended that they should. When they make themselves miserable on your account, it is hard that you will not lend them your countenance and support. This deplorable humour of theirs does not hit any one else. They are useful, but not agreeable people ; they may assist you in your affairs, but they depress and tyrannise over your feelings. When they have made you happy, they will not let you be so—have no enjoyment of the good they have done—will on no account part with their melancholy and desponding tone—and, by their mawkish insensibility and doleful grimaces, throw a damp over the triumph they are called upon to celebrate. They would keep you in hot water, that they may help you out of it. They will nurse you in a fit of sickness (congenial sufferers!)—arbitrate a law-suit for you, and embroil you deeper—procure you a loan of money ;— but all the while they are only delighted with rubbing the sore place, and casting the colour of your mental or other disorders. "The whole need not a physician;" and, being once placed at ease and comfort, they have no farther use for you as subjects for their singular beneficence, and you are not sorry to be quit of their tiresome interference. The old proverb, *A friend in need is a friend indeed,* is not verified in them. The class of persons here spoken of are the very reverse of *summer-friends,* who court you in prosperity, flatter your vanity, are the humble servants of your follies, never see or allude to anything wrong, minister to your gaiety, smooth over every difficulty, and, with the slightest approach of misfortune or of anything unpleasant, take French leave—

> "As when, in prime of June, a burnish'd fly,
> Sprung from the meads, o'er which he sweeps along,
> Cheer'd by the breathing bloom and vital sky,
> Tunes up, amid these airy halls, his song,
> Soothing at first the gay reposing throng;
> And oft he sips their bowl, or, nearly drown'd,
> He thence recovering drives their beds among,
> And scares their tender sleep with trump profound:
> Then out again he flies, to wing his mazy round."[1]

However we may despise such triflers, yet we regret them more than those well-meaning friends on whom a dull melancholy vapour hangs, that drags them and every one about them to the ground.

Again, there are those who might be very agreeable people, if they had but spirit to be so; but there is a narrow, unaspiring, under-bred tone in all they say or do. They have great sense and information—abound in a knowledge of character—have a fund of anecdote—are unexceptionable in manners and appearance—and yet we cannot make up our minds to like them: we are not glad to see them, nor sorry when they go away. Our fami-

[1] Thomson's *Castle of Indolence,* Canto i, st. 64, edit. 1841.

liarity with them, however great, wants the principle of cement, which is a certain appearance of frank cordiality and social enjoyment. They have no pleasure in the subjects of their own thoughts, and therefore can communicate none to others. There is a dry, husky, grating manner—a pettiness of detail—a tenaciousness of particulars, however trifling or unpleasant—a disposition to cavil—an aversion to enlarged and liberal views of things—in short, a hard, painful, unbending *matter-of-factness*, from which the spirit and effect are banished, and the letter only is attended to, which makes it impossible to sympathise with their discourse. To make conversation interesting or agreeable, there is required either the habitual tone of good company, which gives a favourable colouring to everything—or the warmth and enthusiasm of genius, which, though it may occasionally offend or be thrown off its guard, makes amends by its rapturous flights, and flings a glancing light upon all things. The literal and *dogged* style of conversation resembles that of a French picture, or its mechanical fidelity is like evidence given in a court of justice, or a police report.

From the literal to the plain-spoken, the transition is easy. The most efficient weapon of offence is truth. Those who deal in dry and repulsive matters-of-fact, tire out their friends; those who blurt out hard and home truths, make themselves mortal enemies wherever they come. There are your blunt, honest creatures, who omit no opportunity of letting you know their minds, and are sure to tell you all the ill, and conceal all the good they hear of you. They would not flatter you for the world, and to caution you against the malice of others, they think the province of a friend. This is not candour, but impudence; and yet they think it odd you are not charmed with their unreserved communicativeness of disposition. Gossips and tale-bearers, on the contrary, who supply the *tittle-tattle* of the neighbourhood, flatter you to your face, and laugh at you behind your back, are welcome and agreeable guests in all companies. Though you know it will be your turn next, yet for the sake of the immediate gratification, you are contented to pay your share of the public tax upon character, and are better pleased with the falsehoods that never reach your ears, than with the truths that others (less complaisant and more sincere) utter to your face—so short-sighted and willing to be imposed upon is our self-love! There is a man, who has the air of not being convinced without an argument : you avoid him as if he were a lion in your path. There is another, who asks you fifty questions as to the commonest things you advance : you would sooner pardon a fellow who held a pistol to your breast and demanded your money. No one regards a turnpike-keeper, or a custom-house officer, with a friendly eye : he who stops you in an excursion of fancy, or ransacks the articles of your belief obstinately and churlishly, to distinguish the spurious from the genuine, is still more your foe. These inquisitors and cross-examiners upon system make ten enemies for every controversy in which they engage. The world dread nothing so much as being convinced of their errors. In doing them this piece of service, you make war equally on their prejudices, their interests, their pride, and indolence. You not only set up for a superiority of understanding over them, which they hate, but you deprive them of their ordinary grounds of action, their topics of discourse, of their confidence in themselves, and those to whom they have been accustomed to look up for instruction and advice. It is making children of them. You unhinge all their established opinions and trains of thought ; and after leaving them in this listless, vacant, unsettled state—dissatisfied with their own notions and shocked at yours—you expect them to court and be delighted with your company, because, forsooth, you have only expressed your sincere and conscientious convictions. Mankind are not deceived by professions, unless they choose. They think that this pill of true doctrine, however it may be gilded over, is full of gall and bitterness to them; and, again, it is a maxim of which the vulgar are firmly persuaded, that plain-speaking (as it is called). nine parts in ten, is spleen and self-opinion; and the other part, perhaps, honesty. Those who will not abate an inch in argument, and are always seeking to recover the wind of you, are, in the eye of the world, disagreeable, unconscionable people, who ought to be *sent to Coventry*, or left to wrangle by themselves. No persons, however, are more averse to contradiction than these same dogmatists. What shows our susceptibility on this point is, that there is no flattery so adroit or effectual as that of implicit assent. Any one, however mean his capacity or ill-qualified to judge, who gives way to all our sentiments, and never seems to think but as we do, is indeed an *alter idem*—another self; and we admit him without scruple into our entire confidence, "yea, into our heart of hearts."

It is the same in books. Those which, under the disguise of plain-speaking, vent paradoxes, and set their faces against the " common-sense " of mankind, are neither " the volumes

—— " that enrich the shops,
That pass with approbation through the land ;"

nor, I fear, can it be added—

" That bring their authors an immortal fame."

They excite a clamour and opposition at first, and are in general soon consigned to oblivion. Even if the opinions are in the end adopted, the authors gain little by it, and their names remain in their original obloquy; for the public will own no obligations to such ungracious benefactors. In like manner, there are many books written in a very delightful vein, though with little in them, and that are accordingly popular. Their principle is to please, and not to offend; and they succeed in both objects. We are contented with the deference shown to our feelings for the time, and grant a truce both to wit and wisdom. The " courteous reader " and the good-natured author are well matched in this instance, and find their account in mutual tenderness and forbearance to each other's infirmities. I am not sure that Walton's *Angler* is not a book of this last description—

> " That dallies with the innocence of thought,
> Like the old time."

Hobbes and Mandeville are in the opposite extreme, and have met with a correspondent fate. The *Tatler* and *Spectator* are in the golden mean, carry instruction as far as it can go without shocking, and give the most exquisite pleasure without one particle of pain. " *Desire to please, and you will infallibly please*," is a maxim equally applicable to the study or the drawing-room. Thus, also, we see actors of very small pretensions, and who have scarce any other merit than that of being on good terms with themselves, and in high good humour with their parts (though they hardly understand a word of them), who are universal favourites with the audience. Others, who are masters of their art, and in whom no slip or flaw can be detected, you have no pleasure in seeing, from something dry, repulsive, and unconciliating in their manner; and you almost hate the very mention of their names, as an unavailing appeal to your candid decision in their favour, and as taxing you with injustice for refusing it.

We may observe persons who seem to take a peculiar delight in the *disagreeable*. They catch all sorts of uncouth tones and gestures, the manners and dialect of clowns and hoydens, and aim at vulgarity as desperately as others ape gentility. [This is what is often understood by a *love of low life*.] They say the most unwarrantable things, without meaning or feeling what they say. What startles or shocks other people, is to them a sport—an amusing excitement—a fillip to their constitutions; and from the bluntness of their perceptions, and a certain wilfulness of spirit, not being able to enter into the refined and agreeable, they make a merit of despising everything of the kind. Masculine women, for example, are those who, not being distinguished by the charms and delicacy of the sex, affect a superiority over it by throwing aside all decorum. We also find another class, who continually do and say what they ought not, and what they do not intend, and who are governed almost entirely by an instinct of absurdity. Owing to a perversity of imagination or irritability of nerve, the idea that a thing is improper acts as a provocation to it: the fear of committing a blunder is so strong, that in their agitation they *bolt* out whatever is uppermost in their minds, before they are aware of the consequence. The dread of something wrong haunts and rivets their attention to it; and an uneasy, morbid apprehensiveness of temper takes away their self-possession, and hurries them into the very mistakes they are most anxious to avoid.

If we look about us, and ask who are the agreeable and disagreeable people in the world, we shall see that it does not so much depend on their virtues or vices—their understanding or stupidity—as on the degree of pleasure or pain they seem to feel in ordinary social intercourse. What signify all the good qualities any one possesses, if he is none the better for them himself? If the cause is so delightful, the effect ought to be so too. We enjoy a friend's society only in proportion as he is satisfied with ours. Even wit, however it may startle, is only agreeable as it is sheathed in good-humour. There are a kind of *intellectual stammerers*, who are delivered of their good things with pain and effort; and consequently what costs them such evident uneasiness does not impart unmixed delight to the bystanders. There are those, on the contrary, whose sallies cost them nothing—who abound in a flow of pleasantry and good-humour; and who float down the stream with them carelessly and triumphantly—

"Wit at the helm, and Pleasure at the prow."

Perhaps it may be said of English wit in general, that it too much resembles pointed lead : after all, there is something heavy and dull in it! The race of small wits are not the least agreeable people in the world. They have their little joke to themselves, enjoy it, and do not set up any preposterous pretensions to thwart the current of our self-love. Toad-eating is accounted a thriving profession; and a *butt*, according to the *Spectator*, is a highly useful member of society—as one who takes whatever is said of him in good part, and as necessary to conduct off the spleen and superfluous petulance of the company. Opposed to these are the swaggering bullies—the licensed wits—the free-thinkers—the loud talkers, who, in the jockey phrase, have *lost their mouths*, and cannot be reined in by any regard to decency or common-sense. The more obnoxious the subject, the more are they charmed with it, converting their want of feeling into a proof of superiority to vulgar prejudice and squeamish affectation. But there is an unseemly exposure of the mind, as well as of the body. There are some objects that shock the sense, and cannot with propriety be mentioned : there are naked truths that offend the mind, and ought to be kept out of sight as much as possible. For human nature cannot bear to be too hardly pressed upon. One of these cynical truisms, when brought forward to the world, may be forgiven as a slip of the pen : a succession of them, denoting a deliberate purpose and *malice prepense*, must ruin any writer. Lord Byron had got into an irregular course of these a little before his death—seemed desirous, in imitation of Mr. Shelley, to run the gauntlet of public obloquy—and, at the same time, wishing to screen himself from the censure he defied, dedicated his *Cain* to 'Sir Walter Scott—a pretty godfather to such a bantling!

Some persons are of so teazing and fidgetty a turn of mind, that they do not give you a moment's rest. Everything goes wrong with them. They complain of a headache or the weather. They take up a book, and lay it down again—venture an opinion, and retract it before they have half done—offer to serve you, and prevent some one else from doing it. If you dine with them at a tavern, in order to be more at your ease, the fish is too little done—the sauce is not the right one; they ask for a sort of wine which they think is not to be had, or if it is, after some trouble, procured, do not touch it; they give the waiter fifty contradictory orders, and are restless and sit on thorns the whole of dinner-time. All this is owing to a want of robust health, and of a strong spirit of enjoyment: it is a fastidious habit of mind, produced by a valetudinary habit of body: they are out of sorts with everything, and of course their ill-humour and captiousness communicates itself to you, who are as little delighted with them as they are with other things. Another sort of people, equally objectionable with this helpless class, who are disconcerted by a shower of rain or stopped by an insect's wing, are those who, in the opposite spirit, will have everything their own way, and carry all before them—who cannot brook the slightest shadow of opposition—who are always in the heat of an argument—who knit their brows and clench their teeth in some speculative discussion, as if they were engaged in a personal quarrel—and who, though successful over almost every competitor, seem still to resent the very offer of resistance to their supposed authority, and are as angry as if they had sustained some pre meditated injury. There is an impatience of temper and an intolerance of opinion in this that conciliates neither our affection nor esteem. To such persons nothing appears of any moment but the indulgence of a domineering intellectual superiority to the disregard and discomfiture of their own and every body else's comfort. Mounted on an abstract proposition, they trample on every courtesy and decency of behaviour; and though, perhaps, they do not intend the gross personalities they are guilty of, yet they cannot be acquitted of a want of due consideration for others, and of an intolerable egotism in the support of truth and justice. You may hear one of these Quixotic declaimers pleading the cause of humanity in a voice of thunder, or expatiating on the beauty of a Guido with features distorted with rage and scorn. This is not a very amiable or edifying spectacle.

There are persons who cannot make friends. Who are they? Those who cannot be friends. It is not the want of understanding or good-nature, of entertaining or useful qualities, that you complain of: on the contrary, they have probably many points of attraction; but they have one that neutralises all these—they care nothing about you, and are neither the better nor worse for what you think of them. They manifest no joy at your approach; and when you leave them, it is with a feeling that they can do just as well without you. This is not sullenness, nor indifference, nor absence of mind; but they are intent solely on their own thoughts, and you are merely one of the subjects they exercise them upon. They live in society as in a solitude; and, however their brain works, their pulse beats neither faster nor slower for the common accidents of life. There is, therefore, something cold and repulsive in the air that is about them—like that of marble. In a word, they are *modern philosophers;* and the modern philosopher is what the pedant was of old— a being who lives in a world of his own, and has no correspondence with this. It is not that such persons have not done you services—you acknowledge it ; it is not that they have said severe things of you—you submit to it as a necessary evil : but it is the cool manner in which the whole is done that annoys you—the speculating upon you, as if you were nobody—the regarding you, with a view to an experiment *in corpore vili*—the principle of dissection—the determination to spare no blemishes—to cut you down to your real standard ;—in short, the utter absence of the partiality of friendship, the blind enthusiasm of affection, or the delicacy of common decency, that whether they " hew you as a carcase fit for hounds, or carve you as a dish fit for the gods," the operation on your feelings and your sense of obligation is just the same ; and, whether they are demons or angels in themselves, you wish them equally *at the devil !*

Other persons of worth and sense give way to mere violence of temperament (with which the understanding has nothing to do)—are burnt up with a perpetual fury —repel and throw you to a distance by their restless, whirling motion—so that you dare not go near them, or feel as uneasy in their company as if you stood on the edge of a volcano. They have their *tempora mollia fandi ;* but then what a stir may you not expect the next moment ! Nothing is less inviting or less comfortable than this state of uncertainty and apprehension. Then they are those who never approach you without the most alarming advice or information, telling you that you are in a dying way, or that your affairs are on the point of ruin, by way of disburthening their consciences ; and others, who give you to understand much the same thing as a good joke, out of sheer impertinence, constitutional vivacity, and want of something to say. All these, it must be confessed, are disagreeable people ; and you repay their over-anxiety or total forgetfulness of you, by a determination to *cut* them as speedily as possible. We meet with instances of persons

who overpower you by a sort of boisterous mirth and rude
animal spirits, with whose ordinary state of excitement it
is as impossible to keep up as with that of any one really
intoxicated ; and with others who seem scarce alive—who
take no pleasure or interest in anything—who are born to
exemplify the maxim,

> " Not to admire is all the art I know
> To make men happy, or to keep them so,"—

and whose mawkish insensibility or sullen scorn are
equally annoying. In general, all people brought up in
remote country places, where life is crude and harsh—all
sectaries—all partisans of a losing cause, are discontented
and disagreeable. Commend me above all to the Westminster School of Reform, whose blood runs as cold in
their veins as the torpedo's, and whose touch jars like it.
Catholics are, upon the whole, more amiable than
Protestants—foreigners than English people. Among
ourselves, the Scotch, as a nation, are particulary disagreeable. They hate every appearance of comfort themselves,
and refuse it to others. Their climate, their religion,
and their habits are equally averse to pleasure. Their
manners are either distinguished by a fawning sycophancy
(to gain their own ends, and conceal their natural defects),
that makes one sick ; or by a morose, unbending callous-
ness, that makes one shudder. I had forgot to mention
two other descriptions of persons who fall under the scope
of this essay :—those who take up a subject, and run on
with it interminably, without knowing whether their
hearers care one word about it, or in the least minding
what reception their oratory meets with—these are
pretty generally voted *bores* (mostly German ones) :—
and others, who may be designated as practical paradox-
mongers—who discard the "milk of human kindness,"
and an attention to common observances, from all their
actions, as effeminate and puling—who wear an out-of-the

way hat as a mark of superior understanding, and carry home a handkerchief full of mushrooms in the top of it as an original discovery—who give you craw-fish for supper instead of lobsters; seek their company in a garret, and over a gin-bottle, to avoid the imputation of affecting genteel society; and discard their friends after a term of years, and warn others against them, as being *honest fellows*, which is thought a vulgar prejudice. This is carrying the harsh and repulsive even beyond the disagreeable—to the hateful. Such persons are generally people of commonplace understandings, obtuse feelings, and inordinate vanity. They are formidable if they get you in their power—otherwise, they are only to be laughed at.

There are a vast number who are disagreeable from meanness of spirit, downright insolence, from slovenliness of dress or disgusting tricks, from folly or ignorance; but these causes are positive moral or physical defects, and I only meant to speak of that repulsiveness of manners which arises from want of tact and sympathy with others. So far of friendship: a word, if I durst, of love. Gallantry to women (the sure road to their favour) is nothing but the appearance of extreme devotion to all their wants and wishes—a delight in their satisfaction, and a confidence in yourself, as being able to contribute towards it. The slightest indifference with regard to them, or distrust of yourself, are equally fatal. The amiable is the voluptuous in looks, manner, or words. No face that exhibits this kind of expression—whether lively or serious, obvious or suppressed, will be thought ugly—no address, awkward —no lover who approaches every women he meets as his mistress, will be unsuccessful. Diffidence and awkwardness are the two antidotes to love.

To please universally, we must be pleased with ourselves and others. There should be a tinge of the coxcomb, an oil of self-complacency, an anticipation of success —

there should be no gloom, no moroseness, no shyness—in short, there should be very little of the Englishman, and a good deal of the Frenchman. But though, I believe, this is the receipt, we are none the nearer making use of it. It is impossible for those who are naturally disagreeable ever to become otherwise. This is some consolation, as it may save a world of useless pains and anxiety. *" Desire to please, and you will infallibly please,"* is a true maxim; but it does not follow that it is in the power of all to practise it. A vain man, who thinks he is endeavouring to please, is only endeavouring to shine, and is still farther from the mark. An irritable man, who puts a check upon himself, only grows dull, and loses spirit to be anything. Good temper and a happy turn of mind (which are the indispensable requisites) can no more be commanded than good health or good looks; and though the plain and sickly need not distort their features, and may abstain from excess, this is all they can do. The utmost a disagreeable person can do is to hope, by care and study, to become less disagreeable than he is, and to pass unnoticed in society. With this negative character he should be contented, and may build his fame and happiness on other things.

I will conclude with a description of men who neither please nor aspire to please anybody, and who can come in nowhere so properly as at the fag-end of an essay :—I mean that class of discontented but amusing persons, who are infatuated with their own ill success, and reduced to despair by a lucky turn in their favour. While all goes well, they are *like fish out of water*. They have no reliance on or sympathy with their good fortune, and look upon it as a momentary delusion. Let a doubt be thrown on the question, and they begin to be full of lively apprehensions again: let all their hopes vanish, and they feel themselves on firm ground once more. From want of spirit, or from habit, their imaginations cannot rise above the low ground of humility—cannot reflect the gay, flaunting tints of the fancy—flag and droop into despondency —and can neither indulge the expectation, nor employ the means of success. Even when it is within their reach, they dare not lay hands upon it ; and shrink from unlooked for bursts of prosperity, as something of which they are both ashamed and unworthy. The class of *croakers* here spoken of are less delighted with other people's misfortunes than with their own. Their neighbours may have some pretensions—they have none. Querulous complaints and anticipations of discomfort are the food on which they live; and they at last acquire a passion for that which is the favourite theme of their thoughts, and can no more do without it than without the pinch of snuff with which they season their conversation, and enliven the pauses of their daily prognostics.

On Knowledge of the World.

"Who shall go about to cozen fortune, or wear the badge of honour without the stamp of merit ?"

A KNOWLEDGE of the world is generally supposed to be the fruit of experience and observation, or of a various, practical acquaintance with men and things. On the contrary, it appears to me to be a kind of instinct, arising out of a peculiar construction and turn of mind. Some persons display this knowledge at their first outset in life : others, with all their opportunities and dear-bought lessons, never acquire it to the end of their career. In fact, a knowledge of the world only means a knowledge of our own interest; it is nothing but a species of selfishness or ramification of the law of self-preservation. There may be said to be two classes of people in the world, which remain for ever distinct : those who consider things in the abstract, or with a reference to truth, and those who consider them only with a reference to themselves, or to the *main chance.* The first, whatever may be their acquirements or discoveries, wander through life in a sort of absence of mind, or comparative state of sleep-walking: the last, though their attention is riveted to a single point of view, are always on the alert, know perfectly well what they are about, and calculate with the greatest nicety the effect which their words or actions will have on others. They do not trouble themselves about the arguments on any subject; they know the opinion entertained on it, and that is enough for them to regulate themselves by; the rest they regard as quite Utopian, and foreign to the purpose. " Subtle as the fox for prey, like warlike as the wolf for what they eat," they leave mere speculative points to those who, from some unaccountable bias or caprice, take an interest in what does not personally concern them, and make good the old saying, that " the children of the world are wiser in their generation than the children of the light!"

The man of the world is to the man of science very much what the chamelion is to the armadillo: the one takes its hue from every surrounding object, and is undistinguishable from them; the other is shut up in a formal crust of knowledge, and clad in an armour of proof, from which the shaft of ridicule or the edge of disappointment falls equally pointless. It is no uncommon case to see a person come into a room, which he enters awkwardly enough, and has nothing in his dress or appearance to recommend him, but after the first embarrassments are over, sits down, takes his share in the conversation, in which he acquits himself creditably, shows sense, reading, and shrewdness, expresses himself with point, articulates distinctly, when he blunders on some topic which he might see is disagreeable, but persists in it the more as he finds others shrink from it; mentions a book of which you have not heard, and perhaps do not wish to hear, and he therefore thinks himself bound to favour you with the contents; gets into an argument with one, proses on with another on a subject in which his hearer has no interest; and when he goes away, people remark, " What a pity that Mr. —— has not more knowledge of the world, and has so little skill in adapting himself to the tone and manners of society !" But will time and habit cure him of this defect? Never. He wants a certain *tact*, he has not a voluntary power over his ideas, but is like a person reading out of a book, or who can only pour out the budget of knowledge with which his brain is crammed in all places and companies alike. If you attempt to divert his attention from the general subject to the persons he is addressing, you puzzle and stop him quite. He is a mere conversing automaton. He has not the *sense of personality* —the faculty of perceiving the effect (as well as the grounds) of his opinions : and how then should failure or mortification give it him? It must be a painful reflection, and he must be glad to turn from it; or. after a few reluctant and unsuccessful efforts to correct his errors, he will try to forget or harden himself in them. Finding that he makes so slow and imperceptible a progress in amending his faults, he will take his swing in the opposite direction, will triumph and revel in his supposed excellences, will launch out into the wide, untrammelled field of abstract speculation, and silence envious sneers and petty cavils by force of argument and dint of importunity. You will find him the same character at sixty that he was at thirty ; or, should time soften down some of his asperities, and tire him of his absurdities as he has tired others, nothing will transform him into a man of the world, and he will die in a garret, or a paltry second-floor, from not having been able to acquire the art " to see himself as others see him," or to dress his opinions, looks, and actions in the smiles and approbation of the world. On the other hand, take a youth from the same town (perhaps a school-fellow, and the dunce of the neighbourhood); he has "no figures, nor no fantasies which busy thought draws in the brain of men," no preconceived notions by which he must square his conduct or his conversation, no dogma to maintain in the teeth of opposition, no Shibboleth to which he must force others to subscribe; the progress of science or the good of his fellow-creatures are things about which he has not the remotest conception, or the smallest particle of anxiety—

> " His soul proud science never taught to stray
> Far as the solar walk, or milky way;"

all that he sees or attends to is the immediate path before him, or what can encourage or lend him a helping hand through it; his mind is a complete blank, on which the world may write its maxims and customs in what characters it pleases; he has only to study its humours, flatter its prejudices, and take advantage of its foibles; while walking the streets he is not taken up with solving an abstruse problem, but with considering his own appearance and that of others; instead of contradicting a patron, assents to all he hears; and in every proposition that comes before him asks himself only what he can get by it, and whether it will make him friends or enemies: such a one is said to possess great penetration and knowledge of the world, understands his place in society, gets on in it, rises from the counter to the counting-house, from the dependant to be a partner, amasses a fortune, gains in size and respectability as his affairs prosper, has his town and country house, and ends with buying up half the estates in his native county!

The great secret of a knowledge of the world, then, consists in a subserviency to the will of others, and the primary motive to this attention is a mechanical and watchful perception of our own interest. It is not an art that requires a long course of study, the difficulty is in putting one's-self apprentice to it. It does not surely imply any very laborious or profound inquiry into the distinctions of truth or falsehood to be able to assent to whatever one hears; nor any great refinement of moral feeling to approve of whatever has custom, power, or interest on its side. The only question is, "Who is willing to do so?"—and the answer is, those who have no other faculties or pretensions, either to stand in the way of, or to assist their progress through life. Those are slow to wear the livery of the world who have any independent resources of their own. It is not that the philosopher, or the man of genius, does not see and know all this, that he is not constantly and forcibly reminded of it by his own failure or the success of others, but he cannot stoop to practise it. He has a different scale of excellence and mould of ambition, which have nothing in common with current maxims and time-serving calculations. He is a moral and intellectual egotist, not a mere worldly-minded one. In youth, he has sanguine hopes and brilliant dreams, which he cannot sacrifice for sordid realities—as he advances farther in life, habit and pride forbid his turning back. He cannot bring himself to give up his best-grounded convictions to a blockhead, or his conscientious principles to a knave, though he might make his fortune by so doing. The rule holds good here, as well as in another sense—"What shall it profit a man if he gain the whole world and lose his own soul?" If his convictions and principles had been less strong, they would have yielded long ago to the suggestions of his interest, and he would have relapsed into the man of the world, or rather he would never have had the temptation or capacity to be anything else. One thing that keeps men honest, as well as that confirms them knaves, is their incapacity to do any better for themselves than nature has done for them. One person can with difficulty speak the truth, as another lies with a very ill grace. After repeated awkward attempts to change characters. they each very properly fall back into their old *jog-trot* path, as best suited to their genius and habits.

There are individuals who make themselves and every one else uncomfortable by trying to be agreeable, and who are only to be endured in their natural characters of blunt, plain-spoken people. Many a man would have turned rogue if he had known how. *Non ex quotibet ligno fit Mercurius.* The modest man cannot be impudent if he would. The man of sense cannot play the fool to advantage. It is not the mere resolution to act a part that will enable us to do it, without a natural genius and fitness for it. Some men are born to be valets, as others are to be courtiers. There is the climbing *genus* in man as well as in plants. It is sometimes made a wonder how men of "no mark or likelihood" frequently rise to court-preferment, and make their way against all competition. That is the very reason. They present no tangible point; they offend no feeling of self-importance. They are a perfect unresisting medium of patronage and favour. They aspire through servility; they repose in insignificance. A man of talent or pretension in the same circumstances would be kicked out in a week. A look that implied a doubt, a hint that suggested a difference of opinion, would be fatal. It is of no use, in parleying with absolute power, to dissemble, to suppress: there must be no feelings or opinions to dissemble or suppress. The artifice of the dependant is not a match for the jealousy of the patron: "The soul must be subdued to the very quality of its lord." Where all is annihilated in the presence of the Sovereign, is it astonishing that *nothings* should succeed? Ciphers are as necessary in courts as eunuchs in seraglios.

I do not think Mr. Cobbett would succeed in an interview with the Prince [Regent]. Bub Doddington said, " He would not justify before his Sovereign, even where his own character was at stake. I am afraid we could hardly reckon upon the same forbearance in Mr. Cobbett where his country's welfare was at stake, and where he had an opportunity of vindicating it. He might have a great deal of reason on his side; but he might forget, or seem to forget, that as the King is above the law, he is also above reason. Reason is but a suppliant at the foot of thrones, and waits for their approval or rebuke. *Salus populi suprema lex*—may be a truism anywhere else. If reason dares to approach them at all, it must be in the shape of deference and humility, not of headstrong importunity and self-will. Instead of breathless awe, of mild intreaty, of humble remonstrance, it is Mr. Cobbett who, upon very slight encouragement, would give the law, and the Monarch who must kiss the rod. The reformer would be too full of his own opinion to allow an option even to Majesty, and the affair would have the same ending as that of the old ballad—

"Then the Queen, overhearing what Betty did say,
Would send Mr. Roper to take her away."

As I have brought Mr. Cobbett in here by the neck and shoulders, I may add, that I do not think he belongs properly to the class, either of philosophical speculators, or men of the world. He is a political humorist. He is too much taken up with himself either to attend to right reason or to judge correctly of what passes around him. He mistakes strength of purpose and passion, not only for truth, but for success. Because he can give fifty good reasons for a thing, he thinks it not only *ought* to be, but *must* be. Because he is swayed so entirely by his wishes and humours, he believes others will be ready to give up their prejudices, interests, and resentments to oblige him. He persuades himself that he is the fittest person to represent Westminster in parliament, and he considers this point (once proved) tantamount to his return. He knows no more of the disposition or sentiments of the people of

K

Westminster than of the inhabitants of the moon (except from what he himself chooses to say or write of them), and it is this want of sympathy which, as much as anything, prevents his being chosen. The exclusive force and bigotry of his opinions deprives them of half their influence and effect, by allowing no toleration to others, and consequently setting them against him.

Mr. Cobbett seemed disappointed, at one time, at not succeeding in the character of a legacy-hunter. Why, a person, to succeed in this character, ought to be a mere skin or bag to hold money, a place to deposit it in, a shadow, a deputy, a trustee who keeps it for the original owner—so that the transfer is barely nominal, and who, if the donor were to return from the other world, would modestly yield it up—one who has no personal identity of his own, no will to encroach upon or dispose of it, otherwise than his patron would wish after his death—not a hairbrained egotist, a dashing adventurer, to squander, hector, and flourish away with it in wild schemes and ruinous experiments, every one of them at variance with the opinions of the testator, in new methods of turnip-hoeing; in speculations in madder—this would be to tear his soul from his body twice over—

"His patron's ghost from Limbo lake the while
Sees this which more damnation doth upon him pile !"

Mr. Cobbett complained, that in his last interview with Baron Maseres, that gentleman was in his dotage, and that his reverend legatee sat at the bottom of the table, cutting a poor figure, and not contradicting a word the Baron said. No doubt, as he has put this in print in the exuberance of his dissatisfaction, he let both gentlemen see pretty plainly what he thought of them, and fancied that this expression of his contempt, as it gratified him, was the way to ensure the good will of the one to make over his whole estate, or the good word of the other to let him *go snacks.* This is a new way of being *quits* with one's benefactors, and an egregious *quid pro quo.* If Baron Maseres had left Mr. Cobbett 200,000*l.* it must have been not to write his epitaph, or visit him in his last moments!

A gossiping chambermaid who only smiles and assents when her mistress wishes to talk, or an ignorant country clown who stands with his hat off when he has a favour to ask of the squire (and if he is wise, at all other times), knows more of the matter. A knowledge of mankind is little more than Sir Pertinax's instinct of *bowing,* or of "never standing upright in the presence of a great man," or of that great blockhead, the world. It is not a perception of truth, but a sense of power, and an instant determination of the will to submit to it. It is, therefore, less an intellectual acquirement than a natural disposition. It is on this account that I think both cunning and wisdom are a sort of original endowments, or attain maturity much earlier than is supposed, from their being moral qualities, and having their seat in the heart rather than the head. The difference depends on the *manner* of seeing things. The one is a selfish, the other is a disinterested view of nature. The one is the clear open look of integrity, the other is a contracted and blear-eyed obliquity of mental vision. If any one has but the courage and honesty to look at an object as it is in itself, or divested of prejudice, fear, and favour, he will be sure to see it pretty right; as he who regards it through the refractions of opinion and fashion, will be sure to see it distorted and falsified, however the error may redound to his own advantage. Certainly, he who makes the universe tributary to his convenience, and subjects all his impressions of what is right or wrong, true or false, black or white, round or square, to the standard and maxims of the world, who never utters a proposition but he fancies a patron close at his elbow who overhears him, who is even afraid, in private, to suffer an honest conviction to rise in his mind, lest it should mount to his lips, get wind, and ruin his prospects in life, ought to gain something in exchange for the restraint and force put upon his thoughts and faculties : on the contrary, he who is confined by no such petty and debasing trammels, whose comprehension of mind is " in large heart enclosed," finds his inquiries and his views expand in a degree commensurate with the universe around him ; makes truth welcome wherever he meets her, and receives her cordial embrace in return. To see things divested of passion and interest, is to see them with the eye of history and philosophy. It is easy to judge right, or at least to come to a mutual understanding in matters of history, and abstract morality. Why, then, is it so difficult to arrive at the same calm certainty in actual life ? Because the passions and interests are concerned, and it requires so much more candour, love of truth, and independence of spirit to encounter " the world and its dread laugh," to throw aside every sinister consideration, and grapple with the plain merits of the case.• To be wiser than other men is to be honester than they; and strength of mind is only courage to see and speak the truth. Perhaps the courage may be also owing to the strength ; but both go together, and are natural, and not acquired. Do we not see in fables the force of the moral principle in detecting the truth? The only effect of fables is, by making inanimate or irrational things actors in the scene, to remove the case completely from our own sphere, to take our self-love off its guard, to simplify the question ; and yet the result of this obvious appeal is allowed to be universal and irresistible. Is not this another example that " the heart of man is deceitful above all things ;" or, that it is less our incapacity to distinguish what is right, than our secret determination to adhere to what is wrong, that prevents our discriminating one from the other? It is not that great and useful truths are not manifest and discernible in themselves ; but little, dirty objects get between them and us, and from being near and gross, hide the lofty and distant. The first business of the patriot and the philanthropist is to overleap this barrier, to rise out of this material dross. Indignation, contempt of the base and grovelling, makes the philosopher no less than the poet ; and it is the power of looking beyond self that enables each to inculcate moral truth and nobleness of sentiment, the one by general precepts, the other by individual example.

I have no quarrel with men of the world, mere *muck-worms ;* every one after his fashion, " as the flesh and fortune shall serve ;" but I confess I have a little distaste to those who, having set out as loud and vaunting enthusiasts, have turned aside to " tread the primrose path of dalliance," and to revile those who did not choose to follow so edifying an example. The candid brow and elastic spring of youth may be exchanged for the wrinkles and crookedness of age ; but at least we should retain something of the erectness and openness of our first unbiassed thoughts. I cannot understand how any degree of egotism can dispense with the consciousness of personal identity. As we advance farther in life, we are naturally inclined to revert in imagination to its commencement ; but what can those dwell upon there who find only feelings that they despise, and opinions that they have abjured ?

" If thine eye offend thee, pluck it out and cast it from thee :" but the operation is a painful one, and the body remains after it only a mutilated fragment. Generally, those who are cut off from this resource in former recollections, make up for it (as well as they can) by an exaggerated and anxious fondness for their late-espoused convictions—a thing unsightly and indecent. Why does he[1] who at one time despises " the little Chapel Bell," afterwards write " the Book of the Church ?" The one is not an atonement for the other ; each shows only a juvenile or a superannuated precocity of judgment. It is uniting

[1] Southey.—ED.

Camille-Desmoulins and Camille-Jourdan, (Jourdan of the Chimes) in one character. I should like, not out of malice, but from curiosity, to see Mr. Southey re-write the beautiful poem on "his own miniature-picture, when he was two years old," and see what he would substitute for the lines—

> "And it was thought
> That thou shouldst tread preferment's flowery path,
> Young Robert!"

There must here, I think, be *hiatus in manuscriptis:* the verse must halt a little! The laureate and his friends say that they are still labouring in the same design as ever, correcting the outlines and filling up the unfinished sketch of their early opinions. They seem rather to have quite blotted them out, and to have taken a fresh canvas to begin another, and no less extravagant caricature. Or their new and old theories remind one of those heads in picture-dealers' shops, where one half of the face is thoroughly cleaned and repaired, and the other left covered with stains and dirt, to show the necessity of the picture-scourer's art: the transition offends the sight.

It may be made a question whether men grow wiser as they grow older, any more than they grow stronger or healthier or honester. They may, in one sense, imbibe a greater portion of worldly wisdom, and have their romantic flights tamed to the level of every day's practice and experience; but perhaps it would be better if some of the extravagance and enthusiasm of youth could be infused into the latter, instead of being absorbed (perforce) in that sink of pride, envy, selfishness, ignorance, conceit, prejudice, and hypocrisy. One thing is certain, that this is the present course of events, and that if the individual grows wiser as he gains experience, the world does not, and that the tardy penitent who is treading back his steps, may meet the world advancing as he is retreating, and adopting more and more of the genuine impulses and disinterested views of youth into its creed. It is, indeed, only by conforming to some such original and unsophisticated standard, that it can acquire either soundness or consistency. The appeal is a fair one, from the bad habits of society to the unprejudiced aspirations and impressions of human nature.

It seems, in truth, a hard case to have all the world against us, and to require uncommon fortitude (not to say presumption) to stand out single against such a host. The bare suggestion must "give us pause," and has no doubt overturned many an honest conviction. The *opinion of the world* (as it pompously entitles itself), if it means anything more than a set of local and party prejudices, with which only our interest, not truth, is concerned, is a shadow, a bugbear, and a contradiction in terms. *Having all the world against us,* is a phrase without a meaning; for in those points in which all the world agree, no one differs from the world. If all the world were of the same way of thinking, and always kept in the same mind, it would certainly be a little staggering to have them against you. But however widely and angrily they may differ from you, they differ quite as much from one another, and even from themselves. What is gospel at one moment, is heresy the next: different countries and climates have different notions of things. When you are put on your trial, therefore, for impugning the public opinion, you may always *subpœna* this great body against itself. For example, I have been twitted for somewhere calling Tom Paine a great writer, and no doubt his reputation at present "does somewhat smack:" yet in 1792 he was so great, or so popular an author, and so much read and admired by numbers who would not now mention his name, that the Government was obliged to suspend the Constitution, and to go to war to counteract the effects of his popularity. His extreme popularity was then the cause (by a common and vulgar *reaction*) of his extreme

obnoxiousness. If the opinion of the world, then, con-
tradicts itself, why may not I contradict it, or choose at
what time, and to what extent I will agree with it? I
have been accused of abusing dissenters, and saying that
sectaries, in general, are dry and suspicious; and I
believe that all the world will say the same thing except
themselves. I have said that the church people are proud
and overbearing, which has given them umbrage, though
in this I have all the sectaries on my side. I have
laughed at the Methodists,[1] and for this I have been
accused of glancing at religion: yet who but a Methodist
does not laugh at the Methodists as well as myself? But
I also laugh at those who laugh at them. I have pointed
out by turns the weak sides and foibles of different sects
and parties, and they themselves maintain that they
respectively are perfect and infallible: and this is what is
called having all the world against me. I have inveighed
all my life against the insolence of the Tories, and for
this I have the authority both of Whigs and Radicals;
but then I have occasionally spoken against the indecision
of the Whigs, and the extravagance of the Radicals, and
thus have brought all three on my back, though two out
of the three regularly agree with all I say of the third
party. Poets do not approve of what I have said of their
turning prose-writers; nor do the politicians approve of
my tolerating the fooleries of the fanciful tribe at all: so
they make common cause to *damn* me between them.
People never excuse the drawback from themselves, nor
the concessions to an adversary: such is the justice and
candour of mankind! Mr. Wordsworth is not satisfied
with the praise I have heaped upon himself,[2] and still
less, that I have allowed Mr. Moore to be a poet at all.[3]

---

[1] See more particularly a paper in the *Round Table*, edit. 1817,
i. 163, *On the Causes of Methodism.*—Ed.

[2] In the *Lectures on the English Poets*, 1818, and the *Spirit of the
Age*, 1825.—Ed.　　　　[3] *Spirit of the Age*, 1825.—Ed.

I do not think I have ever set my face against the popular idols of the day; I have been among the foremost in crying up Mrs. Siddons, Kean, Sir Walter Scott, Madame Pasta, and others; and as to the great names of former times, my admiration has been lavish, and sometimes almost mawkish. I have dissented, it is true, in one or two instances; but that only shows that I judge for myself, not that I make a point of contradicting the general taste. I have been more to blame in trying to push certain Illustrious Obscure into notice:—they have not forgiven the obligation, nor the world the tacit reproach. As to my personalities, they might quite as well be termed *impersonalities*. I am so intent on the abstract proposition and its elucidation, that I regard everything else of very subordinate consequence: my friends, I conceive, will not refuse to contribute to so laudable an undertaking, and my enemies *must!* I have found fault with the French, I have found fault with the English; and pray, do they not find great, mutual, and just fault with one another? It may seem a great piece of arrogance in any one, to set up his individual and private judgment against that of ten millions of people; but cross the channel, and you will have thirty millions on your side. Even should the thirty millions come over to the opinions of the ten (a thing that may happen to-morrow), still one need not despair. I remember my old friend Peter Finnerty laughing very heartily at something I had written about the Scotch, but it was followed up by a sketch of the Irish, on which he closed the book, looked grave, and said he disapproved entirely of all national reflections. Thus you have all the world on your side, except the party concerned. What any set of people think or say of themselves is hardly a rule for others: yet, if you do not attach yourself to some one set of people and principles, and stick to them through thick and thin, instead of giving your opinion fairly and fully all round, you must expect to have all the world against you, for no other reason than because you express sincerely, and *for their good*, not only what they say of others, but what is said of themselves, which they would fain keep a profound secret, and prevent the divulging of under the severest pains and penalties. When I told Jeffrey that I had composed a work in which I had "in some sort handled" about a score of leading characters, he said, "Then you will have one man against you, and the remaining nineteen for you!"[1] I have not found it so. In fact, these persons would agree pretty nearly to all that I say, and allow that, in nineteen points out of twenty, I am right; but the twentieth, that relates to some imperfection of their own, weighs down all the rest, and produces an unanimous verdict against the author. There is but one thing in which the world agree, a certain bigoted blindness, and conventional hypocrisy, without which, according to Mandeville (that is, if they really spoke what they thought and knew of one another), they would fall to cutting each other's throats immediately.

We find the same contrariety and fluctuation of opinion in different ages, as well as countries and classes. For about a thousand years, during "the high and palmy state" of the Romish hierarchy, it was agreed (*nemine contradicente*) that *two and two made five:* afterwards, for above a century, there was great battling and controversy to prove that they made four and a half; then, for a century more, it was thought a great stride taken to come down to four and a quarter; and, perhaps, in another century or two, it will be discovered for a wonder that *two and two actually make four!* It is said, that this slow advance and perpetual interposition of impediments is a salutary check to the rashness of innovation, and to hazardous experiments. At least, it is a very effectual one,

[1] *The Spirit of the Age, or Contemporary Portraits.* London, 1825, 8vo. Frequently reprinted.—ED.

amounting almost to a prohibition. One age is employed in building up an absurdity, and the next exhausts all its wit and learning, zeal and fury, in battering it down, so that at the end of two generations you come to the point where you set out, and have to begin again. These heats and disputes about external points of faith may be things of no consequence, since under all the variations of form or doctrine the essentials of practice remain the same. It does not seem so ; at any rate, the non-essentials appear to excite all the interest, and " keep this dreadful pudder o'er our heads ;" and when the dogma is once stripped of mystery and intolerance, and reduced to common sense, no one appears to take any furthur notice of it.

The appeal, then, to the authority of the world, chiefly resolves itself into the old proverb, that " when you are at Rome you must do as those at Rome do ; " that is, it is a shifting circle of local prejudices and gratuitous assumptions, a successful conformity to which is best insured by a negation of all other qualities that might interfere with it : solid reason and virtue are out of the question. But it may be insisted, that there are qualities of a more practical order that may greatly contribute to and facilitate our advancement in life, such as presence of mind, convivial talents, insight into character, thorough acquaintance with the profounder principles and secret springs of society, and so forth : I do not deny that all this may be of advantage in extraordinary cases, and often abridge difficulties, but I do not think that it is either necessary or generally useful. For instance, habitual caution and reserve is a surer resource than presence of mind, or quick-witted readiness of expedient, which, though it gets men out of scrapes, as often leads them into them by begetting a false confidence. Persons of agreeable and lively talents often find to their cost that one indiscretion procures them more enemies then ten agreeable sallies do friends. A too great penetration into character is less desirable than a certain power

of hoodwinking ourselves to their defects, unless the
former is accompanied with a profound hypocrisy, which
is also liable to detection and discomfiture : and as to
general maxims and principles of worldly knowledge, I
conceive that an instinctive sympathy with them is much
more profitable than their incautious discovery and formal
announcement.   Thus the politic rule, "When a great
wheel goes up a hill, cling fast to it ; when a great wheel
runs down a hill, let go your hold of it," may be useful as
a hint or warning to the shyness of fidelity of an Englishman ; a North-Briton feels its truth instinctively, and acts
upon it unconsciously.   When it is observed in the *History
of a Foundling*,[1] that "Mr. Alworthy had done so many
charitable actions that he had made enemies of the whole
parish," the sarcasm is the dictate of a generous indignation at ingratitude rather than a covert apology for selfish
niggardliness.   Misanthropic reflections have their source
in philanthropic sentiments ; the real despiser of the world
keeps up appearances with it, and is at pains to varnish
over its vices and follies, even to himself, lest his secret
should be betrayed, and do him an injury.   Those who see
completely into the world begin to play tricks with it, and
over-reach themselves by being too knowing : it is even
possible to *out-cant* it, and get laughed at that way.   Fielding knew something of the world, yet he did not make a
fortune.   Sir Walter Scott has twice made a fortune by
descriptions of nature and character, and has twice lost it
by the fondness for speculative gains.   Wherever there is
a strong faculty for anything, the exercise of that faculty
becomes its own end and reward, and produces an indifference or inattention to other things ; so that the best
security for success in the world is an incapacity for
success in any other way.   A bookseller, to succeed in his
business, should have no knowledge of books, except as
marketable commodities : the instant he has a taste, an

[1] Fielding's *Tom Jones.*—Ed.

opinion of his own on the subject, he may consider himself as a ruined man. In like manner, a picture-dealer should know nothing of pictures but the catalogue price, the cant of the day. The moment he has a feeling for the art, he will be tenacious of it: a Guido, a Salvator "will be the fatal Cleopatra for which he will lose all he is worth, and be content to lose it." Should a general, then, know nothing of war, a physician of medicine? No: because this is an art and not a trick, and the one has to contend with nature, and the other with an enemy, and not to pamper or cajole the follies of the world. It requires also great talents to overturn the world; not to push one's fortune in it: to rule the state like Cromwell or Buonaparte; not, to rise in it like Castlereagh or Croker. Yet, even in times of crisis and convulsion, he who outrages the feeling of the moment and echoes the wildest extravagance, succeeds; as, in times of peace and tranquillity, he does so who acquiesces most tamely in the ordinary routine of things. This may serve to point out another error, common to men of the world, who sometimes, giving themselves credit for more virtue than they possess, declare very candidly that if they had to begin life over again, they would have been *great rogues.* The answer to this is, that then they would have been *hanged.* No: the way to get on in the world is to be neither more nor less wise, neither better nor worse than your neighbours, neither to be a " reformer nor a house-breaker," neither to advance before the age nor lag behind it, but to be as like it as possible, to reflect its image and superscription at every turn, and then you will be its darling and its delight, and it will dandle you and fondle you, and make much of you, as a monkey doats upon its young! The knowledge of vice— that is, of *statutable* vice — is not the knowledge of the world ; otherwise, a Bow-street runner and the keeper of a house of ill fame would be the most knowing characters, and would soon rise above their professions.

July. 1827.

On Fashion. [1]

" Born of nothing, begot of nothing."

" His garment neither was of silk nor say,
　But painted plumes in goodly order dight,
　Like as the sun-burnt Indians do array,
　Their tawny bodies in their proudest plight :
　As those same plumes, so seemed he vain and light,
　That of his gait might easily appear ;
　For still he fared as dancing in delight,
　And in his hands a windy fan did bear,
　That in the idle air he moved still here and there."

FASHION is an odd jumble of contradictions, of sympathies and antipathies. It exists only by its being participated among a certain number of persons, and its essence is destroyed by being communicated to a greater number. It is a continual struggle between " the great vulgar and the small " to get the start of, or keep up with each other in the race of appearances, by an adoption on the part of the one of such external and fantastic symbols as strike the attention and excite the envy or admiration of the beholder, and which are no sooner made known and exposed to public view for this purpose, than they are successfully copied by the multitude, the slavish herd of imitators, who do not wish to be behindhand with their betters in outward show and pretensions, and then sink without any further notice into disrepute and contempt. Thus fashion lives only in a perpetual round of giddy innovation and restless vanity. To be old-fashioned is the greatest crime a coat or a hat can be guilty of. To look like nobody else is a sufficiently mortifying reflection ; to be in danger of being mistaken for one of the rabble is worse. Fashion constantly begins and ends in the two things it abhors most, singularity and vulgarity. It is the perpetual setting up

[1] Written in 1818.—ED.

and then disowning a certain standard of taste, elegance, and refinement, which has no other foundation or authority than that it is the prevailing distraction of the moment, which was yesterday ridiculous from its being new, and to-morrow will be odious from its being common. It is one of the most slight and insignificant of all things. It cannot be lasting, for it depends on the constant change and shifting of its own harlequin disguises; it cannot be sterling, for, if it were, it could not depend on the breath of caprice; it must be superficial, to produce its immediate effect on the gaping crowd; and frivolous, to admit of its being assumed at pleasure, by the numbers of those who affect, by being in the fashion, to be distinguished from the rest of the world. It is not anything in itself, nor the sign of anything but the folly and vanity of those who rely upon it as their greatest pride and ornament. It takes the firmest hold of weak, flimsy, and narrow minds, of those whose emptiness conceives of nothing excellent but what is thought so by others, and whose self-conceit makes them willing to confine the opinion of all excellence to themselves and those like them. That which is true or beautiful in itself, is not the less so for standing alone. That which is good for anything, is the better for being more widely diffused. But fashion is the abortive issue of vain ostentation and exclusive egotism : it is haughty, trifling, affected, servile, despotic, mean and ambitious, precise and fantastical, all in a breath—tied to no rule, and bound to conform to every whim of the minute.

"The fashion of an hour marks the wearer." It is a sublimated essence of levity, caprice, vanity, extravagance, idleness, and selfishness. It thinks of nothing but not being contaminated by vulgar use, and winds and doubles like a hare, and betakes itself to the most paltry shifts to avoid being overtaken by the common hunt that are always in full chase after it. It contrives to keep up its fastidious pretensions, not by the difficulty of the attainment, but by the rapidity and evanescent nature of the changes. It is a sort of conventional badge, or understood passport into select circles, which must still be varying (like the water-mark in bank-notes) not to be counterfeited by those without the pale of fashionable society; for to make the test of admission to all the privileges of that refined and volatile atmosphere depend on any real merit or extraordinary accomplishment, would exclude too many of the pert, the dull, the ignorant, too many shallow, upstart, and self-admiring pretenders, to enable the few that passed muster to keep one another in any tolerable countenance. If it were the fashion, for instance, to be distinguished for virtue, it would be difficult to set or follow the example; but then this would confine the pretension to a small number (not the most fashionable part of the community), and would carry a very singular air with it; or if excellence in any art or science were made the standard of fashion, this would also effectually prevent vulgar imitation, but then it would equally prevent fashionable impertinence. There would be an obscure circle of *vertù* as well as virtue, drawn within the established circle of fashion, a little province of a mighty empire—the example of honesty would spread slowly, and learning would still have to boast of a respectable minority. But of what use would such uncourtly and out-of-the-way accomplishments be to the great and noble, the rich and fair, without any of the *éclat*, the noise and nonsense which belong to that which is followed and admired by all the world alike? The real and solid will never do for the current coin, the common wear and tear of foppery and fashion. It must be the meretricious, the showy, the outwardly fine, and intrinsically worthless—that which lies within the reach of the most indolent affectation, that which can be put on or off at the suggestion of the most wilful caprice, and for which, through all its fluctuations, no mortal reason can be given, but that it is the newest absurdity in vogue! The shape of a head-dress, whether flat or piled (curl on curl) several stories high by the help of pins and pomatum, the size of a pair of paste buckles, the quantity of gold lace on an embroidered waistcoat, the mode of taking a pinch of snuff, or of pulling out a pocket-hand-kerchief, the lisping and affected pronunciation of certain words, the saying Mem for Madam, Lord Foppington's[1] *Tam* and *'Paun honour*, with a regular set of visiting phrases and insipid sentiments ready sorted for the day, were what formerly distinguished the mob of fine gentle-men and ladies from the mob of their inferiors. These marks and appendages of gentility had their day, and were then discarded for others equally peremptory and unequivocal. But in all this chopping and changing, it is generally one folly that drives out another; one trifle that by its specific levity acquires a momentary and surprising ascendancy over the last. There is no striking deformity of appearance or behaviour that has not been made " the outward and visible sign of an inward and invisible grace." Factitious imperfections are laid hold of to hide real defects. Paint, patches, and powder were at one time synonymous with health, cleanliness, and beauty. Obscenity, irreligion, swearing, drinking, gaming, effeminacy in the one sex and Amazon airs in the other, anything, is the fashion while it lasts. In the reign of Charles II., the profession and practice of every species of extravagance and debauchery were looked upon as the indispensable marks of an accomplished cavalier. Since that period the court has reformed, and has had rather a rustic air. Our belles formerly overloaded themselves with dress, of late years they have affected to go almost naked—"and are, when unadorned, adorned the most." The women having left off stays, the men have taken to wear them, if we are to believe the authentic Memoirs

---

[1] The character so called in Vanbrugh's play of *The Relapse.*—ED.

of the Fudge Family.[1] The Niobe head is at present
buried in the *poke* bonnet, and the French milliners and
marchandes des modes have proved themselves an over-
match for the Greek sculptors, in matters of taste and
costume.

A very striking change has, however, taken place in
dress of late years, and some progress has been made in
taste and elegance, from the very circumstance, that as
fashion has extended its empire in that direction, it has
lost its power. While fashion in dress included what was
costly, it was confined to the wealthier classes; even
this was an encroachment on the privileges of rank and
birth, which for a long time were the only things that
commanded or pretended to command respect, and we
find Shakspeare complaining that "the City bears the
cost of princes on unworthy shoulders;" but when the
appearing in the top of the mode no longer depended on
the power of purchasing certain expensive articles of
dress, or in the right of wearing them, the rest was so
obvious and easy, that any one who chose might cut as
coxcombical a figure as the best. It became a matter of
mere affectation on the one side, and gradually ceased to
be made a matter of aristocratic assumption on the other.
"In the grand carnival of this our age," among other
changes, this is not the least remarkable, that the
monstrous pretensions to distinctions in dress have
dwindled away by tacit consent, and the simplest and
most graceful have been in the same request with all
classes. In this respect, as well as some others, "the age
is grown so picked, that the toe of the peasant comes so
near the heel of the courtier he galls his kibe;"[2] a lord is
hardly to be distinguished in the street from an attorney's

---

[1] By Thomas Moore. *The Fudge Family in Paris*, 1818, was
followed up by *The Fudges in England;* but the former is here
referred to.—ED.

[2] *Hamlet*, v, 1. [Dyce's edit. 1868, vii 196.]

clerk; and a plume of feathers is no longer mistaken for the highest distinction in the land! The ideas of natural equality and the Manchester steam-engines together, have, like a double battery, levelled the high towers and artificial structures of fashion in dress, and a white muslin gown is now the common costume of the mistress and the maid, instead of the one wearing, as heretofore, rich silks and satins, and the other coarse linsey-wolsey. It would be ridiculous (on a similar principle) for the courtier to take the wall of the citizen, having no longer a sword by his side to maintain his right of precedence; and, from the stricter notions that have prevailed of a man's personal merit and identity, a cane dangling from his wrist is the greatest extension of his figure that can be allowed to the modern *petit-maître.*

What shows the worthlessness of mere fashion is, to see how easily this vain and boasted distinction is assumed, when the restraint of decency or circumstances is once removed, by the most uninformed and commonest of the people. I know an undertaker that is the greatest prig in the streets of London, and an Aldermanbury haberdasher that has the most military strut of any lounger in Bond-street or St. James's. We may, at any time, raise a regiment of fops from the same number of fools, who have vanity enough to be intoxicated with the smartness of their appearance, and not sense enough to be ashamed of themselves. Every one remembers the story in *Peregrine Pickle,* of the strolling gipsy that he picked up in spite, had well scoured, and introduced her into genteel company, where she met with great applause, till she got into a passion by seeing a fine lady cheat at cards, rapped out a volley of oaths, and let nature get the better of art. Dress is the great secret of address. Clothes and confidence will set anybody up in the trade of modish accomplishment. Look at the two classes of well-dressed females whom we see at the play-house in the boxes.

Both are equally dressed in the height of the fashion, both are *rouged*, and wear their neck and arms bare—both have the same conscious, haughty, theatrical air—the same toss of the head—the same stoop in the shoulders, with all the pride that arises from a systematic disdain of formal prudery—the same pretence and jargon of fashionable conversation—the same mimicry of tones and phrases —the same " lisping, and ambling, and painting, and nicknaming of God's creatures;" the same everything but real propriety of behaviour and real refinement of sentiment.   In all the externals they are as like as the reflection in the looking-glass.   The only difference between the woman of fashion and the woman of pleasure is, that the one *is* what the other only *seems to be;* and yet the victims of dissipation, who thus rival and almost outshine women of the first quality in all the blaze, and pride, and glitter of show and fashion, are, in general, no better than a set of raw, uneducated, inexperienced country girls, or awkward, coarse-fisted servant-maids, who require no other apprenticeship or qualification to be on a level with persons of the highest distinction in society, in all the brilliancy and elegance of outward appearance, than that they have forfeited its common privileges, and every title to its respect.   The truth is, that real virtue, beauty, or understanding, are the same, whether "in a high or low degree;" and the airs and graces of pretended superiority over these which the highest classes give themselves, from mere frivolous and external accomplishments, are easily imitated, with provoking success, by the lowest, whenever they *dare.*

On Nicknames.[1]

"Hæ nugæ in seria ducunt."

THIS is a more important subject than it seems at first sight. It is as serious in its results as it is contemptible in the means by which these results are brought about. Nicknames, for the most part, govern the world. The history of politics, of religion, of literature, of morals, and of private life, is too often little less than the history of nicknames. What are one-half the convulsions of the civilised world—the frequent overthrow of states and kingdoms—the shock and hostile encounters of mighty continents—the battles by sea and land—the intestine commotions—the feuds of the Vitelli and Orsini, of the Guelphs and Ghibellines—the civil wars in England and the League in France—the jealousies and heart-burnings of cabinets and councils—the uncharitable proscriptions of creeds and sects, Turk, Jew, Pagan, Papist and Puritan, Quaker, and Methodist—the persecutions and massacres —the burnings, tortures, imprisonments, and lingering deaths, inflicted for a different profession of faith—but so many illustrations of the power of this principle ? Foxe's *Book of Martyrs*, and Neale's *History of the Puritans*, are comments on the same text. The fires in Smithfield were fanned by nicknames, and a nickname set its seal on the unopened dungeons of the Holy Inquisition. Nicknames are the talismans and spells that collect and set in motion all the combustible part of men's passions and prejudices, which have hitherto played so much more successful a game, and done their work so much more effectually than reason, in all the grand concerns and petty details of human life, and do not yet seem tired of the task assigned

[1] Written in 1818.

them. Nicknames are the convenient, portable tools by
which they simplify the process of mischief, and get
through their job with the least time and trouble. These
worthless, unmeaning, irritating, envemoned words of reproach are the established signs by which the different
compartments of society are ticketed, labelled, and marked
out for each other's hatred and contempt. They are to be
had, ready cut and dry, of all sorts and sizes, wholesale
and retail, for foreign exportation or for home consump-
tion, and for all occasions in life. " The priest calls the
lawyer a cheat, the lawyer beknaves the divine."   The
Frenchman hates the Englishman because he is an Englishman ; and the Englishman hates the Frenchman for as
good a reason.   The Whig hates the Tory, and the Tory
the Whig.   The Dissenter hates the Church-of-England-
man, and the Church-of-England-man hates the Dissenter,
as if they were of a different species, because they have a
different designation. The Mussulman calls the worshipper
of the Cross " Christian dog," spits in his face, and kicks
him from the pavement, by virtue of a nickname ; and the
Christian retorts the indignity upon the Infidel and the
Jew by the same infallible rule of right.   In France they
damn Shakspeare in the lump, by calling him a *barbare;*
and we talk of Racine's *verbiage* with inexpressible contempt
and self-complacency.   Among ourselves, an anti-Jacobin
critic denounces a Jacobin poet and his friends, at a venture, " as infidels and fugitives, who have left their wives
destitute, and their children fatherless "—whether they
have wives and children or not. The unenlightened savage
makes a meal of his enemy's flesh, after reproaching him
with the name of his tribe, because he is differently
tattooed ; and the literary cannibal cuts up the character
of his opponent by the help of a nickname. The jest of
all this is, that a party nickname is always a relative term,
and has its countersign, which has just the same force and
meaning, so that both must be perfectly ridiculous and

insignificant. A Whig implies a Tory ; there must be "Malcontents" as well as "Malignants ;" Jacobins and anti-Jacobins; English and French. These sorts of *noms-de-guerre* derive all their force from their contraries. Take away the meaning of the one, and you take the sting out of the other. They could not exist but upon the strength of mutual and irreconcileable antipathies; there must be no love lost between them. What is there in the names themselves to give them a preference over each other? "Sound them, they do become the mouth as well ; weigh them, they are as heavy ; conjure with them, one will raise a spirit as soon as the other." If there were not fools and madmen who hated both; there could not be fools and madmen bigoted to either. I have heard an eminent character boast that he had done more to produce the late war by nicknaming Buonaparte "the Corsican," than all the state papers and documents on the subject put together. And yet Mr. Southey asks triumphantly, "Is it to be supposed that it is England, *our* England, to whom that war was owing?" As if, in a dispute between two countries, the conclusive argument, which lies in the pronoun *our* belonged only to one of them. I like Shakspeare's version of the matter better :—

> "Hath Britain all the sun that shines? Day, night,
> Are they not but in Britain? I' the world's volume
> *Our* Britain seems as of it, but not in 't ;
> In a great pool a swan's nest, prithee, think
> There's livers out of Britain." [1]

In all national disputes, it is common to appeal to the numbers on your side as decisive on the point. If everybody in England thought the late war right, everybody in France thought it wrong. There were ten millions on one side of the question (or rather of the water), and thirty millions on the other side—that's all. I remember some one arguing, in justification of our Ministers interfering

[1] *Cymbeline*, iii, 4. [Dyce's edit. 1868, vii, 683.]

without occasion, "That governments would not go to war for nothing;" to which I answered: "Then they could not go to war at all; for, at that rate, neither of them could be in the wrong, and yet both of them must be in the right, which was absurd." The only meaning of these vulgar nicknames and party distinctions, where they are urged most violently and confidently, is that others differ from you in some particular or other (whether it be opinion, dress, clime, or complexion), which you highly disapprove of, forgetting that, by the same rule, they have the very same right to be offended at you because you differ from them. Those who have reason on their side do not make the most obstinate and grevious appeals to prejudice and abusive language. I know but of one exception to this general rule, and that is where the things that excite disgust are of such a kind that they cannot well be gone into without offence to decency and good manners; but it is equally certain in this case, that those who are most shocked at the things are not those who are most forward to apply the names. A person will not be fond of repeating a charge, or adverting to a subject, that inflicts a wound on his own feelings, even for the sake of wounding the feelings of another. A man should be very sure that he himself is not what he has always in his mouth. The greatest prudes have been often accounted the greatest hypocrites, and a satirist is at best but a suspicious character. The loudest and most unblushing invectives against vice and debauchery will as often proceed from a desire to inflame and pamper the passions of the writer, by raking into a nauseous subject, as from a wish to excite virtuous indignation against it in the public mind, or to reform the individual. To familiarise the mind to gross ideas is not the way to increase your own or the general repugnance to them. But to return to the subject of nicknames.

The use of this figure of speech is, that it excites a

strong idea without requiring any proof. It is a short-hand, compendious mode of getting at a conclusion, and never troubling yourself or anybody else with the formalities of reasoning or the dictates of common sense. It is superior to all evidence, for it does not rest upon any, and operates with the greatest force and certainty in proportion to the utter want of probability. Belief is only a stray impression, and the malignity or extravagance of the accusation passes for a proof of the crime. " Brevity is the soul of wit;" and of all eloquence a nickname is the most concise, of all arguments the most unanswerable. It gives *carte-blanche* to the imagination, throws the reins on the neck of the passions, and suspends the use of the understanding altogether. It does not stand upon cere-mony, on the nice distinctions of right and wrong. It does not wait the slow processes of reason, or stop to unravel the wit of sophistry. It takes everything for granted that serves for nourishment for the spleen. It is instantaneous in its operations. There is nothing to interpose between the effect and it. It is passion without proof, and action without thought—" the unbought grace of life, the cheap defence of nations." It does not, as Mr. Burke expresses it, "leave the will puzzled, undecided, and sceptical in the moment of action." It is a word and a blow. The " No Popery" cry, raised a little while ago let loose all the lurking spite and prejudice which had lain rankling in the proper receptacles for them for above a century, without any knowledge of the past history of the country which had given rise to them, or any reference to their connection with present circumstances; for the knowledge of the one would have prevented the possi-bility of their application to the other. Facts present a tangible and definite idea to the mind, a train of causes and consequences, accounting for each other, and leading to a positive conclusion—but no farther. But a nickname is tied down to no such limited service; it is a disposable force, that is almost always perverted to mischief. It clothes itself with all the terrors of uncertain abstraction, and there is no end of the abuse to which it is liable but the cunning of those who employ, or the credulity of those who are gulled by it. It is a reserve of the ignorance, bigotry, and intolerance of weak and vulgar minds, brought up where reason fails, and always ready, at a moment's warning, to be applied to any, the most absurd purposes. If you bring specific charges against a man, you thereby enable him to meet and repel them, if he thinks it worth his while ; but a nickname baffles reply, by the very vagueness of the inferences from it, and gives increased activity to the confused, dim, and imperfect notions of dislike connected with it, from their having no settled ground to rest upon. The mind naturally irritates itself against an unknown object of fear or jealousy, and makes up for the blindness of its zeal by an excess of it. We are eager to indulge our hasty feelings to the utmost, lest, by stopping to examine, we should find that there is no excuse for them. The very consciousness of the injustice we may be doing another makes us only the more loud and bitter in our invectives against him. We keep down the admonitions of returning reason, by calling up a double portion of gratuitous and vulgar spite. The will may be said to act with most force *in vacuo;* the passions are the most ungovernable when they are blindfolded. That malignity is always the most implacable which is accompanied with a sense of weakness, because it is never satisfied of its own success or safety. A nickname carries the weight of the pride, the indolence, the cowardice, the ignorance, and the ill-nature of mankind on its side. It acts by mechanical sympathy on the nerves of society. Any one who is without character himself may make himself master of the reputation of another by the application of a nickname, as, if you do not mind soiling your fingers, you may always throw dirt on another. No matter how undeserved the imputation, it will stick; for, though it is sport to the bystanders to see you bespattered, they will not stop to see you wipe out the stains. You are not heard in your own defence; it has no effect, it does not tell, excites no sensation, or it is only felt as a disappointment of their triumph over you. Their passions and prejudices are inflamed by the charge, " As rage with rage doth sympathise ;" by vindicating yourself, you merely bring them back to common-sense, which is a very sober, mawkish state. *Give a dog an ill name and hang him,* is a proverb. " A nickname is the heaviest stone that the devil can throw at a man." It is a bugbear to the imagination, and, though we do not believe in it, it still haunts our apprehensions. Let a nickname be industriously applied to our dearest friend, and let us know that it is ever so false and malicious, yet it will answer its end ; it connects the person's name and idea with an ugly association, you think of them with pain together, or it requires an effort of indignation or magnanimity on your part to disconnect them ; it becomes an uneasy subject, a sore point, and you will sooner desert your friend, or join in the conspiracy against him, than be constantly forced to repel charges without truth or meaning, and have your penetration or character called in question by a rascal. Nay, such is the unaccountable construction of language and of the human mind, that the affixing the most innocent or praiseworthy appellation to any individual, or set of individuals, *as a nickname,* has all the effect of the most opprobrious epithets. Thus the cant name, " the Talents," was successfully applied as a stigma to the Whigs at one time ; it held them up to ridicule, and made them obnoxious to public feeling, though it was notorious to everybody that the Whig leaders were " the Talents," and that their adversaries nicknamed them so from real hatred and pretended derision. Call a man short by his Christian name, as Tom or Dick such-a-one, or by his profession (however respectable), as Canning pelted a noble lord with his left-off title of Doctor, and you undo him for ever, if he has a reputation to lose. Such is the tenaciousness of spite and ill-nature, or the jealousy of public opinion, even this will be peg enough to hang doubtful inuendos, weighty dilemmas upon. "With so small a web as this will I catch so great a fly as Cassio." The public do not like to see their favourites treated with impertinent familiarity ; it lowers the tone of admiration very speedily. It implies that some one stands in no great awe of their idol, and he perhaps may know as much about the matter as they do. It seems as if a man whose name, with some contemptuous abbreviation, is always dinned in the public ear, was distinguished for nothing else. By repeating a man's name in this manner you may soon make him sick of it, and of his life too. Children do not like to be *called out of their names :* it is questioning their personal identity. There are political writers who have fairly worried their readers into conviction by abuse and nicknames. People surrender their judgments to escape the persecution of their style, and the disgust and indignation which their incessant violence and vulgarity excite, at last make you hate those who are the objects of it. *Causa causæ causa causati.* They make people sick of a subject by making them sick of their arguments.

A parrot may be taught to call names; and if the person who keeps the parrot has a spite to his neighbours, he may give them a great deal of annoyance without much wit, either in the employer or the puppet. The insignificance of the instrument has nothing to do with the efficacy of the means. Hotspur would have had "a *starling* taught to speak nothing but Mortimer," in the ears of his enemy. Nature, it is said, has given arms to all creatures the most proper to defend themselves, and annoy others : to the lowest she has given the use of nicknames.

There are some droll instances of the effect of proper names combined with circumstances. A young student had come up to London from Cambridge, and went in the evening and planted himself in the pit of the playhouse. He had not been seated long, when in one of the front boxes near him he discovered one of his college tutors, with whom he felt an immediate and strong desire to claim acquaintance, and accordingly he called out, in a low and respectful voice, "Dr. Topping!" The appeal was, however, ineffectual. He then repeated in a louder tone, but still in an under key, so as not to excite the attention of any one but his friend, "Dr. Topping!" The Doctor took no notice. He then grew more impatient, and repeated "Dr. Topping, Dr. Topping!" two or three times pretty loud, to see whether the Doctor did not or would not hear him. Still the Doctor remained immovable. The joke began at length to get round, and one or two persons, as he continued his invocation of the Doctor's name, joined in with him ; these were reinforced by others calling out, "Dr. Topping, Dr. Topping!" on all sides, so that he could no longer avoid perceiving it, and at length the whole pit rose and roared, "Dr. Topping!" with loud and repeated cries, and the Doctor was forced to retire precipitately, frightened at the sound of his own name.

The calling people by their Christian or surname is a proof of affection, as well as of hatred. They are generally the best of good fellows with whom their friends take this sort of liberty. *Diminutives* are titles of endearment. Dr. Johnson's calling Goldsmith "Goldy" did equal honour to both. It showed the regard he had for him. This familiarity may perhaps imply a certain want of formal respect ; but formal respect is not neccessary to, if it is consistent with, cordial friendship. Titles of honour are the reverse of nicknames : they convey the idea of respect, as the others do of contempt, but they equally mean little or nothing. Junius's motto, *Stat nominis 'umbra,* is a very significant one; it might be extended farther. A striking instance of the force of names, standing by themselves, is in the respect felt towards Michael Angelo in this country. We know nothing of him but his name. It is an abstraction of fame and greatness. Our admiration of him supports itself, and our idea of his superiority seems self-evident, because it is attached to his name only.

On Taste.[1]

TASTE is nothing but sensibility to the different degrees and kinds of excellence in the works of Art or Nature. This definition will perhaps be disputed; for I am aware the general practice is to make it consist in a disposition to find fault.

A French man or woman will in general conclude their account of Voltaire's denunciation of Shakspeare and Milton as barbarians, on the score of certain technical improprieties, with assuring you that "he (Voltaire) had a great deal of taste." It is their phrase, *Il avait beaucoup de goût.* To which the proper answer is, that this may be, but that he did not show it in this case; as the overlooking great and countless beauties, and being taken up only with petty or accidental blemishes, shows as little strength or understanding as it does refinement or elevation of taste. The French author, indeed, allows of Shakspeare, that "he had found a few pearls on his enormous dunghill." But there is neither truth nor proportion in this sentence, for his works are (to say the least)—

"Rich with praise
As is the ooze and bottom of the sea
With sunken wreck and sumless treasuries."[2]

---

[1] Written in 1819.　　　[2] *Henry V.,* i, 2, edit. 1868, iv, 429.

Genius is the power of producing excellence: taste is the power of perceiving the excellence thus produced in its several sorts and degrees, with all their force, refinement, distinctions, and connections. In other words, taste (as it relates to the productions of art) is strictly the power of being properly affected by works of genius. It is the proportioning admiration to power, pleasure to beauty; it is entire sympathy with the finest impulses of the imagination, not antipathy, not indifference to them. The eye of taste may be said to reflect the impressions of real genius, as the even mirror reflects the objects of Nature in all their clearness and lustre, instead of distorting or diminishing them;

> " Or, like a gate of steel,
> Fronting the sun, receives and renders back
> His figure and his heat."

To take a pride and pleasure in nothing but defects (and these perhaps of the most paltry, obvious, and mechanical kind)—in the disappointment and tarnishing of our faith in substantial excellence, in the proofs of weakness, not of power (and this where there are endless subjects to feed the mind with wonder and increased delight through years of patient thought and fond remembrance), is not a sign of uncommon refinement, but of unaccountable perversion of taste. So, in the case of Voltaire's hypercriticisms on Milton and Shakspeare, the most common-place and prejudiced admirer of these authors knows, as well as Voltaire can tell him, that it is a fault to make a sea-port (we will say) in Bohemia, or to introduce artillery and gunpowder in the war in heaven. This is common to Voltaire, and the merest English reader: there is nothing in it either way. But what he differs from us in, and, as it is supposed, greatly to his advantage, and to our infinite shame and mortification, is, that this is all that he perceives, or will hear of in Milton or Shakspeare, and that he either knows, or pretends to know, nothing of that prodigal waste, or studied accumulation of grandeur, truth, and beauty, which are to be found in each of these authors. Now, I cannot think that, to be dull and insensible to so great and such various excellence—to have no feeling in unison with it, no latent suspicion of the treasures hid beneath our feet, and which we trample upon with ignorant scorn—to be cut off, as by a judicial blindness, from that universe of thought and imagination that shifts its wondrous pageant before us— to turn aside from the throng and splendour of airy shapes that fancy weaves for our dazzled sight, and to strut and vapour over a little pettifogging blunder in geography or chronology, which a school-boy or village pedagogue would be ashamed to insist upon, is any proof of the utmost perfection of taste, but the contrary. At this rate, it makes no difference whether Shakspeare wrote his works or not, or whether the critic, who " damns him into everlasting redemption " for a single slip of the pen, ever read them; he is absolved from all knowledge, taste, or feeling, of the different excellences, and inimitable creations of the poet's pen—from any sympathy with the wanderings and the fate of *Imogen,* the beauty and tenderness of *Ophelia,* the thoughtful abstraction of *Hamlet ;* his soliloquy on life may never have given him a moment's pause, or touched his breast with one solitary reflection; the *Witches* in *Macbeth* may " lay their choppy fingers upon their skinny lips " without making any alteration in his pulse, and *Lear's* heart may break in vain for him; he may hear no strange noises in *Prospero's* island, and the moonlight that sleeps on beds of flowers, where fairies couch in the *Midsummer Night's Dream,* may never once have steeped his senses in repose. Nor will it avail Milton to " have built high towers in heaven," nor to have brought down heaven upon earth, nor that he has made Satan rear his giant form before us, " Majestic though in ruin," or decked the bridal bed of Eve with beauty, or clothed her with innocence, "likest heaven," as she ministered to Adam and his Angel-guest. Our critic knows nothing of all this, of beauty or sublimity, of thought or passion, breathed in sweet or solemn sounds, with all the magic of verse "in tones and numbers fit;" he lays his finger on the map, and shows you that there is no sea-port for Shakspeare's weather-beaten travellers to land at in Bohemia, and takes out a list of mechanical inventions, and proves that gunpowder was not known till long after Milton's "Battle of the Angels;" and concludes, that every one who, after these profound and important discoveries, finds anything to admire in these two writers, is a person without taste, or any pretensions to it. By the same rule, a thorough-bred critic might prove that Homer was no poet, and the *Odyssey* a vulgar performance, because *Ulysses* makes a pun on the name of *Noman;* or some other disciple of the same literal school might easily set aside the whole merit of Racine's *Athalie,* or Molière's *Ecole des Femmes,* and pronounce these *chef-d'œuvres* of art barbarous and gothic, because the characters in the first address one another (absurdly enough) as *Monsieur* and *Madame,* and because the latter is written in rhyme, contrary to all classical precedent. These little false measures of criticism may be misapplied, and retorted without end, and require to be eked out by national antipathy or political prejudice to give them currency and weight. Thus it was in war time that the author of the *Friend* ventured to lump all the French tragedies together as a smart collection of ·epigrams, and that the author of the *Excursion,* a poem, being portion[1] of

---

[1] Why is the word *portion* here used, as if it were a portion of Scripture?

"Those strains that once did sweet in Zion glide,
He wales a *portion* with judicious care."

Cottar's Saturday Night.

Now, Mr. Wordsworth's poems, though not profane, yet neither

M

a larger poem, to be named the *Recluse,* made bold to call Voltaire a dull prose-writer with impunity. Such pitiful quackery is a cheap way of setting up for exclusive taste and wisdom, by pretending to despise what is most generally admired, as if nothing could come up to or satisfy that ideal standard of excellence, of which the person bears about the select pattern in his own mind. "Not to admire anything" is as bad a test of wisdom as it is a rule for happiness. We sometimes meet with individuals who have formed their whole character on this maxim, and who ridiculously affect a decided and dogmatical tone of superiority over others, from an uncommon degree both of natural and artificial stupidity. They are blind to painting—deaf to music—indifferent to poetry; and they triumph in the catalogue of their defects as the fault of these arts, because they have not sense enough to perceive their own want of perception. To treat any art or science with contempt, is only to prove your own incapacity and want of taste for it: to say that what has been done best in any kind is good for nothing, is to say that the utmost exertion of human ability is not equal to the lowest, for the productions of the lowest are worth something, except by comparison with what is better. When we hear persons exclaiming that the pictures at the Marquis of Stafford's[1] or Mr. Angerstein's, or those at the British Gallery, are a heap of trash, we might tell them that they betray in this a want, not of taste only,

---

are they sacred, to deserve this solemn style, though some of his admirers have gone so far as to compare them, for primitive, patriarchal simplicity, to the historical parts of the Bible. Much has been said of the merits and defects of this large poem, which is "portion of a larger;" perhaps Horace's rule has been a double bar to its success—*Non satis est pulchra poemata esse, dulcia sunto.* The features of this author's muse want sweetness of expression as well as regularity of outline.

[1] Now transferred to Bridgewater House.—ED.

but of common-sense, for that these collections contain some of the finest specimens of the greatest masters, and that *that* must be excellent in the productions of human art, beyond which human genius, in any age or country, has not been able to go.. Ask these very fastidious critics what it is that they *do* like, and you will soon find, from tracing out the objects of their secret admiration, that their pretended disdain of first-rate excellence is owning either to ignorance of the last refinements of works of genius, or envy at the general admiration which they have called forth. I have known a furious philippic against the faults of shining talents and established reputation subside into complacent admiration of dull mediocrity, that neither tasked the kindred sensibility of its admirers beyond its natural inertness, nor touched his self-love with a consciousness of inferiority; and that, by never attempting original beauties, and never failing, gave no opportunity to intellectual ingratitude to be plausibly revenged for the pleasure or instruction it had reluctantly received. So there are judges who cannot abide Mr. Kean, and think Mr. Young an incomparable actor, for no other reason than because he never shocks them with an idea which they had not before. The only excuse for the over-delicacy and supercilious indifference here described, is when it arises from an intimate acquaintance with, and intense admiration of, other and higher degrees of perfection and genius. A person whose mind has been worked up to a lofty pitch of enthusiasm in this way cannot, perhaps, condescend to notice, or be much delighted with inferior beauties; but, then, neither will he dwell upon, and be preposterously offended with, slight faults. So that the ultimate and only conclusive proof of taste is, even here, not indifference but enthusiasm; and before a critic can give himself airs of superiority for what he despises, he must first lay himself open to reprisals, by telling us what he admires. There we may fairly join issue with him. Without this indispensable condition of all true taste, absolute stupidity must be more than on a par with the most exquisite refinement; and the most formidable Drawcansir of all would be the most impenetrable blockhead. Thus, if we know that Voltaire's contempt of Shakspeare arose from his idolatry of Racine, this may excuse him in a national point of view; but he has no longer any advantage over us; and we must console ourselves as well as we can for Mr. Wordsworth's not allowing us to laugh at the wit of Voltaire, by laughing now and then at the only author whom he is known to understand and admire![1]

Instead of making a disposition to find fault a proof of taste, I would reverse the rule, and estimate every one's pretensions to taste by the degree of their sensibility to the highest and most various excellence. An indifference to less degrees of excellence is only excusable as it arises from a knowledge and admiration of higher ones; and a readiness in the detection of faults should pass for refinement only as it is owing to a quick sense and impatient love of beauties. In a word, fine taste consists in sympathy, not in antipathy; and the rejection of what is bad is only to be accounted a virtue when it implies a preference of and attachment to what is better.

There is a certain point which may be considered as the highest point of perfection at which the human faculties can arrive in the conception and execution of certain things; to be able to reach this point in reality is the greatest proof of genius and power; and I imagine that the greatest proof of taste is given in being able to appreciate it when done. For instance, I have heard

---

[1] A French teacher, in reading *Titus and Berenice* with an English pupil, used to exclaim, in raptures, at the best passages, "What have you in Shakespeare equal to this?" This showed that he had a taste for Racine, and a power of appreciating his beauties, though he might want an equal taste for Shakspeare.

(and I can believe) that Madame Catalani's manner of
singing *Hope told a flattering tale* was the perfection of
singing ; and I cannot conceive that it would have been
the perfection of taste to have thought nothing at all of
it.   There was, I understand, a sort of fluttering of the
voice and a breathless palpitation of the heart (like the
ruffling of the feathers of the robin-redbreast), which
completely gave back all the uneasy and thrilling voluptuousness of the sentiment ; and I contend that the person
on whom not a particle of this expression was lost (or
would have been lost, if it had been even finer), into whom
the tones of sweetness or tenderness sink deeper and
deeper as they approach the farthest verge of ecstacy or
agony, he who has an ear attuned to the trembling harmony, and a heart " pierceable" by pleasure's finest point,
is the best judge of music—not he who remains insensible
to the matter himself, or, if you point it out to him, asks,
" What of it ? " I fancied that I had a triumph, some time
ago, over a critic and connoisseur in music, who thought
little of the minuet in *Don Giovanni ;* but the same person
redeemed his pretensions to musical taste, in my opinion,
by saying of some passage in Mozart, " This is a soliloquy
equal to any in *Hamlet.*"   In hearing the accompaniment
in the *Messiah,* of angels' voices to the shepherds keeping
watch at night, who has the most taste and delicacy—he
who listens in silent rapture to the silver sounds, as they
rise in sweetness and soften into distance, drawing the
soul from earth to heaven, and making it partake of the
music of the spheres—or he who remains deaf to the
summons, and remarks that it is an allegorical conceit?
Which would Handel have been most pleased with, the
man who was seen standing at the performance of the
Coronation Anthem in Westminster Abbey, with his face
bathed in tears, and mingling " the drops which sacred
joy had engendered" with that ocean of circling sound, or
with him who sat with frigid, critical aspect, his heart

untouched and his looks unaltered as the statues on the wall?[1] Again, if any one, in looking at Rembrandt's picture of *Jacob's Dream*, should not be struck with the solemn awe that surrounds it, and with the dazzling flights of angels' wings, like steps of golden light, emanations of flame or spirit hovering between earth and sky, and should observe very wisely that Jacob was thrown in one corner of the picture like a bundle of clothes, without power, form, or motion, and should think this a defect, I should say that such a critic might possess great knowledge of the mechanical part of painting, but not an atom of feeling or imagination. Or who is it that, looking at the productions of Raphael or Titian, is the person of true taste, he who finds what there is, or he who finds what there is not, in each? Not he who picks a petty, vulgar quarrel with the colouring of Raphael, or the drawing of Titian, is the true critic and judicious spectator, but he who broods over the expression of the one till it takes possession of his soul, and who dwells on the tones and hues of the other till his eye is saturated with truth and beauty; for by this means he moulds his mind to the study and reception of what is most perfect in form and colour, instead of letting it remain empty, " swept and garnished," or rather a dull blank, with " knowledge at each entrance quite shut out." He who cavils at the want of drawing in Titian is not the most sensible to it in Raphael; in-

---

[1] It is a fashion among the scientific, or pedantic part of the musical world, to decry Miss Stephens's singing as feeble and insipid. This it is to take things by their contraries. Her excellence does not lie in force or contrast, but in sweetness and simplicity. To give only one instance. Any person who does not feel the beauty of her singing the lines in *Artaxerxes*, " What was my pride is now my shame," &c., in which the notes seem to fall from her lips like languid drops from the bending flower, and her voice flutters and dies away with the expiring conflict of passion in her bosom, may console himself with the possession of other faculties, but assuredly he has no ear for music.

stead of that he only insists on the latter's want of colouring. He who is offended at Raphael's hardness and
monotony is not delighted with the soft, rich pencilling of
Titian; he only takes care to find fault with him for
wanting that which, if he possessed it in the highest
degree, he would not admire or understand. And this is
easy to be accounted for. First, such a critic has been
told what to do, and follows his instructions; secondly, to
perceive the height of any excellence, it is necessary to
have the most exquisite sense of that kind of excellence
through all its gradations: to perceive the want of any
excellence, it is merely necessary to have a negative or
abstract notion of the thing, or perhaps only of the name;
or, in other words, any, the most crude and mechanical
idea of a given quality is a measure of positive deficiency,
whereas none but the most refined idea of the same quality
can be a standard of superlative merit. To distinguish
the finest characteristics of Titian or Raphael—to go
along with them in their imitation of nature, is to be so
far like them—to be occupied only with that in which
they fell short of others, instead of that in which they
soared above them, shows a vulgar, narrow capacity, insensible to anything beyond mediocrity, and an ambition
still more grovelling. To be dazzled by admiration of
the greatest excellence, and of the highest works of genius,
is natural to the best capacities and the best natures;
envy and dulness are most apt to detect minute blemishes
and unavoidable inequalities, as we see the spots in the
sun by having its rays blunted by mist or smoke. It may
be asked, then, whether mere extravagance and enthusiasm
are proofs of taste? And I answer, no; where they are
without reason and knowledge. Mere sensibility is not
true taste, but sensibility to real excellence is. To admire
and be wrapt up in what is trifling or absurd, is a proof
of nothing but ignorance or affectation: on the contrary,
he who admires most what is most worthy of admiration

(let his raptures or his eagerness to express them be what they may), shows himself neither extravagant nor unwise. When Mr. Wordsworth once said that he could read the description of Satan in Milton—

> " Nor seem'd
> Less than arch-angel ruin'd, and the excess
> Of glory obscur'd "—

till he felt a certain faintness come over his mind from a sense of beauty and grandeur, I saw no extravagance in this, but the utmost truth of feeling. When the same author, or his friend Mr. Southey, says, that the *Excursion* is better worth preserving than the *Paradise Lost*, this appears to me a great piece of impertinence, or an unwarrantable stretch of friendship.

The highest taste is shown in habitual sensibility to the greatest beauties ; the most general taste is shown in a perception of the greatest variety of excellence. Many people admire Milton, and as many admire Pope, while there are but few who have any relish for both. Almost all the disputes on this subject arise, not so much from false as from confined taste. We suppose that only one thing can have merit ; and that, if we allow it to anything else, we deprive the favourite object of our critical faith of the honours due to it. We are generally right in what we approve ourselves, for liking proceeds from a certain conformity of objects to the taste ; as we are generally wrong in condemning what others admire, for our dislike mostly proceeds from a want of taste for what pleases them. Our being totally senseless to what excites extreme delight in those who have as good a right to judge as we have, in all human probability, implies a defect of faculty in us rather than a limitation in the resources of nature or art. Those who are pleased with the fewest things, know the least ; as those who are pleased with everything, know nothing. Shakspeare makes *Mrs. Quickly* say of *Falstaff*, by a pleasant blunder,

that "A' could never abide carnation."[1] So there are
persons who cannot like Claude, because he is not
Salvator Rosa; some who cannot endure Rembrandt, and
others who would not cross the street to see a Vandyke;
one reader does not like the neatness of Junius, and
another objects to the extravagance of Burke; and they
are all right, if they expect to find in others what is only
to be found in their favourite author or artist, but equally
wrong if they mean to say that each of those they would
condemn by a narrow and arbitrary standard of taste, has
not a peculiar and transcendent merit of his own. The
question is not whether *you* like a certain excellence (it is
your own fault if you do not), but whether another possessed it in a very eminent degree. If he did not, who is
there that possessed it in a greater—that ranks above him
in that particular? Those who are accounted the best,
are the best in their line. When we say that Rembrandt
was a master of *chiaro-scuro*, for instance, we do not say
that he joined to this the symmetry of the Greek statues,
but we mean that we must go to him for the perfection of
chiaro-scuro, and that a Greek statue has not *chiaro-scuro*.
If any one objects to Junius's *Letters*, that they are a
tissue of epigrams, we answer, be it so; it is for that very
reason that we admire them. Again, should any one find
fault with Mr. Burke's writings as a collection of rhapsodies, the proper answer always would be, " Who is there
that has written finer rhapsodies?" I know an admirer
of *Don Quixote* who can see no merit in *Gil Blas*, and an
admirer of *Gil Blas* who could never get through *Don
Quixote*. I myself have great pleasure in reading both
these works, and in that respect think I have an advantage
over both these critics. It always struck me as a singular
proof of good taste, good sense, and liberal thinking, in
an old friend,[2] who had Paine's *Rights of Man* and Burke's

---

[1] *Henry V.,* ii, 3.

[2] The Rev. Joseph Fawcett; see *Memoirs,* 1867, i. 81, and ii.
291.—Ed.

Reflections on the French Revolution bound up in one volume, and who said, that, both together, they made a very good book. To agree with the greatest number of sound judges is to be in the right, and sound judges are persons of natural sensibility and acquired knowledge.[1] On the other hand, it must be owned, there are critics whose praise is a libel, and whose recommendation of any work is enough to condemn it. Men of the greatest genius are not always persons of the most liberal and unprejudiced taste. They have a strong bias to certain qualities themselves, are for reducing others to their own standard, and lie less open to the general impressions of things. This exclusive preference of their own peculiar excellences to those of others, in writers whose merits have not been sufficiently understood or acknowledged by their contemporaries, chiefly because they were *not* commonplace, may sometimes be seen mounting up to a degree of bigotry and intolerance, little short of insanity. There are some critics I have known who never allow an author any merit till all the world "cry out upon him," and others who never allow another any merit that any one can discover but themselves. If there are connoisseurs who spend their lives and waste their breath in extolling sublime passages in obscure writers, and lovers who choose their mistresses for their ugly faces, this is not taste but affectation. What is popular is not necessarily vulgar; and that which we try to rescue from fatal obscurity, had in general much better remain where it is.

Taste relates to that which, either in the objects of nature, or the imitation of them or the Fine Arts in general is calculated to give pleasure. Now, to know what is calculated to give pleasure, the way is to enquire what does

---

[1] I apprehend that natural is of more importance than acquired sensibility. Thus, any one, without having been at an opera, may judge of opera dancing, only from having seen (with judicious eyes) a stag bound across a lawn, or a tree wave its branches in the air. In all, the general principles of motion are the same.

give pleasure : so that taste is, after all, much more a matter of fact and less of theory than might be imagined. We may hence determine another point, *viz.*—whether there is any universal or exclusive standard of taste, since this is to inquire, in other words, whether there is any one thing that pleases all the world alike, or whether there is only one thing that pleases anybody, both which questions carry their own answers with them. Still it does not follow, because there is no dogmatic or bigoted standard of taste, like a formula of faith, which whoever does not believe without doubt he shall be dammed everlastingly, that there is no standard of taste whatever, that is to say, that certain things are not more apt to please than others, that some do not please more generally, that there are not others that give most pleasure to those who have studied the subject, that one nation is most susceptible of a particular kind of beauty, and another of another, according to their characters, &c. It would be a difficult attempt to force all these into one general rule or system, and yet equally so to deny that they are absolutely capricious, and without any foundation or principle whatever. There are, doubtless, books for children that we discard as we grow up ; yet, what are the majority of mankind, or even readers, but grown children ? If put to the vote of all the milliners' girls in London, *Old Mortality*, or even *Heart of Mid-Lothian*, would not carry the day (or, at least, not very triumpantly) over a common Minerva-press novel ; and I will hazard another opinion, that no women ever liked Burke. Mr. Pratt, on the contrary, said that he had to " boast of many learned and beautiful suffrages." [1] It is not, then, solely from the greatest number of voices, but from the opinion of the greatest number of well-informed minds, that we can establish, if not an absolute standard, at least a comparative scale, of taste. Certainly,

[1] In answer to a criticism by Mr. Godwin on his poem called *Sympathy.*

it can hardly be doubted that the greater the number of
persons of strong natural sensibility or love for any art,
and who have paid the closest attention to it, who agree
in their admiration of any work of art, the higher do its
pretensions rise to classical taste and intrinsic beauty.   In
this way, as the opinion of a thousand good judges may
outweigh that of nearly all the rest of the world, so there
may be one individual among them whose opinion may
outweigh that of the other nine hundred and ninety-nine;
that is, one of a still stronger and more refined perception
of beauty than all the rest, and to whose opinion that of
the others and of the world at large would approximate and
be conformed, as their taste or perception of what was
pleasing became stronger and more confirmed by exercise
and proper objects to call it forth.   Thus, if we were still
to insist on an universal standard of taste, it must be that,
not which *does*, but which *would* please universally, supposing all men to have paid an equal attention to any
subject and to have an equal relish for it, which can only
be guessed at by the imperfect and yet more than casual
agreement among those who have done so from choice and
feeling.   Taste is nothing but an enlarged capacity for
receiving pleasure from works of imagination, &c.   It is
time, however, to apply this rule.   There is, for instance,
a much greater number of habitual readers and play-goers
in France, who are devoted admirers of Racine or Molière
than there are in England of Shakspeare: does Shakspeare's fame rest, then, on a less broad and solid foundation than that of either of the others?   I think not,
supposing that the class of judges to whom Shakspeare's
excellences appeal are a higher, more independent, and
more original court of criticism, and that their suffrages
are quite as unanimous (though not so numerous) in the
one case as in the other.   A simile or a sentiment is not
the worse in common opinion for being somewhat superficial and hackneyed, but it is the worse in poetry.   The

perfection of *commonplace* is that which would unite the greatest number of suffrages, if there were not a tribunal above *commonplace.* For instance, in Shakspeare's description of flowers, primroses are mentioned—

> " That come before the swallow dares, and take
> The winds of March with beauty :" [1]

Now, I do not know that this expression is translatable into French, or intelligible to the common reader of either nation, but raise the scale of fancy, passion, and observation of nature to a certain point, and I will be bold to say that there will be no scruple entertained whether this single metaphor does not contain more poetry of the kind than is to be found in all Racine. As no Frenchman coüld write it, so I believe no Frenchman can understand it. We cannot take this insensibility on their part as a mark of our superiority, for we have plenty of persons among ourselves in the same predicament, but not the wisest or most refined, and to these the appeal is fair from the many—" and fit audience find, though few." So I think it requires a higher degree of taste to judge of Titian's portraits than Raphael's scripture pieces : not that I think more highly of the former than the latter, but the world and connoisseurs in general think there is no comparison (from the dignity of the subject), whereas I think it difficult to decide which are the finest. Here again we have a commonplace, a preconception, the moulds of the judgment preoccupied by certain assumptions of degrees and classes of excellence, instead of judging from the true and genuine impressions of things. Men of genius, or those who can produce excellence would be the best judges of it—poets of poetry, painters of painting, &c.—but that persons of original and strong powers of mind are too much disposed to refer everything to their own peculiar bias, and are comparatively indif-

[1] *Winter's Tale,* iv. 3, edit. 1868, iii. 469.

ferent to merely passive impressions. On the other hand, it is wholly wrong to oppose taste to genius, for genius in works of art is nothing but the power of producing what is beautiful (which, however, implies the intimate sense of it), though this is something very different from mere negative or formal beauties, which have as little to do with taste as genius.

I have, in a former essay, ascertained one principal of taste or excellence in the arts of imitation, where it was shown that objects of sense are not as it were simple and self-evident propositions, but admit of endless analysis and the most subtle investigation. We do not see nature with our eyes, but with our understandings and our hearts. To suppose that we see the whole of any object, merely by looking at it, is a vulgar error: we fancy that we do, because we are, of course, conscious of no more than we see in it, but this circle of our knowledge enlarges with further acquaintance and study, and we then perceive that what we perhaps barely distinguished in the gross, or regarded as a dull blank, is full of beauty, meaning, and curious details. He sees most of nature who understands its language best, or connects one thing with the greatest number of other things. Expression is the key to the human countenance, and unfolds a thousand imperceptible distinctions. How, then, should every one be a judge of pictures, when so few are of faces? A merely ignorant spectator, walking through a gallery of pictures, no more distinguishes the finest than your dog would, if he was to accompany you. Do not even the most experienced dispute on the preference, and shall the most ignorant decide? A vulgar connoisseur would even prefer a Denner to a Titian, because there is more of merely curious and specific detail. We may hence account for another circumstance, why things please in the imitation which do not in reality. If we saw the whole of anything, or if the object in nature were merely one thing, this could not be the case. But the fact is, that in the imitation, or in the scientific study of any object, we come to an analysis of the details or some other abstract view of the subject which we had overlooked in a cursory examination, and these may be beautiful or curious, though the object in the gross is disgusting, or connected with disagreeable or uninteresting associations. Thus, in a picture of *still life*, as a shell or a marble chimney-piece, the stains or the gradations of colour may be delicate, and subjects for a new and careful imitation, though the *tout ensemble* has not, like a living face, the highest beauty of intelligence and expression. Here lie and here return the true effects and triumphs of art. It is not in making the eye a microscope, but in making it the interpreter and organ of all that can touch the soul and the affections, that the perfection of fine art is shown. Taste, then, does not place in the first rank of merit what merely proves difficulty or gratifies curiosity, unless it is combined with excellence and sentiment, or the pleasures of imagination and the moral sense. In this case the pleasure is more than doubled, where not only the imitation but the thing imitated, is fine in itself. Hence the preference given to Italian over Dutch pictures.

In respect to the imitation of nature, I would further observe that I think Sir Joshua Reynolds was wrong in making the grandeur of the design depend on the omission of the details, or the want of finishing. This seems also to proceed on the supposition that there cannot be two views of nature, but that the details are opposed to and inconsistent with an attention to general effect. Now this is evidently false, since the two things are undoubtedly combined by nature. For instance, the grandeur of design or character in the arch of an eyebrow is not injured or destroyed in reality by the hair-lines of which it is composed. Nor is the general form or outline of the eyebrow altered in the imitation, whether you make it one rude mass or descend into the minutiæ of the parts, which are arranged in such a manner as to produce the arched form and give the particular expression. So the general form of a nose, say an aquiline one, is not affected, whether I paint a wart which may happen to be on it or not, and so of the outline and proportions of the whole face. That is, general effect is consistent with individual details, and though these are not necessary to it, yet they often assist it, and always confirm the sense of verisimilitude. The most finished paintings, it is true, are not the grandest in effect; but neither is it true that the greatest daubs are the most sublime in character and composition. The best painters have combined an eye to the whole with careful finishing, and as there is a medium in all things, so the rule here seems to be not to go on *ad infinitum* with the details, but to stop when the time and labour necessary seem, in the judgment of the artist, to exceed the benefit produced.

Beauty does not consist in a medium, but in gradation or harmony. It has been the fashion of late to pretend to refer everything to association of ideas (and it is difficult to answer this appeal, since association, by its nature, mixes up with everything), but as Hartley has himself observed, who carried this principle to the utmost extent, and might be supposed to understand its limits, association implies something to be associated, and if there is a pleasing association, there must be first something naturally pleasing from which the secondary satisfaction is reflected, or to which it is conjoined. The chirping of a sparrow is as much a rural and domestic sound as the notes of the robin or the thrush, but it does not serve as a point to link other interests to because it wants beauty in itself; and, on the other hand, the song of the nightingale draws more attention to itself as a piece of music, and conveys less sentiment than the simple note of the cuckoo, which, from its solitary singularity, acts as the warning voice of time. Those who deny that there is a natural and pleasing softness arising from harmony or gradation, might as well affirm that sudden and abrupt transitions do not make our impressions more distinct as that they do not make them more harsh and violent. Beauty consists in gradation of colours or symmetry of form (conformity): strength or sublimity arises from the sense of power, and is aided by contrast. The ludicrous is the incoherent, arising, not from a conflicting power, but from weakness or the inability of any habitual impulse to sustain itself. The *ideal* is not confined to creation, but takes place in imitation, where a thing is subjected to one view, as all the parts of a face to the same expression. Invention is only feigning according to nature, or with a certain proportion between causes and effects. Poetry is infusing the same spirit into a number of things, or bathing them all, as it were, in the same overflowing sense of delight (making the language also soft and musical), as the same torch kindles a number of lamps. I think invention is chiefly confined to poetry and words or ideas, and has little place in painting or concrete imagery, where the want of truth, or of the actual object, soon spoils the effect and force of the representation. Indeed, I think all genius is, in a great measure, national and local, arising out of times and circumstances, and being sustained at its full height by these alone, and that originality is not a deviation from, but a recurrence to nature. Rules and models destroy genius and art; and the excess of the artificial in the end cures itself, for it in time becomes so uniform and vapid as to be altogether contemptible, and to seek *perforce* some other outlet or purchase for the mind to take hold of.

The metaphysical theory above premised will account not only for the difficulty of imitating nature, but for the excellence of various masters, and the diversity and popularity of different styles. If the truth of sense and nature were one, there could be but one mode of representing it, more or less correct. But nature contains an

N

infinite variety of parts, with their relations and significations, and different artists take these, and all together do not give the whole. Thus Titian coloured, Raphael designed, Rubens gave the florid hue and motions, Rembrandt *chiaro-scuro*, &c.; but none of these reached perfection in their several departments, much less with reference to the whole circumference of art. It is ridiculous to suppose there is but one standard or one style. One artist looks at objects with as different an eye from another, as he does from the mathematician. It is erroneous to tie down individual genius to ideal models. Each person should do that, not which is best in itself, even supposing this could be known, but that which he can do best, which he will find out if left to himself. Spenser could not have written *Paradise Lost*, nor Milton the *Faërie Queene*. Those who aim at faultless regularity will only produce mediocrity, and no one ever approaches perfection except by stealth, and unknown to themselves. Did Correggio know what he had done when he had painted the "St. Jerome"—or Rembrandt when he made the sketch of "Jacob's Dream?" Oh, no! Those who are conscious of their powers never do anything.

Why the Heroes of Romances are Insipid.

BECAUSE it is taken for granted that they must be amiable and interesting, in the first instance, which, like other things that are taken for granted, is but indifferently, or indeed cannot be, made out at all in the sequel. To put it to the proof, to give illustrations of it, would be to throw a doubt upon the question. They have only to show themselves to ensure conquest. Indeed, the reputation of their victories goes before them, and is a pledge of their success before they even appear. They are, or are supposed to be, so amiable, so handsome, so accomplished, so captivating, that all hearts bow before them, and all the women are in love with them without knowing why or wherefore, except that it is understood that they are to be so. All obstacles vanish without a finger lifted or a word spoken, and the effect is produced without a blow being struck. When there is this imaginary charm at work, everything they could do or say must weaken the impression, like arguments brought in favour of a self-evident truth: they very wisely say or do little or nothing, rely on their names and the author's good word, look, smile, and are adored; but to all but the heroines of romance and their confidantes, are exceedingly uninteresting and *commonplace* personages, either great coxcombs or wonderfully insipid. When a lover is able to look unutterable things which produce the desired effect, what occasion for him to exert his eloquence or make an impassioned speech, in order to bring about a revolution in his favour, which is already accomplished by other less doubtful means? When the impression at first sight is complete and irresistible, why throw away any farther thoughts or words to make it more so? This were "to gild refined gold, to paint the lily, to smooth the ice, to throw a perfume on the violet, or add another hue unto the rainbow, or seek with taper-light the beauteous eye of Heaven to garnish," which has been pronounced to be " wasteful and superfluous excess." Authors and novel-writers therefore reserve for their second-rate and less prominent characters, the artillery of words, the arts of persuasion, and all the unavailing battery of hopeless attentions and fine sentiment, which are of no use to the more accomplished gallant, who makes his triumphant approaches by stolen glances and breathing sighs, and whose appearance alone supersedes the disclosure of all his other implied perfections and an importunate display of a long list of titles to the favour of the fair, which, as they are not insisted on, it would be vain and unbecoming to produce to the gaze of the world, or for the edification of the curious reader. It is quite enough if the lady is satisfied with her choice, and if (as generally happens both as a cause and consequence in such cases) the gentleman is satisfied with himself. If he indeed seemed to entertain a doubt upon the subject, the spell of his fascination would be broken, and the author would be obliged to derogate from the *beau ideal* of his character, and make him do something to deserve the good opinion that might be entertained of him, and to which he himself had not led the way by boundless self-complacency and the conscious assurance of infallible success.

Another circumstance that keeps our novel heroes in the background is, that if there was any doubt of their success, or they were obliged to employ the ordinary and vulgar means to establish their superiority over every one else, they would be no longer those " faultless monsters " which it is understood that they must be to fill their part in the drama. The discarded or despairing, not the favoured lovers, are unavoidably the most interesting persons in the story. In fact, the principals are already disposed of in the first page ; they are destined for each other by an unaccountable and uncontrollable sympathy : the ceremony is in a manner over, and they are already married people, with all the lawful attributes and indifference belonging to the character. To produce an interest, there must be mixed motives, alternate hope and fear, difficulties to struggle with, sacrifices to make ; but the true hero of romance is too fine a gentleman to be subjected to this rude ordeal or mortifying exposure, which devolves upon some much more unworthy and unpretending personage. The beauty of the outline must not be disturbed by the painful conflicts of passion or the strong contrast of light and shade. The taste of the heroic cannot swerve for a moment from the object of its previous choice, who must never be placed in disdvantageous circumstances. The top characters occupy a certain prescriptive rank in the world of romance, by the rules of etiquette and laws of this sort of fictitious composition, reign like princes, and have only to do nothing to forfeit their privileges or compromise their supposed dignity.

The heroes of the old romances, the Grand Cyruses, the Artamenes, and Oroondates, are in this respect better than the moderns. They had their steel helmet and plume of feathers, the glittering spear and shield, the barbed steed, and the spread banner, and had knightly service to perform in joust and tournament, in the field of battle or the deep forest, besides the duty which they owed to their "mistress' eyebrow," and the favours they received at her hands. They were comparatively picturesque and adventurous personages, and men of action in the tented field, and lost all title to the smile of beauty if they did not deserve it by feats of prowess, and by the valour of their arms. However insipid they might be as accepted lovers, in their set speeches and improgressive languishments by which they paid their court to their hearts' idols, the "fairest of the fair," yet in their character of warriors and heroes, they were men of mettle, and had something in them. They did not merely sigh and smile and kneel in the presence of their mistresses— they had to unhorse their adversaries in combat, to storm castles, to vanquish giants, and lead armies. So far, so well. In the good old times of chivalry and romance, favour was won and maintained by the bold achievements and fair fame of the chosen knight, which keeps up a show of suspense and dramatic interest, instead of depending, as in more effeminate times, on taste, sympathy, and a refinement of sentiment and manners, of the delicacy of which it is impossible to convey any idea by words or actions. Even in the pompous and affected courtship of the romances of the seventeenth century (now, alas!

exploded) the interviews between the lovers are so rare
and guarded, their union, though agreed upon and inevitable, is so remote, the smile with which the lady
regards her sworn champion, though as steady as that of
one of the fixed stars, is like them so cold, as to give a
tone of passion and interest to their enamoured flights as
though they were affected by the chances and changes of
sublunary affairs.   I confess I have read some of these
fabulous folios formerly with no small degree of delight
and breathless anxiety, particularly that of *Cassandra;*
and would willingly indeed go over it again to catch even
a faint, a momentary glimpse of the pleasure with which
I used at one period to peruse its prolix descriptions and
high-flown sentiments.   Not only the Palmerins of England and Amadises of Gaul, who made their way to their
mistresses' hearts by slaying giants and taming dragons,
but the heroes of the French romances of intrigue and
gallantry which succeeded those of necromancy and chivalry, and where the adventurers for the prize have to
break through the fences of morality and scruples of
conscience instead of stone-walls and enchantments dire,
are to be excepted from the censure of downright insipidity, which attaches to those ordinary drawing-room heroes,
who are installed in the good graces of their divinities by
a look, and keep their places there by the force of *still
life!*   It is Gray who cries out, " Be mine to read eternal
new romances of Marivaux and Crebillon!"   I could say
the same of those of Madame La Fayette and the Duke de
la Rochefoucault.   *The Princess of Cleves* is a most charming work of this kind; and the *Duc de Nemours* is a great
favourite with me.   He is perhaps the most brilliant
personage that ever entered upon the *tapis* of a drawing-
room, or trifled at a lady's toilette.
   I prefer him, I own, vastly to Richardson's *Sir Charles
Grandison,* whom I look upon as the prince of coxcombs;
and so much the more impertinent as he is a moral one.

His character appears to me "ugly all over with affectation." There is not a single thing that Sir Charles Grandison does or says all through the book from liking to any person or object but himself, and with a view to answer to a certain standard of perfection for which he pragmatically sets up. He is always thinking of himself, and trying to show that he is the wisest, happiest, and most virtuous person in the whole world. He is (or would be thought) a code of Christian ethics—a compilation and abstract of all gentlemanly accomplishments. There is nothing, I conceive, that excites so little sympathy as this inordinate egotism; or so much disgust as this everlasting self-complacency. Yet his self-admiration, brought forward on every occasion as the incentive to every action and reflected from all around him, is the burden and pivot of the story. "Is not the man Sir Charles Grandison?" is what he and all the other persons concerned are continually repeating to themselves. His preference of the little, insignificant, selfish, affected, puritanical Miss Byron, who is remarkable for nothing but her conceit of herself and her lover, to the noble Clementina, must for ever stamp him for the poltroon and blockhead that he was. What a contrast between these two females—the one, the favourite heroine, settling her idle punctilios and the choice of her ribbons for the wedding-day with equal interest, the other, self-devoted, broken-hearted, generous, disinterested, pouring out her whole soul in the fervent expressions and dying struggles of an unfortunate and hopeless affection! It was impossible indeed for the genius of the author (strive all he could) to put the prettiness and coquettish scruples of the bride elect upon a par with the eloquent despair and impassioned sentiments of her majestic but unsuccessful rival. Nothing can show more clearly that the height of good fortune, and of that conventional faultlessness which is supposed to secure it, is incompatible with any great degree of interest. Lady Clementina should have been married to Sir Charles to surfeit her of a coxcomb—Miss Byron to Lovelace to plague her with a rake! Have we not sometimes seen such matches? A slashing critic of my acquaintance once observed, that " Richardson would be surprised in the next world to find Lovelace in Heaven and Grandison in Hell!" Without going this orthodox length, I must say there is something in Lovelace's vices more attractive than in the other's best virtues. Clarissa's attachment seems as natural as Clementina's is romantic. There is a *regality* about Lovelace's manner, and he appears clothed in a panoply of wit, gaiety, spirit, and enterprise, that is criticism-proof. If he had not possessed these dazzling qualities, nothing could have made us forgive for an instant his treatment of the spotless Clarissa ; but indeed they might be said to be mutually attracted to and extinguished in each other's dazzling lustre! When we think of Lovelace and his luckless exploits, we can hardly be persuaded at this time of day that he wore a wig. Yet that he did so is evident ; for Miss Howe, when she gave him that spirited box on the ear, struck the powder out of it! Mr. B. in *Pamela* has all the insipidity that arises from patronising beauty and condescending to virtue. Pamela herself is delightfully made out; but she labours under considerable disadvantages, and is far from a *regular* heroine.

Sterne (thank God!) has neither hero nor heroine, and he does very well without them.

Many people find fault with Fielding's *Tom Jones* as gross and immoral. For my part, I have doubts of his being so very handsome, from the author's always talking about his beauty, and I suspect he was a clown, from being constantly assured he was so very genteel. Otherwise, I think Jones acquits himself very well both in his actions and speeches, as a lover and as a *trencher-man*, whenever he is called upon. Some persons, from their antipathy to that headlong impulse, of which Jones was the slave, and to that morality of good-nature which in him is made a foil to principle, have gone so far as to prefer Blifil as the *prettier fellow* of the two. I certainly cannot subscribe to this opinion, which perhaps was never meant to have followers, and has nothing but its singularity to recommend it. Joseph Andrews is a hero of the shoulder-knot : it would be hard to canvass his pretensions too severely, especially considering what a patron he has in Parson Adams. That one character would cut up into a hundred fine gentlemen and novel heroes ! Booth is another of the good-natured tribe, a fine man, a very fine man ! But there is a want of spirit to animate the well-meaning mass. He hardly deserved to have the hashed mutton kept waiting for him. The author has redeemed himself in Amelia ; but a heroine with a *broken nose*, and who was a married woman besides, must be rendered truly interesting and amiable to make up for superficial objections. The character of the Nobleman in this novel is *not* insipid. If Fielding could have made virtue as admirable as he could make vice detestable, he would have been a greater master even than he was. I do not understand what those critics mean who say he got all his characters out of ale-houses. It is true he did some of them.

Smollett's heroes are neither one thing nor the other ; neither very refined nor very insipid. Wilson in *Humphrey Clinker* comes the nearest to the *beau ideal* of this character, the favourite of the novel-reading and boarding-school girl. Narcissa and Emilia Gauntlet are very charming girls ; and Monimia in *Count Fathom* is a fine monumental beauty. But perhaps he must be allowed to be most *at home* in Winifred Jenkins !

The women have taken this matter up in our own time : let us see what they have made of it. Mrs. Radcliffe's heroes and lovers are perfect in their kind; nobody can find any fault with them, for nobody knows anything about them. They are described as very handsome, and quite unmeaning and inoffensive.

> " Her heroes have no character at all."

Theodore, Valancourt,—what delightful names! and there is nothing else to distinguish them by. Perhaps, however, this indefiniteness is an advantage. We add expression to the inanimate outline, and fill up the blank with all that is amiable, interesting, and romantic. A long ride without a word spoken, a meeting that comes to nothing, a parting look, a moonlight scene, or evening skies that paint their sentiments for them better than the lovers can do for themselves, farewells too full of anguish, deliverances too big with joy to admit of words, suppressed sighs, faint smiles, the freshness of the morning, pale melancholy, the clash of swords, the clank of chains that make the fair one's heart sink within her, these are the chief means by which the admired authoress of the *Romance of the Forest* and the *Mysteries of Udolpho* keeps alive an ambiguous interest in the bosom of her fastidious readers, and elevates the lover into the hero of the fable. Unintelligible distinctions, impossible attempts, a delicacy that shrinks from the most trifling objection, and an enthusiasm that rushes on its fate, such are the charming and teazing contradictions that form the flimsy texture of a modern romance! If the lover in such critical cases was anything but a lover, he would cease to be the most amiable of all characters in the abstract and by way of excellence, and would be a traitor to the cause; to give reasons or to descend to particulars, is to doubt the omnipotence of love and shake the empire of credulous fancy; a sounding name, a graceful form, are all that is necessary to suspend the whole train of tears, sighs, and the softest emotions upon; the ethereal nature of the passion requires ethereal food to sustain it; and our youthful hero, in order to be perfectly interesting, must be drawn as perfectly insipid!

I cannot, however, apply this charge to Mrs. Inchbald's heroes or heroines. However finely drawn, they are an essence of sentiment. Their words are composed of the warmest breath, their tears scald, their sighs stifle. Her characters seem moulded of a softer clay, the work of fairest hands. Miss Milner is enchanting. Doriforth indeed is severe, and has a very stately opinion of himself, but he has spirit and passion. Lord Norwynne is the most unpleasant and obdurate. He seduces by his situation and kills by indifference, as is natural in such cases But still through all these the fascination of the writer's personal feelings never quits you. On the other hand, Miss Burney's (Madame D'Arblay's) *forte* is ridicule, or an exquisite tact for minute absurdities; when she aims at being fine, she only becomes affected. No one had ever much less of the romantic. Lord Orville is a condescending suit of clothes; yet, certainly, the sense which Evelina has of the honour done her is very prettily managed. Sir Clement Willoughby is a much gayer and more animated person, though his wit outruns his discretion. Young Delville is the hero of punctilio—a perfect diplomatist in the art of love-making—and draws his parallels and sits down as deliberately before the citadel of his mistress' heart, as a cautious general lays siege to an impregnable fortress. Cecilia is not behindhand with him in the game of studied cross-purposes and affected delays, and is almost the veriest and most provoking trifler on record. Miss Edgeworth, I believe, has no heroes. Her *trenchant* pen cuts away all extravagance and idle pretence, and leaves nothing but common sense, prudence, and propriety behind it, wherever it comes.

I do not apprehend that the heroes of the author of

Waverley form any very striking exception to the common rule. They conform to their designation and follow the general law of their being. They are, for the most part, very equivocal and undecided personages, who receive their governing impulse from accident, or are puppets in the hands of their mistresses, such as Ivanhoe, Frank Osbaldistone, Henry Morton, &c. I do not say that any of these are absolutely insipid, but they have in themselves no leading or master-traits, and they are worked out of very listless and inert materials, into a degree of force and prominence, solely by the genius of the author. Instead of acting, they are acted upon, and keep in the back-ground and in a neutral posture, till they are absolutely forced to come forward, and it is then with a very amiable reservation of modest scruples. Does it not seem almost, or generally speaking, as if a character. to be put in this responsible situation of candidate for the highest favour of the public at large, or of the fair in particular, who is to conciliate all suffrages and concentrate all interests, must really have nothing in him to please or give offence, that he must be left a negative, feeble character, without untractable or uncompromising points, and with a few slight recommendations and obvious good qualities, which every one may be supposed to improve upon and fill up according to his or her inclination or fancy and the model of perfection previously existing in the mind? It is a privilege claimed, no doubt, by the fair reader to make out the object of her admiration and interest according to her own choice; and the same privilege, if not openly claimed, may be covertly exercised by others. We are all fond of our own creations; and if the author does little to his chief character, and allows us to have a considerable hand in it, it may not suffer in our opinion from this circumstance. In fact, the hero of the work is not so properly the chief object in it, as a sort of blank left open to the imagination, or a lay-figure on which the reader disposes whatever drapery he pleases! Of all Sir Walter's male characters the most dashing and spirited is the Sultan Saladin. But he is not meant for a hero, nor fated to be a lover. He is a collateral and incidental performer in the scene. His movements therefore remain free, and he is master of his own resplendent energies, which produce so much the more daring and felicitous an effect. So far from being intended to please all tastes, or the most squeamish, he is not meant for any taste. He has no pretensions, and stands upon the sole ground of his own heroic acts and sayings. The author has none of the timidity or mawkishness arising from a fear of not coming up to his own professions, or to the expectations excited in the reader's mind. Any striking trait, any interesting exploit, is more than was bargained for—is heaped measure, running over. There is no idle, nervous apprehension of falling short of perfection, arresting the hand or diverting the mind from truth and nature. If the Pagan is not represented as a monster and barbarian, all the rest is a god-send. Accordingly all is spontaneous, bold, and original in this beautiful and glowing design, which is as magnificent as it is magnanimous.—Lest I should forget it, I will mention, while I am on the subject of Scotch novels, that Mackenzie's *Man of Feeling* is not without interest, but it is an interest brought out in a very singular and unprecedented way. He not merely says or does nothing to deserve the approbation of the goddess of his idolatry, but, from extreme shyness and sensitiveness, instead of presuming on his merits, gets out of her way, and only declares his passion on his death-bed. Poor Harley!—Mr. Godwin's Falkland is a very high and heroic character: he, however, is not a love-hero; and the only part in which an eposide of this kind is introduced, is of the most trite and mawkish description. The case is different in *St. Leon*. The author's resuscitated hero there quaffs joy, love, and immortality with a considerable *gusto*, and with appropriate manifestations of triumph.

As to the heroes of the philosophical school of romance, such as Goethe's *Werter*, &c., they are evidently out of the pale of this reasoning. Instead of being commonplace and insipid, they are one violent and startling paradox from beginning to end. They run a-tilt at all established usages and prejudices, and overset all the existing order of society. There is plenty of interest here; and, instead of complaining of a calm, we are borne along by a hurricane of passion and eloquence, certainly without anything of "temperance that may give it smoothness." Schiller's *Moor*, Kotzebue's heroes, and all the other German prodigies are of this stamp.

Shakspeare's lovers and Boccaccio's I like much: they seem to me full of tenderness and manly spirit, and free from insipidity and cant. Otway's *Jaffier* is, however, the true woman's man—full of passion and effeminacy, a mixture of strength and weakness. Perhaps what I have said above may suggest the true reason and apology for Milton's having unwittingly made Satan the hero of *Paradise Lost*. He suffers infinite losses, and makes the most desperate efforts to recover or avenge them; and it is the struggle with fate and the privation of happiness that sharpens our desires, or enhances our sympathy with good or evil. We have little interest in unalterable felicity, nor can we join with heart and soul in the endless symphonies and exalting hallelujahs of the spirits of the blest. The remorse of a fallen spirit, or " tears such as angels shed," touch us more nearly.

On the Conversation of Lords.

"An infinite deal of nothing."—SHAKESPEARE.

THE conversation of lords is very different from that of authors. Mounted on horseback, they stick at nothing in the chase, and clear every obstacle with flying leaps, while we poor devils have no chance of keeping up with them with our clouten shoes and long hunting-poles. They have all the benefit of education, society, confidence; they read books, purchase pictures, breed horses, learn to ride, dance, and fence, look after their estates, travel abroad: authors have none of these advantages, or inlets of knowledge, to assist them, except one, reading; and this is still more impoverished and clouded by the painful exercise of their own thoughts. The knowledge of the great has a character of wealth and property in it, like the stores of the rich merchant or manufacturer, who lays his hands on all within his reach: the understanding of the student is like the workshop of the mechanic, who has nothing but what he himself creates. How difficult is the production, how small the display in the one case compared to the other! Most of Correggio's designs are contained in one small room at Parma: how different from the extent and variety of some hereditary and princely collections!

The human mind has a trick (probably a very natural and consoling one) of striking a balance between the favours of wisdom and of fortune, and of making a gratuitous and convenient foil to another. Whether this is owing to envy or to a love of justice, I will not say; but whichever it is owing to, I must own I do not think it well founded. A scholar is without money: therefore (to make the odds even) we argue (not very wisely) that a rich man must be without ideas. This does not follow: "the wish is father to that thought;" and the thought is a spurious one. We might as well pretend, that because a man has the advantage of us in height, he is not strong or in good health; or because a woman is handsome, she is not at the same time young, accomplished and well-bred. Our fastidious self-love or our rustic prejudices may revolt at the accumulation of advantages in others;

but we must learn to submit to the mortifying truth, which every day's experience points out, with what grace we may. There were those who grudged to Lord Byron the name of a poet because he was of noble birth; as he himself could not endure the praises bestowed upon Wordsworth, whom he considered as a clown. He carried this weakness so far, that he even seemed to regard it as a piece of presumption in Shakspeare *to be preferred before him* as a dramatic author, and contended that Milton's writing an epic poem and the *Answer to Salmasius* was entirely owing to vanity—so little did he relish the superiority of the old blind school-master. So it is that one party would arrogate every advantage to themselves, while those on the other side would detract from all in their rivals that they do not themselves possess. Some will not have the statue painted : others can see no beauty in the clay-model.

The man of rank and fortune, besides his chance for the common or (now and then) an uncommon share of wit and understanding, has it in his power to avail himself of everything that is to be taught of art and science ; he has tutors and valets at his beck ; he may master the dead languages, he *must* acquire the modern ones ; he moves in the highest circles, and may descend to the lowest ; the paths of pleasure, of ambition, of knowledge, are open to him ; he may devote himself to a particular study, or skim the cream of all ; he may read books or men or things, as he finds most convenient or agreeable ; he is not forced to confine his attention to some one dry, uninteresting pursuit ; he has a single *hobby*, or half a dozen ; he is not distracted by care, by poverty and want of leisure ; he has every opportunity and facility afforded him for acquiring various accomplishments of body or mind, and every encouragement, from confidence and success, for making an imposing display of them ; he may laugh with the gay, jest with the witty, argue with the wise ; he has been in courts, in colleges, and camps, is familiar with playhouses and taverns, with the riding-house and the dissecting-room, has been present at or taken part in the debates of both Houses of Parliament, was in the O. P. row, and is deep in the Fancy, understands the broadsword exercise, is a connoisseur in regimentals, plays the whole game at whist, is a tolerable proficient at backgammon, drives four-in-hand, skates, rows, swims, shoots; knows the different sorts of game and modes of agriculture in the different counties of England, the manufactures and commerce of the different towns, the politics of Europe, the campaigns in Spain, has the Gazette, the newspapers, and reviews at his fingers' ends, has visited the finest scenes of Nature and beheld the choicest works of Art, and is in society where he is continually hearing or talking of all these things: and yet we are surprised to find that a person so circumstanced and qualified has any ideas to communicate or words to express himself, and is not, as by patent and prescription he was bound to be, a mere well-dressed fop of fashion or a booby lord! It would be less remarkable if a poor author, who has none of this giddy range and scope of information, who pores over the page till it fades from his sight, and refines upon his style till the words stick in his throat, should be dull as a beetle and mute as a fish, instead of spontaneously pouring out a volume of wit and wisdom on every subject that can be started.

An author lives out of the world, or mixes chiefly with those of his own class; which renders him pedantic and pragmatical, or gives him a reserved, hesitating, and *interdicted* manner. A lord or gentleman-commoner goes into the world, and this imparts that fluency, spirit, and freshness to his conversation, which arises from the circulation of ideas and from the greater animation and excitement of unrestrained intercourse. An author's tongue is tied for want of somebody to speak to: his ideas rust and become obscured, from not being brought out in company and exposed to

the gaze of instant admiration. A lord has always some
one at hand on whom he can "bestow his tediousness,"
and grows voluble, copious, inexhaustible in consequence :
his wit is polished, and the flowers of his oratory expanded
by his smiling commerce with the world, like the figures
in tapestry, that after being thrust into a corner and folded
up in closets, are displayed on festival and gala-days.
Again, the man of fashion and fortune reduces many of
those arts and mysteries to practice, of which the scholar
gains all his knowledge from books and vague description.
Will not the rules of architecture find a readier reception
and sink deeper into the mind of the proprietor of a noble
mansion, or of him who means to build one, than of the
half-starved occupier of a garret? Will not the political
economist's insight into Mr. Ricardo's doctrine of Rent, or
Mr. Malthus's theory of Population, be vastly quickened
by the circumstance of his possessing a large landed estate
and having to pay enormous poor-rates? And, in general,
is it not self-evident that a man's knowledge of the true
interests of the country will be enlarged just in proportion
to the *stake* he has in it? A person may have read
accounts of different cities and the customs of different
nations : but will this give him the same accurate idea of
the situation of celebrated places, of the aspect and
manners of the inhabitants, or the same lively impulse
and ardour and fund of striking particulars in expatiating
upon them, as if he had run over half the countries of
Europe, for no other purpose than to satisfy his own
curiosity, and excite that of others on his return? I
many years ago looked into the Duke of Newcastle's[1]
Treatise on Horsemanship ; all I remember of it is some
quaint cuts of the Duke and his riding-master introduced
to illustrate the lessons. Had I myself possessed a stud
of Arabian coursers, with grooms and a master of the

---

[1] William, Duke of Newcastle, husband of the poetical Duchess.
—ED.

horse to assist me in reducing these precepts to practice, they would have made a stronger impression on my mind; and what interested myself from vanity or habit, I could have made interesting to others.   I am sure I could have learnt to *ride the Great Horse*, and do twenty other things, in the time I have employed in endeavouring to make something out of nothing, or in conning the same problem fifty times over, as monks count over their beads!   I have occasionally in my life bought a few prints, and hung them up in my room with great satisfaction; but is it to be supposed possible, from this casual circumstance, that I should compete in taste or in the knowledge of *vertu* with a peer of the realm, who has in his possession the costly designs, or a wealthy commoner, who has spent half his fortune in learning to distinguish copies from originals?   "A question not to be asked!"   Nor is it likely that the having dipped into the *Memoirs of Count Grammont*, or of Lady Vane in *Peregrine Pickle*, should enable any one to sustain a conversation on subjects of love and gallantry with the same ease, grace, brilliancy, and spirit as the having been engaged in a hundred adventures of one's own, or heard the scandal and tittle-tattle of fashionable life for the last thirty years canvassed a hundred times.   Books may be manufactured from other books by some dull, mechanical process: it is conversation and the access to the best society that alone fit us for society; or "the act and practique part of life must be the mistress to our theorique," before we can hope to shine in mixed company, or bend our previous knowledge to ordinary and familiar uses out of that plaster-cast mould which is as brittle as it is formal!

There is another thing which tends to produce the same effect, viz., that lords and gentlemen seldom trouble themselves about the knotty and uninviting parts of a subject : they leave it to " the dregs of earth " to drain the cup or find the bottom.   They are attracted by the frothy and sparkling. If a question puzzles them, or is not likely to amuse others, they leave it to its fate, or to those whose business it is to contend with difficulty, and to pursue truth for its own sake. They string together as many available *off-hand* topics as they can procure for love or money; and, aided by a good person or address, sport them with very considerable effect at the next rout or party they go to. They do not *bore* you with pedantry, or tease you with sophistry. Their conversation is not made up of *moot-points* or *choke-pears.* They do not willingly forego "the feast of reason or the flow of soul" to grub up some solitary truth or dig for hidden treasure. They are amateurs, not professors; the patrons, not the drudges of knowledge. An author loses half his life, and *stultifies* his faculties, in hopes to find out something which perhaps neither he nor any one else can ever find out. For this he neglects half a hundred acquirements, half a hundred accomplishments. *Aut Cæsar aut nihil.* He is proud of the discovery or of the fond pursuit of one truth—a lord is vain of a thousand ostentatious commonplaces. If the latter ever devotes himself to some crabbed study, or sets about finding out the longitude, he is then to be looked upon as a humorist if he fails—a genious if he succeeds—and no longer belongs to the class I have been speaking of.

Perhaps a multiplicity of attainments and pursuits is not very favourable to their selectness; as a local and personal acquaintance with objects of imagination takes away from, instead of adding to, their romantic interest. Familiarity is said to breed contempt; or at any rate, the being brought into contact with places, persons, or things that we have hitherto only heard or read of, removes a certain aerial, delicious veil of refinement from them, and strikes at that *ideal* abstraction which is the charm and boast of a life conversant chiefly with books. The huddling a number of tastes and studies together tends to degrade and vulgarise each, and to give a crude, unconcocted, dissipated turn to the mind. Instead of stuffing it full of gross, palpable, immediate objects of excitement, a wiser plan would be to leave something in reserve, something hovering in airy space to draw our attention out of ourselves, to excite hope, curiosity, wonder, and never to satisfy it. The great art is not to throw a glare of light upon all objects, or to lay the whole extended landscape bare at one view; but so to manage as to see the more amiable side of things, and through the narrow vistas and loop-holes of retreat—

"Catch glimpses that may make us less forlorn."

I hate to annihilate air and distance by the perpetual use of an opera-glass, to run everything into foreground, and to interpose no medium between the thought and the object. The breath of words stirs and plays idly with the gossamer web of fancy; the touch of things destroys it. I have seen a good deal of authors; and I believe that they (as well as I) would quite as lieve I had not. Places I have seen, too, that did not answer my expectation. Pictures, (that is, some few of them) are the only things that are the better for our having studied them "face to face, not in a glass darkly," and that in themselves surpass any description we can give, or any notion we can form of them. But I do not think seriously, after all, that those who possess are the best judges of them. They become furniture, property in their hands. The purchasers look to the price they will fetch, or turn to that which they have cost. They consider not beauty or expression, but the workmanship, the date, the pedigree, the school—something that will figure in the description in a catalogue or in a puff in a newspaper. They are blinded by silly admiration of whatever belongs to themselves, and warped so as to eye "with jealous leer malign" all that is not theirs. Taste is melted down in the crucible of avarice and vanity, and leaves a wretched *caput mortuum* of pedantry and conceit. As to books, they " best can feel them who have read them most," and who rely on them for their only support and their only chance of distinction. They most keenly relish the graces of style who have in vain tried to make them their own : they alone understand the value of a thought who have gone through the trouble of thinking. The privation of other advantages is not a clear loss, if it is counterbalanced by a proportionable concentration and unity of interest in what is left. The love of letters is the forlorn hope of the man of letters. His ruling passion is the love of fame. A member of the Roxburghe Club has a certain work (let it be the *Decameron* of Boccaccio) splendidly bound, and in the old quarto edition, we will say. In this not only his literary taste is gratified, but the pride of property, the love of external elegance and decoration. The poor student has only a paltry and somewhat worn copy of the same work (or perhaps only a translation) which he picked up at a stall, standing out of a shower of rain. What then! has not the Noble Virtuoso doubly the advantage, and a much higher pleasure in the perusal of the work? No; for these are vulgar and mechanical helps to the true enjoyment of letters. From all this mock-display and idle parade of binding and arms and dates, his unthought-of rival is precluded, and sees only the talismanic words, feels only the spirit of the author, and in that author reads " with sparkling eyes "

> " His title to a mansion in the skies."

Oh! divine air of learning, fanned by the undying breath of genius, still let me taste thee, free from all adventitious admixtures,

> " Pure in the last recesses of the soul !"

We are far, at present, from the style of Swift's *Polite Conversation.* The fashionable tone has quite changed in

this respect, and almost gone into the opposite extreme.
At that period the polite world seems to have been nearly
at a stand, in a state of intellectual *abeyance ;* or, in the
interval between the disuse of chivalrous exercises and
the introduction of modern philosophy, not to have known
how to pass its time, and to have sunk into the most
commonplace formality and unmeaning apathy.   But lo !
at a signal given, or rather prompted by that most
powerful of all calls, the want of something to do, all
rush into the lists, having armed themselves anew with
the shining panoply of science and of letters, with an
eagerness, a perseverance, a dexterity, and a success, that
are truly astonishing.   The higher classes have of late
taken the lead almost as much in arts as they formerly
did in arms, when the last was the only prescribed mode
of distinguishing themselves from the rabble, whom they
treated as serfs and churls.   The prevailing cue at present
is to regard mere authors (who are not also of gentle
blood) as dull, illiterate, poor creatures, a sort of pretenders to taste and elegance, and adventurers in intellect.
The true adepts in black-letter are knights of the shire :
the sworn patentees of Parnassus are Peers of the Realm.
Not to pass for a literary quack, you must procure a
diploma from the College of Heralds.   A dandy conceals
a bibliomanist : our belles are *blue-stockings.*   The Press
is so entirely monopolised by beauty, birth, or importance
in the State,[1] that an author by profession resigns the
field to the crowd of well-dressed competitors, out of
modesty or pride ; is fain to keep out of sight—

    " Or write by stealth, and blush to find it fame !"

Lord Byron used to boast that he could bring forward

---

[1] This was written when the *mania* for fashionable novels by
Noble Authors was at its height.—ED. of *Sketches and Essays,* 1839.
See the criticism on Disraeli's *Vivian Grey* by the author, in the
Examiner for 1827, under the title of the *Dandy School.*

a dozen young men of fashion who would beat all the regular authors at their several weapons of wit or argument; and though I demur to the truth of the assertion, yet there is no saying till the thing is tried. Young gentlemen make *very pretty sparrers*, but are not the "ugliest customers" when they take off the gloves. Lord Byron himself was in his capacity of author an *out-and-outer;* but then it was at the expense of other things, for he could not talk except in short sentences and sarcastic allusions, he had no ready resources; all his ideas moulded themselves into stanzas, and all his ardour was carried off in rhyme. The channel of his pen was worn deep by habit and power; the current of his thoughts flowed strong in it, and nothing remained to supply the neighbouring flats and shallows of miscellaneous conversation, but a few sprinklings of wit or gushes of spleen. An intense purpose concentrated and gave a determined direction to his energies, that "held on their way, unslacked of motion." The track of his genius was like a volcanic eruption, a torrent of burning lava, full of heat and splendour and headlong fury, that left all dry, cold, hard, and barren behind it! To say nothing of a host of female authors, a bright galaxy above our heads, there is no young lady of fashion in the present day, scarce a boarding-school girl, that is not mistress of as many branches of knowledge as would set up half a dozen literary hacks. In lieu of the sampler and the plain-stitch of our grandmothers, they have so many hours for French, so many for Italian, so many for English grammar and composition, so many for geography and the use of the globes, so many for history, so many for botany, so many for painting, music, dancing, riding, &c. One almost wonders how so many studies are crammed into the twenty-four hours; or how such fair and delicate creatures can master them without spoiling the smoothness of their brows, the sweetness of their tempers, or the graceful simplicity of their manners. A girl learns French (not only to read, but to speak it) in a few months, while a boy is as many years in learning to construe Latin. Why so? Chiefly because the one is treated as a *bagatelle* or agreeable relaxation; the other as a serious task or necessary evil. Education, a very few years back, was looked upon as a hardship, and enforced by menaces and blows, instead of being carried on (as now) as an amusement and under the garb of pleasure, and with the allurements of self-love. It is found that the products of the mind flourish better and shoot up more quickly in the sunshine of good-humour and in the air of freedom, than under the frowns of sullenness, or the shackles of authority. "The labour we delight in physics pain." The idlest people are not those who have most leisure-time to dispose of as they choose: take away the feeling of compulsion, and you supply a motive for application, by converting a toil into a pleasure. This makes nearly all the difference between the hardest drudgery and the most delightful exercise—not the degree of exertion, but the motive and the accompanying sensation. Learning does not gain proselytes by the austerity or awfulness of its looks. By representing things as so difficult, and as exacting such dreadful sacrifices, and to be acquired under such severe penalties, we not only deter the student from the attempt, but lay a dead-weight upon the imagination, and destroy that cheerfulness and alacrity of spirit which is the spring of thought and action. But to return. An author by profession reads a few works that he intends to criticise and cut up "for a consideration;" a *blue-stocking* by profession reads all that come out to pass the time or satisfy her curiosity. The author has something to say about Fielding, Richardson, or even the Scotch novels; but he is soon distanced by the fair critic, or overwhelmed with the contents of whole Circulating Libraries poured out upon his head without stint or intermission. He reads for an object, and to live; she for the sake of reading, or to talk. Be this as it may, the idle reader at present reads twenty-times as many books as the learned one. The former skims the surface of knowledge, and carries away the striking points and a variety of amusing detail, while the latter reserves himself for great occasions, or perhaps does nothing under the pretence of having so much to do.

> "From every work he challenges *essoin*,
> For contemplation's sake."

The *literati* of Europe threaten at present to become the Monks of letters, and from having taken up learning as a profession, to live on the reputation of it. As gentlemen have turned authors, authors seem inclined to turn gentlemen; and enjoying the *otium cum dignitate*, to be much too refined and abstracted to condescend to the subordinate or mechanical parts of knowledge. They are too wise in general to be acquainted with anything in particular; and remain in a proud and listless ignorance of all that is within the reach of the vulgar. They are not, as of old, walking libraries or Encyclopædias, but rather certain faculties of the mind personified. They scorn the material and instrumental branches of inquiry, the husk and bran, and affect only the fine flour of literature—they are only to be called in to give the last polish to style, the last refinement to thought. They leave it to their drudges, the Reading Public, to accumulate the facts, to arrange the evidence, to make out the *data*, and like great painters whose pupils have got in the ground-work and the established proportions of a picture, come forward to go over the last thin glazing of the colours, or throw in the finer touches of expression. On my excusing myself to North-cote for some blunder in history, by saying, "I really had not time to read,"—he said, "No, but you have time to write!" And once a celebrated critic taking me to task as to the subject of my pursuits, and receiving regularly the same answer to his queries, that I knew nothing of chemistry, nothing of astronomy, of botany, of law, of politics, &c., at last exclaimed, somewhat impatiently, "What the devil is it, then, you *do* know?" I laughed, and was not very much disconcerted at the reproof, as it was just.

Modern men of letters may be divided into three classes; the mere scholar or *book-worm*, all whose knowledge is taken from books, and who may be passed by as an obsolete character, little inquired after—the literary *hack* or coffee-house politician, who gets his information mostly from hearsay, and who makes some noise indeed, but the echo of it does not reach beyond his own club or circle—and the man of real or of pretended genius, who aims to draw upon his own resources of thought or feeling, and to throw a new light upon nature and books. This last personage (if he acts up to his supposed character) has too much to do to lend himself to a variety of pursuits, or to lay himself out to please in all companies. He has a task in hand, a vow to perform; and he cannot be diverted from it by incidental or collateral objects. All the time that he does not devote to this paramount duty, he should have to himself, to repose, to lie fallow, to gather strength and recruit himself. A boxer is led into the lists that he may not waste a particle of vigour needlessly; and a leader in Parliament, on the day that he is expected to get up a grand attack or defence, is not to be pestered with the ordinary news of the day. So an author (who is, or would be thought original) has no time for *spare* accomplishments or ornamental studies. All that he intermeddles with must be marshalled to bear upon his purpose. He must be acquainted with books and the thoughts of others, but only so far as to assist him on his way, and " to take progression from them." He starts from the point where *they* left off. All that does not aid him in his new career goes for nothing, is thrown out of the account, or is a useless and splendid incumbrance. Most of his time he passes in brooding over some wayward hint or suggestion of a thought, nor is he bound to give any explanation of what he does with the rest. He tries to melt down truth into essences—to express some fine train of feeling, to solve some difficult problem, to start what is new, or to perfect what is old; in a word, not to do what others can do (which in the division of mental labour he holds to be unnecessary), but to do what they all with their joint efforts cannot do. For this he is in no hurry, and must have the disposal of his leisure and the choice of his subject. The public can wait. He deems with a living poet, who is an example of his own doctrine—

> ———" That there are powers
> Which of themselves our minds impress;
> That we can feed this mind of ours
> In a wise passiveness."

Or I have sometimes thought that the dalliance of the mind with Fancy or with Truth might be described almost in the words of Andrew Marvell's address " To his Coy Mistress :"

> " Had we but world enough and time,
> This toying, lady, were no crime;
> We would sit down, and think which way
> To walk and pass our love's long day.
> Thou by the Indian Ganges' side
> Shouldst rubies find: I by the tide
> Of Humber would complain. I would
> Love you ten years before the flood;
> And you should, if you please, refuse
> Till the conversion of the Jews.
> My contemplative love should grow
> Vaster than empires, and more slow.
> An hundred years should go to praise
> Thine eyes, and on thy forehead gaze;
> Two hundred to adore each breast,
> But thirty thousand to the rest;

An age at least to every part,
And the last age should show your heart:
For, lady, you deserve this state;
Nor would I love at lower rate!"

The aspiring poet or prose-writer undertakes to do a certain thing; and if he succeeds, it is enough. While he is intent upon that or asleep, others may amuse themselves how they can with any topic that happens to be afloat, and all the eloquence they are masters of, so that they do not disturb the champion of truth, or the proclaimer of beauty to the world. The Conversation of Lords, on the contrary, is to this like a newspaper to a book—the latter treats well or ill of one subject, and leads to a conclusion on one point; the other is made up of all sorts of things jumbled together, debates in parliament, law reports, plays, operas, concerts, routs, levees, fashions, auctions, the last fight, foreign news, deaths, marriages, and *crim.-cons.*, bankruptcies, and quack medicines; and a large allowance is frequently to be made, besides the natural confusion of the subjects, for *cross-readings* in the speaker's mind![1] Or, to take another illustration, fashionable conversation has

[1] As when a person asks you "whether you do not find a strong resemblance between Rubens's pictures and Quarles's poetry?"—which is owing to the critic's having lately been at Antwerp and bought an edition of Quarles's '*Emblems.*' Odd combinations must take place where a number of ideas are brought together, with only a thin, hasty partition between them, and without a sufficient quantity of judgment to discriminate. An Englishman, of some apparent consequence, passing by the St. Peter Martyr of Titian at Venice, observed, "It was a copy of the same subject by Domenichino at Bologna." This betrayed an absolute ignorance both of Titian and of Domenichino, and of the whole world of art; yet, unless I had also seen the St. Peter at Bologna, this connoisseur would have had the advantage of me, two to one, and might have disputed the precedence of the two pictures with me, but that chronology would have come to my aid. Thus persons who travel from place to place, and roam from subject to subject, make up by the extent and discursiveness of their knowledge for the want of truth and refinement in their conception of the objects of it.

something theatrical or *melo-dramatic* in it ; it is got up
for immediate effect, it is calculated to make a great display, there is a profusion of paint, scenery, and dresses,
the music is loud, there are banquets and processions, you
have the dancers from the Opera, the horses from Astley's,
and the elephant from Exeter 'Change, the stage is all life,
bustle, noise, and glare, the audience brilliant and delighted, and the whole goes off in a blaze of phosphorus ;
but the dialogue is poor, the story improbable, the critics
shake their heads in the pit, and the next day the piece is
damned !

In short, a man of rank and fortune takes the adventitious and ornamental part of letters, the obvious, the
popular, the fashionable, that serves to amuse at the time,
or minister to the cravings of vanity, without laying a very
heavy tax on his own understanding, or the patience of his
hearers. He furnishes his mind as he does his house, with
what is showy, striking, and of the newest pattern : he
mounts his *hobby* as he does his horse, which is brought to
his door for an airing, and which (should it prove restive
or sluggish) he turns away for another ; or, like a child at a
fair, gets into a round-about of knowledge, till his head becomes giddy, runs from sight to sight, from booth to booth,
and, like the child, goes home loaded with trinkets, gew-
gaws and rattles. He does not pore and pine over an idea
(like some poor hypochondriac) till it becomes impracticable, unsociable, incommunicable, absorbed in mysticism,
and lost in minuteness : he is not upon oath never to utter
anything but oracles, but rattles away in a fine careless,
hair-brained, dashing manner, hit or miss, and succeeds
the better for it. Nor does he prose over the same stale
round of politics and the state of the nation (with the
coffee-house politician), but launches out with freedom and
gaiety into whatever has attraction and interest in it,
" runs the great circle, and is still at home." He is
inquisitive, garrulous, credulous, sanguine, florid—neither

pedantic nor vulgar. Neither is he intolerant, exclusive, bigoted to one set of opinions or one class of individuals. He clothes an abstract theory with illustrations from his own experience and observation, hates what is dry and dull, and throws in an air of high health, buoyant spirits, fortune and splendid connections to give animation and vividness to what perhaps might otherwise want it. He selects what is palpable without being gross or trivial, lends it colour from the flush of success, and elevation from the distinctions of rank. He runs on and never stops for an answer, rather dictating to others than endeavouring to ascertain their opinions, solving his own questions, improving upon their hints, and bearing down or precluding opposition by a good-natured loquacity or stately dogmatism. All this is perhaps more edifying as a subject of speculation than delightful in itself. Shakspeare says, " A man's mind is parcel of his fortunes"—and I think the inference will be borne out in the present case. I should guess that in the prevailing tone of fashionable society or aristocratic literature would be found all that variety, splendour, facility, and startling effect which corresponds with external wealth, magnificence of appearance, and a command of opportunity ; while there would be wanting whatever depends chiefly on intensity of pursuit, on depth of feeling, and on simplicity and independence of mind joined with straitened fortune. Prosperity is a great teacher ; adversity is a greater. Possession pampers the mind ; privation trains and strengthens it. Accordingly, we find but one really great name (Bacon) in this rank of English society, where superiority is taken for granted, and reflected from outward circumstances. The rest are in the second class. Lord Bolingbroke, whom Pope idolised (and it pains me that all his idols are not mine), was a boastful, empty mouther ! I never knew till the other day, that Lord Bolingbroke was the model on which Mr. Pitt formed himself. He was his *Magnus*

Apollo; and no wonder. The late Minister used to lament it as the great desideratum of English literature, that there was no record anywhere existing of his speeches as they were spoken, and declared that he would give any price for one of them, reported as speeches were reported in the newspapers in our time. Being asked which he thought the best of his written productions, he would answer, raising his eyebrows and deepening the tones of his voice to a sonorous bass—"Why, undoubtedly, Sir, the *Letter to Sir William Wyndham* is the most masterly of all his writings, and the first composition for wit and eloquence in the English language ;"—and then he would give his reasons at great length and *con amore*, and say that Junius had formed himself entirely upon it. Lord Bolingbroke had, it seems, a house next door to one belonging to Lord Chatham at Walham Green ; and as the gardens joined, they could hear Lord Bolingbroke walking out with the company that came to see him in his retirement, and elaborately declaiming politics to the old lords and statesmen that were with him, and philosophy to the younger ones. Pitt learned this story from his father when a boy. This account, interesting in itself, was to me the more interesting and extraordinary, as it had always appeared to me that Mr. Pitt was quite an original, *sui generis*—

> "As if a man were author of himself,
> And own'd no other kin ;"

that so far from having a model or idol that he looked up to and grounded himself upon, he had neither admiration nor consciousness of anything existing out of himself, and that he lived solely in the sound of his own voice and revolved in the circle of his own hollow and artificial periods. I have it from the same authority that he thought Cobbett the best writer and Horne Tooke the cleverest man of the day. His hatred of Wyndham was excessive and mutual. Perhaps it may be said that Lord Chatham was a first-rate man in his way, and I incline to think it but he was a self-made man, bred in a camp, not in a court, and his rank was owing to his talents.[1]

The Letter-Bell.

COMPLAINTS are frequently made of the vanity and shortness of human life, when, if we examine its smallest details, they present a world by themselves. The most trifling objects, retraced with the eye of memory, assume the vividness, the delicacy, and importance of insects seen through a magnifying glass. There is no end of the brilliancy or the variety. The habitual feeling of the love of life may be compared to "one entire and perfect chrysolite," which, if analysed, breaks into a thousand shining fragments. Ask the sum-total of the value of human life, and we are puzzled with the length of the account, and the multiplicity of items in it : take any one of them apart, and it is wonderful what matter for reflection will be found in it ! As I write this, the *Letter-Bell* passes; it has a lively, pleasant sound with it, and not only fills the street with its importunate clamour, but rings clear through the length of many half-forgotten years. It strikes upon the ear, it vibrates to the brain, it wakes me from the dream of time, it flings me back upon my first entrance into life, the period of my first coming up to town, when all around was strange, uncertain, ad-

[1] There are few things more contemptible than the conversation of mere *men of the town*. It is made up of the technicalities and cant of all professions, without the spirit or knowledge of any. It is flashy and vapid, or is like the rinsings of different liquors at a night-cellar instead of a bottle of fine old port. It is without body or clearness, and a heap of affectation. In fact, I am very much of the opinion of that old Scotch gentleman who owned that " he preferred the dullest book he had ever read to the most brilliant conversation it had ever fallen to his lot to hear !"

verse—a hubbub of confused noises, a chaos of shifting objects—and when this sound alone, startling me with the recollection of a letter I had to send to the friends I had lately left, brought me as it were to myself, made me feel that I had links still connecting me with the universe, and gave me hope and patience to persevere. At that loud-tinkling, interrupted sound, the long line of blue hills near the place where I was brought up waves in the horizon,[1] a golden sunset hovers over them, the dwarf-oaks rustle their red leaves in the evening-breeze, and the road from Wem to Shrewsbury, by which I first set-out on my journey through life, stares me in the face as plain, but, from time and change, not less visionary and mysterious than the pictures in the *Pilgrim's Progress.* Or if the Letter-Bell does not lead me a dance into the country, it fixes me in the thick of my town recollections, I know not how long ago. It was a kind of alarm to break off from my work when there happened to be company to dinner or when I was going to the play. *That* was going to the play, indeed, when I went twice a year, and had not been more than half a dozen times in my life. Even the idea that any one else in the house was going, was a sort of reflected enjoyment, and conjured up a lively anticipation of the scene. I remember a Miss D——, a maiden lady from Wales (who in her youth was to have been married to an earl), tantalised me greatly in this way, by talking all day of going to see Mrs. Siddons' " airs and graces " at night in some favourite part; and when the Letter-Bell announced that the time was approaching, and its last receding sound lingered on the ear, or was lost in silence, how anxious and uneasy I became, lest she and her companion should not be in time to get good places— lest the curtain should draw up before they arrived—and lest I should lose one line or look in the intelligent report which I should hear the next morning! The punctuating

---

[1] Compare *Memoirs*, i. 32-3.—Ed.

of time at that early period—every thing that gives it an articulate voice—seems of the utmost consequence ; for we do not know what scenes in the *ideal* world may run out of them : a world of interest may hang upon every instant, and we can hardly sustain the weight of future years which are contained in embryo in the most minute and inconsiderable passing events. How often have I put off writing a letter till it was too late ! How often have I had to run after the postman with it—now missing, now recovering the sound of his bell—breathless, angry with myself—then hearing the welcome sound come full round a corner—and seeing the scarlet costume which set all my fears and self-reproaches at rest ! I do not recollect having ever repented giving a letter to the postman or wishing to retrieve it after he had once deposited it in his bag. What I have once set my hand to, I take the consequences of, and have been always pretty much of the same humour in this respect. I am not like the person who, having sent off a letter to his mistress, who resided a hundred and twenty miles in the country, and disapproving, on second thoughts, of some expressions contained in it, took a post-chaise and four to·follow and intercept it the next morning. At other times, I have sat and watched the decaying embers in a little back painting-room (just as the wintry day declined), and brooded over the half-finished copy of a Rembrandt, or a landscape by Vangoyen, placing it where it might catch a dim gleam of light from the fire ; while the Letter-Bell was the only sound that drew my thoughts to the world without, and reminded me that I had a task to perform in it. As to that landscape, methinks I see it now—

"The slow canal, the yellow-blossomed vale,
The willow-tufted bank, the gliding sail."

There was a windmill, too, with a poor low clay-built cottage beside it : how delighted I was when I had made the tremulous, undulating reflection in the water, and saw the dull canvas become a lucid mirror of the commonest features of nature! Certainly, painting gives one a strong interest in nature and humanity (it is not the *dandy-school* of morals or sentiment)—

> " While with an eye made quiet by the power
> Of harmony and the deep power of joy,
> We see into the life of things."

Perhaps there is no part of a painter's life (if we must tell " the secrets of the prison-house ") in which he has more enjoyment of himself and his art, than that in which, after his work is over, and with furtive, sidelong glances at what he has done, he is employed in washing his brushes and cleaning his pallet for the day. Afterwards, when he gets a servant in livery to do this for him, he may have other and more ostensible sources of satisfaction—greater splendour, wealth, or fame; but he will not be so wholly in his art, nor will his art have such a hold on him as when he was too poor to transfer its meanest drudgery to others—too humble to despise aught that had to do with the object of his glory and his pride, with that on which all his projects of ambition or pleasure were founded. " Entire affection scorneth nicer hands." When the professor is above this mechanical part of his business, it may have become a *stalking-horse* to other worldly schemes, but is no longer his *hobby-horse* and the delight of his inmost thoughts.

I used sometimes to hurry through this part of my occupation, while the Letter-Bell (which was my dinner-bell) summoned me to the fraternal board, where youth and hope

> " Made good digestion wait on appetite
> And health on both ;"

or oftener I put it off till after dinner, that I might loiter longer and with more luxurious indolence over it, and connect it with the thoughts of my next day's labours.

The dustman's-bell, with its heavy monotonous noise,

and the brisk, lively tinkle of the muffin-bell, have something in them, but not much. They will bear dilating upon with the utmost licence of inventive prose. All things are not alike *conductors* to the imagination. A learned Scotch professor found fault with an ingenious friend and arch-critic for cultivating a rookery on his grounds : the professor declared " he would as soon think of encouraging a *froggery*." This was barbarous as it was senseless. Strange, that a country that has produced the *Scotch Novels* and *Gertrude of Wyoming* should want sentiment !

The postman's double knock at the door the next morning is " more germain to the matter." How that knock often goes to the heart ! We distinguish to a nicety the arrival of the Twopenny or the General Post. The summons of the latter is louder and heavier, as bringing news from a greater distance, and as, the longer it has been delayed, fraught with a deeper interest. We catch the sound of what is to be paid — eightpence, ninepence, a shilling — and our hopes generally rise with the postage. How we are provoked at the delay in getting change — at the servant who does not hear the door ! Then if the postman passes, and we do not hear the expected knock, what a pang is there ! It is like the silence of death — of hope ! We think he does it on purpose, and enjoys all the misery of our suspense. I have sometimes walked out to see the Mail-Coach pass, by which I had sent a letter, or to meet it when I expected one. I never see a Mail-Coach, for this reason, but I look at it as the bearer of glad tidings — the messenger of fate. I have reason to say so. The finest sight in the metropolis is that of the Mail-Coaches setting off from Piccadilly. The horses paw the ground, and are impatient to be gone, as if conscious of the precious burden they convey. There is a peculiar secrecy and despatch, significant and full of meaning, in all the proceedings concerning them. Even the outside passengers have an erect and supercilious air, s if proof against the accidents of the journey. In fact, it seems indifferent whether they are to encounter the summer's heat or winter's cold, since they are borne on through the air in a winged chariot. The Mail-Carts drive up; the transfer of packages is made; and, at a signal given, they start off, bearing the irrevocable scrolls that give wings to thought, and that bind or sever hearts for ever. How we hate the Putney and Brentford stages that draw up in a line after they are gone! Some persons think the sublimest object in nature is a ship launched on the bosom of the ocean; but give me, for my private satisfaction, the Mail-Coaches that pour down Piccadilly of an evening, tear up the pavement, and devour the way before them to the Land's-End!

In Cowper's time, Mail-Coaches were hardly set up; but he has beautifully described the coming-in of the Post-Boy:—

> " Hark! 'tis the twanging horn o'er yonder bridge,
> That with its wearisome but needful length
> Bestrides the wintry flood, in which the moon
> Sees her unwrinkled face reflected bright:
> He comes, the herald of a noisy world,
> With spattered boots, strapped waist, and frozen locks;
> News from all nations lumbering at his back.
> True to his charge, the close-packed load behind.
> Yet careless what he brings, his one concern
> Is to conduct it to the destined inn;
> And having dropped the expected bag, pass on.
> He whistles as he goes, light-hearted wretch!
> Cold and yet cheerful; messenger of grief
> Perhaps to thousands, and of joy to some;
> To him indifferent whether grief or joy.
> Houses in ashes and the fall of stocks,
> Births, deaths, and marriages, epistles wet
> With tears that trickled down the writer's cheeks
> Fast as the periods from his fluent quill,
> Or charged with amorous sighs of absent swains
> Or nymphs responsive, equally affect
> His horse and him, unconscious of them all."

And yet, notwithstanding this, and so many other passages that seem like the very marrow of our being. Lord Byron denies that Cowper was a poet!—The Mail-Coach is an improvement on the Post-Boy ; but I fear it will hardly bear so poetical a description. The picturesque and dramatic do not keep pace with the useful and mechanical. The telegraphs that lately communicated the intelligence of the new revolution to all France within a few hours, are a wonderful contrivance ; but they are less striking and appalling than the beacon-fires (mentioned by Æschylus), which, lighted from hill top to hill top, announced the taking of Troy, and the return of Agamemnon.

Envy.[1]

ENVY is the *grudging* or receiving pain from any accomplishment or advantage possessed by another. It is one of the most tormenting and odious of the passions, inasmuch as it does not consist in the enjoyment or pursuit of any good to ourselves, but in the hatred and jealousy of the good fortune of others, and the debarring and defrauding them of their due and what is of no use to us, on the *dog in the manger* principle ; and it is at the same time as mean as it is revolting, as being accompanied with a sense of weakness, and a desire to conceal and tamper with the truth and its own convictions, out of paltry spite and vanity. It is, however, but an excess or excrescence of the other passions (such as pride or avarice), or of a wish to monopolise all the good things of life to ourselves, which makes us impatient and dissatisfied at seeing any one else in possession of that to which we think we have the only fair title. Envy is the deformed and distorted offspring of *egotism ;* and when we reflect on

[1] Another and different paper on this subject will be found in *The Plain Speaker*, 1826 [edit. 1870, pp. 132-47].—ED.

the strange and disproportioned character of the parent, we cannot wonder at the perversity and waywardness of the child. Such is the absorbing and exorbitant quality of our self-love, that it represents us as of infinitely more importance in our own eyes than the whole universe put together, and would sacrifice the claims and interest of all the world beside to the least of its caprices or extravagances : need we be surprised, then, that this little, upstart, overweening self, that would trample on the globe itself, and then weep for new ones to conquer, should be uneasy, mad, mortified, eaten up with chagrin and melancholy, and hardly able to bear its own existence, at seeing a simple competitor among the crowd cross its path, jostle its pretensions, and stagger its opinion of its exclusive right to admiration and superiority ? This it is that constitutes the offence, that gives the shock, that inflicts the wound, that some poor creature (as we would fain suppose) whom we had before overlooked and entirely disregarded as not worth our notice, should of a sudden enter the lists and challenge comparison with us. The presumption is excessive; and so is our thirst of revenge. From the moment, however, that the eye fixes on another as the object of envy, we cannot take it off; for our pride and self-conceit magnify that which obstructs our success and lessens our self-importance into a monster; we see nothing else, we hear of nothing else, we dream of nothing else; it haunts us and takes possession of our whole souls; and as we are engrossed by it ourselves, so we fancy that all the rest of the world are equally taken up with our petty annoyances and disappointed pride. Hence the "jealous leer malign" of envy, which, not daring to look that which provokes it in the face, cannot yet keep its eyes from it, and gloats over and becomes as it were enamoured of the very object of its loathing and deadly hate. We pay off the score which our littleness and vanity has been running up, by ample and gratuitous concessions to the first person that gives a check to our swelling self-complacency, and forces us to drag him into an unwilling comparison with ourselves. It is no matter who the person is, or what his pretensions—if they are a counterpoise to our own, we think them of more consequence than anything else in the world. This often gives rise to laughable results. We see the jealousies among servants, hackney-coachmen, cobblers in a stall: we are amused with the rival advertisements of quacks and stage-coach proprietors, and smile to read the significant intimation on some shop window, " No connection with next door;" but the same folly runs through the whole of life; each person thinks that he who stands in his way or outstrips him in a particular pursuit, is the most enviable, and at the same time the most hateful character in the world. Nothing can show the absurdity of the passion of envy in a more striking point of view than the number of rival claims which it entirely overlooks, while it would arrogate all excellence to itself. The loftiness of our ambition and the narrowness of our views are equal, and, indeed, both depend upon the same cause. The player envies only the player, the poet envies only the poet, because each confines his idea of excellence to his own profession and pursuit, and thinks, if he could but remove some one particular competitor out of his way, he should have a clear stage to himself, and be a " Phœnix gazed by all :" as if, though we crushed one rival, another would not start up; or as if there were not a thousand other claims, a thousand other modes of excellence and praiseworthy acquirements, to divide the palm and defeat his idle pretension to the sole and unqualified admiration of mankind. Professors of every class see merit only in their own line; yet they would blight and destroy that *little bit* of excellence which alone they acknowledge to exist, except as it centres in themselves. Speak in praise of an actor to another actor, and he turns away with

impatience and disgust: speak disparagingly of the first
as an actor in general, and the latter eagerly takes up the
quarrel as his own: thus the *esprit de corps* only comes in
as an appendage to our self-love. It is, perhaps, well
that we are so blind to merit out of our immediate sphere,
for it might only prove an additional *eye-sore*, increase the
obliquity of our mental vision, multiply our antipathies,
or end in total indifference and despair. There is nothing
so bad as a cynical apathy and contempt for every art and
science from a superficial *smattering* and general acquaintance with them all. The merest pedantry and the
most tormenting jealousy and heart-burning of envy are
better than this. Those who are masters of different
advantages and accomplishments are seldom the more
satisfied with them: they still aim at something else
(however contemptible) which they have not or cannot do.
So Pope says of Wharton—

> " Though wondering senates hung on all he spoke,
>   The club must hail him master of the joke.
>   Shall parts so various aim at nothing new?
>   He'll shine a Tully and a Wilmot too."

The world, indeed, are pretty even with these constel-
lations of splendid and superfluous qualities in their
fastidious estimate of their own pretensions, for (if possible) they never give any individual credit for more than
one leading attainment, if that. If a man is an artist, his
being a fine musician adds nothing to his fame. When
the public strain a point to own one claim, it is on condition that the fortunate candidate waves every other.
The mind is prepared with a plausible antithesis in such
cases against the formidable encroachment of vanity: one
qualification is regularly made a foil to another. We
allow no one to be two things at a time: it quite unsettles
our notion of personal identity. If we allow a man wit,
it is part of the bargain that he wants judgment: if style,

he wants matter. Rich, but a fool or miser: a beauty, but vain, and no better than she should be;—*so runs the bond.* "But" is the favourite monosyllable of envy and self-love. Raphael could draw and Titian could colour: we shall never get beyond these points while the world stands; the human understanding is not cast in a mould to receive double proofs of entire superiority to itself. It is folly to expect it. If a further claim be set up, we call in question the solidity of the first, incline to retract it, and suspect that the whole is a juggle and a piece of impudence, as we threaten a common beggar with the stocks for following us to ask a second alms. This is, in fact, one source of the prevalence and deep root which envy has in the human mind: we are incredulous as to the truth and justice of the demands which are so often made upon our pity or our admiration; but let the distress or the merit be established beyond all controversy, and we open our hearts and purses on the spot, and sometimes run into the contrary extreme when charity or admiration becomes the fashion. No one envies the Author of *Waverley*, because all admire him, and are sensible that admire him as they will, they can never admire him enough. We do not envy the sun for shining when we feel the warmth and see the light. When some persons start an injudicious parallel between Sir Walter and Shakspeare, we then may grow jealous and uneasy, because this interferes with our older and more firmly-rooted conviction of genius, and one which has stood a surer and severer test. Envy has, then, some connection with a sense of justice—it is a defence against imposture and quackery. Though we do not willingly give up the secret and silent consciousness of our own worth to vapouring and false pretences, we do homage to the true candidate for fame when he appears, and even exult and take a pride in our capacity to appreciate the highest desert. This is one reason why we do not envy the dead—less because they are removed out of our way, than because all doubt and diversity of opinion is dismissed from the question of their title to veneration and respect. Our tongue, having a licence, grows wanton in their praise. We do not envy or stint our admiration of Rubens, because the mists of uncertainty or prejudice are withdrawn by the hand of time from the splendour of his works. Fame is to genius

> ——" Like a gate of steel,
> Fronting the sun, receives and renders back
> His figure and his heat."

We give full and unbounded scope to our impressions when they are confirmed by successive generations, as we form our opinions coldly and slowly while we are afraid our judgment may be reversed by posterity. We trust the testimony of ages, for it is true; we are no longer in pain lest we should be deceived by varnish and tinsel, and feel assured that the praise and the work are both sterling. In contemporary reputation, the greater and more transcendent the merit, the less is the envy attending it, which shows that this passion is not, after all, a mere barefaced hatred and detraction from acknowledged excellence. Mrs. Siddons was not an object of envy; her unrivalled powers defied competition or gainsayers. If Kean had a party against him, it was composed of those who could not or would not see his merits through his defects; and, in like manner, John Kemble's elevation to the tragic throne was not carried by loud and tumultuous acclamation, because the stately height which he attained was the gradual result of labour and study, and his style of acting did not flash with the inspiration of the god. We are backward to bestow a heaped measure of praise whenever there is any inaptitude or incongruity that acts to damp or throw a stumbling-block in the way of our enthusiasm. Hence the jealousy and dislike shown towards upstart wealth, as we cannot in our imaginations reconcile the

former poverty of the possessors with their present magnificence—we despise fortune-hunters in ambition as well
as in love—and hence, no doubt, one strong ground of
hereditary right. We acquiesce more readily in an
assumption of superiority that in the first place implies
no merit (which is a great relief to the baser sort), and in
the second, that baffles opposition by seeming a thing
inevitable, taken for granted, and transmitted in the
common course of nature. In contested elections, where
the precedence is understood to be awarded to rank and
title, there is observed to be less acrimony and obstinacy
than when it is supposed to depend on individual merit
and fitness for the office ; no one willingly allows
another more ability or honesty than himself, but he cannot deny that another may be better born. Learning.
again, is more freely admitted than genius, because it is
of a more positive quality, and is felt to be less essentially
a part of a man's self ; and with regard to the grosser and
more invidious distinction of wealth, it may be difficult to
substitute any finer test of respectability for it, since it is
hard to fathom the depth of a man's understanding, but
the length of his purse is soon known ; and besides there
is a little collusion in the case.

"The learned pate ducks to the golden fool."

We bow to a patron who gives us a good dinner and his
countenance for our pains, and interest bribes and lulls
envy asleep. The most painful kind of envy is the envy
towards inferiors ; for we cannot bear to think that a
person (in other respects utterly insignificant) should have
or seem to have an advantage over us in anything we have
set our hearts upon, and it strikes at the very root of
our self-love to be foiled by those we despise. There
is some dignity in a contest with power and acknowledged reputation ; but a triumph over the sordid and the
mean is itself a mortification, while a defeat is intolerable.

On the Spirit of Partisanship.[1]

I HAVE in my time known few thorough partisans, at least on my own side of the question. I conceive, however, that the honestest and strongest-minded men have been so. In general, interest, fear, vanity, the love of contradiction, even a scrupulous regard to truth and justice, come to divert them from the popular cause. It is a character that requires very opposite and almost incompatible qualities—reason and prejudice, a passionate attachment founded on an abstract idea. He who can take up a speculative question, and pursue it with the same zeal and unshaken constancy that he does his immediate interests or private animosities—he who is as faithful to his principles as he is to himself, is the true partisan. I do not here speak of the bigot, or the mercenary or cowardly tool of a party. There are plenty of this description of persons (a considerable majority of the inhabitants of every country)—who are " ever strong upon the stronger side," staunch, thorough-paced sticklers for their passions and prejudices, and who stand by their party as long as their party can stand by them. I speak of those who espouse a cause from liberal motives and with liberal views, and of the obstacles that are so often found to relax their perseverance or impair their zeal. These may, I think, be reduced chiefly to the heads of obligations to friends, of vanity, or the desire of the lead and distinction, to an over-squeamish delicacy in regard to appearances, to fickleness of purpose, or to natural timidity and weakness of nerve.

There is nothing more contemptible than party-spirit in one point of view; and yet it seems inseparable in practice from public principle. You cannot support

[1] Written in 1820.

measures unless you support men; you cannot carry any point or maintain any system without acting in concert with others. In theory, it is all very well. We may refine in our distinctions, and elevate our language to what point we please. But in carrying the most sounding words and stateliest propositions into effect, we must make use of the instrumentality of men; and some of the alloy and imperfection of the means may insinuate itself into the end. If we do not go all lengths with those who are embarked with us in the same views; if we are not hearty in the defence of their interests and motives; if we are not fully in their confidence and they in ours; if we do not ingraft on the stock of public virtue the charities and sentiments of private affection and esteem; if the bustle and anxiety and irritation of the state-affairs do not kindle into the glow of friendship, as well as patriotism; if we look distant, suspicious, lukewarm at one another; if we criticise, carp at, pry into the conduct of our party with watchful, jealous eyes; it is to be feared we shall play the game into the enemy's hands, and not co-operate together for the common good with all the steadiness and cordiality that might be wished. On the other hand, if we lend ourselves to the foibles and weaknesses of our friends; if we suffer ourselves to be implicated in their intrigues, their scrambles and bargainings for place and power; if we flatter their mistakes, and not only screen them from the eyes of others, but are blind to them ourselves; if we compromise a great principle in the softness of a womanish friendship; if we entangle ourselves in needless family ties; if we sell ourselves to the vices of a patron, or become the mouthpiece and echo of a *coterie;* we shall be in that case slaves of a faction, not servants of the public, nor shall we long have a spark of the old Roman or the old English virtue left. Good-nature, conviviality, hospitality, habits of acquaintance and regard, favours received or conferred,

spirit and eloquence to defend a friend when pressed hard
upon, courtesy and good-breeding, are one thing—
patriotism, firmness of principle, are another.   The true
patriot knows when to make each of these in turn give
way to or control the other, in furtherance of the common
good, just as the accomplished courtier makes all other
interests, friendships, cabals, resentments, reconciliations,
subservient to his attachment to the person of the king.
He has the welfare of his country, the cause of mankind
at heart, and makes that the scale in which all other
motives are weighed as in a balance.   With this inward
prompter he knows when to speak and when to hold his
tongue, when to temporise, and when to throw away the
scabbard, when to make men of service to principles, and
when to make principles the sole condition of popularity
—nearly as well as if he had a title or a pension depending in reversion on his success : for it is true that
" in their generation the children of this world are wiser
than the children of light."   In my opinion, Charles Fox
had too much of what we mean by " the milk of human
kindness " to be a practical statesman, particularly in
critical times, and with a cause of infinite magnitude at
stake.   He was too easy a friend, and too generous an
enemy.   He was willing to think better of those with
whom he acted, or to whom he was opposed, than they
deserved.   He was the creature of temperament and
sympathy, and suffered his feelings to be played upon,
and to get the better of his principles, which were not
of the most rigid kind—not " stuff o' the conscience."
With all the power of the crown, and all the strongholds
of prejudice and venality opposed to him, " instead of a
softness coming over the heart of a man," he should (in
such a situation) have " turned to the stroke his adamantine scales that feared no discipline of human hands,"
and made it a struggle *ad internecionem* on the one side,
as it was on the other.   There was no place for

moderation, much less for huckstering and trimming.
Mr. Burke saw the thing right enough. It was a question
about a principle—about the existence or extinction of
human rights in the abstract. He was on the side of
legitimate slavery; Mr. Fox on that of natural liberty.
That was no reason he should be less bold or jealous
in her defence, because he had everything to contend
against. But he made too many coalitions, too many com-
promises with flattery, with friendship (to say nothing
of the baits of power), not to falter and be defeated at
last in the noble stand he had made for the principles of
freedom.

Another sort are as much too captious and precise, as
these are lax and *cullible* in their notions of political
warfare. Their fault is an overweening egotism, as that
of the former was too great a facility of temper. They
will have everything their own way to the minutest tittle,
or they cannot think of giving it their sanction and
support. The cause must come to them, they will not
go to the cause. They stand upon their punctilio. They
have a character at stake, which is dearer to them than
the whole world. They have an idea of perfect truth
and beauty in their own minds, the contemplation of
which is a never-failing source of delight and consolation
to them,

"Though sun and moon were in the flat sea sunk,"

and which they will not soil by mixing it up with the
infirmities of any cause or any party. They will not,
"to do a great right, do a little wrong." They will let
the lofty pillar inscribed to human liberty fall to the
ground sooner than extend a finger to save it, on account
of the dust and cobwebs that cling to it. It is not this
great and mighty object they are thinking of all the
time, but their own fantastic reputation and puny pretensions. While the world is tumbling about our ears,

Q

and the last hold of liberty, the ark containing our birthright, the only possible barrier against bare-faced tyranny, is tottering—instead of setting the engines and the mortal instruments at work to prop it, and fighting in the trenches to the last drop, they are washing their hands of all imaginary imperfections, and looking in the glass of their own vanity, with an air of heightened self-complacency. Alas! they do not foresee the fatal consequences; they have an eye only to themselves. While all the power, the prejudice, and ignorance of mankind are drawn up in deadly array against the advance of truth and justice, they owe it to themselves, forsooth! to state the naked merits of the question (heat and passion apart), and pick out all the faults of which their own party has been guilty, to fling as a make-weight into the adversary's scale of unmeasured abuse and execration. They will not take their ready stand by the side of him who was "the very arm and burgonet of man," and like a demi-Atlas, could alone prop a declining world, because for themselves they have some objections to the individual instrument, and they think principles more important than persons. No, they think persons of more consequence than principles, and themselves most of all. They injure the principle through the person most able to protect it. They betray the cause by not defending it as it is attacked, tooth and nail, might and main, without exception and without remorse. When everything is at stake, dear and valuable to man, as man; when there is but the one dreadful alternative of entire loss, or final recovery of truth and freedom, it is no time to stand upon trifles and moot-points: the great object is to be secured first, and at all hazards.

But there is a third thing in their minds, a fanciful something which they prefer to both contending parties. It may be so; but neither they nor we can get it. We must have one of the two things imposed upon us, not by choice but by hard necessity. "Our bane and antidote are both before us;" and if we do anything to neglect the one, we justly incur the heavy, intolerable, unredeemed penalty of the other. If our pride is stung, if we have received a blow or the lie in our own persons, we know well enough what to do: our blood is up, we have an actual feeling and object to satisfy; and we are not to be diverted from our purpose by sophistry or mere words. The quarrel is personal to ourselves; and we feel the whole stress of it, rousing every faculty and straining every nerve. But if the quarrel is general to mankind; if it is one in which the rights, freedom, hopes, and happiness of the whole world are embarked; if we see the dignity of our common nature prostrate, trampled upon and mangled before the brute image of power, this gives us little concern; our reason may disapprove, but our passions, our prejudices, are not touched; and therefore our reason, our humanity, our abstract love of right (not "screwed to the sticking-place" by some paltry interest of our own) are easily satisfied with any hollow professions of good-will, or put off with vague excuses, or staggered with open defiance. We are here, where a principle only is in danger, at leisure to calculate consequences, prudently for ourselves, or favourably for others: were it a point of honour (we think the honour of human nature is not our honour, that its disgrace is not our disgrace—we are not the *rabble!*) we should throw consideration and compassion to the dogs, and cry—"Away to heaven respective lenity, and fire-eyed fury be my conduct now!" But charity is cold. We are the dupes of the flatteries of our opponents, because we are indifferent to our own object: we stand in awe of their threats, because in the absence of passion we are tender of our persons. They beat us in courage and in intellect, because we have nothing but the common good to sharpen our faculties or goad our will; they have no

less an alternative in view than to be uncontrolled masters
of mankind, or to be hurled from high—

> " To grinning scorn a sacrifice,
> And endless infamy !"

They do not celebrate the triumphs of their enemies as
their own : it is with them a more feeling disputation.
They never give an inch of ground that they can keep ;
they keep all that they can get ; they make no concessions
that can redound to their own discredit; they assume all
that makes for them ; if they pause it is to gain time ;
if they offer terms it is to break them : they keep no faith
with enemies : if you relax in your exertions, they persevere the more : if you make new efforts, they redouble
theirs.   While they give no quarter, you stand upon more
ceremony.   While they are cutting your throat, or putting
the gag in your mouth, you talk of nothing but liberality,
freedom of inquiry, and *douce humanité.* Their object is to
destroy you, your object is to spare them—to treat them
according to your own fancied dignity. They have sense
and spirit enough to take all advantages that will further
their cause : you have pedantry and pusillanimity enough
to undertake the defence of yours, in order to defeat it.
It is the difference between the efficient and the inefficient; and this again resolves itself into the difference
between a speculative proposition and a practical interest.
    One thing that makes tyrants bold is, that they have
the power to justify their wrong. They lay their hands
upon the sword, and ask who will dispute their commands.
The friends of humanity and justice have not in general
this ark of confidence to recur to, and can only appeal to
reason and propriety. They oppose power on the plea of
right and conscience; and shall they, in pursuance of
their claims, violate in the smallest tittle what is due to
truth and justice ? So that the one have no law but their
wills, and the absolute extent of their authority, in attain-

ing or securing their ends, because they make no preten
sions to scrupulous delicacy : the others are cooped and
cabined in by all sorts of nice investigations in philosophy,
and misgivings of the moral sense ; that is, are deprived
or curtailed of the means of succeeding in their ends,
because those ends are not bare-faced violence and wrong.
It might as well be said that a man has a right to knock
me on the head on the highway, and that I am only to
use mildness and persuasion in return, as best suited to
the justice of my cause ; as that I am not to retaliate
and make reprisals on the common enemies of mankind
in their own style and mode of execution. Is not a man
to defend his liberty, or the liberties of his fellow men,
as strenuously and remorselessly as he would his life or
his purse ? Men are Quakers in political principle, Turks
and Jews in private conscience.

The whole is an error arising from confounding the
distinction between theory and practice, between the still-
life of letters and the tug and onset of contending factions.
I might recommend to our political mediators the advice
which *Henry V.* addressed to his soldiers on a critical
occasion :—

> "In peace there's nothing so becomes a man
>   As modest stillness and humility ;
>   But when the blast of war blows in our ears,
>   Then imitate the action of the tiger ;
>   Stiffen the sinews, summon up the blood,
>   Disguise fair nature with hard-favour'd rage ;
>   Then lend the eye a terrible aspèct ;
>   Let it pry through the portage of the head,
>   Like the brass-cannon : let the brow o'erwhelm it
>   As fearfully as doth a gallèd rock
>   O'erhang and jutty his confounded base,
>   Swill'd with the wild and wasteful ocean :
>   Now set the teeth, and stretch the nostril wide ;
>   Hold hard the breath, and bend up every spirit
>   To his full height."[1]

---

[1] *Henry V.*, iii. 1 [edit. *ut supra*].

So, in speculation refine as much as you please, intellectually and morally speaking, and you may do it with advantage. Reason is then the instrument you use, and you cannot raise the standard of perfection you fix upon and propose to others too high, or proceed with too much candour and moderation in the advancement of truth : but in practice you have not your choice of ends or means. You have two things to decide between, the extreme, probably, of an evil and a considerable good ; and if you will not make your mind up to take the best of the two with all its disadvantages and drawbacks, you must be contented to take the worst : for as you cannot alter the state of the conflicting parties who are carrying their point by force, or dictate what is best by a word speaking ; so by finding fault with the attainable good, and throwing cold water on it, you add fuel to your enemy's courage and assist his success. " Those who are not for us are against us." You create a diversion in his favour, by distracting and enervating men's minds, as much as by questioning the general's orders, or drawing off a strong detachment in the heat of a battle. Political is like military warfare. There are but two sides ; and after you have once chosen your party, it will not do to stand in the midway, and say you like neither. There is no other to like, in the eye of common sense, or in the practical and inevitable result of the thing. As active partisans, we must take up with the best we can get in the circumstances, and defend it with all our might against a worse cause (which will prevail, if this does not), instead of " letting our frail thoughts dally with faint surmise ;" or, while dreaming of an ideal perfection, we shall find ourselves surprised into the train, and gracing the triumph, of the common enemy. It is sufficient if our objects and principles are sound and disinterested. If we were engaged in a friendly contest, where integrity and fair dealing were the order of the day, our means might be as unimpeachable as our ends ; but in a struggle with the passions, interests, and prejudices of men, right reason, pure intention, are hardly competent to carry us through : we want another stimulus. The vices may be opposed to each other sometimes with advantage and propriety. A little of the alloy of human frailty may be allowed to lend its aid to the service of humanity; and if we have only so much obstinacy or insensibility as enables us to persevere in the path of public duty with more determination and effect, both our motives and conduct will be above the ordinary standard of political morality. To suppose that we can do much more than this, or that we can set up our individual opinion of what is best in itself, or of the best means of attaining it, and be listened to by the world at large, is egregiously to overrate their docility or our own powers of persuasion.

It is the same want of a centripetal force, of a ruling passion, of a moral instinct of union and co-operation for a general purpose, that makes men fly off into knots and factions, and each set up for the leader of a party himself. Where there is a strong feeling of interest at work, it reconciles and combines the most discordant materials, and fits them to their place in the social machine. But in the conduct and support of the public good, we see "nothing but vanity, chaotic vanity." There is no forbearance, no self-denial, no magnanimity of proceeding. Every one is seeking his own aggrandisement, or to supplant his neighbour, instead of advancing the popular cause. It is because they have no real regard for it but as it serves as a stalking horse to their ambition, restless inquietude, or love of cabal. They abuse and vilify their own party, just as they do the ministers.

> " Each lolls his tongue out at the other,
>   And shakes his empty noddle at his brother."

John Bull does not aim so maliciously, or hit so hard at

Whigs and Reformers, as Cobbett. The reason is, that a very large proportion of these Marplots and regenerators of the world are actuated by no love of their species or zeal for a general question, but by envy, malice, and all uncharitableness. They are discontented with themselves and with everything about them. They object to, they dissent from every measure. Nothing pleases their fastidious tastes. For want of something to exercise their ill-humour and troublesome officiousness upon, they abuse the government: when they are baulked or tired of this they fall foul of one another. The slightest slip or difference of opinion is never forgiven, but gives birth to a deadly feud. Touch but their petty self-importance, and out comes a flaming denunciation of their own cabal, and all they know about the individuals composing it. This is not patriotism but spleen—a want of something to do and to talk about—of sense, honesty, and feeling. To wreak their spite on an individual, they will ruin the cause, and serve up the friend and idol of the people sliced and carbonadoed, a delicious mortal to the other side. There is a strange want of keeping in this. They are true neither to themselves nor to their principles. The Reformers are in general, it must be confessed, an ill-conditioned set; and they should be told of this infirmity that most easily besets them. When they find their gall and bitterness overflowing on the very persons who take the lead, and deservedly take the lead, in their affairs, for some slight flaw or misunderstanding, they should be taught to hold their tongues, or be drummed out of the regiment as spies and informers.

Trimming, and want of spirit to declare the honest truth, arise in part from the same source. When a man is not thoroughly convinced of an opinion, or where he does not feel a deep interest in it, he does not like to make himself obnoxious by avowing it; is willing to make all the allowance he can for difference of sentiment, and consults his own safety by retiring from a sinking cause. This is the very time when the genuine partisan, who has a rooted attachment to a principle, and feels it as a part of himself, finds himself most called upon to come forward in its support. His anxiety for truth and justice leaves him in no fear for himself, and the sincerity of his motives makes him regardless of censure or obloquy. His profession of hearty devotion to freedom was not an ebullition called forth by the sunshine of prosperity, a lure for popularity and public favour; and when these desert it, he still maintains his post with his integrity. There is a natural timidity of mind, also, which can never go the whole length of any opinion, but is always interlarding its qualified assent with unmeaning *buts* and *ifs;* as there is a levity and discursiveness of imagination which cannot settle finally in any belief, and requires a succession of glancing views, topics, and opposite conclusions, to satisfy its appetite for intellectual variety. I have known persons leave the cause of independence and freedom, not because they found it unprofitable, but because they found it flat and stale for want of novelty. At the same time, interest is a great stimulator; and perhaps the success of their early principles might have reconciled them to their embarrassing monotony. Few persons have strength and simplicity of mind (without some additional inducement) to be always harping on the same string, or to put up with the legitimate variety to be found in an abstract principle, applicable to all emergencies. They like changeable silks better than lasting homespun. A sensible man once mentioned to me his having called on —— that morning, who entertained with him a *tirade* against the Bourbons for two hours; but he said he did not at all feel convinced that he might not have been writing ultra-royalist paragraphs for the ——, just, before he came, in their favour, and only shifted his side of the argument, as a man who is tired of lying too long on one side of his body is glad to turn to the other. There was much shrewdness, and equal probability in this conjecture.

I think the spirit of partisanship is of use in a point of view that has not been distinctly adverted to. It serves as a conductor to carry off our antipathies and ill-blood in a quarter and a manner that is least hurtful to the general weal. A thorough partisan is a good hater; but he hates only one side of a question, and that the *outside*. His bigotry throws human nature into strong light and shade; he has his sympathies as well as his antipathies; it is not all black or a dull drab-colour. He does not generalise in his contempt or disgust, or proceed from individuals to universals. He lays the faults and vices of mankind to the account of sects and parties, creeds and classes. Man in himself is a good sort of animal. It is the being a Tory or a Whig (as it may happen) that makes a man a knave or fool; but then we hardly look upon him as of the same species with ourselves. Kings are not arbitrary, nor priests hypocritical, because they are men, but because they are kings and priests. We form certain nominal abstractions of these classes, which the more we dislike them the less natural do they seem, and leave the general character of the species untouched, or act as a foil to it. There is nothing that is a greater damper to party spirit than to suggest that the errors and enormities of both sides arise from certain inherent dispositions common to the species. It shocks the liberal and enlightened among us, to suppose that under any circumstances they could become bigots, tools, persecutors. They wipe their hands clean of all such aspersions. There is a great gulf of prejudice and passion placed between us and our opponents; and this is interpreted into a natural barrier and separation of sentiment and feeling. "Our withers are unwrung." Burke represented modern revolutionists to himself under the equivocal similitude of " green-eyed,

spring-nailed, velvet-pawed philosophers, whether going
on two legs or on four;" and thus removed to a distance
from his own person all the ill attributes with which he
had complimented the thorough-bred metaphysician. By
comparing the plausible qualities of a minister of state to
the sleekness of the panther, I myself seem to have no
more affinity with that whole genus, than with the
whiskers and claws of that formidable and spirited
animal. Bishop Taylor used to reprimand his rising
pride by saying, at the sight of a reprobate, " There goes
my wicked self:" we do not apply the same method
politically, and say, " There goes my Tory or my Jacobin
self." We suppose the two things incompatible. The
Calvinist damns the Arminian, the Protestant the Papist,
&c., but it is not for a difference of nature, but an opposition of opinion. The spirit of partisanship is not a
spirit of our misanthropy. But for the vices and errors
of example and institution, mankind are (on this principle)
only a little lower than the angels; it is false doctrine
and absurd prejudices that make demons of them. The
only original sin is differing in opinion with us: of that
they are curable like any occasional disorder, and the
man comes out, from beneath the husk of his party
and prejudices, pure and immaculate. Make proselytes of
them, let them come over to our way of thinking, and they
are a different race of beings quite. This is to be effected
by the force of argument and the progress of knowledge.
It is well, it is perfectly well. We cast the slough of our
vices with the shibboleth of our party; a real Reform in
Parliament would banish all knavery and folly from the
land. It is not the same wretched little mischievous
animal, man, that is alike under all denominations and all
systems, and in whom different situations and notions only
bring out different inherent, incorrigible vices and propensities; but the professions and the theory being
changed for the one which we think the only true and

infallible one, the whole world, by the mere removal of our arbitrary prejudices and modes of thinking, would become as sincere, as benevolent, as independent, and as worthy people as we are! To hate and proscribe half the species under various pretexts and nicknames, seems, therefore, the only way to entertain a good opinion of ourselves and mankind in general.

Footmen.

FOOTMEN are no part of Christianity; but they are a very necessary appendage to our happy Constitution in Church and State. What would the bishop's mitre be without these grave supporters to his dignity? Even the plain presbyter does not dispense with his decent serving-man to stand behind his chair and load his duly emptied plate with beef and pudding, at which the genius of Ude turns pale. What would become of the coronet-coach filled with elegant and languid forms, if it were not for the triple row of powdered, laced, and liveried footmen, clustering, fluttering, and lounging behind it? What an idea do we not conceive of the fashionable *belle*, who is making the most of her time and tumbling over silks and satins within at Howell and James's, or at the Bazaar in Soho-square, from the tall lacquey in blue and silver with gold-headed cane, cocked-hat, white thread stockings and large calves to his legs, who stands as her representative without! The sleek shopman appears at the door, at an understood signal the livery-servant starts from his position, the coach-door flies open, the steps are let down, the young lady enters the carriage as young ladies are taught to step into carriages, the footman closes the door, mounts behind, and the glossy vehicle rolls off, bearing its lovely burden and her gaudy attendant from the gaze of the gaping crowd! Is there not a spell in beauty, a charm in rank and fashion, that one would almost wish to be this fellow—to obey its nod, to watch its looks, to breathe but by its permission, and to live but for its use, its scorn, or pride ?

Footmen are in general looked upon as a sort of super-numeraries in society—they have no place assigned them in any Encyclopædia—they do not come under any of the heads in Mr. Mill's *Elements,* or Mr. Macculloch's *Principles of Political Economy;* and they nowhere have had im-partial justice done them, except in Lady Booby's love for one of that order. But if not " the Corinthian capitals of polished society," they are " a graceful ornament to the civil order." Lords and ladies could not do without them. Nothing exists in this world but by contrast. A foil is necessary to make the plainest truths self-evident. It is the very insignificance, the nonentity, as it were, of the gentlemen of the cloth, that constitutes their importance, and makes them an indispensable feature in the social sys-tem, by setting off the pretensions of their superiors to the best advantage. What would be the good of having a will of our own, if we had not others about us who are deprived of all will of their own, and who wear a badge to say, " I serve ? " How can we show that we are the lords of the creation but by reducing others to the condition of machines, who never move but at the beck of our caprices ? Is not the plain suit of the master wonderfully relieved by the borrowed trappings and mock-finery of his servant ? You see that man on horseback who keeps at some distance behind another, who follows him as his shadow, turns as he turns, and as he passes or speaks to him, lifts his hand to his hat and observes the most profound attention —what is the difference between these two men ? The one is as well mounted, as well fed, is younger and seemingly in better health than the other ; but between these two there are perhaps seven or eight classes of society each of whom is dependent on and trembles at the frown of the other—it is a nobleman and his lacquey. Let any one take a stroll towards the West-end of the town, South Audley or Upper Grosvenor-streets; it is then he will feel himself first entering into the *beau ideal* of civilised life, a society composed entirely of lords and footmen! Deliver me from the filth and cellars of St. Giles's, from the shops of Holborn and the Strand, from all that appertains to middle and to low life; and commend me to the streets with the straw at the doors and hatchments over head to tell us of those who are just born or who are just dead, and with groups of footmen lounging on the steps and insulting the passengers—it is then I feel the true dignity and imaginary pretensions of human nature realised! There is here none of the squalidness of poverty, none of the hardships of daily labour, none of the anxiety and petty artifice of trade; life's business is changed into a romance, a summer's dream, and nothing painful, disgusting, or vulgar intrudes. All is on a liberal and handsome scale. The true ends and benefits of society are here enjoyed and bountifully lavished, and all the trouble and misery banished, and not even allowed so much as to exist in thought. Those who would find the real Utopia, should look for it somewhere about Park-lane or May-fair. It is there only any feasible approach to equality is made—for it is *like master like man.* Here, as I look down Curzon-street, or catch a glimpse of the taper spire of South Audley Chapel, or the family arms on the gate of Chesterfield House, the vista of years opens to me, and I recall the period of the triumph of Mr. Burke's *Reflections on the French Revolution,* and the overthrow of *The Rights of Man!* You do not, indeed, penetrate to the interior of the mansion where sits the stately possessor, luxurious and refined; but you draw your inference from the lazy, pampered, motley crew poured forth from his portals. This mealy-coated, moth-like, butterfly generation, seem to have no earthly business but to enjoy themselves. Their green liveries accord with the budding leaves and spreading branches of the trees in Hyde Park—they seem " like brothers of the groves "—their red faces and powdered heads harmonise with the blossoms of the neighbouring almond-trees, that shoot their sprays over old-fashioned brick walls, They come forth like grasshoppers in June, as numerous and as noisy. They bask in the sun and laugh in your face. Not only does the master enjoy an uninterrupted leisure and tranquillity—those in his employment have nothing to do. He wants drones, not drudges, about him, to share his superfluity, and give a haughty pledge of his exemption from care. They grow sleek and wanton, saucy and supple. From being in-dependent of the world, they acquire the look of *gentle-men's gentlemen*. There is a cast of the aristocracy, with a slight shade of distinction. The saying, " Tell me your company, and I'll tell you your manners," may be ap-plied *cum grano salis* to the servants in great families. Mr. Northcote knew an old butler who had lived with a nobleman so long, and had learnt to imitate his walk, look, and way of speaking, so exactly that it was next to impossible to tell them apart. See the porter in the great leather chair in the hall—how big, and burly, and self-important he looks; while my Lord's gentleman (the politician of the family) is reading the second edition of *The Courier* (once more in request) at the side window, and the footman is romping, or taking tea with the maids in the kitchen below. A match-girl meanwhile plies her shrill trade at the railing ; or a gipsy-woman passes with her rustic wares through the street, avoiding the closer haunts of the city. What a pleasant farce is that of *High Life Below Stairs !* What a careless life do the domestics of the great lead ! For, not to speak of the reflected self-importance of their masters and mistresses, and the con-tempt with which they look down on the herd of mankind, they have only to eat and drink their fill, talk the scandal of the neighbourhood, laugh at the follies, or assist the intrigues of their betters, till they themselves fall in love, marry, set up a public-house (the only thing they are fit for), and without habits of industry, resources in themselves, or self-respect, and drawing fruitless comparisons with the past, are, of all people, the most miserable! Service is no inheritance; and when it fails, there is not a more helpless, or more worthless set of devils in the world. Mr. C—— used to say he should like to be a footman to some elderly lady of quality, to carry her prayer-book to church, and place her hassock right for her. There can be no doubt that this would have been better, and quite as useful as the life he has led, dancing attendance on Prejudice, but flirting with Paradox in such a way as to cut himself out of the old lady's will. For my part, if I had to choose, I should prefer the service of a young mistress, and might share the fate of the footmen recorded in heroic verse by Lady Wortley Montagu. Certainly it can be no hard duty, though a sort of *forlorn hope*, to have to follow three sisters, or youthful friends (resembling the three Graces), at a slow pace, and with grave demeanour, from Cumberland-gate to Kensington-gardens—to be there shut out, a privation enhancing the privilege, and making the sense of distant, respectful, idolatrous admiration more intense—and then, after a brief interval lost in idle chat, or idler reverie, to have to follow them back again, observing, not observed, to keep within call, to watch every gesture, to see the breeze play with the light tresses or lift the morning robe aside, to catch the half-suppressed laugh, and hear the low murmur of indistinct words and wishes, like the music of the spheres. An *amateur footman* would seem a more rational occupation than that of an amateur author, or an amateur artist. An insurmountable barrier, if it excludes passion, does not banish sentiment, but draws an atmosphere of superstitious, trembling apprehension round the object of so much attention and respect; nothing makes women seem so much like angels as always to see, never to converse with them; and those whom he has to dangle a cane after, must, to a lacquey of any spirit, appear worthy to wield sceptres.

But of all situations of this kind, the most enviable is that of a lady's maid in a family travelling abroad. In the obtuseness of foreigners to the nice gradations of English refinement and manners, the maid has not seldom a chance of being taken for the mistress—a circumstance never to be forgot! See our Abigail mounted in the *dickey* with John, snug and comfortable—setting out on the grand tour as fast as four horses can carry her, whirled over the " vine-covered hills and gay regions of France," crossing the Alps and Apennines in breathless terror and wonder—frightened at a precipice, laughing at her escape—coming to the inn, going into the kitchen to see what is to be had—not speaking a word of the language, except what she picks up " as pigeons pick up peas:"—the bill paid, the passport *visé*, the horses put to, and *en route* again—seeing everything, and understanding nothing, in a full tide of health, fresh air, and animal spirits, and without one qualm of taste or sentiment, and arriving at Florence, the city of palaces, with its amphitheatre of hills and olives, without suspecting that such persons as Boccaccio, Dante, or Galileo, had ever lived there, while her young mistress is puzzled with the varieties of the Tuscan dialect, is disappointed in the Arno, and cannot tell what to make of the statue of David by Michael Angelo, in the Great Square. The difference is, that the young lady, on her return, has something to think of; but the maid absolutely forgets everything, and is only giddy and out of breath, as if she had been up in a balloon.

> " No more : where ignorance is bliss,
> 'Tis folly to be wise !"

English servants abroad, notwithstanding the comforts

R

they enjoy, and though travelling as it were *en famille*, must be struck with the ease and familiar footing on which foreigners live with their domestics, compared with the distance and reserve with which they themselves are treated. The *bonne* sits down in the room, or walks abreast with you in the street; and the valet, who waits behind his master's chair at table, gives Monsieur his advice or opinion without being asked for it. We need not wonder at this familiarity and freedom, when we consider that those who allowed it could (formerly, at least, when the custom began) send those who transgressed but in the smallest degree to the Bastille or the galleys at their pleasure. The licence was attended with perfect impunity. With us the law leaves less to discretion; and by interposing a real independence (and plea of right) between the servant and master, does away with the appearance of it on the surface of manners. The insolence and tyranny of the Aristocracy fell more on the tradespeople and mechanics than on their domestics, who were attached to them by a semblance of feudal ties. Thus, an upstart lady of quality (an imitator of the old school) would not deign to speak to a milliner while fitting on her dress, but gave her orders to her waiting-women to tell her what to do. Can we wonder at twenty *reigns of terror* to efface such a feeling?

I have alluded to the inclination in servants in great houses to ape the manners of their superiors, and to their sometimes succeeding. What facilitates the metamorphosis is, that the Great, in their character of *courtiers*, are a sort of footmen in their turn. There is the same crouching to interest and authority in either case, with the same surrender or absence of personal dignity—the same submission to the trammels of outward form, with the same suppression of inward impulses—the same degrading finery, the same pretended deference in the eye of the world, and the same lurking contempt from being admitted behind the scenes, the same heartlessness, and the same eye-service—in a word, they are alike puppets governed by motives not their own, machines made of ‚coarser or finer materials. It is not, therefore, surprising, if the most finished courtier of the day cannot, by a vulgar eye, be distinguished from a gentleman's servant. M. de Bausset, in his amusing and excellent *Memoirs*, makes it an argument of the legitimacy of Napoleon's authority, that from denying it, it would follow that his lords of the bed-chamber were valets, and he himself (as prefect of the palace) no better than head cook. The inference is logical enough. According to the author's view, there was no other difference between the retainers of the court and the kitchen than the rank of the master !

I remember hearing it said that "all men were equal but footmen." But of all footmen the lowest class is *literary footmen.* These consist of persons who, without a single grain of knowledge, taste, or feeling, put on the livery of learning, mimic its phrases by rote, and are retained in its service by dint of quackery and assurance alone. As they have none of the essence, they have all the externals of men of gravity and wisdom. They walk with a peculiar strut, thrust themselves into the acquaintance of persons they hear talked of, get introduced into the clubs, are seen reading books they do not understand at the Museum and public libraries, dine (if they can) with lords or officers of the Guards, abuse any party as *low* to show what fine gentlemen they are, and the next week join the same party to raise their own credit and gain a little consequence, give themselves out as wits, critics, and philosophers (and as they have never done anything, no man can contradict them), and have a great knack of turning editors, and not paying their contributors. If you get five pounds from one of them, he never forgives it. With the proceeds thus appropriated, the book-worm graduates a dandy, hires expensive apartments, sports a tandem, and it is inferred that he must be a great author who can support such an appearance with his pen, and a great genius who can conduct so many learned works while his time is devoted to the gay, the fair, and the rich. This introduces him to new editorships, to new and more select friendships, and to more rrequent and importunate demands from debts and duns. At length the bubble bursts and disappears, and you hear no more of our classical adventurer, except from the invectives and self-reproaches of his dupes. Such a candidate for literary honours bears the same relation to the man of letters that the valet, with his second-hand finery and servile airs, does to his master.

A Chapter on Editors.

EDITORS are a "sort of *tittle-tattle*"—difficult to deal with, dangerous to discuss. They in general partake of the usual infirmity of human nature, and of persons placed in high and honorary situations. Like other individuals raised to authority, they are chosen to fill a certain post for qualities useful or ornamental to the *reading public;* but they soon fancy that the situation has been invented for their own honour and profit, and sink the use in the abuse. Kings are not the only servants of the public who imagine that they are the *state.* Editors are but men, and easily " lay the flattering unction to their souls" that they *are* the Magazine, the Newspaper, or the Review they conduct. They have got a little power in their hands, and they wish to employ that power (as all power is employed) to increase the sense of self-importance ; they borrow a certain dignity from their situation as arbiters and judges of taste and elegance, and they are determined to keep it to the detriment of their employers and of every one else. They are dreadfully afraid there should be anything behind the Editor's chair, greater than the

Editor's chair. That is a scandal to be prevented at all risks. The publication they are entrusted with for the amusement and edification of the town, they convert, in theory and practice, into a stalking horse of their own vanity, whims, and prejudices. They cannot write a whole work themselves, but they take care that the whole is such as they might have written : it is to have the Editor's mark, like the broad R, on every page, or the N. N. at the Tuileries; it is to bear the same image and superscription—every line is to be upon oath : nothing is to be differently conceived or better expressed than the Editor could have done it. The whole begins in vanity, and ends too often in dulness and insipidity.

It is utterly impossible to persuade an Editor that he is nobody. As Mr. Horne Tooke said, on his trial for a libel before Lord Kenyon, " There are two parties in this cause—myself and the jury; the judge and the crier of the court attend in their respective places :" so, in every periodical miscellany, there are two essential parties—the writers and the public; the Editor and the printer's devil are merely the mechanical instruments to bring them together. There is a secret consciousness of this on the part of the Conductor of the Literary Diligence, that his place is one for show and form rather than use ; and as he cannot maintain his pretended superiority by what he does himself, he thinks to arrive at the same end by hindering others from doing their best. The " dog-in-the-manger" principle comes into full play. If an article has nothing to recommend it, is one of no mark or likelihood, it goes in ; there is no offence in it. If it is likely to strike, to draw attention, to make a noise, then every syllable is scanned, every objection is weighed : if grave, it is too grave; if witty, it is too witty. One way or other, it might be better ; and while this nice point is pending, it gives place, as a matter of course, to something that there is no question about.

The responsibility, the delicacy, the nervous apprehension of the Editor, naturally increase with the probable effect and popularity of the contributions on which he has to pass judgment; and the nearer an effusion approaches to perfection, the more fatal is a single flaw, or its falling short of that superhuman standard by a hair's-breadth difference, to its final reception. If people are likely to ask, " Who wrote a certain paper in the last number of ———?" the Editor is bound, as a point of honour, to baulk that impertinent curiosity on the part of the public. He would have it understood that all the articles are equally good, and may be equally his own. If he inserts a paper of more than the allowed average merit, his next care is to spoil by revising it. The sting, with the honey, is sure to be left out. If there is anything that pleased you in the writing, you look in vain for it in the proof. What might electrify the reader, startles the Editor. With a paternal regard for the interests of the public, he takes care that their tastes should not be pampered, and their expectations raised too high, by a succession of fine passages, of which it is impossible to continue a supply. He interposes between the town and their vicious appetite for the piquant and high-seasoned, as we forbid children to indulge in sweetmeats. The trite and superficial are always to be had *to order*, and present a beautiful uniformity of appearance. There is no unexpected relief, no unwelcome inequality of style, to disorder the nerves, or perplex the understanding : the reader may read, and smile, and sleep, without meeting a single idea to break his repose.

Some Editors, moreover, have a way of altering the first paragraph : they have then exercised their privileges, and let you alone for the rest of the chapter. This is like paying " a pepper-corn rent," or making one's bow on entering a room : it is being let off cheap. Others add a pointless conclusion of their own : it is like signing their names to the article. Some have a passion for sticking in the word *however* at every opportunity, in order to impede the march of the style ; and others are contented and take great pains (with Lindley Murray's Grammar lying open before them) to alter " if it *is* " into " if it *be*." An Editor abhors an ellipsis. If you fling your thoughts into continued passages, they set to work to cut them up into short paragraphs : if you make frequent breaks, they turn the tables on you that way, and throw the whole composition into masses. Anything to preserve the form and appearance of power, to make the work their own by mental stratagem, to stamp it by some fiction of criticism with their personal identity, to enable them to run away with the credit, and look upon themselves as the master-spirits of the work and of the age ! If there is any point they do not understand, they are sure to meddle with it, and mar the sense ; for it piques their self-love, and they think they are bound *ex-officio* to know better than the writer. Thus they substitute (at a venture, and merely for the sake of altering) one epithet for another, when perhaps the same word has occurred just before, and produces a cruel tautology, never considering the trouble you have taken to compare the context and vary the phraseology.

Editors have no misplaced confidence in the powers of their contributors : they think by the supposition they must be in the right from a single supercilious glance— and you in the wrong, after poring over a subject for a month. There are Editors who, if you insert the name of a popular actor, strike it out, and, in virtue of their authority, insert a favourite of their own—as a dexterous attorney substitutes the name of a friend in a will. Some Editors will let you praise nobody ; others will let you blame nobody. The first excites their jealousy of contemporary merit ; the last excites their fears, and they do not like to make enemies. Some insist upon giving no opinion at all, and observe an *unarmed neutrality* as to all parties and persons : it is no wonder the world think very little of them in return. Some Editors stand upon their characters for this ; others for that. Some pique themselves upon being genteel and well-dressed ; others on being moral and immaculate, and do not perceive that the public never trouble their heads about the matter. I knew one Editor who openly discarded all regard to character and decency, and who throve by the dissolution of partnership, if indeed the articles were ever drawn up. Some Editors drink tea with a set of *blue-stockings* and literary ladies : not a whisper, not a breath that might blow away those fine cobwebs of the brain—

> " More subtle web Arachne cannot spin ;
> Nor those fine threads which oft we woven see
> Of scorched dew, do not in the air more lightly flee !"

Others dine with Lords and Academicians—for God's sake, take care what you say ! Would you strip the Editor's mantel-piece of the cards of invitation that adorn it to select parties for the next six months ? An Editor takes a turn in St. James's-street, and is congratulated by the successive literary or political groups on all he does not write ; and when the mistake is found out, the true Simon Pure is dismissed. We have heard that it was well said by the proprietor of a leading journal, that he would take good care never to write a line in his own paper, as he had conflicting interests enough to manage, without adding literary jealousies to the number. On the other hand, a very good-natured and warm-hearted individual declared, " he would never have another man of talents for an Editor " (the Editor, in this case, is to the proprietor as the author to the Editor), " for he was tired of having their good things thrust in his teeth." Some Editors are scrubs, mere drudges, newspaper-puffs ; others are bullies or quacks ; others are nothing at all—they have the name, and receive a salary for it! A literary sinecure is at once lucrative and highly respectable. At Lord's Ground there are some old hands that are famous for "*blocking out and staying in :*" it would seem that some of our literary veterans had taken a lesson from their youthful exercises at Harrow or Eton.

All this is bad enough ; but the worst is, that Editors, besides their own failings, have *friends* who aggravate and take advantage of them. These self-styled friends are the nightshade and hemlock clinging to the work, preventing its growth and circulation, and dropping a slumberous poison from its jaundiced leaves. They form a *cordon*, an opaque mass round the Editor, and persuade him that they are the support, the prop, and pillar of his reputation. They get between him and the public, and shut out the light, and set aside common-sense. They pretend anxiety for the interest of some established organ of opinion, while all they want is to make it the organ of their dogmas, prejudices, or party. They want to be the Magazine or the Review—to wield that power covertly, to warp that influence to their own purposes. If they cannot do this, they care not if it sinks or swims. They prejudge every question—fly-blow every writer who is not of their own set. A friend of theirs has three articles in the last number of ————; they strain every nerve and make pressing instances to throw a slur on a popular contribution by another hand, in order that he may write a fourth in the next number. The short articles which are read by the vulgar, are cut down to make room for the long ones, which are read by nobody but the writers and their friends. If an opinion is expressed contrary to the shibboleth of the party, it is represented as an outrage on decency and public opinion, when in truth the public are delighted with the candour and boldness displayed. They would convert the most valuable and spirited journal into a dull pamphleteer, stuffed with their own lucubrations on certain heavy topics. The self-importance of these people is in proportion to their insignificance; and what they cannot do by an appeal to argument or sound policy, they effect by importunity and insinuation. They keep the Editor in continual alarm as to what will be said of him by the public, when in fact the public will think (in nine cases out of ten) just what he tells them.

These people create much of the mischief. An Editor should have no friends—his only prompter should be the number of copies of the work that sell. It is superfluous to strike off a large impression of a work for those few squeamish persons who prefer lead to tinsel. Principle and good manners are barriers that are, in our estimate, inviolable: the rest is open to popular suffrage, and is not to be prejudged by a *coterie* with closed doors. Another difficulty lies here. An Editor should, in one sense, be a respectable man—a distinguished character; otherwise he cannot lend his name and sanction to the work. But "here's the rub"—that one so graced and gifted can neither have his time nor his thoughts to himself. He who dines out loses his free agency. He may improve in politeness, he falls off in the pith and pungency of his style. A poem is dedicated to the son of the Muses: can the critic do otherwise than praise it? A tragedy is brought out by a noble friend and patron: the severe rules of the drama must yield in some measure to the amenities of private life. On the contrary, Mr. ——— is a garretteer—a person that nobody knows; his work has nothing but the *contents* to recommend it; it sinks into obscurity, or addresses itself to the *canaille*. An Editor, then, should be an abstraction—a being in the clouds—a mind without a body—reason without passion.——But where find such a one?

WINTERSLOW:

ESSAYS AND CHARACTERS.

WRITTEN THERE.

PREFACE TO THE EDITION OF 1850.

WINTERSLOW is a village of Wiltshire, between Salisbury and Andover, where my father, during a considerable portion of his life, spent several months of each year, latterly, at an ancient inn on the Great Western Road, called Winterslow Hut. One of his chief attractions hither were the noble woods of Tytherleigh or Tudorleigh. round Norman Court, the seat of Mr. Baring Wall, M.P., whose proffered kindness to my father, on a critical occasion, was thoroughly appreciated by the very sensitiveness which declined its acceptance, and will always be gratefully remembered by myself. Another feature was Clarendon Wood—whence the noble family of Clarendon derived their title—famous besides for the Constitutions signed in the palace which once rose proudly amongst its stately trees, but of which scarce a vestige remains. In another direction, within easy distance, gloams Stonehenge, visited by my father, less perhaps for its historical associations than for its appeal to the imagination, the upright stones seeming in the dim twilight, or in the drizzling mist, almost continuous in the locality, so many spectre-Druids, moaning over the past, and over their brethren prostrate about them. At no great distance, in another direction, are the fine pictures of Lord Radnor, and somewhat further, those of Wilton House. But the chief happiness was the thorough quiet of the place, the sole interruption of which was the passage, to and fro, of the London mails. The Hut stands in a valley, equidistant about a mile from two tolerably high hills, at the summit of which, on their approach either way, the guards used to blow forth their admonition to the hostler. The sound, coming through the clear, pure air, was another agreeable feature in the day, reminiscentiary of the great city that my father so loved and so loathed. In olden times, when we lived in the village itself—a mile up the hill opposite—behind the Hut, Salisbury Plain stretches away mile after mile of open space—the reminiscence of the metropolis would be, from time to time, furnished in the pleasantest of ways by the presence of some London friends; among these, dearly loved and honoured there, as everywhere else, Charles and Mary Lamb paid us frequent visits, rambling about all the time, thorough Londoners in a thoroughly country place, delighted and wondering and wondered at. For such reasons, and for the other reason, which I mention incidentally, that Winterslow is my own native place, I have given its name to this collection of " Essays and Characters written there;" as, indeed, practically were very many of his works, for it was there that most of his thinking was done.

WILLIAM HAZLITT.

CHELSEA, *Jan.* 1850.

ESSAY I.[1]

My First Acquaintance with Poets.

My father was a Dissenting Minister, at Wem, in Shropshire; and in the year 1798 (the figures that compose the date are to me like the "dreaded name of Demogorgon") Mr. Coleridge came to Shrewsbury, to succeed Mr. Rowe in the spiritual charge of a Unitarian Congregation there. He did not come till late on the Saturday afternoon before he was to preach; and Mr. Rowe, who himself went down to the coach, in a state of anxiety and expectation, to look for the arrival of his successor, could find no one at all answering the description but a round-faced man, in a short black coat (like a shooting jacket) which hardly seemed to have been made for him, but who seemed to be talking at a great rate to his fellow passengers. Mr. Rowe had scarce returned to give an account of his disappointment when the round-faced man in black entered, and dissipated all doubts on the subject by beginning to talk. He did not cease while he stayed; nor has he since, that I know of. He held the good town of Shrewsbury in delightful suspense for three weeks that he remained there, "fluttering the *proud Salopians*, like an eagle in a dove-cote;" and the Welch mountains that skirt the horizon with their tempestuous confusion, agree to have heard no such mystic sounds since the days of

"High-born Hoel's harp or soft Llewellyn's lay."

As we passed along between Wem and Shrewsbury, and I eyed their blue tops seen through the wintry branches, or

[1] First printed as a sketch in the *Examiner* newspaper in 1817, and republished, without alteration, in *Political Essays*, 1819. In its present form it originally appeared in the first volume of the *Liberal: Verse and Prose from the South*, 1823. It is reprinted in the *Literary Remains*, 1836.—ED.

the red rustling leaves of the sturdy oak-trees by the road-side, a sound was in my ears as of a Syren's song; I was stunned, startled with it, as from deep sleep; but I had no notion then that I should ever be able to express my admiration to others in motley imagery or quaint allusion, till the light of his genius shone into my soul, like the sun's rays glittering in the puddles of the road. I was at that time dumb, inarticulate, helpless, like a worm by the way-side, crushed, bleeding, lifeless; but now, bursting the deadly bands that " bound them,

" With Styx nine times round them,"

my ideas float on winged words, and as they expand their plumes, catch the golden light of other years. My soul has indeed remained in its original bondage, dark, obscure, with longings infinite and unsatisfied; my heart, shut up in the prison-house of this rude clay, has never found, nor will it ever find, a heart to speak to ; but that my understanding also did not remain dumb and brutish, or at length found a language to express itself, I owe to Coleridge. But this is not to my purpose.

My father lived ten miles from Shrewsbury, and was in the habit of exchanging visits with Mr. Rowe, and with Mr. Jenkins of Whitchurch (nine miles farther on), according to the custom of Dissenting Ministers in each other's neighbourhood. A line of communication is thus established, by which the flame of civil and religious liberty is kept alive, and nourishes its smouldering fire unquenchable, like the fires in the *Agamemnon* of Æschylus, placed at different stations, that waited for ten long years to announce with their blazing pyramids the destruction of Troy. Coleridge had agreed to come over and see my father, according to the courtesy of the country, as Mr. Rowe's probable successor; but in the meantime, I had gone to hear him preach the Sunday after his arrival. A poet and a philosopher getting up into a

Unitarian pulpit to preach the gospel, was a romance in these degenerate days, a sort of revival of the primitive spirit of Christianity, which was not to be resisted.

It was in January of 1798, that I rose one morning before daylight, to walk ten miles in the mud, to hear this celebrated person preach. Never, the longest day I have to live, shall I have such another walk as this cold, raw, comfortless one, in the winter of the year 1798. *Il y a des impressions que ni le tems ni les circonstances peuvent effacer. Dusse-je vivre des siècles entiers, le doux tems de ma jeunesse ne peut renaître pour moi, ni s'effacer jamais dans ma mémoire.* When I got there, the organ was playing the 100th Psalm, and when it was done, Mr. Coleridge rose and gave out his text, "And he went up into the mountain to pray, HIMSELF, ALONE." As he gave out this text, his voice "rose like a steam of rich distilled perfumes," and when he came to the two last words, which he pronounced loud, deep, and distinct, it seemed to me, who was then young, as if the sounds had echoed from the bottom of the human heart, and as if that prayer might have floated in solemn silence through the universe. The idea of St. John came into my mind, "of one crying in the wilderness, who had his loins girt about, and whose food was locusts and wild honey." The preacher then launched into his subject, like an eagle dallying with the wind. The sermon was upon peace and war; upon church and state—not their alliance but their separation—on the spirit of the world and the spirit of Christianity, not as the same, but as opposed to one another. He talked of those who had "inscribed the cross of Christ on banners dripping with human gore." He made a poetical and pastoral excursion—and to show the fatal effects of war, drew a striking contrast between the simple shepherd-boy, driving his team afield, or sitting under the hawthorn, piping to his flock, "as though he should never be old," and the same poor country lad,

s

crimped, kidnapped, brought into town, made drunk at an alehouse, turned into a wretched drummer-boy, with his hair sticking on end with powder and pomatum, a long cue at his back, and tricked out in the loathsome finery of the profession of blood :

"Such were the notes our once-loved poet sung."

And for myself, I could not have been more delighted if I had heard the music of the spheres. Poetry and Philosophy had met together. Truth and Genius had embraced, under the eye and with the sanction of Religion. This was even beyond my hopes. I returned home well satisfied. The sun that was still labouring pale and wan through the sky, obscured by thick mists, seemed an emblem of the *good cause ;* and the cold dank drops of dew, that hung half melted on the beard of the thistle, had something genial and refreshing in them ; for there was a spirit of hope and youth in all nature, that turned everything into good. The face of nature had not then the brand of Jus Divinum on it :

" Like to that sanguine flower inscrib'd with woe."

On the Tuesday following, the half-inspired speaker came. I was called down into the room where he was, and went half-hoping, half-afraid. He received me very graciously, and I listened for a long time without uttering a word. I did not suffer in his opinion by my silence. "For those two hours," he afterwards was pleased to say, "he was conversing with William Hazlitt's forehead!" His appearance was different from what I had anticipated from seeing him before. At a distance, and in the dim light of the chapel, there was to me a strange wildness in his aspect, a dusky obscurity, and I thought him pitted with the small-pox. His complexion was at that time clear, and even bright—

"As are the children of yon azure sheen."

His forehead was broad and high, light as if built of ivory, with large projecting eyebrows, and his eyes rolling beneath them, like a sea with darkened lustre. " A certain tender bloom his face o'erspread," a purple tinge as we see it in the pale thoughtful complexions of the Spanish portrait-painters, Murillo and Valasquez. His mouth was gross, voluptuous, open, eloquent ; his chin good-humoured and round ; but his nose, the rudder of the face, the index of the will, was small, feeble, nothing—like what he has done. It might seem that the genius of his face as from a height surveyed and projected him (with sufficient capacity and huge aspiration) into the world unknown of thought and imagination, with nothing to support or guide his veering purpose, as if Columbus had launched his adventurous course for the New World in a scallop, without oars or compass. So, at least, I comment on it after the event. Coleridge, in his person, was rather above the common size, inclining to the corpulent, or like Lord Hamlet, "somewhat fat and pursy." His hair (now, alas ! grey) was then black and glossy as the raven's, and fell in smooth masses over his forehead. This long pendulous hair is peculiar to enthusiasts, to those whose minds tend heavenward ; and is traditionally inseparable (though of a different colour) from the pictures of Christ. It ought to belong, as a character, to all who preach *Christ crucified*, and Coleridge was at that time one of those !

It was curious to observe the contrast between him and my father, who was a veteran in the cause, and then declining into the vale of years. He had been a poor Irish lad, carefully brought up by his parents, and sent to the University of Glasgow (where he studied under Adam Smith) to prepare him for his future destination. It was his mother's proudest wish to see her son a Dissenting Minister. So, if we look back to past generations (as far as eye can reach), we see the same hopes, fears, wishes, followed by the same disappointments, throbbing in the

human heart; and so we may see them (if we look forward)
rising up for ever, and disappearing, like vapourish bubbles,
in the human breast! After being tossed about from congregation to congregation in the heats of the Unitarian
controversy, and squabbles about the American war, he
had been relegated to an obscure village, where he was to
spend the last thirty years of his life, far from the only
converse that he loved, the talk about disputed texts of
Scripture, and the cause of civil and religious liberty.
Here he passed his days, repining, but resigned, in the
study of the Bible, and the perusal of the Commentators
—huge folios, not easily got through, one of which would
outlast a winter! Why did he pore on these from morn
to night (with the exception of a walk in the fields or a
turn in the garden to gather broccoli-plants or kidney
beans of his own rearing, with no small degree of pride
and pleasure)? Here were "no figures nor no fantasies"—
neither poetry nor philosophy—nothing to dazzle, nothing
to excite modern curiosity; but to his lack-lustre eyes
there appeared within the pages of the ponderous, un-
wieldy, neglected tomes, the sacred name of JEHOVAH
in Hebrew capitals: pressed down by the weight of the
style, worn to the last fading thinness of the understanding,
there were glimpses, glimmering notions of the patriarchal
wanderings, with palm-trees hovering in the horizon, and
processions of camels at the distance of three thousand
years; there was Moses with the Burning Bush, the
number of the Twelve Tribes, types, shadows, glosses
on the law and the prophets; there were discussions (dull
enough) on the age of Methuselah, a mighty speculation!
there were outlines, rude guesses at the shape of Noah's
Ark and of the riches of Solomon's Temple; questions as
to the date of the creation, predictions of the end of all
things; the great lapses of time, the strange mutations of
the globe were unfolded with the voluminous leaf, as it
turned over; and though the soul might slumber with an

hieroglyphic veil of inscrutable mysteries drawn over it, yet it was in a slumber ill-exchanged for all the sharpened realities of sense, wit, fancy, or reason. My father's life was comparatively a dream; but it was a dream of infinity and eternity, of death, the resurrection, and a judgment to come!

No two individuals were ever more unlike than were the host and his guest. A poet was to my father a sort of nondescript; yet whatever added grace to the Unitarian cause was to him welcome. He could hardly have been more surprised or pleased, if our visitor had worn wings. Indeed, his thoughts had wings: and as the silken sounds rustled round our little wainscoted parlour, my father threw back his spectacles over his forehead, his white hairs mixing with its sanguine hue; and a smile of delight beamed across his rugged, cordial face, to think that Truth had found a new ally in Fancy![1] Besides, Coleridge seemed to take considerable notice of me, and that of itself was enough. He talked very familiarly, but agreeably, and glanced over a variety of subjects. At dinner-time he grew more animated, and dilated in a very edifying manner on Mary Wolstonecraft and Mackintosh. The last, he said, he considered (on my father's speaking of his *Vindiciæ Gallicæ* as a capital performance) as a clever, scholastic man—a master of the topics—or, as the ready warehouseman of letters, who knew exactly where to lay his hand on what he wanted, though the goods were not his own. He thought him no match for Burke, either in

[1] My father was one of those who mistook his talent, after all. He used to be very much dissatisfied that I preferred his *Letters* to his *Sermons.* The last were forced and dry; the first came naturally from him. For ease, half-plays on words, and a supine, monkish, indolent pleasantry, I have never seen them equalled. [The *Sermons* of the Rev. William Hazlitt were printed by subscription in 1808, 2 vols. 8vo. He published other tracts and discourses. A letter of his, contributed to the *Monthly Repository* in July, 1808, will be found reprinted in the *Memoirs of William Hazlitt*, 1867, i, 267-9]

style or matter. Burke was a metaphysician, Mackintosh a mere logician. Burke was an orator (almost a poet) who reasoned in figures, because he had an eye for nature: Mackintosh, on the other hand, was a rhetorician, who had only an eye to commonplaces. On this I ventured to say that I had always entertained a great opinion of Burke, and that (as far as I could find) the speaking of him with contempt might be made the test of a vulgar, democratical mind. This was the first observation I ever made to Coleridge, and he said it was a very just and striking one. I remember the leg of Welsh mutton and the turnips on the table that day had the finest flavour imaginable. Coleridge added that Mackintosh and Tom Wedgwood (of whom, however, he spoke highly) had expressed a very indifferent opinion of his friend Mr. Wordsworth, on which he remarked to them—"He strides on so far before you, that he dwindles in the distance!" Godwin had once boasted to him of having carried on an argument with Mackintosh for three hours with dubious success ; Coleridge told him—"If there had been a man of genius in the room he would have settled the question in five minutes." He asked me if I had ever seen Mary Wolstonecraft, and I said, I had once for a few moments, and that she seemed to me to turn off Godwin's objections to something she advanced with quite a playful, easy air. He replied, that " this was only one instance of the ascendency which people of imagination exercised over those of mere intellect." He did not rate Godwin very high[1] (this was caprice or prejudice, real or affected), but he had a great idea of Mrs. Wolstonecraft's powers of conversation ; none at all of her talent for book-making. We talked a

---

[1] He complained in particular of the presumption of his attempting to establish the future immortality of man, " without " (as he said) " knowing what Death was or what Life was "—and the tone in which he pronounced these two words seemed to convey a complete image of both.

little about Holcroft. He had been asked if he was not much struck *with* him, and he said, he thought himself in more danger of being struck *by* him. I complained that he would not let me get on at all, for he required a definition of every the commonest word, exclaiming, "What do you mean by a *sensation*, Sir? What do you mean by an *idea?*" This, Coleridge said, was barricadoing the road to truth; it was setting up a turnpike-gate at every step we took. I forget a great number of things, many more than I remember; but the day passed off pleasantly, and the next morning Mr. Coleridge was to return to Shrewsbury. When I came down to breakfast, I found that he had just received a letter from his friend, T. Wedgwood, making him an offer of 150*l.* a year if he chose to waive his present pursuit, and devote himself entirely to the study of poetry and philosophy. Coleridge seemed to make up his mind to close with this proposal in the act of tying on one of his shoes. It threw an additional damp on his departure. It took the wayward enthusiast quite from us to cast him into Deva's winding vales, or by the shores of old romance. Instead of living at ten miles' distance, of being the pastor of a Dissenting congregation at Shrewsbury, he was henceforth to inhabit the Hill of Parnassus, to be a Shepherd on the Delectable Mountains. Alas! I knew not the way thither, and felt very little gratitude for Mr. Wedgwood's bounty. I was presently relieved from this dilemma; for Mr. Coleridge, asking for a pen and ink, and going to a table to write something on a bit of card, advanced towards me with undulating step, and giving me the precious document, said that that was his address, *Mr. Coleridge, Nether-Stowey, Somersetshire;* and that he should be glad to see me there in a few weeks' time, and, if I chose, would come half-way to meet me. I was not less surprised than the shepherd-boy (this simile is to be found in *Cassandra*), when he sees a thunderbolt fall close at his feet. I stammered out my acknowledgments and acceptance of this offer (I thought Mr. Wedgwood's annuity a trifle to it) as well as I could ; and this mighty business being settled, the poet preacher took leave, and I accompanied him six miles on the road. It was a fine morning in the middle of winter, and he talked the whole way. The scholar in Chaucer is described as going

——" Sounding on his way."

So Coleridge went on his. In digressing, in dilating, in passing from subject to subject, he appeared to me to float in air, to slide on ice. He told me in confidence (going along) that he should have preached two sermons before he accepted the situation at Shrewsbury, one on Infant Baptism, the other on the Lord's Supper, showing that he could not administer either, which would have effectually disqualified him for the object in view. I observed that he continually crossed me on the way by shifting from one side of the footpath to the other. This struck me as an odd movement; but I did not at that time connect it with any instability of purpose or involuntary change of principle, as I have done since. He seemed unable to keep on in a straight line. He spoke slightingly of Hume (whose *Essay on Miracles* he said was stolen from an objection started in one of South's sermons— *Credat Judæus Appella !*) I was not very much pleased at this account of Hume, for I had just been reading, with infinite relish, that completest of all metaphysical *chokepears*, his *Treatise on Human Nature*, to which the *Essays* in point of scholastic subtilty and close reasoning, are mere elegant trifling, light summer reading. Coleridge even denied the excellence of Hume's general style, which I think betrayed a want of taste or candour. He however made me amends by the manner in which he spoke of Berkeley. He dwelt particularly on his *Essay on Vision* as a masterpiece of analytical reasoning. So it undoubtedly is. He was exceedingly angry with Dr. Johnson

for striking the stone with his foot, in allusion to this
author's *Theory of Matter and Spirit*, and saying, "Thus
I confute him, Sir." Coleridge drew a parallel (I don't
know how he brought about the connection) between
Bishop Berkeley and Tom Paine. He said the one was
an instance of a subtle, the other of an acute mind, than
which no two things could be more distinct. The one
was a shop-boy's quality, the other the characteristic of a
philosopher. He considered Bishop Butler as a true
philosopher, a profound and conscientious thinker, a
genuine reader of nature and his own mind. He did not
speak of his *Analogy*, but of his *Sermons at the Rolls'
Chapel*, of which I had never heard. Coleridge somehow
always contrived to prefer the *unknown* to the *known*. In
this instance he was right. The *Analogy* is a tissue of
sophistry, of wire-drawn, theological special-pleading;
the *Sermons* (with the preface to them) are in a fine vein
of deep, matured reflection, a candid appeal to our observation of human nature, without pedantry and without bias.
I told Coleridge I had written a few remarks, and was
sometimes foolish enough to believe that I had made a
discovery on the same subject (the *Natural disinterestedness of the Human Mind*)[1]—and I tried to explain my view
of it to Coleridge, who listened with great willingness,
but I did not succeed in making myself understood. I
sat down to the task shortly afterwards for the twentieth
time, got new pens and paper, determined to make clear
work of it, wrote a few meagre sentences in the skeleton
style of a mathematical demonstration, stopped half-way
down the second page; and, after trying in vain to pump
up any words, images, notions, apprehensions, facts, or
observations, from that gulf of abstraction in which I
had plunged myself for four or five years preceding, gave
up the attempt as labour in vain, and shed tears of help-

---

[1] The *Essay on the Principles of Human Action*, begun about this
time, but not completed and published till 1805.—ED.

less despondency on the blank, unfinished paper. I can write fast enough now. Am I better than I was then? Oh no! One truth discovered, one pang of regret at not being able to express it, is better than all the fluency and flippancy in the world. Would that I could go back to what I then was! Why can we not revive past times as we can revisit old places? If I had the quaint Muse of Sir Philip Sidney to assist me, I would write a *Sonnet to the Road between Wem and Shrewsbury*, and immortalise every step of it by some fond enigmatical conceit. I would swear that the very milestones had ears, and that Harmer-hill stooped with all its pines, to listen to a poet, as he passed! I remember but one other topic of discourse in this walk. He mentioned Paley, praised the naturalness and clearness of his style, but condemned his sentiments, thought him a mere time-serving casuist, and said that "the fact of his work on Moral and Political Philosophy being made a text-book in our Universities was a disgrace to the national character." We parted at the six-mile stone; and I returned homeward, pensive, but much pleased. I had met with unexpected notice from a person whom I believed to have been prejudiced against me. "Kind and affable to me had been his condescension, and should be honoured ever with suitable regard." He was the first poet I had known, and he certainly answered to that inspired name. I had heard a great deal of his powers of conversation and was not disappointed. In fact, I never met with anything at all like them, either before or since. I could easily credit the accounts which were circulated of his holding forth to a large party of ladies and gentlemen, an evening or two before, on the Berkeleian Theory, when he made the whole material universe look like a transparency of fine words; and another story (which I believe he has somewhere told himself) of his being asked to a party at Birmingham, of his smoking tobacco and going to sleep after dinner on a sofa,

where the company found, him to their no small surprise, which was increased to wonder when he started
up of a sudden, and rubbing his eyes, looked about him,
and launched into a three-hours' description of the third
heaven, of which he had had a dream, very different from
Mr. Southey's *Vision of Judgment*, and also from that
other *Vision of Judgment*, which Mr. Murray, the Secretary
of the Bridge-street Junta, took into his especial keeping.

On my way back I had a sound in my ears—it was the
voice of Fancy; I had a light before me—it was the face
of Poetry. The one still lingers there, the other has not
quitted my side! Coleridge, in truth, met me half-way on
the ground of philosophy, or I should not have been won
over to his imaginative creed. I had an uneasy, pleasurable sensation all the time, till I was to visit him. During
those months the chill breath of winter gave me a welcom-
ing; the vernal air was balm and inspiration to me. The
golden sunsets, the silver star of evening, lighted me on
my way to new hopes and prospects. *I was to visit Coleridge in the spring.* This circumstance was never absent
from my thoughts, and mingled with all my feelings. I
wrote to him at the time proposed, and received an answer
postponing my intended visit for a week or two, but very
cordially urging me to complete my promise then. This
delay did not damp, but rather increased my ardour. In
the meantime, I went to Llangollen Vale, by way of in-
itiating myself in the mysteries of natural scenery; and I
must say I was enchanted with it. I had been reading
Coleridge's description of England in his fine *Ode on the
Departing Year*, and I applied it, *con amore*, to the objects
before me. That valley was to me (in a manner) the
cradle of a new existence: in the river that winds through
it, my spirit was baptized in the waters of Helicon!

I returned home, and soon after set out on my journey
with unworn heart, and untired feet. My way lay through
Worcester and Gloucester, and by Upton, where I thought

of Tom Jones and the adventure of the muff. I remember getting completely wet through one day, and stopping at an inn (I think it was at Tewkesbury) where I sat up all night to read *Paul and Virginia*. Sweet were the showers in early youth that drenched my body, and sweet the drops of pity that fell upon the books I read! I recollect a remark of Coleridge's upon this very book that nothing could show the gross indelicacy of French manners and the entire corruption of their imagination more strongly than the behaviour of the heroine in the last fatal scene, who turns away from a person on board the sinking vessel, that offers to save her life, because he has thrown off his clothes to assist him in swimming. Was this a time to think of such a circumstance? I once hinted to Wordsworth, as we were sailing in his boat on Grasmere lake, that I thought he had borrowed the idea of his *Poems on the Naming of Places* from the local inscriptions of the same kind in *Paul and Virginia*. He did not own the obligation, and stated some distinction without a difference in defence of his claim to originality. Any, the slighest variation, would be sufficient for this purpose in his mind; for whatever *he* added or altered would inevitably be worth all that any one else had done, and contain the marrow of the sentiment. I was still two days before the time fixed for my arrival, for I had taken care to set out early enough. I stopped these two days at Bridgewater; and when I was tired of sauntering on the banks of its muddy river, returned to the inn and read *Camilla*. So have I loitered my life away, reading books, looking at pictures, going to plays, hearing, thinking, writing on what pleased me best. I have wanted only one thing to make me happy; but wanting that have wanted everything!

I arrived, and was well received. The country about Nether Stowey is beautiful, green and hilly, and near the sea-shore. I saw it but the other day, after an interval

of twenty years, from a hill near Taunton. How was
the map of my life spread out before me, as the map of
the country lay at my feet! In the afternoon, Coleridge
took me over to All-Foxden, a romantic old family mansion
of the St. Aubins, where Wordsworth lived. It was then
in the possession of a friend of the poet's, who gave him
the free use of it. Somehow, that period (the time just
after the French Revolution) was not a time when *nothing
was given for nothing.* The mind opened and a softness
might be perceived coming over the heart of individuals,
beneath "the scales that fence" our self-interest. Wordsworth himself was from home, but his sister kept house,
and set before us a frugal repast; and we had free access
to her brother's poems, the *Lyrical Ballads*,[1] which were
still in manuscript, or in the form of *Sybilline Leaves.* I
dipped into a few of these with great satisfaction, and with
the faith of a novice. I slept that night in an old room
with blue hangings, and covered with the round-faced
family portraits of the age of George I. and II., and from
the wooded declivity of the adjoining park that overlooked
my window, at the dawn of day, could

——"hear the loud stag speak."

In the outset of life (and particularly at this time I
felt it so) our imagination has a body to it. We are in a
state between sleeping and waking, and have indistinct
but glorious glimpses of strange shapes, and there is always
something to come better than what we see. As in our
dreams the fulness of the blood gives warmth and reality
to the coinage of the brain, so in youth our ideas are
clothed, and fed, and pampered with our good spirits; we
breathe thick with thoughtless happiness, the weight of
future years presses on the strong pulses of the heart, and
we repose with undisturbed faith in truth and good. As

[1] The *Ballads* were not published till this year. Wordsworth,
however, was known as the author of *Descriptive Sketches*, 1793, and
the *Evening Walk*, 1793.—ED.

we advance, we exhaust our fund of enjoyment and of hope. We are no longer wrapped in *lamb's-wool*, lulled in Elysium. As we taste the pleasures of life, their spirit evaporates, the sense palls; and nothing is left but the phantoms, the lifeless shadows of what *has been!*

That morning, as soon as breakfast was over, we strolled out into the park, and seating ourselves on the trunk of an old ash-tree that stretched along the ground, Coleridge read aloud with a sonorous and musical voice, the ballad of *Betty Foy*. I was not critically or sceptically inclined. I saw touches of truth and nature, and took the rest for granted. But in the *Thorn*, the *Mad Mother*, and the *Complaint of a Poor Indian Woman*, I felt that deeper power and pathos which have been since acknowledged,

> "In spite of pride, in erring reason's spite,"

as the characteristics of this author; and the sense of a new style and a new spirit in poetry came over me. It had to me something of the effect that arises from the turning up of the fresh soil, or of the first welcome breath of Spring:

> "While yet the trembling year is unconfirmed."

Coleridge and myself walked back to Stowey that evening, and his voice sounded high

> "Of Providence, foreknowledge, will, and fate,
> Fix'd fate, free-will, foreknowledge absolute,"

as we passed through echoing grove, by fairy stream or waterfall, gleaming in the summer moonlight! He lamented that Wordsworth was not prone enough to believe in the traditional superstitions of the place, and that there was a something corporeal, a *matter-of-fact-ness*, a clinging to the palpable, or often to the petty, in his poetry, in consequence. His genius was not a spirit that descended to him through the air; it sprung out of the

ground like a flower, or unfolded itself from a green
spray, on which the goldfinch sang. He said, however (if
I remember right), that this objection must be confined to
his descriptive pieces, that his philosophic poetry had a
grand and comprehensive spirit in it, so that his soul
seemed to inhabit the universe like a palace, and to
discover truth by intuition, rather than by deduction.
The next day Wordsworth arrived from Bristol at
Coleridge's cottage. I think I see him now. He
answered in some degree to his friend's description of
him, but was more gaunt and Don Quixote-like. He was
quaintly dressed (according to the *costume* of that uncon-
strained period) in a brown fustian jacket and striped
pantaloons. There was something of a roll, a lounge in
his gait, not unlike his own *Peter Bell*. There was a
severe, worn pressure of thought about his temples, a
fire in his eye (as if he saw something in objects more
than the outward appearance), an intense, high, narrow
forehead, a Roman nose, cheeks furrowed by strong
purpose and feeling, and a convulsive inclination to
laughter about the mouth, a good deal at variance with
the solemn, stately expression of the rest of his face.
Chantrey's bust wants the marking traits; but he was
teased into making it regular and heavy : Haydon's
head of him, introduced into the *Entrance of Christ
into Jerusalem*, is the most like his drooping weight of
thought and expression. He sat down and talked very
naturally and freely, with a mixture of clear, gushing
accents in his voice, a deep guttural intonation, and a
strong tincture of the northern *burr*, like the crust on
wine. He instantly began to make havoc of the half of a
Cheshire cheese on the table, and said, triumphantly, that
" his marriage with experience had not been so productive
as Mr. Southey's in teaching him a knowledge of the good
things of this life." He had been to see the *Castle
Spectre* by Monk Lewis, while at Bristol, and described it

very well. He said "it fitted the taste of the audience like a glove." This *ad captandum* merit was however by no means a recommendation of it, according to the severe principles of the new school, which reject rather than court popular effect. Wordsworth, looking out of the low, latticed window, said, "How beautifully the sun sets on that yellow bank!" I thought within myself, "With what eyes these poets see nature!" and ever after, when I saw the sun-set stream upon the objects facing it, conceived I had made a discovery, or thanked Mr. Wordsworth for having made one for me! We went over to All-Foxden again the day following, and Wordsworth read us the story of *Peter Bell* in the open air; and the comment upon it by his face and voice was very different from that of some later critics! Whatever might be thought of the poem, "his face was as a book where men might read strange matters," and he announced the fate of his hero in prophetic tones. There is a *chaunt* in the recitation both of Coleridge and Wordsworth, which acts as a spell upon the hearer, and disarms the judgment. Perhaps they have deceived themselves by making habitual use of this ambiguous accompaniment. Coleridge's manner is more full, animated, and varied; Wordsworth's more equable, sustained, and internal. The one might be termed more *dramatic*, the other more *lyrical*. Coleridge has told me that he himself liked to compose in walking over uneven ground, or breaking through the straggling branches of a copse-wood; whereas Wordsworth always wrote (if he could) walking up and down a straight gravel walk, or in some spot where the continuity of his verse met with no collateral interruption. Returning that same evening, I got into a metaphysical argument with Wordsworth, while Coleridge was explaining the different notes of the nightingale to his sister, in which we neither of us succeeded in making ourselves perfectly clear and intelligible. Thus I passed three weeks at Nether Stowey

and in the neighbourhood, generally devoting the after-
noons to a delightful chat in an arbour made of bark
by the poet's friend Tom Poole, sitting under two fine
elm-trees, and listening to the bees humming round us,
while we quaffed our *flip*. It was agreed, among other
things, that we should make a jaunt down the Bristol
Channel, as far as Linton. We set off together on foot,
Coleridge, John Chester, and I. This Chester was a
native of Nether Stowey, one of those who were attracted
to Coleridge's discourse as flies are to honey, or bees in
swarming-time to the sound of a brass pan. He "followed
in the chase like a dog who hunts, not like one that made
up the cry." He had on a brown cloth coat, boots, and
corduroy breeches, was low in stature, bow-legged, had a
drag in his walk like a drover, which he assisted by a
hazel switch, and kept on a sort of trot by the side of
Coleridge, like a running footman by a state coach, that
he might not lose a syllable or sound that fell from
Coleridge's lips. He told me his private opinion, that
Coleridge was a wonderful man. He scarcely opened his
lips, much less offered an opinion the whole way : yet of
the three, had I to choose during that journey, I would be
John Chester. He afterwards followed Coleridge into
Germany, where the Kantean philosophers were puzzled
how to bring him under any of their categories. When
he sat down at table with his idol, John's felicity was
complete ; Sir Walter Scott's, or Mr. Blackwood's, when
they sat down at the same table with the King, was not
more so. We passed Dunster on our right, a small town
between the brow of a hill and the sea. I remember
eyeing it wistfully as it lay below us : contrasted with the
woody scene around, it looked as clear, as pure, as
embrowned and ideal as any landscape I have seen since, of
Gaspar Poussin's or Domenichino's. We had a long day's
march (our feet kept time to the echoes of Coleridge's
tongue) through Minehead and by the Blue Anchor,

and on to Linton, which we did not reach till near midnight, and where we had some difficulty in making a lodgment. We, however, knocked the people of the house up at last, and we were repaid for our apprehensions and fatigue by some excellent rashers of fried bacon and eggs. The view in coming along had been splendid. We walked for miles and miles on dark brown heaths overlooking the Channel, with the Welsh hills beyond, and at times descended into little sheltered valleys close by the sea-side, with a smuggler's face scowling by us, and then had to ascend conical hills with a path winding up through a coppice to a barren top, like a monk's shaven crown, from one of which I pointed out to Coleridge's notice the bare masts of a vessel on the very edge of the horizon, and within the red-orbed disk of the setting sun, like his own spectre-ship in the *Ancient Mariner.* At Linton the character of the sea-coast becomes more marked and rugged. There is a place called the *Valley of Rocks* (I suspect this was only the poetical name for it), bedded among precipices overhanging the sea, with rocky caverns beneath, into which the waves dash, and where the sea-gull for ever wheels its screaming flight. On the tops of these are huge stones thrown transverse, as if an earthquake had tossed them there, and behind these is a fretwork of perpendicular rocks, something like the *Giant's Causeway.* A thunder-storm came on while we were at the inn, and Coleridge was running out bareheaded to enjoy the commotion of the elements in the *Valley of Rocks,* but as if in spite, the clouds only muttered a few angry sounds, and let fall a few refreshing drops. Coleridge told me that he and Wordsworth were to have made this place the scene of a prose-tale, which was to have been in the manner of, but far superior to, the *Death of Abel,* but they had relinquished the design. In the morning of the second day, we breakfasted luxuriously in an old-fashioned parlour on tea, toast, eggs, and honey, in the very sight of the bee-hives from which it had been taken, and a garden full of thyme and wild flowers that had produced it. On this occasion Coleridge spoke of Virgil's *Georgics*, but not well. I do not think he had much feeling for the classical or elegant.[1] It was in this room that we found a little worn-out copy of the *Seasons*, lying in a window-seat, on which Coleridge exclaimed, "*That* is true fame!" He said Thomson was a great poet, rather than a good one; his style was as meretricious as his thoughts were natural. He spoke of Cowper as the best modern poet. He said the *Lyrical Ballads* were an experiment about to be tried by him and Wordsworth, to see how far the public taste would endure poetry written in a more natural and simple style than had hitherto been attempted; totally discarding the artifices of poetical diction, and making use only of such words as had probably been common in the most ordinary language since the days of Henry II. Some comparison was introduced between Shakspeare and Milton. He said "he hardly knew which to prefer. Shakspeare appeared to him a mere stripling in the art; he was as tall and as strong, with infinitely more activity than Milton, but he never appeared to have come to man's estate; or if he had, he would not have been a man, but a monster." He spoke with contempt of Gray, and with intolerance of Pope. He did not like the versification of the latter. He observed that "the ears of these couplet-writers might be charged with having short memories, that could not retain the harmony of whole passages." He thought

---

[1] He had no idea of pictures, of Claude or Raphael, and at this time I had as little as he. He sometimes gives a striking account at present of the Cartoons at Pisa by Buffamalco and others; of one in particular, where Death is seen in the air brandishing his scythe, and the great and mighty of the earth shudder at his approach, while the beggars and the wretched kneel to him as their deliverer. He would, of course, understand so broad and fine a moral as this at any time.

little of Junius as a writer; he had a dislike of Dr. Johnson; and a much higher opinion of Burke as an orator and politician, than of Fox or Pitt. He, however, thought him very inferior in richness of style and imagery to some of our elder prose-writers, particularly Jeremy Taylor. He liked Richardson, but not Fielding; nor could I get him to enter into the merits of *Caleb Williams*.[1] In short, he was profound and discriminating with respect to those authors whom he liked, and where he gave his judgment fair play; capricious, perverse, and prejudiced in his antipathies and distastes. We loitered on the " ribbed sea sands," in such talk as this a whole morning, and, I recollect, met with a curious seaweed, of which John Chester told us the country name! A fisherman gave Coleridge an account of a boy that had been drowned the day before, and that they had tried to save him at the risk of their own lives. He said " he did not know how it was that they ventured, but, Sir, we have a *nature* towards one another." This expression, Coleridge remarked to me, was a fine illustration of that theory of disinterestedness which I (in common with Butler) had adopted. I broached to him an argument of mine to prove that *likeness* was not mere association of ideas. I said that the mark in the sand put one in mind of a man's foot, not because it was part of a former impression of a man's foot (for it was quite new), but because it was like the shape of a man's foot. He assented to the justness of this distinction (which I have explained at length elsewhere, for the benefit of the curious) and John Chester listened; not from any interest in the subject, but because he was astonished that I should be able to suggest anything to Coleridge that he did not already know. We returned on the third morning, and Coleridge remarked the silent cottage-smoke curling up the valleys where, a few

[1] By William Godwin. *Things as they are, or the Adventures of Caleb Williams.* London, 1794, 12mo, 3 vols.—ED.

evenings before, we had seen the lights gleaming through the dark.

In a day or two after we arrived at Stowey, we set ou , I on my return home, and he for Germany. It was a Sunday morning, and he was to preach that day for Dr. Toulmin of Taunton. I asked him if he had prepared anything for the occasion? He said he had not even thought of the text, but should as soon as we parted. I did not go to hear him—this was a fault—but we met in the evening at Bridgewater. The next day we had a long day's walk to Bristol, and sat down, I recollect, by a well-side on the road, to cool ourselves and satisfy our thirst, when Coleridge repeated to me some descriptive lines of his tragedy of *Remorse ;* which I must say became his mouth and that occasion better than they, some years after, did Mr. Elliston's and the Drury-lane boards—

> "Oh memory! shield me from the world's poor strife,
> And give those scenes thine everlasting life."

I saw no more of him for a year or two, during which period he had been wandering in the Hartz Forest, in Germany; and his return was cometary, meteorous, unlike his setting out. It was not till some time after that I knew his friends Lamb and Southey. The last always appears to me (as I first saw him) with a commonplace book under his arm, and the first with a *bon-mot* in his mouth. It was at Godwin's that I met him with Holcroft and Coleridge, where they were disputing fiercely which was the best—*Man as he was, or man as he is to be.* "Give me," says Lamb, "man as he is *not* to be." This saying was the beginning of a friendship between us, which I believe still continues. Enough of this for the present.

> "But there is matter for another rhyme,
> And I to this may add a second tale."

ESSAY II.

Of Persons one would wish to have seen.[1]

"Come like shadows—so depart."

LAMB it was, I think, who suggested this subject, as well as the defence of Guy Faux, which I urged him to execute. As, however, he would undertake neither, I suppose I must do both,[2] a task for which he would have been much fitter, no less from the temerity than the felicity of his pen—

"Never so sure our rapture to create
As when it touch'd the brink of all we hate."

Compared with him, I shall, I fear, make but a common-place piece of business of it; but I should be loth the idea was entirely lost, and besides I may avail· myself of some hints of his in the progress of it. I am sometimes, I suspect, a better reporter of the ideas of other people than expounder of my own. I pursue the one too far into paradox or mysticism; the others I am not bound to follow farther than I like, or than seems fair and reasonable.

On the question being started, Ayrton said, " I suppose the two first persons you would choose to see would be the two greatest names in English literature, Sir Isaac Newton and Mr. Locke?" In this Ayrton, as usual, reckoned without his host. Every one burst out a laughing at the expression of Lamb's face, in which impatience was restrained by courtesy. "Yes, the greatest names," he stammered out hastily, "but they were not persons—not

[1] Printed in the *Literary Remains*, 1836.—ED. The paper was written about 1820, but the event which it purports to describe occurred many years before.

[2] *A Defence of Guy Faux, with some Observations on Heroism*, appeared in the *Examiner* for 1821; but see *Memoirs of William Hazlitt*, 1867, i. 316–17.—ED.

persons."—" Not persons?" said Ayrton, looking wise and foolish at the same time, afraid his triumph might be premature. "That is," rejoined Lamb, "not characters, you know. By Mr. Locke and Sir Isaac Newton, you mean the *Essay on the Human Understanding*, and the *Principia*, which we have to this day. Beyond their contents there is nothing personally interesting in the men. But what we want to see any one *bodily* for, is when there is something peculiar, striking in the individuals, more than we can learn from their writings, and yet are curious to know. I dare say Locke and Newton were very like Kneller's portraits of them. But who could paint Shakspeare?"—" Ay," retorted Ayrton, "there it is; then I suppose you would prefer seeing him and Milton instead?"—"No," said Lamb, "neither. I have seen so much of Shakspeare on the stage and on book-stalls, in frontispieces and on mantel-pieces, that I am quite tired of the everlasting repetition : and as to Milton's face, the impressions that have come down to us of it I do not like ; it is too starched and puritanical ; and I should be afraid of losing some of the manna of his poetry in the leaven of his countenance and the precisian's band and gown."—" I shall guess no more," said Ayrton. " Who is it, then, you would like to see ' in his habit as he lived,' if you had your choice of the whole range of English literature ?" Lamb then named Sir Thomas Browne and Fulke Greville, the friend of Sir Philip Sidney, as the two worthies whom he should feel the greatest pleasure to encounter on the floor of his apartment in their night-gown and slippers, and to exchange friendly greeting with them. At this Ayrton laughed outright, and conceived Lamb was jesting with him ; but as no one followed his example, he thought there might be something in it, and waited for an explanation in a state of whimsical suspense. Lamb then (as well as I can remember a conversation that passed twenty years ago—how time slips!) went on as follows. "The reason why I pitch upon these two authors is, that their writings are riddles, and they themselves the most mysterious of personages. They resemble the soothsayers of old, who dealt in dark hints and doubtful oracles; and I should like to ask them the meaning of what no mortal but themselves, I should suppose, can fathom. There is Dr. Johnson : I have no curiosity, no strange uncertainty about him; he and Boswell together have pretty well let me into the secret of what passed through his mind. He and other writers like him are sufficiently explicit : my friends whose repose I should be tempted to disturb (were it in my power), are implicit, inextricable, inscrutable.

"When I look at that obscure but gorgeous prose composition the *Urn-burial,* I seem to myself to look into a deep abyss, at the bottom of which are hid pearls and rich treasure; or it is like a stately labyrinth of doubt and withering speculation, and I would invoke the spirit of the author to lead me through it. Besides, who would not be curious to see the lineaments of a man who, having himself been twice married, wished that mankind were propagated like trees! As to Fulke Greville, he is like nothing but one of his own 'Prologues spoken by the ghost of an old king of Ormus,' a truly formidable and inviting personage : his style is apocalyptical, cabalistical, a knot worthy of such an apparition to untie; and for the unravelling a passage or two, I would stand the brunt of an encounter with so portentous a commentator!"—I am afraid, in that case," said Ayrton, "that if the mystery were once cleared up, the merit might be lost;" and turning to me, whispered a friendly apprehension, that while Lamb continued to admire these old crabbed authors, he would never become a popular writer. Dr. Donne was mentioned as a writer of the same period, with a very interesting countenance, whose history was singular, and whose meaning was often quite as *uncomeatable,* without a personal citation from the dead, as that of any of his contemporaries. The volume was produced; and while some one was expatiating on the exquisite simplicity and beauty of the portrait prefixed to the old edition, Ayrton got hold of the poetry, and exclaiming " What have we here ?" read the following :

> " Here lies a She-Sun and a He-Moon there—
> She gives the best light to his sphear,
> Or each is both, and all, and so
> They unto one another nothing owe." [1]

There was no resisting this, till Lamb, seizing the volume, turned to the beautiful *Lines to his Mistress*,[2] dissuading her from accompanying him abroad, and read them with suffused features and a faltering tongue :

> " By our first strange and fatal interview,
> By all desires which thereof did ensue,
> By our long starving hopes, by that remorse
> Which my words' masculine perswasive force
> Begot in thee, and by the memory
> Of hurts, which spies and rivals threatned me,
> I calmely beg. But by thy father's wrath,
> By all paines which want and divorcement hath,
> I conjure thee; and all the oathes which I
> And thou have sworne to seale joynt constancy
> Here I unsweare, and overswear them thus—
> Thou shalt not love by wayes so dangerous.
> Temper, O fair love! love's impetuous rage,
> Be my true mistris still, not my faign'd Page ;
> I'll goe, and, by thy kinde leave, leave behinde
> Thee ! onely worthy to nurse in my minde.
> Thirst to come backe ; O, if thou die before,
> My soule, from other lands to thee shall soare.
> Thy (else almighty) beautie cannot move
> Rage from the seas, nor thy love teach them love.
> Nor tame wild Boreas' harshnesse ; thou hast reade
> How roughly hee in peeces shivered

---

[1] Epithalamion on Frederick, Count Palatina of the Rhyne and the Lady Elizabeth.

[2] Foolishly put among *Funeral Elegies*, forgetting the sense of *Elegy.* Davies's *Nosce Teipsum* is so called.

Fair Orithea, whom he swore he lov'd.
Fall ill or good, 'tis madnesse to have prov'd
Dangers unurg'd : Feed on this flattery,
That absent lovers one in th' other be.
Dissemble nothing, not a boy ; nor change
Thy bodie's habite, nor minde ; be not strange
To thyeselfe onely.   All will spie in thy face
A blushing, womanly, discovering grace.
Richly-clouth'd apes are call'd apes, and as soone
Eclips'd as bright, we call the moone the moon.
Men of France, chaugeable camelions,
Spittles of diseases, shops of fashions,
Love's fuellers, and the rightest company
Of players, which upon the world's stage be,
Will quickly know thee . . [seven lines left out].
O stay here ! for for thee
England is onely a worthy gallerie,
To walke in expectation ; till from thence
Our greatest King call thee to his presence.
When I am gone, dreame me some happinesse,
Nor let thy lookes our long-hid love confesse,
Nor praise, nor dispraise me ; nor blesse, nor curse
Openly love's force, nor in bed fright thy nurse
With midnight's startings, crying out, Oh, oh,
Nurse, oh, my love is slaine, I saw him goe
O'er the white Alpes alone ; I saw him, I, aye,
Assail'd, fight, taken, stabb'd, bleed, fall, and die.
Augure me better chance, except dread Jove
Thinke it enough for me to have had thy love."

Some one then inquired of Lamb if we could not see
from the window the Temple walk in which Chaucer used
to take his exercise ; and on his name being put to the
vote, I was pleased to find that there was a general
sensation in his favour in all but Ayrton, who said something about the ruggedness of the metre, and even objected
to the quaintness of the orthography.   I was vexed at this
superficial gloss, pertinaciously reducing everything to its
own trite level, and asked " if he did not think it would
be worth while to scan the eye that had first greeted the
Muse in that dim twilight and early dawn of English

literature; to see the head round which the visions of
fancy must have played like gleams of inspiration or a
sudden glory; to watch those lips that "lisped in
numbers, for the numbers came"—as by a miracle, or as
if the dumb should speak? Nor was it alone that he had
been the first to tune his native tongue (however imperfectly to modern ears); but he was himself a noble,
manly character, standing before his age and striving to
advance it; a pleasant humourist withal, who has not
only handed down to us the living manners of his time,
but had, no doubt, store of curious and quaint devices,
and would make as hearty a companion as mine Host of
the Tabard. His interview with Petrarch is fraught with
interest. Yet I would rather have seen Chaucer in
company with the author of the *Decameron,* and have heard
them exchange their best stories together—the *Squire's
Tale* against the Story of the *Falcon,* the *Wife of Bath's
Prologue* against the *Adventures of Friar Albert.* How
fine to see the high mysterious brow which learning then
wore, relieved by the gay, familiar tone of men of the
world, and by the courtesies of genius! Surely, the
thoughts and feelings which passed through the minds of
these great revivers of learning, these Cadmuses who
sowed the teeth of letters, must have stamped an expression on their features as different from the moderns
as their books, and well worth the perusal. Dante," I
continued, "is as interesting a person as his own Ugolino,
one whose lineaments curiosity would as eagerly devour
in order to penetrate his spirit, and the only one of the
Italian poets I should care much to see. There is a fine
portrait of Ariosto by no less a hand than Titian's; light,
Moorish, spirited, but not answering our idea. The same
artist's large colossal profile of Peter Aretine is the only
likeness of the kind that has the effect of conversing with
'the mighty dead;' and this is truly spectral, ghastly,
necromantic." Lamb put it to me if I should like to see

284 Of Persons one would wish to have seen.

Spenser as well as Chaucer; and I answered, without hesitation, "No; for that his beauties were ideal, visionary, not palpable or personal, and therefore connected with less curiosity about the man. His poetry was the essence of romance, a very halo round the bright orb of fancy; and the bringing in the individual might dissolve the charm. No tones of voice could come up to the mellifluous cadence of his verse; no form but of a winged angel could vie with the airy shapes he has described. He was (to my apprehension) rather a 'creature of the element, that lived in the rainbow and played in the plighted clouds,' than an ordinary mortal. Or if he did appear, I should wish it to be as a mere vision, like one of his own pageants, and that he should pass by unquestioned like a dream or sound—

—' *That* was Arion crown'd :
So went he playing on the wat'ry plain.'"

Captain Burney muttered something about Columbus, and Martin Burney hinted at the Wandering Jew; but the last was set aside as spurious, and the first made over to the New World.

"I should like," said Mrs. Reynolds, "to have seen Pope talk with Patty Blount; and I *have* seen Goldsmith." Every one turned round to look at Mrs. Reynolds, as if by so doing they could get a sight at Goldsmith.

"Where," asked a harsh, croaking voice, "was Dr. Johnson in the years 1745-6? He did not write anything that we know of, nor is there any account of him in Boswell during those two years. Was he in Scotland with the Pretender? He seems to have passed through the scenes in the Highlands in company with Boswell, many years after, 'with lack-lustre eye,' yet as if they were familiar to him, or associated in his mind with interests that he durst not explain. If so, it would be an additional reason for my liking him; and I would give something to have seen him seated in the tent with the youthful Majesty of Britain, and penning the Proclamation to all true subjects and adherents of the legitimate Government."

"I thought," said Ayrton, turning short round upon Lamb, "that you of the Lake School did not like Pope?" —"Not like Pope! My dear sir, you must be under a mistake—I can read him over and over for ever!"— "Why, certainly, the *Essay on Man* must be allowed to be a masterpiece."—"It may be so, but I seldom look into it."—"Oh! then it's his Satires you admire?"—"No, not his Satires, but his friendly Epistles and his compliments." —"Compliments! I did not know he ever made any."— "The finest," said Lamb, "that were ever paid by the wit of man. Each of them is worth an estate for life—nay, is an immortality. There is that superb one to Lord Cornbury:

> 'Despise low joys, low gains;
> Disdain whatever Cornbury disdains;
> Be virtuous, and be happy for your pains.'

Was there ever more artful insinuation of idolatrous praise? And then that noble apotheosis of his friend Lord Mansfield (however little deserved), when, speaking of the House of Lords, he adds:

> 'Conspicuous scene! another yet is nigh,
> (More silent far) where kings and poets lie;
> Where Murray (long enough his country's pride)
> Shall be no more than Tully or than Hyde!'

And with what a fine turn of indignant flattery he addresses Lord Bolingbroke:

> 'Why rail they then, if but one wreath of mine,
> Oh! all-accomplish'd St. John, deck thy shrine?'

Or turn," continued Lamb, with a slight hectic on his cheek and his eye glistening, "to his list of early friends:

> 'But why then publish? Granville the polite,
> And knowing Walsh, would tell me I could write;

Well-natured Garth inflamed with early praise,
And Congreve loved, and Swift endured my lays:
The courtly Talbot, Somers, Sheffield read,
Ev'n mitred Rochester would nod the head;
And St. John's self (great Dryden's friend before)
Received with open arms one poet more.
Happy my studies, if by these approved!
Happier their author, if by these beloved!
From these the world will judge of men and books,
Not from the Burnets, Oldmixons, and Cooks.'"

Here his voice totally failed him, and throwing down the book, he said, "Do you think I would not wish to have been friends with such a man as this?"

"What say you to Dryden?"—"He rather made a show of himself, and courted popularity in that lowest temple of fame, a coffee-shop, so as in some measure to vulgarise one's idea of him. Pope, on the contrary, reached the very *beau ideal* of what a poet's life should be; and his fame while living seemed to be an emanation from that which was to circle his name after death. He was so far enviable (and one would feel proud to have witnessed the rare spectacle in him) that he was almost the only poet and man of genius who met with his reward on this side of the tomb, who realised in friends, fortune, the esteem of the world, the most sanguine hopes of a youthful ambition, and who found that sort of patronage from the great during his lifetime which they would be thought anxious to bestow upon him after his death. Read Gay's verses to him on his supposed return from Greece, after his translation of Homer was finished, and say if you would not gladly join the bright procession that welcomed him home, or see it once more land at Whitehall stairs."—"Still," said Mrs. Reynolds, "I would rather have seen him talking with Patty Blount, or riding by in a coronet-coach with Lady Mary Wortley Montagu!"

Erasmus Phillips, who was deep in a game of piquet at the other end of the room, whispered to Martin Burney to ask if Junius would not be a fit person to invoke from the dead. "Yes," said Lamb, "provided he would agree to lay aside his mask."

We were now at a stand for a short time, when Fielding was mentioned as a candidate; only one, however, seconded the proposition. "Richardson?"—"By all means, but only to look at him through the glass door of his back shop, hard at work upon one of his novels (the most extraordinary contrast that ever was presented between an author and his works); not to let him come behind his counter, lest he should want you to turn customer, or to go upstairs with him, lest he should offer to read the first manuscript of Sir Charles Grandison, which was originally written in eight-and-twenty volumes octavo, or get out the letters of his female correspondents, to prove that Joseph Andrews was low."

There was but one statesman in the whole of English history that any one expressed the least desire to see— Oliver Cromwell, with his fine, frank, rough, pimply face, and wily policy; and one enthusiast, John Bunyan, the immortal author of the *Pilgrim's Progress.* It seemed that if he came into the room, dreams would follow him, and that each person would nod under his golden cloud, "nigh-sphered in heaven," a canopy as strange and stately as any in Homer.

Of all persons near our own time, Garrick's name was received with the greatest enthusiasm, who was proposed by Barron Field. He presently superseded both Hogarth and Handel, who had been talked of, but then it was on condition that he should act in tragedy and comedy, in the play and the farce, *Lear* and *Wildair* and *Abel Drugger.* What a *sight for sore eyes* that would be! Who would not part with a year's income at least, almost with a year of his natural life, to be present at it? Besides, as he could not act alone, and recitations are unsatisfactory things, what a troop he must bring with him—the silver-

tongued Barry, and Quin, and Shuter and Weston, and
Mrs. Clive and Mrs. Pritchard, of whom I have heard my
father speak as so great a favourite when he was young!
This would indeed be a revival of the dead, the restoring
of art; and so much the more desirable, as such is the
lurking scepticism mingled with our overstrained admiration of past excellence, that though we have the speeches
of Burke, the portraits of Reynolds, the writings of Goldsmith, and the conversation of Johnson, to show what
people could do at that period, and to confirm the universal testimony to the merits of Garrick; yet, as it was
before our time, we have our misgivings, as if he was
probably, after all, little better than a Bartlemy-fair actor,
dressed out to play *Macbeth* in a scarlet coat and laced
cocked-hat.   For one, I should like to have seen and
heard with my own eyes and ears.   Certainly, by all
accounts, if any one was ever moved by the true his-
trionic *œstus*, it was Garrick.   When he followed the
Ghost in *Hamlet*, he did not drop the sword, as most
actors do, behind the scenes, but kept the point raised the
whole way round, so fully was he possessed with the idea,
or so anxious not to lose sight of his part for a moment.
Once at a splendid dinner-party at Lord ——'s, they
suddenly missed Garrick, and could not imagine what was
become of him, till they were drawn to the window by the
convulsive screams and peals of laughter of a young
negro boy, who was rolling on the ground in an ecstasy of
delight to see Garrick mimicking a turkey-cock in the
court-yard, with his coat-tail stuck out behind, and in a
seeming flutter of feathered rage and pride.   Of our party
only two persons present had seen the British Roscius;
and they seemed as willing as the rest to renew their
acquaintance with their old favourite.

   We were interrupted in the hey-day and mid-career of
this fanciful speculation, by a grumbler in a corner, who
declared it was a shame to make all this rout about a

mere player and farce-writer, to the neglect and exclusion
of the fine old dramatists, the contemporaries and rivals
of Shakspeare. Lamb said he had anticipated this objection when he had named the author of *Mustapha* and
Alaham; and, out of caprice, insisted upon keeping him to
represent the set, in preference to the wild, hair-brained
enthusiast, Kit Marlowe; to the sexton of St. Ann's,
Webster, with his melancholy yew-trees and death's-
heads; to Decker, who was but a garrulous proser; to
the voluminious Heywood; and even to Beaumont and
Fletcher, whom we might offend by complimenting the
wrong author on their joint productions. Lord Brooke,
on the contrary, stood quite by himself, or, in Cowley's
words, was "a vast species alone." Some one hinted at
the circumstance of his being a lord, which rather startled
Lamb, but he said a *ghost* would perhaps dispense with
strict etiquette, on being regularly addressed by his title.
Ben Jonson divided our suffrages pretty equally. Some
were afraid he would begin to traduce Shakspeare, who
was not present to defend himself. "If he grows disagreeable," it was whispered aloud, "there is Godwin can
match him." At length, his romantic visit to Drummond
of Hawthornden was mentioned, and turned the scale in
his favour.

Lamb inquired if there was any one that was hanged
that I would choose to mention? And I answered, Eugene
Aram. The name of the " Admirable Crichton " was
suddenly started as a splendid example of *waste* talents, so
different from the generality of his countrymen. This
choice was mightily approved by a North-Briton present,
who declared himself descended from that prodigy of
learning and accomplishment, and said he had family plate
in his possession as vouchers for the fact, with the initials
A. C.—*Admirable Chricton!* Hunt laughed, or rather
roared, as heartily at this as I should think he has done
for many years.

The last named Mitre-courtier[1] then wished to know whether there were any metaphysicians to whom one might be tempted to apply the wizard spell? I replied, there were only six in modern times deserving the name —Hobbes, Berkeley, Butler, Hartley, Hume, Leibnitz; and perhaps Jonathan Edwards, a Massachusetts man.[2] As to the French, who talked fluently of having *created* this science, there was not a tittle in any of their writings that was not to be found literally in the authors I had mentioned. [Horne Tooke, who might have a claim to come in under the head of Grammar, was still living.] None of these names seemed to excite much interest, and I did not plead for the re-appearance of those who might be thought best fitted by the abstracted nature of their studies for the present spiritual and disembodied state, and who, even while on this living stage, were nearly divested of common flesh and blood. As Ayrton, with an uneasy, fidgetty face, was about to put some question about Mr. Locke and Dugald Stewart, he was prevented by Martin Burney, who observed, "If J—— was here, he would undoubtedly be for having up those profound and redoubted socialists, Thomas Aquinas and Duns Scotus." I said this might be fair enough in him who had read, or fancied he had read, the original works, but I did not see how we could have any right to call up these authors to give an account of themselves in person, till we had looked into their writings.

[1] Lamb at this time occupied chambers in Mitre-court, Temple.

[2] Bacon is not included in this list, nor do I know where he should come in. It is not easy to make room for him and his reputation together. This great and celebrated man in some of his works recommends it to pour a bottle of claret into the ground of a morning, and to stand over it, inhaling the perfumes. So he sometimes enriched the dry and barren soil of speculation with the fine aromatic spirit of his genius. His *Essays* and his *Advancement of Learning* are works of vast depth and scope of observation. The last, though it contains no positive discoveries, is a noble chart of the human intellect, and a guide to all future inquirers.

By this time it should seem that some rumour of our whimsical deliberation had got wind, and had disturbed the *irritable genus* in their shadowy abodes, for we received messages from several candidates that we had just been thinking of. Gray declined our invitation, though he had not yet been asked : Gay offered to come, and bring in his hand the Duchess of Bolton, the original Polly : Steele and Addison left their cards as Captain Sentry[1] and Sir Roger de Coverley : Swift came in and sat down without speaking a word, and quitted the room as abruptly : Otway and Chatterton were seen lingering on the opposite side of the Styx, but could not muster enough between them to pay Charon his fare : Thomson fell asleep in the boat, and was rowed back again ; and Burns sent a low fellow, one John Barleycorn, an old companion of his, who had conducted him to the other world, to say that he had during his lifetime been drawn out of his retirement as a show, only to be made an exciseman of, and that he would rather remain where he was. He desired, however, to shake hands by his representative—the hand, thus held out, was in a burning fever, and shook prodigiously.

The room was hung round with several portraits of eminent painters. While we were debating whether we should demand speech with these masters of mute eloquence, whose features were so familiar to us, it seemed that all at once they glided from their frames, and seated themselves at some little distance from us. There was Leonardo, with his majestic beard and watchful eye, having a bust of Archimedes before him ; next him was Raphael's graceful head turned round to the Fornarina ; and on his other side was Lucretia Borgia, with calm, golden locks ; Michael Angelo had placed the model of St. Peter's on the table before him ; Correggio had an angel at his side ; Titian was seated with his mistress between himself and Giorgione ; Guido was accompanied by his own Aurora,

[1] A member of the *Spectator* Club.—ED.

who took a dice-box from him; Claude held a mirror in
his hand; Rubens patted a beautiful panther (led in by a
satyr) on the head; Vandyke appeared as his own Paris,
and Rembrandt was hid under firs, gold chains, and jewels,
which Sir Joshua eyed closely, holding his hand so as to
shade his forehead.   Not a word was spoken; and as we
rose to do them homage, they still presented the same
surface to the view.   Not being *bonâ-fide* representations
of living people, we got rid of the splendid apparitions by
signs and dumb show.   As soon as they had melted into
thin air, there was a loud noise at the outer door, and we
found it was Giotto, Cimabue, and Ghirlandaio, who had
been raised from the dead by their earnest desire to see
their illustrious successors—

> " Whose names on earth
> In Fame's eternal records live for aye !"

Finding them gone, they had no ambition to be seen after
them, and mournfully withdrew.   " Egad !" said Lamb,
" these are the very fellows I should like to have had
some talk with, to know how they could see to paint when
all was dark around them."
    " But shall we have nothing to say," interrogated
G. J——, " to the *Legend of Good Women ?*"—" Name,
name, Mr. J——," cried Hunt in a boisterous tone of
friendly exultation, " name as many as you please, without
reserve or fear of molestation !"   J—— was perplexed
between so many amiable recollections, that the name of
the lady of his choice expired in a pensive whiff of his
pipe ; and Lamb impatiently declared for the Duchess of
Newcastle.   Mrs. Hutchinson was no sooner mentioned,
than she carried the day from the Duchess.   We were the
less solicitous on this subject of filling up the posthumous
lists of Good Women, as there was already one in the
room as good, as sensible, and in all respects as exemplary,
as the best of them could be for their lives !   " I should

like vastly to have seen Ninon de l'Enclos," said that incomparable person ; and this immediately put us in mind that we had neglected to pay honour due to our friends on the other side of the Channel : Voltaire, the patriarch of levity, and Rousseau, the father of sentiment ; Montaigne and Babelais (great in wisdom and in wit) ; Molière and that illustrious group that are collected round him (in the print of that subject) to hear him read his comedy of the *Tartuffe* at the house of Ninon ; Racine, La Fontaine, Rochefoucalt, St. Evremont, &c.

"There is one person," said a shrill, querulous voice, " I would rather see than all these—Don Quixote !"

" Come, come !" said Hunt ; " I thought we should have no heroes, real or fabulous. What say you, Mr. Lamb ? Are you for eking out your shadowy list with such names as Alexander, Julius Cæsar, Tamerlane, or Ghengis Khan ?"—" Excuse me," said Lamb ; " on the subject of characters in active life, plotters and disturbers of the world, I have a crotchet of my own, which I beg leave to reserve."—" No, no ! come, out with your worthies !"— " What do you think of Guy Fawkes and Judas Iscariot ?" Hunt turned an eye upon him like a wild Indian, but cordial and full of smothered glee. " Your most exquisite reason !" was echoed on all sides ; and Ayrton thought that Lamb had now fairly entangled himself. " Why I cannot but think," retorted he of the wistful countenance, " that Guy Fawkes, that poor, fluttering annual scarecrow of straw and rags, is an ill-used gentleman. I would give something to see him sitting pale and emaciated, sur- rounded by his matches and his barrels of gunpowder, and expecting the moment that was to transport him to Paradise for his heroic self-devotion ; but if I say any more, there is that fellow Godwin will make something of it. And as to Judas Iscariot, my reason is different. I would fain see the face of him who, having dipped his hand in the same dish with the Son of Man, could afterwards betray him. I have no conception of such a thing; nor have I ever seen any picture (not even Leonardo's very fine one) that gave me the least idea of it."—"You have said enough, Mr. Lamb, to justify your choice."

" Oh ! ever right, Menenius—ever right !"

" There is only one other person I can ever think of after this," continued Lamb; but without mentioning a name that once put on a semblance of mortality. "If Shakspeare was to come into the room, we should all rise up to meet him; but if that person was to come into it, we should all fall down and try to kiss the hem of his garment !"

As a lady present seemed now to get uneasy at the turn the conversation had taken, we rose up to go. The morning broke with that dim, dubious light by which Giotto, Cimabue, and Ghirlandaio must have seen to paint their earliest works; and we parted to meet again and renew similar topics at night, the next night, and the night after that, till that night overspread Europe which saw no dawn. The same event, in truth, broke up our little Congress that broke up the great one. But that was to meet again : our deliberations have never been resumed.

ESSAY III.

On Party Spirit.

PARTY spirit is one of the *profoundnesses of Satan*, or, in modern language, one of the dexterous *equivoques* and contrivances of our self-love, to prove that we, and those who agree with us, combine all that is excellent and praiseworthy in our own persons (as in a ring-fence), and that all the vices and deformity of human nature take refuge with those who differ from us. It is extending and fortifying the principle of the *amour-propre*, by calling to its aid the *espirit de corps,* and screening and surrounding our favourite propensities and obstinate caprices in the hollow squares or dense phalanxes of sects and parties. This is a happy mode of pampering our self-complacency, and persuading ourselves that we, and those that side with us, are "the salt of the earth;" of giving vent to the morbid humours of our pride, envy, hatred, malice, and all uncharitableness, those natural secretions of the human heart, under the pretext of self-defence, the public safety, or a voice from heaven, as it may happen ; and of heaping every excellence into one scale, and throwing all the obloquy and contempt into the other, in virtue of a nick-name, a watchword of party, a badge, the colour of a ribbon, the cut of a dress. We thus desolate the globe, or tear a country in pieces, to show that we are the only people fit to live in it; and fancy ourselves angels, while we are playing the devil. In this manner the Huron devours the Iroquois, because he is an Iroquois ; and the Iroquois the Huron, for a similar reason : neither suspects that he does it because he himself is a savage, and no better than a wild beast ; and is convinced in his own breast that the difference of man and tribe makes a total difference in the case. The Papist persecutes the Protestant, the Protestant persecutes the Papist in his turn ; and each fancies that he has a plenary right to do so, while he keeps in view only the offensive epithet which "cuts the common link of brotherhood between them." The Church of England ill-treated the Dissenters, and the Dissenters, when they had the opportunity, did not spare the Church of England. The Whig calls the Tory a knave, the Tory compliments the Whig with the same title, and each thinks the abuse sticks to the party-name, and has nothing to do with himself or the generic name of *man.* On the contrary, it cuts both ways ; but while the Whigs say "The Tory is a knave, because he is a Tory," this is as much as to say, "I cannot be a knave, because I am a Whig ;" and by exaggerating the profligacy of his opponent, he imagines he is laying the sure foundation, and raising the lofty superstructure, of his own praises. But if he says, which is the truth, " The Tory is not a rascal, because he is a Tory, but because human nature in power, and with the temptation, is a rascal," then this would imply that the seeds of depravity are sown in his own bosom, and might shoot out into full growth and luxuriance if he got into place, and this he does not wish to develop till he *does* get into place.

We may be intolerant even in advocating the cause of toleration, and so bent on making proselytes to free-thinking as to allow no one to think freely but ourselves. The most boundless liberality in appearance may amount in reality to the most monstrous ostracism of opinion—not condemning this or that tenet, or standing up for this or that sect or party, but in a supercilious superiority to all sects and parties alike, and proscribing in one sweeping clause, all arts, sciences, opinions, and pursuits but our own. Till the time of Locke and Toland a general toleration was never dreamt of : it was thought right on all hands to punish and discountenance heretics and schismatics, but each party alternately claimed to be true Christians and Orthodox believers. Daniel De Foe, who spent his whole life, and wasted his strength, in asserting the right of the Dissenters to a Toleration (and got nothing for his pains but the pillory), was scandalised at the proposal of the general principle, and was equally strenuous in excluding Quakers, Anabaptists, Socinians, Sceptics, and all who did not agree in the *essentials* of Christianity — that is, who did not agree with him—from the benefit of such an indulgence to tender consciences. We wonder at the cruelties formerly practised upon the Jews : is there anything wonderful in it ? They were at that time the only people to make a butt and a bugbear of, to set up as a mark of indignity, and as a foil to our self-love, for the

feræ naturæ principle that is within us, and always craving
its prey to run down, to worry and make sport of at discretion, and without mercy—the unvarying uniformity
and implicit faith of the Catholic Church had imposed
silence, and put a curb on our jarring dissensions, heart-
burnings, and ill-blood, so that we had no pretence for
quarrelling among ourselves for the glory of God or the
salvation of men :—a JORDANUS BRUNO, an Atheist or
sorcerer, once in a way, would hardly suffice to stay the
stomach of our theological rancour ; we therefore fell with
might and main upon the Jews as a forlorn hope in this
dearth of objects of spite or zeal ; or when the whole
of Europe was reconciled to the bosom of holy Mother
Church, went to the Holy Land in search of a difference
of opinion, and a ground of mortal offence : but no sooner
was there a division of the Christian World, than Papist
fell on Protestants or Schismatics, and Schismatics upon
one another, with the same loving fury as they had before
fallen upon Turks and Jews. The disposition is always
there, like a muzzled mastiff; the pretext only is wanting;
and this is furnished by a name, which, as soon as it is
affixed to different sects or parties, gives us a licence, we
think, to let loose upon them all our malevolence, domineering humour, love of power, and wanton mischief, as
if they were of different species. The sentiment of the
pious English Bishop was good, who, on seeing a criminal
led to execution, exclaimed, "There goes my wicked
self !"

If we look at common patriotism, it will furnish an
illustration of party spirit. One would think by an
Englishman's hatred of the French, and his readiness to
die fighting with and for his countrymen, that all the
nation were united as one man, in heart and hand—and so
they are in war-time and as an exercise of their loyalty
and courage : but let the crisis be over, and they cool
wonderfully; begin to feel the distinctions of English,

Irish, and Scotch; fall out among themselves upon some minor distinction; the same hand that was eager to shed the blood of a Frenchman, will not give a crust of bread or a cup of cold water to a fellow countryman in distress; and the heroes who defended the "wooden walls of old England" are left to expose their wounds and crippled limbs to gain a pittance from the passengers, or to perish of hunger, cold, and neglect, in our highways. Such is the effect of our boasted nationality : it is active, fierce in doing mischief; dormantly lukewarm in doing good. We may also see why the greatest stress is laid on trifles in religion, and why the most violent animosities arise out of the smallest differences, either in this or in politics.

In the first place, it would never do to establish our superiority over others by the acquisition of greater virtues, or by discarding our vices; but it is charming to do this by merely repeating a different formula of prayer, turning to the east instead of the west. He should fight boldly for such a distinction, who is persuaded it will furnish him a passport to the other world, and entitle him to look down on the rest of his fellows as *given over to perdition*. Secondly, we often hate those most with whom we have only a slight shade of difference, whether in politics or religion; because as the whole is a contest for precedence and infallibility, we find it more difficult to draw the line of distinction where so many points are conceded, and are staggered in our conviction by the arguments of those whom we cannot despise as totally and incorrigibly in the wrong. The High Church party in Queen Anne's time were disposed to sacrifice the Low Church and Dissenters to the Papists, because they were more galled by their arguments and disconcerted with their pretensions. In private life the reverse of the foregoing holds good : that is, trades and professions present a direct contrast to sects and parties. A conformity in sentiment strengthens our party and opinion, but those who have a similarity of pursuit, are rivals in interest; and hence the old maxim, that *two of a trade can never agree.*

1830.

ESSAY IV.

On the Feeling of Immortality in Youth.

No young man believes he shall ever die. It was a saying of my brother's,[1] and a fine one. There is a feeling of Eternity in youth which makes us amends for everything. To be young is to be as one of the Immortals. One half of time indeed is spent—the other half remains in store for us with all its countless treasures, for there is no line drawn, and we see no limit to our hopes and wishes. We make the coming age our own—

"The vast, the unbounded prospect lies before us."

Death, old age, are words without a meaning, a dream, a fiction, with which we have nothing to do. Others may have undergone, or may still undergo them—we "bear a charmed life," which laughs to scorn all such idle fancies. As, in setting out on a delightful journey, we strain our eager sight forward,

"Bidding the lovely scenes at distance hail,"

and see no end to prospect after prospect, new objects presenting themselves as we advance, so in the outset of life we see no end to our desires nor to the opportunities of gratifying them. We have as yet found no obstacle, no disposition to flag, and it seems that we can go on so for ever. We look round in a new world, full of life and motion, and ceaseless progress, and feel in ourselves all the vigour and spirit to keep pace with it, and do not

[1] John Hazlitt, the miniature painter.—ED.

foresee from any present signs how we shall be left behind
in the race, decline into old age, and drop into the grave.
It is the simplicity and, as it were, abstractedness of our
feelings in youth that (so to speak) identifies us with
nature and (our experience being weak and our passions
strong) makes us fancy ourselves immortal like it.   Our
short-lived connection with being, we fondly flatter ourselves, is an indissoluble and lasting union.   As infants
smile and sleep, we are rocked in the cradle of our desires,
and hushed into fancied security by the roar of the universe around us—we quaff the cup of life with eager thirst
without draining it, and joy and hope seem ever mantling
to the brim—objects press around us, filling the mind
with their magnitude and with the throng of desires that
wait upon them, so that there is no room for the thoughts
of death.   We are too much dazzled by the gorgeousness
and novelty of the bright waking dream about us to discern the dim shadow lingering for us in the distance.
Nor would the hold that life has taken of us permit us to
detach our thoughts that way, even if we could.   We are
too much absorbed in present objects and pursuits.
While the spirit of youth remains unimpaired, ere "the
wine of life is drunk," we are like people intoxicated or in
a fever, who are hurried away by the violence of their
own sensations : it is only as present objects begin to pall
upon the sense, as we have been disappointed in our
favourite pursuits, cut off from our closest ties, that we by
degrees become weaned from the world, that passion
loosens its hold upon futurity, and that we begin to
contemplate as in a glass darkly the possibility of parting
with it for good.   Till then, the example of others has no
effect upon us.   Casualties we avoid ; the slow approaches
of age we play at *hide and seek* with.   Like the foolish fat
scullion in Sterne, who hears that Master Bobby is dead,
our only reflection is, "So am not I !"   The idea of death,
instead of staggering our confidence, only seems to

strengthen and enhance our sense of the possession and enjoyment of life. Others may fall around us like leaves, or be mowed down by the scythe of Time like grass : these are but metaphors to the unreflecting, buoyant ears and overweening presumption of youth. It is not till we see the flowers of Love, Hope, and Joy withering around us, that we give up the flattering delusions that before led us on, and that the emptiness and dreariness of the prospect before us reconciles us hypothetically to the silence of the grave.

Life is indeed a strange gift, and its privileges are most mysterious. No wonder when it is first granted to us, that our gratitude, our admiration, and our delight should prevent us from reflecting on our own nothingness, or from thinking it will ever be recalled. Our first and strongest impressions are borrowed from the mighty scene that is opened to us, and we unconsciously transfer its durability as well as its splendour to ourselves. So newly found, we cannot think of parting with it yet, or at least put off that consideration *sine die*. Like a rustic at a fair, we are full of amazement and rapture, and have no thought of going home, or that it will soon be night. We know our existence only by ourselves, and confound our knowledge with the objects of it. We and Nature are therefore one. Otherwise the illusion, the " feast of reason and the flow of soul," to which we are invited, is a mockery and a cruel insult. We do not go from a play till the last act is ended, and the lights are about to be extinguished. But the fairy face of Nature still shines on : shall we be called away before the curtain falls, or ere we have scarce had a glimpse of what is going on? Like children, our step-mother Nature holds us up to see the raree-show of the universe, and then, as if we were a burden to her to support, lets us fall down again. Yet what brave sub-lunary things does not this pageant present, like a ball or *fête* of the universe !

To see the golden sun, the azure sky, the out-stretched ocean; to walk upon the green earth, and be lord of a thousand creatures; to look down yawning precipices or over distant sunny vales; to see the world spread out under one's feet on a map; to bring the stars near; to view the smallest insects through a microscope; to read history, and consider the revolutions of empire and the successions of generations; to hear of the glory of Tyre, of Sidon, of Babylon, and of Susa, and to say all these were before me and are now nothing; to say I exist in such a point of time, and in such a point of space; to be a spectator and a part of its ever-moving scene; to witness the change of season, of spring and autumn, of winter and summer; to feel hot and cold, pleasure and pain, beauty and deformity, right and wrong; to be sensible to the accidents of nature; to consider the mighty world of eye and ear; to listen to the stock-dove's notes amid the forest deep; to journey over moor and mountain; to hear the midnight sainted choir; to visit lighted halls, or the cathedral's gloom, or sit in crowded theatres and see life itself mocked; to study the works of art and refine the sense of beauty to agony; to worship fame, and to dream of immortality; to look upon the Vatican, and to read Shakspeare; to gather up the wisdom of the ancients, and to pry into the future; to listen to the trump of war, the shout of victory; to question history as to the movements of the human heart; to seek for truth; to plead the cause of humanity; to overlook the world as if time and nature poured their treasures at our feet—to be and to do all this, and then in a moment to be nothing—to have it all snatched from us as by a juggler's trick, or a phantasmagoria! There is something in this transition from all to nothing that shocks us and damps the enthusiasm of youth new flushed with hope and pleasure, and we cast the comfortless thought as far from us as we can. In the first enjoyment of the estate of life we discard the fear of debts and duns,

and never think of the final payment of our great debt to
Nature. Art we know is long ; life, we flatter ourselves,
should be so too. We see no end of the difficulties and
delays we have to encounter : perfection is slow of attainment, and we must have time to accomplish it in. The
fame of the great names we look up to is immortal : and
shall not we who contemplate it imbibe a portion of
ethereal fire, the *divinæ particula auræ,* which nothing can
extinguish ? A wrinkle in Rembrandt or in Nature takes
whole days to resolve itself into its component parts, its
softenings and its sharpnesses ; we refine upon our
perfections, and unfold the intricacies of nature. What a
prospect for the future ! What a task have we not begun !
And shall we be arrested in the middle of it ? We do not
count our time thus employed lost, or our pains thrown
away ; we do not flag or grow tired, but gain new vigour
at our endless task. Shall Time, then, grudge us to finish
what we have begun, and have formed a compact with
Nature to do ? Why not fill up the blank that is left us in
this manner ? I have looked for hours at a Rembrandt
without being conscious of the flight of time, but with
ever new wonder and delight, have thought that not only
my own but another existence I could pass in the same
manner. This rarefied, refined existence seemed to have
no end, nor stint, nor principle of decay in it. The print
would remain long after I who looked on it had become
the prey of worms. The thing seems in itself out of all
reason : health, strength, appetite are opposed to the idea
of death, and we are not ready to credit it till we have
found our illusions vanished, and our hopes grown cold.
Objects in youth, from novelty, &c., are stamped upon
the brain with such force and integrity that one thinks
nothing can remove or obliterate them. They are riveted
there, and appear to us as an element of our nature. It must
be a mere violence that destroys them, not a natural decay.
In the very strength of this persuasion we seem to enjoy an

age by anticipation. We melt down years into a single moment of intense sympathy, and by anticipating the fruits defy the ravages of time. If, then, a single moment of our lives is worth years, shall we set any limits to its total value and extent? Again, does it not happen that so secure do we think ourselves of an indefinite period of existence, that at times, when left to ourselves, and impatient of novelty, we feel annoyed at what seems to us the slow and creeping progress of time, and argue that if it always moves at this tedious snail's pace it will never come to an end? How ready are we to sacrifice any space of time which separates us from a favourite object, little thinking that before long we shall find it move too fast.

For my part, I started in life with the French Revolution, and I have lived, alas! to see the end of it. But I did not foresee this result. My sun arose with the first dawn of liberty, and I did not think how soon both must set. The new impulse to ardour given to men's minds imparted a congenial warmth and glow to mine; we were strong to run a race together, and I little dreamed that long before mine was set, the sun of liberty would turn to blood, or set once more in the night of despotism. Since then, I confess, I have no longer felt myself young, for with that my hopes fell.

I have since turned my thoughts to gathering up some of the fragments of my early recollections, and putting them into a form to which I might occasionally revert. The future was barred to my progress, and I turned for consolation and encouragement to the past. It is thus that, while we find our personal and substantial identity vanishing from us, we strive to gain a reflected and vicarious one in our thoughts: we do not like to perish wholly, and wish to bequeath our names, at least, to posterity. As long as we can make our cherished thoughts and nearest interests live in the minds of others, we do not appear to have retired altogether from the stage. We still occupy the breasts of others, and exert an influence and power over them, and it is only our bodies that are reduced to dust and powder. Our favourite speculations still find encouragement, and we make as great a figure in the eye of the world, or perhaps a greater, than in our life-time. The demands of our self-love are thus satisfied, and these are the most imperious and unremitting. Besides, if by our intellectual superiority we survive ourselves in this world, by our virtues and faith we may attain an interest in another, and a higher state of being, and may thus be recipients at the same time of men and of angels.

> "E'en from the tomb the voice of Nature cries,
> E'en in our ashes live their wonted fires."

As we grow old, our sense of the value of time becomes vivid. Nothing else, indeed, seems of any. consequence. We can never cease wondering that that which has ever been should cease to be. We find many things remain the same: why then should there be change in us. This adds a convulsive grasp of whatever is, a sense of a falla-cious hollowness in all we see. Instead of the full, pulpy feeling of youth tasting existence and every object in it, all is flat and vapid,—a whited sepulchre, fair without but full of ravening and all uncleanness within. The world is a witch that puts us off with false shows and appearances. The simplicity of youth, the confiding expectation, the boundless raptures, are gone: we only think of getting out of it as well as we can, and without any great mischance or annoyance. The flush of illusion, even the complacent retrospect of past joys and hopes, is over: if we can slip out of life without indignity, can escape with little bodily infirmity, and frame our minds to the calm and respectable composure of *still-life* before we return to physical nothingness, it is as much as we can

X

expect. We do not die wholly at our deaths: we have mouldered away gradually long before. Faculty after faculty, interest after interest, attachment after attachment disappear: we are torn from ourselves while living, year after year sees us no longer the same, and death only consigns the last fragment of what we were to the grave. That we should wear out by slow stages, and dwindle at last into nothing, is not wonderful, when even in our prime our strongest impressions leave little trace but for the moment, and we are the creatures of petty circumstance. How little effect is made on us in our best days by the books we have read, the scenes we have witnessed, the sensations we have gone through! Think only of the feelings we experience in reading a fine romance (one of Sir Walter's, for instance); what beauty, what sublimity, what interest, what heart-rending emotions! You would suppose the feelings you then experienced would last for ever, or subdue the mind to their own harmony and tone: while we are reading it seems as if nothing could ever put us out of our way, or trouble us :—the first splash of mud that we get on entering the street, the first twopence we are cheated out of, the feeling vanishes clean out of our minds, and we become the prey of petty and annoying circumstance. The mind soars to the lofty: it is at home in the grovelling, the disagreeable, and the little. And yet we wonder that age should be feeble and querulous, —that the freshness of youth should fade away. Both worlds would hardly satisfy the extravagance of our desires and of our presumption.

ESSAY V.

On Public Opinion.

" Scared at the sound itself has made."

ONCE asking a friend why he did not bring forward an explanation of a circumstance, in which his conduct had been called in question, he said, " His friends were satisfied on the subject, and he cared very little about the opinion of the world." I made answer that I did not consider this a good ground to rest his defence upon, for that a man's friends seldom thought better of him than the world did. I see no reason to alter this opinion. Our friends, indeed, are more apt than a mere stranger to join in with, or be silent under any imputation thrown out against us, because they are apprehensive they may be indirectly implicated in it, and they are bound to betray us to save their own credit. To judge of our jealousy, our sensibility, our high notions of responsibility, on this score, only consider if a single individual lets fall a solitary remark implying a doubt of the wit, the sense, the courage of a friend—how it staggers us—how it makes us shake with fear—how it makes us call up all our eloquence and airs of self-consequence in his defence, lest our partiality should be supposed to have blinded our perceptions, and we should be regarded as the dupes of a mistaken admiration. We already begin to meditate an escape from a losing cause, and try to find out some other fault in the character under discussion, to show that we are not behind-hand (if the truth must be spoken) in sagacity, and a sense of the ridiculous. If, then, this is the case with the first flaw, the first doubt, the first speck that dims the sun of friendship, so that we are ready to turn our backs on our sworn attachments and well-known professions the instant we have not all the world with us, what must it be when we have all the world against us; when our friend, instead of a single stain, is covered with mud from head to foot; how shall we expect our feeble voices not to be drowned in the general clamour? how shall we dare to oppose our partial and mis-timed suffrages to the just indignation of the public? Or if it should not amount to this, how shall we answer the silence and contempt with which his name is received. How shall we animate the great mass of indifference or distrust with our private enthusiasm? how defeat the involuntary smile, or the suppressed sneer, with the burst of generous feeling and the glow of honest conviction? It is a thing not to be thought of, unless we would enter into a crusade against prejudice and malignity, devote ourselves as martyrs to friendship, raise a controversy in every company we go into, quarrel with every person we meet, and after making ourselves and every one else uncomfortable, leave off, not by clearing our friend's reputation, but by involving our own pretensions to decency and common sense. People will not fail to observe that a man may have his reasons for his faults or vices; but that for another to volunteer a defence of them, is without excuse. It is, in fact, an attempt to deprive them of the great and only benefit they derive from the supposed errors of their neighbours and contemporaries—the pleasure of backbiting and railing at them, which they call *seeing justice done.* It is not a single breath of rumour or opinion; but the whole atmosphere is infected with a sort of aguish taint of anger and suspicion, that relaxes the nerves of fidelity, and makes our most sanguine resolutions sicken and turn pale; and he who is proof against it, must either be armed with a love of truth, or a contempt for mankind, which places him out of the reach of ordinary rules and calculations. For myself, I do not shrink from defending a cause or a friend *under a cloud ;* though in neither case will cheap or common efforts suffice. But, in the first, you merely stand up for your own judgment and principles against fashion and prejudice, and thus assume a sort of manly and heroic attitude of defiance : in the last (which makes it a matter of greater nicety and nervous sensibility), you sneak behind another to throw your gauntlet at the whole world, and it requires a double stock of stoical firmness not to be laughed out of your boasted zeal and independence as a romantic and *amiable weakness.*[1]

There is nothing in which all the world agree but in running down some obnoxious individual. It may be supposed that this is not for nothing, and that they have good reasons for what they do. On the contrary, I will undertake to say, that so far from there being invariably just grounds for such an universal outcry, the universality of the outcry is often the only ground of the opinion ; and that it is purposely raised upon this principle, that all other proof or evidence against the person meant to be run down is wanting. Nay, further, it may happen, that while the clamour is at the loudest ; while you hear it from all quarters ; while it blows a perfect hurricane ; while " the world rings with the vain stir "—not one of those who are most eager in hearing and echoing knows what it is about, or is not fully persuaded that the charge is equally false, malicious, and absurd. It is like the wind, that " no man knoweth whence it cometh, or whither it goeth." It is *vox et præterea nihil.* What, then, is it that gives it its confident circulation and its irresistible force ? It is the loudness of the organ with which it is pronounced, the stentorian lungs

---

[1] The only friends whom we defend with zeal and obstinacy are our relations. They seem part of ourselves. For our other friends we are only answerable, so long as we countenance them ; and therefore cut the connection as soon as possible. But who ever willingly gave up the good dispositions of a child, or the honour of a parent ?

of the multitude ; the number of voices that take it up and repeat it, because others have done so ; the rapid flight and the impalpable nature of common fame, that makes it a desperate undertaking for any individual to inquire into or arrest the mischief that, in the deafening buzz or loosened roar of laughter or indignation, renders it impossible for the still small voice of reason to be heard, and leaves no other course to honesty or prudence than to fall flat on the face before it, as before the pestilential blast of the desert, and wait till it has passed over.   Thus every one joins in asserting, propagating, and in outwardly approving what every one, in his private and unbiassed judgment, believes and knows to be scandalous and untrue.   For every one in such circumstances keeps his own opinion to himself, and only attends to or acts upon that which he conceives to be the opinion of every one but himself.   So that public opinion is not seldom a farce, equal to any acted upon the stage.   Not only is it spurious and hollow in the way that Mr. Locke points out, by one man's taking up at second hand the opinion of another, but worse than this, one man takes up what he believes another *will* think, and which the latter professes only because he believes it held by the first !   All, therefore, that is necessary to control public opinion, is to gain possession of some organ loud and lofty enough to make yourself heard, that has power and interest on its side ; and then, no sooner do you blow a blast in this trump of *ill-fame*, like the horn hung up on an old castle-wall, than you are answered, echoed, and accredited on all sides : the gates are thrown open to receive you, and you are admitted into the very heart of the fortress of public opinion, and can assail from the ramparts with every engine of abuse, and with privileged impunity, all those who may come forward to vindicate the truth, or to rescue their good name from the unprincipled keeping of authority, servility, sophistry, and venal falsehood !   The only thing wanted is to give an alarm—to excite a panic in the public mind of being left *in the lurch,* and the rabble (whether in the ranks of literature or war) will throw away their arms, and surrender at discretion to any bully or impostor who, for a *consideration,* shall choose to try the experiment upon them!

What I have here described is the effect even upon the candid and well-disposed : what must it be to the malicious and idle, who are eager to believe all the ill they can hear of every one; or to the prejudiced and interested, who are determined to credit all the ill they hear against those who are not of their own side? To these last it is only requisite to be understood that the butt of ridicule or slander is of an opposite party, and they presently give you *carte blanche* to say what you please of him. Do they know that it is true? No; but they believe what all the world says, till they have evidence to the contrary. Do you prove that it is false? They dare say, that if not that something worse remains behind; and they retain the same opinion as before, for the honour of their party. They hire some one to pelt you with mud, and then affect to avoid you in the street as a dirty fellow. They are told that you have a hump on your back, and then wonder at your assurance or want of complaisance in walking into a room where they are, without it. Instead of apologising for the mistake, and, from finding one aspersion false, doubting all the rest, they are only the more confirmed in the remainder from being deprived of one handle against you, and resent their disappointment, instead of being ashamed of their credulity. People talk of the bigotry of the Catholics, and treat with contempt the absurd claim of the Popes to infallibility—I think with little right to do so. Walk into a church in Paris, you are struck with a number of idle forms and ceremonies, the chanting of the service in Latin, the shifting of the surplices, the sprinkling of holy water, the painted windows " casting a dim religious light," the wax tapers, the pealing organ: the common people seem attentive and devout, and to put entire faith in all this—Why? Because they imagine others to do so; they see and hear certain signs and supposed evidences of it, and it amuses and fills up the void of the mind, the love of the mysterious and wonderful, to lend their assent to it. They have assuredly, in general, no better reason—all our Protestant divines will tell you so. Well, step out of the church of St. Roche, and drop into an English reading-room hard by: what are you the better? You see a dozen or score of your countrymen with their faces fixed, and their eyes glued to a newspaper, a magazine, a review—reading, swallowing, profoundly ruminating on the lie, the cant, the sophism of the day! Why? It saves them the trouble of thinking; it gratifies their ill-humour, and keeps off *ennui!* Does a gleam of doubt, an air of ridicule, or a glance of impatience pass across their features at the shallow and monstrous things they find? No, it is all passive faith and dull security; they cannot take their eyes from the page, they cannot live without it. They believe in their adopted oracle (you see it in their faces) as implicitly as in Sir John Barleycorn, as in a sirloin of beef, as in quarter-day—as they hope to receive their rents, or to see Old England again! Are not the Popes, the Fathers, the Councils, as good as their oracles and champions? They know the paper before them to be a hoax, but do they believe in the ribaldry, the calumny, the less on that account? They believe the more in it, because it is got up solely and expressly to serve a cause that needs such support—and they swear by whatever is devoted to this object.

The greater the profligacy, the effrontery, the servility, the greater the faith. Strange! That the British public, whether at home or abroad, should shake their heads at the Lady of Loretto, and repose deliciously on Mr. Theodore Hook. It may well be thought that the enlightened part of the British public, persons of family and fortunes, who have had a college education, and received the benefit of foreign travel, see through the quackery, which they encourage for a political purpose, without being themselves the dupes of it. This scarcely mends the matter. Suppose an individual, of whom it has been repeatedly asserted that he has warts on his nose, were to enter the reading-room aforesaid, is there a single red-faced country squire who would not be surprised at not finding this story true, would not persuade himself five minutes after that he could not have seen correctly, or that some art had been used to conceal the defects, or would be led to doubt, from this instance, the general candour and veracity of his oracle? He would disbelieve his own senses rather. Seeing is believing, it is said: lying is believing I say. We do not even see with our own eyes, but must "wink and shut our apprehension up," that we may be able to agree to the report of others, as a piece of good manners and a point of established etiquette. Besides, the supposed deformity answered his wishes; the abuse fed fat the ancient grudge he owed some presumptuous scribbler, for not agreeing in a number of points with his betters; it gave him a personal advantage over a man he did not like—and who will give up what tends to strengthen his aversion for another? To Tory prejudice, dire as it is—to English imagination, morbid as it is, a nickname, a ludicrous epithet, a malignant falsehood, when it has been once propagated and taken to the bosom as a welcome consolation, becomes a precious property, a vested right; and people would as soon give up a sinecure, or a share in a close borough, as this sort of plenary indulgence to speak and think with contempt of those who would abolish the one, or throw open the other. Party-spirit is the best reason in the world for personal antipathy and vulgar abuse.

"But, do you not think, Sir" (some dialectician may ask), "that belief is involuntary, and that we judge in all cases according to the precise degree of evidence and the positive facts before us?"[1]

No, Sir.

" You believe, then, in the doctrine of philosophical free-will?"

Indeed, Sir, I do not.

" How then, Sir, am I to understand so unaccountable a diversity of opinion from the most approved writers on the philosophy of the human mind?"

May I ask, my dear Sir, did you ever read Mr. Words-worth's poem of *Michael?*

" I cannot charge my memory with the fact."

Well, Sir, this Michael is an old shepherd, who has a son who goes to sea, and who turns out a great reprobate, by all the accounts received of him. Before he went, how-ever, the father took the boy with him into a mountain-glen, and made him lay the first stone of a sheep-fold, which was to be a covenant and a remembrance between them if anything ill happened. For years after, the old man used to go and work at the sheep-fold—

> " Among the rocks
> He went, and still look'd up upon the sun,
> And listen'd to the wind,"

and sat by the half-finished work, expecting the lad's re-turn, or hoping to hear some better tidings of him. Was this hope founded on reason—or was it not owing to the strength of affection, which in spite of everything could not relinquish its hold of a favourite object, indeed the only one that bound it to existence?

Not being able to make my dialectician answer kindly to interrogatories, I must get on without him. In matters of absolute demonstration and speculative in-differences, I grant, that belief is involuntary, and the

---

[1] See a paper in the *Literary Remains*, 1836, i. 81 *et. seq.*, where this point is argued in greater detail.—ED.

proof not to be resisted; but then, in such matters, there is no difference of opinion, or the difference is adjusted amicably and rationally. Hobbes is of opinion, that if their passions or interests could be implicated in the question, men would deny stoutly that the three angles of a right-angled triangle are equal to two right ones : and the disputes in religion look something like it. I only contend, however, that in all cases not of this peremptory and determinate cast, and where disputes commonly arise, inclination, habit, and example have a powerful share in throwing in the casting-weight to our opinions; and that he who is only tolerably free from these, and not their regular dupe or slave, is indeed " a man of ten thousand." Take, for instance, the example of a Catholic clergyman in a Popish country : it will generally be found that he lives and dies in the faith in which he was brought up, as the Protestant clergyman does in his—shall we say that the necessity of gaining a livelihood, or the prospect of preferment, that the early bias given to his mind by education and study, the pride of victory, the shame of defeat, the example and encouragement of all about him, the respect and love of his flock, the flattering notice of the great, have no effect in giving consistency to his opinions and carrying them through to the last? Yet, who will suppose that in either case this apparent uniformity is mere hypocrisy, or that the intellects of the two classes of divines are naturally adapted to the arguments in favour of the two religions they have occasion to profess? No; but the understanding takes a tincture from outward impulses and circumstances, and is led to dwell on those suggestions which favour, and to blind itself to the objections which impugn, the side to which it previously and morally inclines. Again, even in those who oppose established opinions, and form the little, firm, formidable phalanx of dissent, have not early instruction, spiritual pride, the love of contradiction, a resistance to usurped authority, as much to do with keeping up the war of sects and schisms as the abstract love of truth or conviction of the understanding? Does not persecution fan the flame in such fiery tempers, and does it not expire, or grow lukewarm, with indulgence and neglect? I have a sneaking kindness for a Popish priest in this country; and to a Catholic peer I would willingly bow in passing. What are national antipathies, individual attachments, but so many expressions of the *moral* principle in forming our opinions? All our opinions become grounds on which we act, and build our expectations of good or ill; and this good or ill mixed up with them is soon changed into the ruling principle which modifies or violently supersedes the original cool determination of the reason and senses. The will, when it once gets a footing, turns the sober judgment out of doors. If we form an attachment to any one, are we not slow in giving it up? Or, if our suspicions are once excited, are we not equally rash and violent in believing the worst? Othello characterises himself as one

> ——" That loved not wisely, but too well;
> Of one not easily jealous—but, being wrought,
> Perplex'd in the extreme."[1]

And this answers to the movements and irregularities of passion and opinion which take place in human nature. If we wish a thing we are disposed to believe it: if we have been accustomed to believe it, we are the more obstinate in defending it on that account: if all the world differ from us in any question of moment, we are ashamed to own it; or are hurried by peevishness and irritation into extravagance and paradox. The weight of example presses upon us (whether we feel it or not) like the law of gravitation. He who sustains his opinion by the strength of conviction and evidence alone, unmoved by ridicule, neglect, obloquy, or privation, shows no less resolution

[1] *Othello*, v. 2 [edit. 1868, vii. 469].

than the Hindoo who makes and keeps a vow to hold his right arm in the air till it grows rigid and callous.

To have all the world against us is trying to a man's temper and philosophy. It unhinges even our opinion of our own motives and intentions. It is like striking the actual world from under our feet : the void that is left, the death-like pause, the chilling suspense, is fearful. The growth of an opinion is like the growth of a limb; it receives its actual support and nourishment from the general body of the opinions, feelings, and practice of the world; without that, it soon withers, festers, and becomes useless. To what purpose write a good book, if it is sure to be pronounced a bad one, even before it is read ? If our thoughts are to be blown stifling back upon ourselves, why utter them at all ? It is only exposing what we love most to contumely and insult, and thus depriving ourselves of our own relish and satisfaction in them. Language is only made to communicate our sentiments, and if we can find no one to receive them, we are reduced to the silence of dumbness, we live but in the solitude of a dungeon. If we do not vindicate our opinions, we seem poor creatures who have no right to them; if we speak out, we are involved in continual brawls and controversy. If we contemn what others admire, we make ourselves odious; if we admire what they despise, we are equally ridiculous. We have not the applause of the world nor the support of a party; we can neither enjoy the freedom of social intercourse, nor the calm of privacy. With our respect for others, we lose confidence in ourselves : everything seems to be a subject of litigation—to want proof or confirmation; we doubt, by degrees, whether we stand on our head or our heels—whether we know our right hand from our left. If I am assured that I never wrote a sentence of common English in my life, how can I know that this is not the case ? If I am told at one time that my writings are as heavy as lead, and at another, that they are more light and flimsy than the gossamer—what resource have I but to choose between the two? I could say, if this were the place, what those writings are.— "Make it the place, and never stand upon punctilio!"

They are not, then, so properly the works of an author by profession, as the thoughts of a metaphysician expressed by a painter. They are subtle and difficult problems translated into hieroglyphics. I thought for several years on the hardest subjects, on Fate, Free Will, Foreknowledge absolute, without ever making use of words or images at all, and that has made them come in such throngs and confused heaps when I burst from that void of abstraction. In proportion to the tenuity to which my ideas had been drawn, and my abstinence from ornament and sensible objects, was the tenaciousness with which actual circumstances and picturesque imagery laid hold of my mind, when I turned my attention to them, or had to look round for illustrations. Till I began to paint, or till I became acquainted with the author of *The Ancient Mariner*, I could neither write nor speak. He encouraged me to write a book, which I did according to the original bent of my mind, making it as dry and meagre as I could, so that it fell still-born from the press, and none of those who abuse me for a shallow *catch-penny* writer have so much as heard of it. Yet, let me say, that work contains an important metaphysical discovery, supported by a continuous and severe train of reasoning, nearly as subtle and original as anything in Hume or Berkeley. I am not accustomed to speak of myself in this manner, but impudence may provoke modesty to justify itself. Finding this method did not answer, I despaired for a time; but some trifle I wrote in the *Morning Chronicle*[1] meeting the approbation of the editor[2] and the town, I

---

[1] Probably the *Illustrations of Vetus* in 1813, written in answer to the *Times.* They are reprinted in *Political Essays*, 1819.—ED.

[2] Mr. James Perry.—ED.

resolved to turn over a new leaf—to take the public at its word, to muster all the tropes and figures I could lay hands on, and, though I am a plain man, never to appear abroad but in an embroidered dress. Still, old habits will prevail; and I hardly ever set about a paragraph or a criticism, but there was an undercurrent of thought, or some generic distinction on which the whole turned. Having got my clue, I had no difficulty in stringing pearls upon it; and the more recondite the point, the more I laboured to bring it out and set it off by a variety of ornaments and allusions. This puzzled the scribes whose business it was to crush me. They could not see the meaning: they would not see the colouring, for it hurt their eyes. One cried out, it was dull; another, that it was too fine by half: my friends took up this last alternative as the most favourable; and since then it has been agreed that I am a florid writer, somewhat flighty and paradoxical. Yet, when I wished to unburthen my mind in the *Edinburgh* by an article on English metaphysics, the editor, who echoes this *florid* charge, said he preferred what I wrote for effect, and was afraid of its being thought heavy! I have accounted for the flowers; the paradoxes may be accounted for in the same way. All abstract reasoning is in extremes, or only takes up one view of a question, or what is called the principle of the thing; and if you want to give this popularity and effect, you are in danger of running into extravagance and hyperbole. I have had to bring out some obscure distinction, or to combat some strong prejudice, and in doing this with all my might, may have often overshot the mark. It was easy to correct the excess of truth afterwards. I have been accused of inconsistency, for writing an essay, for instance, on the *Advantages of Pedantry*,[1] and another on the *Ignorance of the Learned*,[2] as if ignorance had not its

[1] The essay *On Pedantry* occurs in the *Round Table*, 1817, i, 27.--ED
[2] Printed in *Table Talk*, 1821 [edit. 1870, p. 93 *et seq*].—ED.

comforts as well as knowledge. The personalities I have
fallen into have never been gratuitous. If I have sacrificed my friends, it has always been to a theory. I have
been found fault with for repeating myself, and for a
narrow range of ideas. To a want of general reading, I
plead guilty, and am sorry for it; but perhaps if I had
read more, I might have thought less. As to my barren-
ness of invention, I have at least glanced over a number
of subjects—painting, poetry, prose, plays, politics, parliamentary speakers, metaphysical lore, books, men, and
things. There is some point, some fancy, some feeling,
some taste, shown in treating of these. Which of my
conclusions has been reversed? Is it what I said ten
years ago of the Bourbons which raised the war-whoop
against me? Surely all the world are of that opinion
now. I have, then, given proofs of some talent, and of
more honesty: if there is haste or want of method, there
is no commonplace, nor a line that licks the dust; and if
I do not appear to more advantage, I at least appear such
as I am. If the Editor of the *Atlas* will do me the favour
to look over my *Essay on the Principles of Human Action*,
will dip into any essay I ever wrote, and will take a
sponge and clear the dust from the face of my *Old Woman*,
I hope he will, upon second thoughts, acquit me of an
absolute dearth of resources and want of versatility in the
direction of my studies.

1828.

ESSAY VI.

On Personal Identity.

" Ha ! here's three of us are sophisticated."—LEAR.

"If I were not Alexander, I would be Diogenes!" said
the Macedonian hero; and the cynic might have retorted
the compliment upon the prince by saying, that, " were he

not Diogenes, he would be Alexander!" This is the universal exception, the invariable reservation that our self-love makes, the utmost point at which our admiration or envy ever arrives—to wish, if we were not ourselves, to be some other individual. No one ever wishes to be another, *instead* of himself. We may feel a desire to change places with others—to have one man's fortune—another's health or strength—his wit or learning, or accomplishments of various kinds—

> " Wishing to be like one more rich in hope,
>   Featured like him, like him with friends possessed,
>   Desiring this man's art, and that man's scope ;"

but we would still be ourselves, to possess and enjoy all these, or we would not give a doit for them. But, on this supposition, what in truth should we be the better for them? It is not we, but another, that would reap the benefit ; and what do we care about that other? In that case, the present owner might as well continue to enjoy them. *We* should not be gainers by the change. If the meanest beggar who crouches at a palace gate, and looks up with awe and suppliant fear to the proud inmate as he passes, could be put in possession of all the finery, the pomp, the luxury, and wealth that he sees and envies, on the sole condition of getting rid, together with his rags and misery, of all recollection that there ever was such a wretch as himself, he would reject the proffered boon with scorn. He might be glad to change situations ; but he would insist on keeping his own thoughts, to *compare notes*, and point the transition by the force of contrast. He would not, on any account, forego his self-congratulation on the unexpected accession of good fortune, and his escape from past suffering. All that excites his cupidity, his envy, his repining or despair, is the alternative of some great good to himself ; and if, in order to attain that object, he is to part with his own existence to take that of another, he can feel no farther interest in it. This is the language both of passion and reason.

Here lies " the rub that makes calamity of so long life :" for it is not barely the apprehension of the ills that " in that sleep of death may come," but also our ignorance and indifference to the promised good, that produces our repugnance and backwardness to quit the present scene. No man, if he had his choice, would be the angel Gabriel to-morrow! What is the angel Gabriel to him but a splendid vision? He might as well have an ambition to be turned into a bright cloud, or a particular star. The interpretation of which is, he can have no sympathy with the angel Gabriel. Before he can be transformed into so bright and ethereal an essence, he must necessarily " put off this mortal coil "—be divested of all his old habits, passions, thoughts, and feelings—to be endowed with other attributes, lofty and beatific, of which he has no notion; and, therefore, he would rather remain a little longer in this mansion of clay, which, with all its flaws, inconveniences, and perplexities, contains all that he has any real knowledge of, or any affection for. When, indeed, he is about to quit it in spite of himself, and has no other chance left to escape the darkness of the tomb, he may then have no objection (making a virtue of necessity) to put on angel's wings, to have radiant locks, to wear a wreath of amaranth, and thus to masquerade it in the skies.

It is an instance of the truthful beauty of the ancient mythology, that the various transmutations it recounts are never voluntary, or of favourable omen, but are interposed as a timely release to those who, driven on by fate, and urged to the last extremity of fear or anguish, are turned into a flower, a plant, an animal, a star, a precious stone, or into some object that may inspire pity or mitigate our regret for their misfortunes. Narcissus was transformed into a flower; Daphne into a laurel; Arethusa into a fountain (by the favour of the gods)—but not till no other remedy was left for their despair. It is a sort of smiling cheat upon death, and graceful compromise with annihilation. It is better to exist by proxy, in some softened type and soothing allegory, than not at all—to breathe in a flower or shine in a constellation, than to be utterly forgot; but no one would change his natural condition (if he could help it) for that of a bird, an insect, a beast, or a fish, however delightful their mode of existence, or however enviable he might deem their lot compared to his own. Their thoughts are not our thoughts—their happiness is not our happiness; nor can we enter into it, except with a passing smile of approbation, or as a refinement of fancy. As the poet sings:

> " What more felicity can fall to creature
> Than to enjoy delight with liberty,
> And to be lord of all the works of nature ?
> To reign in the air from earth to highest sky ;
> To feed on flowers and weeds of glorious feature ;
> To taste whatever thing doth please the eye ?—
> Who rests not pleased with such happiness,
> Well worthy he to taste of wretchedness !"

This is gorgeous description and fine declamation: yet who would be found to act upon it, even in the forming of a wish ; or would not rather be the thrall of wretchedness, than launch out (by the aid of some magic spell) into all the delights of such a butterfly state of existence? The French (if any people can) may be said to enjoy this airy, heedless gaiety and unalloyed exuberance of satisfaction : yet what Englishman would deliberately change with them? We would sooner be miserable after our own fashion than happy after theirs. It is not happiness, then, in the abstract, which we seek, that can be addressed as

> " That something still that prompts th' eternal sigh,
> For which we wish to live or dare to die."

but a happiness suited to our tastes and faculties—that

has become a part of ourselves, by habit and enjoyment—
that is endeared to us by a thousand recollections, privations, and sufferings. No one, then, would willingly
change his country or his kind for the most plausible
pretences held out to him. The most humiliating punishment inflicted in ancient fable is the change of sex: not
that it was any degradation in itself—but that it must
occasion a total derangement of the moral economy and
confusion of the sense of personal propriety. The thing
is said to have happened *au sens contraire,* in our time.
The story is to be met with in " very choice Italian ; " and
Lord D—— tells it in very plain English!

We may often find ourselves envying the possessions of
others, and sometimes inadvertently indulging a wish to
change places with them altogether ; but our self-love
soon discover some excuse to be off the bargain we were
ready to strike, and retracts " vows made in haste, as
violent and void." We might make up our minds to the
alteration in every other particular ; but, when it comes
to the point, there is sure to be some trait or feature of
character in the object of our admiration to which we
cannot reconcile ourselves—some favourite quality or
darling foible of our own. with which we can by no means
resolve to part. The more enviable the situation of
another, the more entirely to our taste, the more reluctant
we are to leave any part of ourselves behind that would
be so fully capable of appreciating all the exquisiteness of
its new situation, or not to enter into the possession of
such an imaginary reversion of good fortune with all our
previous inclinations and sentiments. The outward circumstances were fine: they only wanted a *soul* to enjoy
them, and that soul is ours (as the costly ring wants the
peerless jewel to perfect and set it off). The humble
prayer and petition to sneak into visionary felicity by
personal adoption, or the surrender of our own personal
pretentions, always ends in a daring project of usurpation,

and a determination to expel the actual proprietor, and supply his place so much more worthily with our own identity—not bating a single jot of it. Thus, in passing through a fine collection of pictures, who has not envied the privilege of visiting it every day, and wished to be the owner? But the rising sigh is soon checked, and " the native hue of emulation is sicklied o'er with the pale cast of thought," when we come to ask ourselves, not merely whether the owner has any taste at all for these splendid works, and does not look upon them as so much expensive furniture, like his chairs and tables—but whether he has the same precise (and only true) taste that we have— whether he has the very same favourites that we have— whether he may not be so blind as to prefer a Vandyke to a Titian, a Ruysdael to a Claude; nay, whether he may not have other pursuits and avocations that draw off his attention from the sole objects of our idolatry, and which seem to us mere impertinences and waste of time? In that case, we at once lose all patience, and exclaim indignantly, " Give us back our taste, and keep your pictures!" It is not we who should envy them the possession of the treasure, but they who should envy us the true and exclusive enjoyment of it. A similar train of feeling seems to have dictated Warton's spirited *Sonnet on visiting Wilton House :*

> " From Pembroke's princely dome, where mimic art
> Decks with a magic hand the dazzling bowers,
> Its living hues where the warm pencil pours,
> And breathing forms from the rude marble start,
> How to life's humbler scene can I depart ?
> My breast all glowing from those gorgeous towers,
> In my low cell how cheat the sullen hours ?
> Vain the complaint ! For fancy can impart
> (To fate superior and to fortune's power)
> Whate'er adorns the stately storied-hall :
> She, mid the dungeon's solitary gloom,
> Can dress the Graces in their attic-pall;

Bid the green landscape's vernal beauty bloom ;
And in bright trophies clothe the twilight wall.'

One sometimes passes by a gentleman's park, an old family-seat, with its moss-grown, ruinous paling, its "glades mild-opening to the genial day," or embrowned with forest-trees. Here one would be glad to spend one's life, "shut up in measureless content," and to grow old beneath ancestral oaks, instead of gaining a precarious, irksome, and despised livelihood, by indulging romantic sentiments, and writing disjointed descriptions of them. The thought has scarcely risen to the lips, when we learn that the owner of so blissful a seclusion is a thorough-bred fox-hunter, a preserver of the game, a brawling electioneerer, a Tory member of parliament, a "No-Popery" man !—"I'd sooner be a dog, and bay the moon !" Who would be Sir Thomas Lethbridge for his title and estate ? asks one man. But would not almost any one wish to be Sir Francis Burdett, the man of the people, the idol of the electors of Westminster ? says another. I can only answer for myself. Respectable and honest as he is, there is something in his white boots, and white breeches, and white coat, and white hair, and white hat, and red face, that I cannot, by any effort of candour, confound my personal identity with ! If Mr. —— can prevail on Sir Francis to exchange, let him do so by all means. Perhaps they might contrive to *club* a soul between them ! Could I have had my will, I should have been born a lord : but one would not be a booby lord neither. I am haunted by an odd fancy of driving down the Great North Road in a chaise and four, about fifty years ago, and coming to the inn at Ferry-bridge with outriders, white favours, and a coronet on the panels; and then, too, I choose my companion in the coach. Really there is a witchcraft in all this that makes it necessary to turn away from it, lest, in the conflict between imagination and impossibility, I should grow feverish and light-headed! But, on the other hand, if one was a born lord, should one have the same idea (that every one else has) of *a peeress in her own right?* Is not distance, giddy elevation, mysterious awe, an impassable gulf, necessary to form this idea in the mind, that fine ligament of "ethereal braid, sky-woven," that lets down heaven upon earth, fair as enchantment, soft as Berenice's hair, bright and garlanded like Ariadne's crown; and is it not better to have had this idea all through life—to have caught but glimpses of it, to have known it but in a dream—than to have been born a lord ten times over, with twenty pampered menials at one's beck, and twenty descents to boast of? It is the envy of certain privileges, the sharp privations we have undergone, the cutting neglect we have met with from the want of birth or title, that gives its zest to the distinction: the thing itself may be indifferent or contemptible enough. It is the *becoming* a lord that is to be desired; but he who becomes a lord in reality may be an upstart—a mere pretender, without the sterling essence; so that all that is of any worth in this supposed transition is purely imaginary and impossible.[1] Kings are so accustomed to look down on all the rest of the world, that they consider the condition of mortality as vile and intolerable, if stripped of royal state, and cry out in the bitterness of their despair, "Give me a crown, or a tomb!" It should seem from this as if all mankind would change with the first crowned head that could propose the alternative, or that it would be only the presumption of the supposition, or a sense of their own unworthiness, that would deter them. Perhaps there is

[1] When Lord Byron was cut by the great, on account of his quarrel with his wife, he stood leaning on a marble slab at the entrance of a room, while troops of duchesses and countesses passed out. One little, pert, red-haired girl staid a few paces behind the rest; and, as she passed him, said with a nod, "Aye, you should have married me, and then all this wouldn't have happened to you!"

not a single throne that, if it was to be filled by this sort of voluntary metempsychosis, would not remain empty. Many would, no doubt, be glad to "monarchise, be feared, and kill with looks" in their own persons and after their own fashion : but who would be the *double* of those shadows of a shade—those "tenth transmitters of a foolish face"—Charles X. and Ferdinand VII.? If monarchs have little sympathy with mankind, mankind have even less with monarchs. They are merely to us a sort of state-puppets, or royal wax-work, which we may gaze at with superstitious wonder, but have no wish to become; and he who should meditate such a change must not only feel by anticipation an utter contempt for the *slough* of humanity which he is prepared to cast, but must feel an absolute void and want of attraction in those lofty and incomprehensible sentiments which are to supply its place. With respect to actual royalty, the spell is in a great measure broken. But, among ancient monarchs, there is no one, I think, who envies Darius or Xerxes. One has a different feeling with respect to Alexander or Pyrrhus; but this is because they were great men as well as great kings, and the soul is up in arms at the mention of their names as at the sound of a trumpet. But as to all the rest—those "in the catalogue who go for kings"— the praying, eating, drinking, dressing monarchs of the earth, in time past or present—one would as soon think of wishing to personate the Golden Calf, or to turn out with Nebuchadnezzar to graze, as to be transformed into one of that "swinish multitude." There is no point of affinity. The extrinsic circumstances are imposing; but, within, there is nothing but morbid humours and proud flesh! Some persons might vote for Charlemagne; and there are others who would have no objection to be the modern Charlemagne, with all he inflicted and suffered, even after the necromantic field of Waterloo, and the bloody wreath on the vacant brow of the conqueror, and that fell jailer, set over him by a craven foe, that " glared round his soul, and mocked his closing eyelids ! "

It has been remarked, that could we at pleasure change our situation in life, more persons would be found anxious to descend than to ascend in the scale of society. One reason may be, that we have it more in our power to do so; and this encourages the thought, and makes it familiar to us. A second is, that we naturally wish to throw off the cares of state, of fortune or business, that oppress us, and to seek repose before we find it in the grave. A third reason is, that, as we descend to common life, the pleasures are simple, natural, such as all can enter into, and therefore excite a general interest, and combine all suffrages. Of the different occupations of life, none is beheld with a more pleasing emotion, or less aversion to a change for our own, than that of a shepherd tending his flock : the pastoral ages have been the envy and the theme of all succeeding ones ; and a beggar with his crutch is more closely allied than the monarch and his crown to the associations of mirth and heart's-ease. On the other hand, it must be admitted that our pride is too apt to prefer grandeur to happiness ; and that our passions make us envy great vices oftener than great virtues.

The world show their sense in nothing more than in a distrust and aversion to those changes of situation which only tend to make the successful candidates ridiculous, and which do not carry along with them a mind adequate to the circumstances. The common people, in this respect, are more shrewd and judicious than their superiors, from feeling their own awkwardness and incapacity, and often decline, with an instinctive modesty, the troublesome honours intended for them. They do not overlook their original defects so readily as others overlook their acquired advantages. It is not wonderful, therefore, that opera-singers and dancers refuse or only *con-*

descend as it were, to accept lords, though the latter are to often fascinated by them. The fair performer knows (better than her unsuspecting admirer) how little conᴴection there is between the dazzling figure she makes on the stage and that which she may make in private life, and is in no hurry to convert "the drawing-room into a Green-room." The nobleman (supposing him not to be very wise) is astonished at the miraculous powers of art in

"The fair, the chaste, the inexpressive *she;*"

aud thinks such a paragon must easily conform to the routine of manners and society which every trifling woman of quality of his acquaintance, from sixteen to sixty, gocs through without effort. This is a hasty or a wilful conclusion. Things of habit only come by habit, and inspiration here avails nothing. A man of fortune who marries an actress for her fine performance of tragedy, has been well compared to the person who bought Punch. The lady is not unfrequently aware of the inconsequentiality, and unwilling to be put on the shelf, and hid in the nursery of some musty country mansion. Servant girls, of any sense and spirit, treat their masters (who make serious love to them) with suitable contempt. What is it but a proposal to drag an unmeaning trollop at his heels through life, to her own annoyance and the ridicule of all his friends? No woman, I suspect, ever forgave a man who raised her from a low condition in life (it is a perpetual obligation and reproach); though I believe, men often feel the most disinterested regard for women under such circumstances. Sancho Panza discovered no less folly in his eagerness to enter upon his new government, than wisdom in quitting it as fast as possible. Why will Mr. Cobbett persist in getting into Parliament? He would find himself no longer the same man. What member of Parliament, I should like to know, could write his *Register?* As a popular partisan, he may (for aught

I can say) be a match for the whole Honourable House; but, by obtaining a seat in St. Stephen's Chapel, he would only be equal to a 576th part of it. It was surely a puerile ambition in Mr. Addington to succeed Mr. Pitt as prime minister. The situation was only a foil to his imbecility. Gipsies have a fine faculty of evasion; catch them who can in the same place or story twice! Take them; teach them the comforts of civilisation; confine them in warm rooms, with thick carpets and down beds; and they will fly out of the window—like the bird, described by Chaucer, out of its golden cage. I maintain that there is no common language or medium of understanding between people of education and without it— between those who judge of things from books or from their senses. Ignorance has so far the advantage over learning; for it can make an appeal to you from what you know; but you cannot react upon it through that which it is a perfect stranger to. Ignorance is, therefore, power. This is what foiled Buonaparte in Spain and Russia. The people can only be gained over by informing them, though they may be enslaved by fraud or force. "What is it, then, he does like?"—"Good victuals and drink!" As if you had these not too; but because he has them not, he thinks of nothing else, and laughs at you and your refinements, supposing you live upon air. To those who are deprived of every other advantage, even nature is a *book sealed.* I have made this capital mistake all my life, in imagining that those objects which lay open to all, and excited an interest merely from the *idea* of them, spoke a common language to all; and that nature was a kind of universal home, where all ages, sexes, classes meet. Not so. The vital air, the sky, the woods, the streams—all these go for nothing, except with a favoured few. The poor are taken up with their bodily wants—the rich, with external acquisitions: the one, with the sense of property —the other, of its privation. Both have the same distaste

for *sentiment.* The *genteel* are the slaves of appearances
—the vulgar, of necessity; and neither has the smallest
regard to worth, refinement, generosity. All savages are
irreclaimable. I can understand the Irish character
better than the Scotch. I hate the formal crust of circumstances and the mechanism of society. I have been
recommended, indeed, to settle down into some respectable
profession for life :

> " Ah ! why so soon the blossom tear ?"

I am " in no haste to be venerable ! "

　In thinking of those one might wish to have been, many
people will exclaim, " Surely, you would like to have
been Shakspeare ? " Would Garrick have consented to
the change ? No, nor should he ; for the applause which
he received, and on which he lived, was more adapted to
his genius and taste. If Garrick had agreed to be Shakspeare, he would have made it a previous condition that
he was to be a better player. He would have insisted
on taking some higher part than *Polonius* or the *Grave-
digger.* Ben Jonson and his companions at the Mermaid
would not have known their old friend Will in his new
disguise. The modern Roscius would have scouted the
halting player. He would have shrunk from the parts of
the inspired poet. If others are unlike us, we feel it as a
presumption and an impertinence to usurp their place ; if
they are like us, it seems a work of supererogation. We
are not to be cozened out of our existence for nothing. It
has been ingeniously urged, as an objection to having
been Milton, that " then we should not have had the
pleasure of reading *Paradise Lost.*" Perhaps I should
incline to draw lots with Pope, but that he was deformed,
and did not sufficiently relish Milton and Shakspeare.
As it is, we can enjoy his verses and theirs too. Why,
having these, need we ever be dissatisfied with ourselves ?
Goldsmith is a person whom I considerably affect notwith-

standing his blunders and his misfortunes. The author of the *Vicar of Wakefield*, and of *Retaliation*, is one whose temper must have had something eminently amiable, delightful, gay, and happy in it.

" A certain tender bloom his fame o'erspreads."

But then I could never make up my mind to his preferring Rowe and Dryden to the worthies of the Elizabethan age ; nor could I, in like manner, forgive Sir Joshua—whom I number among those whose existence was marked with a *white stone*, and on whose tomb might be inscribed " Thrice Fortunate !"—his treating Nicholas Poussin with contempt. Differences in matters of taste and opinion are points of honour—" stuff o' the conscience "—stumbling-blocks not to be got over. Others, we easily grant, may have more wit, learning, imagination, riches, strength, beauty, which we should be glad to borrow of them ; but that they have sounder or better views of things, or that we should act wisely in changing in this respect, is what we can by no means persuade ourselves. We may not be the lucky possessors of what is best or most desirable ; but our notion of what is best and most desirable we will give up to no man by choice or compulsion ; and unless others (the greatest wits or brightest geniuses) can come into our way of thinking, we must humbly beg leave to remain as we are. A Calvinistic preacher would not relinquish a single point of faith to be the Pope of Rome ; nor would a strict Unitarian acknowledge the mystery of the Holy Trinity to have painted Raphael's *Assembly of the Just*. In the range of *ideal* excellence, we are distracted by variety and repelled by differences : the imagination is fickle and fastidious, and requires a combination of all possible qualifications, which never met. Habit alone is blind and tenacious of the most homely advantages ; and after running the tempting round of nature, fame and fortune we wrap ourselves

up in our familiar recollections and humble pretensions—
as the lark, after long fluttering on sunny wing, sinks into
its lowly bed!

We can have no very importunate craving, nor very great
confidence, in wishing to change characters, except with
those with whom we are intimately acquainted by their
works; and having these by us (which is all we know or
covet in them), what would we have more? We can
have *no more of a cat than her skin*; nor of an author than
his brains.   By becoming Shakspeare in reality we cut
ourselves out of reading Milton, Pope, Dryden, and a
thousand more—all of whom we have in our possession,
enjoy, and *are*, by turns, in the best part of them, their
thoughts, without any metamorphosis or miracle at all.
What a microcosm is ours!   What a Proteus is the
human mind!   All that we know, think of, or can admire,
in a manner becomes ourselves.   We are not (the meanest
of us) a volume, but a whole library!   In this calculation
of problematical contingencies, the lapse of time makes no
difference.   One would as soon have been Raphael as any
modern artist.   Twenty, thirty, or forty years of elegant
enjoyment and lofty feeling were as great a luxury in the
fifteenth as in the nineteenth century.   But Raphael did
not live to see Claude, nor Titian Rembrandt.   Those
who found arts and sciences are not witnesses of their
accumulated results and benefits; nor, in general, do they
reap the meed of praise which is their due.   We who come
after in some " laggard age," have more enjoyment of their
fame than they had.   Who would have missed the sight
of the Louvre in all its glory to have been one of those
whose works enriched it?   Would it not have been giving
a certain good for an uncertain advantage?   No : I am as
sure (if it is not presumption to say so) of what passed
through Raphael's mind as of what passes through my
own ; and I know the difference between seeing (though
even that is a rare privilege) and producing such per-

fection. At one time I was so devoted to Rembrandt, that I think if the Prince of Darkness had made me the offer in some rash mood, I should have been tempted to close with it, and should have become (in happy hour, and in downright earnest) the great master of light and shade!

I have run myself out of my materials for this Essay, and want a well-turned sentence or two to conclude with; like Benvenuto Cellini, who complains that, with all the brass, tin, iron, and lead he could muster in the house, his statue of Perseus was left imperfect, with a dent in the heel of it. Once more, then—I believe there is one character that all the world would like to change with—which is that of a favoured rival. Even hatred gives way to envy. We would be anything—a toad in a dungeon—to live upon her smile, which is our all of earthly hope and happiness; nor can we, in our infatuation, conceive that there is any difference of feeling on the subject, or that the pressure of her hand is not in itself divine, making those to whom such bliss is deigned like the Immortal Gods!

1828.

ESSAY VII.

Mind and Motive.

"The web of our lives is of a mingled yarn."

" Anthony Codrus Urceus, a most learned and unfortunate Italian, born 1446, was a striking instance " (says his biographer) " of the miseries men bring upon themselves by setting their affections unreasonably on trifles. This learned man lived at Forli, and had an apartment in the palace. His room was so very dark, that he was forced to use a candle in the day time; and one day, going abroad without putting it out, his library was set on fire, and some papers which he had prepared for the press were burned. The instant he was informed of this ill news, he was affected even to madness. He ran furiously to the palace, and, stopping at the door of his apartment, he cried aloud, ' Christ Jesus! what mighty crime have I committed? whom of your followers have I ever injured, that you thus rage with inexpiable hatred against me ?' Then turning himself to an image of the Virgin Mary near at hand, ' Virgin' (says he) ' hear what I have to say, for I speak in earnest, and with a composed spirit. If I shall happen to address you in my dying moments, I humbly entreat you not to hear me, nor receive me into heaven, for I am determined to spend all eternity in hell.' Those who heard these blasphemous expressions endeavoured to comfort him, but all to no purpose; for the society of mankind being no longer supportable to him, he left the city, and retired, like a savage, to the deep solitude of a wood. Some say that he was murdered there by ruffians ; others that he died at Bologna, in 1500, after much contrition and penitence."

Almost every one may here read the history of his own life. There is scarcely a moment in which we are not in some degree guilty of the same kind of absurdity, which was here carried to such a singular excess. We waste our regrets on what cannot be recalled, or fix our desires on what we know cannot be attained. Every hour is the slave of the last; and we are seldom masters either of our thoughts or of our actions. We are the creatures of imagination, passion, and self-will, more than of reason or self-interest. Rousseau, in his *Emilius*, proposed to educate a perfectly reasonable man, who was to have passions and affections like other men, but with an absolute control over them. He was to love and to be wise. This is a contradiction in terms. Even in the common transactions and daily intercourse of life, we are governed by whim, caprice, prejudice, or accident. The falling of

a tea-cup puts us out of temper for the day; and a quarrel
that commenced about the pattern of a gown may end only
with our lives.

> " Friends now fast sworn,
> On a dissension of a doit, break out
> To bitterest enmity. So fellest foes,
> Whose passions and whose plots have broke their sleep.
> To take the one the other, by some chance,
> Some trick not worth an egg, shall grow dear friends,
> And interjoin their issues."

We are little better than humoured children to the last,
and play a mischievous game at cross purposes with our
own happiness and that of others.

We have given the above story as a striking contradiction to the prevailing doctrine of modern systems of
morals and metaphysics, that man is purely a sensual and
selfish animal, governed solely by a regard either to his
immediate gratification or future interest. This doctrine
we mean to oppose with all our might, whenever we meet
with it. We are, however, less disposed to quarrel with
it, as it is opposed to reason and philosophy, than as it
interferes with common sense and observation. If the
absurdity in question had been confined to the schools,
we should not have gone out of our way to meddle with
it : but it has gone abroad in the world, has crept into
ladies' boudoirs, is entered in the commonplace book of
beaux, is in the mouth of the learned and ignorant, and
forms a part of popular opinion. It is perpetually applied
as a false measure to the characters and conduct of men
in the common affairs of the world, and it is therefore our
business to rectify it, if we can. In fact, whoever sets out
on the idea of reducing all our motives and actions to a
simple principle, must either take a very narrow and
superficial view of human nature, or make a very perverse
use of his understanding in reasoning on what he sees.
The frame of our minds, like that of his body, is exceed-

ingly complicated. Besides mere sensibility to pleasure
and pain, there are other original independent principles,
necessarily interwoven with the nature of man as an active
and intelligent being, and which, blended together in
different proportions, give their form and colour to our
lives. Without some other essential faculties, such as
will, imagination, &c., to give effect and direction to our
physical sensibility, this faculty could be of no possible
use or influence; and with those other faculties joined to
it, this pretended instinct of self-love will be subject to be
everlastingly modified and controlled by those faculties,
both in what regards our own good and that of others;
that is, must itself become in a great measure dependent
on the very instruments it uses. The two most predomi-
nant principles in the mind, besides sensibility and self-
interest, are imagination and self-will, or (in general) the
love of strong excitement, both in thought and action. To
these sources may be traced the various passions, pursuits,
habits, affections, follies and caprices, virtues and vices
of mankind. We shall confine ourselves, in the present
article, to give some account of the influence exercised by
the imagination over the feelings. To an intellectual
being, it cannot be altogether arbitrary what ideas it
shall have, whether pleasurable or painful. Our ideas
do not originate in our love of pleasure, and they cannot,
therefore, depend absolutely upon it. They have another
principle. If the imagination were " the servile slave "
of our self-love, if our ideas were emanations of our
sensitive nature, encouraged if agreeable, and excluded
the instant they became otherwise, or encroached on the
former principle, then there might be a tolerable pretence
for the epicurean philosophy which is here spoken of.
But for any such entire and mechanical subserviency of
the operations of the one principle to the dictates of the
other, there is not the slightest foundation in reality.
The attention which the mind gives to its ideas is not

always owing to the gratification derived from them, but to the strength and truth of the impressions themselves, *i. e.*, to their involuntary power over the mind. This observation will account for a very general principle in the mind, which cannot, we conceive, be satisfactorily explained in any other way, we mean *the power of fascination.* Every one has heard the story of the girl who, being left alone by her companions, in order to frighten her, in a room with a dead body, at first attempted to get out, and shrieked violently for assistance, but finding herself shut in, ran and embraced the corpse, and was found senseless in its arms.

It is said that in such cases there is a desperate effort made to get rid of the dread by converting it into the reality. There may be some truth in this account, but we do not think it contains the whole truth. The event produced in the present instance does not bear out the conclusion. The progress of the passion does not seem to have been that of diminishing or removing the terror by coming in contact with the object, but of carrying this terror to its height from an intense and irresistible impulse overcoming every other feeling.

It is a well-known fact that few persons can stand safely on the edge of a precipice, or walk along the parapet wall of a house, without being in danger of throwing themselves down; not, we presume, from a principle of self-preservation; but in consequence of a strong idea having taken possession of the mind from which it cannot well escape, which absorbs every other consideration, and confounds and overrules all self-regards. The impulse cannot in this case be resolved into a desire to remove the uneasiness of fear, for the only danger arises from the fear. We have been told by a person not at all given to exaggeration, that he once felt a strong propensity to throw himself into a cauldron of boiling lead, into which he was looking. These are what Shakspeare calls "the toys of desperation." People sometimes marry, and even fall in love on this principle—that is, through mere apprehension, or what is called a fatality. In like manner, we find instances of persons who are, as it were, naturally delighted with whatever is disagreeable—who catch all sorts of unbecoming tones and gestures—who always say what they should not, and what they do not mean to say—in whom intemperance of imagination and incontinence of tongue are a disease, and who are governed by an almost infallible instinct of absurdity.

The love of imitation has the same general source. We dispute for ever about Hogarth, and the question can never be decided according to the common ideas on the subject of taste. His pictures appeal to the love of truth, not to the sense of beauty: but the one is as much an essential principle of our nature as the other. They fill up the void of the mind; they present an everlasting succession and variety of ideas. There is a fine observation somewhere made by Aristotle, that the mind has a natural appetite of curiosity or desire to know; and most of that knowledge which comes in by the eye, for this presents us with the greatest variety of differences. Hogarth is relished only by persons of a certain strength of mind and penetration into character; for the subjects in themselves are not pleasing, and this objection is only redeemed by the exercise and activity which they give to the understanding. The great difference between what is meant by a severe and an effeminate taste or style, depends on the distinction here made.

Our teasing ourselves to recollect the names of places or persons we have forgotten, the love of riddles and of abstruse philosophy, are all illustrations of the same general principle of curiosity, or the love of intellectual excitement. Again, our impatience to be delivered of a secret that we know; the necessity which lovers have for confidants, auricular confession, and the declarations so commonly made by criminals of their guilt, are effects of the involuntary power exerted by the imagination over the feelings. Nothing can be more untrue, than that the whole course of our ideas, passions, and pursuits, is regulated by a regard to self-interest. Our attachment to certain objects is much oftener in proportion to the strength of the impression they make on us, to their power of riveting and fixing the attention, than to the gratification we derive from them. We are, perhaps, more apt to dwell upon circumstances that excite disgust and shock our feelings, than on those of an agreeable nature. This, at least, is the case where this disposition is particularly strong, as in people of nervous feelings and morbid habits of thinking. Thus the mind is often haunted with painful images and recollections, from the hold they have taken of the imagination. We cannot shake them off, though we strive to do it : nay, we even court their company ; we will not part with them out of our presence ; we strain our aching sight after them ; we anxiously recall every feature, and contemplate them in all their aggravated colours. There are a thousand passions and fancies that thwart our purposes and disturb our repose. Grief and fear are almost as welcome inmates of the breast as hope or joy, and more obstinately cherished. We return to the objects which have excited them, we brood over them, they become almost inseparable from the mind, necessary to it ; they assimilate all objects to the gloom of our own thoughts, and make the will a party against itself. This is one chief source of most of the passions that prey like vultures on the heart, and embitter human life. We hear moralists and divines perpetually exclaiming, with mingled indignation and surprise, at the folly of mankind in obstinately persisting in these tormenting and violent passions, such as envy, revenge, sullenness, despair, &c. This is to them a mystery ; and it will always remain an inexplicable one, while the love of happiness is considered as the only spring of human conduct and desires.[1]

The love of power or action is another independent principle of the human mind, in the different degrees in which it exists, and which are not by any means in exact proportion to its physical sensibility. It seems evidently absurd to suppose that sensibility to pleasure or pain is the only principle of action. It is almost too obvious to remark, that sensibility alone, without an active principle in the mind, could never produce action. The soul might lie dissolved in pleasure, or be agonised with woe; but the impulses of feeling, in order to excite passion, desire, or will, must be first communicated to some other faculty. There must be a principle, a fund of activity somewhere, by and through which our sensibility operates; and that this active principle owes all its force, its precise degree of direction, to the sensitive faculty, is neither self-evident nor true. Strength of will is not always nor generally in proportion to strength of feeling. There are different degrees of activity, as of sensibility, in the mind; and our passions, characters, and pursuits, often depend no less upon the one than on the other. We continually make a distinction in common discourse between sensibility and irritability between passion and feeling, between the nerves and muscles; and we find that the most voluptuous people are in general the most indolent. Every one who has looked closely into human nature must have observed persons who are naturally and habitually restless in the extreme, but without any extraordinary susceptibility to

[1] As a contrast to the story at the beginning of this article, it will be not amiss to mention that of Sir Isaac Newton, on a somewhat similar occasion. He had prepared some papers for the press with great care and study, but happening to leave a lighted candle on the table with them, his dog Diamond overturned the candle, and the labour of several years was destroyed. This great man, on seeing what was done, only shook his head, and said with a smile, "Ah, Diamond, you don't know what mischief you have done!"

pleasure or pain, always making or finding excuses to do something—whose actions constantly outrun the occasion, and who are eager in the pursuit of the greatest trifles—whose impatience of the smallest repose keeps them always employed about nothing—and whose whole lives are a continued work of supererogation. There are others, again, who seem born to act from a spirit of contradiction only, that is, who are ready to act not only without a reason, but against it—who are ever at cross-purposes with themselves and others—who are not satisfied unless they are doing two opposite things at a time—who contradict what you say, and if you assent to them, contradict what they have said—who regularly leave the pursuit in which they are successful to engage in some other in which they have no chance of success—who make a point of encountering difficulties and aiming at impossibilities, that there may be no end of their exhaustless task: while there is a third class whose *vis inertiæ* scarcely any motives can overcome—who are devoured by their feelings, and the slaves of their passions, but who can take no pains and use no means to gratify them—who, if roused to action by any unforeseen accident, require a continued stimulus to urge them on—who fluctuate between desire and want of resolution—whose brightest projects burst like a bubble as soon as formed—who yield to every obstacle—who almost sink under the weight of the atmosphere—who cannot brush aside a cobweb in their path, and are stopped by an insect's wing. Indolence is want of will—the absence or defect of the active principle—a repugnance to motion ; and whoever has been much tormented with this passion, must, we are sure, have felt that the inclination to indulge it is something very distinct from the love of pleasure or actual enjoyment. Ambition is the reverse of indolence, and is the love of power or action in great things. Avarice, also, as it relates to the acquisition of riches, is, in a great measure, an active and enterprising feeling; nor does the hoarding of wealth, after it is acquired, seem to have much connection with the love of pleasure. What is called niggardliness, very often, we are convinced from particular instances that we have known, arises less from a selfish principle than from a love of contrivance—from the study of economy as an art, for want of a better — from a pride in making the most of a little, and in not exceeding a certain expense previously determined upon; all which is wilfulness, and is perfectly consistent, as it is frequently found united, with the utmost lavish expenditure and the utmost disregard for money on other occasions. A miser may, in general, be looked upon as a particular species of *virtuoso.* The constant desire in the rich to leave wealth in large masses, by aggrandising some branch of their families, or sometimes in such a manner as to accumulate for centuries, shows that the imagination has a considerable share in this passion. Intemperance, debauchery, gluttony, and other vices of that kind, may be attributed to an excess of sensuality or gross sensibility; though, even here, we think it evident that habits of intoxication are produced quite as much by the strength as by the agreeableness of the excitement; and with respect to some other vicious habits, curiosity makes many more votaries than inclination. The love of truth, when it predominates, produces inquisitive characters, the whole tribe of gossips, tale-bearers, harmless busy-bodies, your blunt honest creatures, who never conceal what they think and who are the more sure to tell it you the less you want to hear it—and now and then a philosopher.

Our passions in general are to be traced more immediately to the active part of our nature, to the love of power, or to strength of will. Such are all those which arise out of the difficulty of accomplishment, which become more intense from the efforts made to attain the object, and which derive their strength from opposition. Mr. Hobbes says well on this subject :

"But for an utmost end, in which the ancient philosophers placed felicity, and disputed much concerning the way thereto, there is no such thing in this world, nor way to it, more than to Utopia ; for while we live, we have desires, and desire presupposeth a further end. Seeing all delight is appetite, and desire of something further, there can be no contentment but in proceeding, and therefore we are not to marvel, when we see that as men attain to more riches, honour, or other power, so their appetite continually groweth more and more; and when they are come to the utmost degree of some kind of power they pursue some other, as long as in any kind they think themselves behind any other. Of those, therefore, that have attained the highest degree of honour and riches, some have affected mastery in some art, as Nero in music and poetry, Commodus in the art of a gladiator; and such as affect not some such thing, must find diversion and recreation of their thoughts in the contention either of play or business, and men justly complain as of a great grief that they know not what to do. Felicity, therefore, by which we mean continual delight, consists not in having prospered, but in prospering."

This account of human nature, true as it is, would be a mere romance, if physical sensibility were the only faculty essential to man, that is, if we were the slaves of voluptuous indolence. But our desires are kindled by their own heat, the will is urged on by a restless impulse, and without action, enjoyment becomes insipid. The passions of men are not in proportion only to their sensibility, or to the desirableness of the object, but to the violence and irritability of their tempers, and the obstacles to their success. Thus an object to which we were almost indifferent while we thought it in our power, often excites the most ardent pursuit or the most painful regret, as soon as

it is placed out of our reach. How eloquently is the contradiction between our desires and our success described in
Don Quixote, where it is said of the lover, that " he courted
a statue, hunted the wind, cried aloud to the desert !"

The necessity of action to the mind, and the keen edge
it gives to our desires, is shown in the different value we
set on past and future objects. It is commonly, and we
might almost say universally, supposed, that there is an
essential difference in the two cases. In this instance,
however, the strength of our passions has converted an
evident absurdity into one of the most inveterate prejudices
of the human mind. That the future is really or in itself
of more consequence than the past, is what we can neither
assent to nor even conceive. It is true, the past has
ceased to be, and is no longer anything, except to the
mind ; but the future is still to come, and has an existence
in the mind only. The one is at an end, the other has
not even had a beginning ; both are purely ideal : so that
this argument would prove that the present only is of any
real value, and that both past and future objects are
equally indifferent, alike nothing. Indeed, the future is,
if possible, more imaginary than the past ; for the past
may in some sense be said to exist in its consequences ; it
acts still ; it is present to us in its effects ; the mouldering
ruins and broken fragments still remain; but of the future
there is no trace. What a blank does the history of the
world for the next six thousand years present to the mind,
compared with that of the last ? All that strikes the
imagination, or excites any interest in the mighty scene is
what has been. Neither in reality, then, nor as a subject
of general contemplation, has the future any advantage
over the past ; but with respect to our own passions and
pursuits it has. We regret the pleasures we have enjoyed.
and eagerly anticipate those which are to come ; we dwell
with satisfaction on the evils from which we have escaped,
and dread future pain. The good that is past is like

money that is spent, which is of no use, and about which we give no further concern. The good we expect is like a store yet untouched, in the enjoyment of which we promise ourselves infinite gratification. What has happened to us we think of no consequence—what is to happen to us, of the greatest. Why so ? Because the one is in our power, and the other not ; because the efforts of the will to bring an object to pass or to avert it, strengthen our attachment to or our aversion from that object ; because the habitual pursuit of any purpose redoubles the ardour of our pursuit, and converts the speculative and indolent interest we should otherwise take in it into real passion. Our regrets, anxiety, and wishes, are thrown away upon the past, but we encourage our disposition to exaggerate the importance of the future, as of the utmost use in aiding our resolutions and stimulating our exertions.

It in some measure confirms this theory, that men attach more or less importance to past and future events, according as they are more or less engaged in action and the busy scenes of life. Those who have a fortune to make, or are in pursuit of rank and power, are regardless of the past, for it does not contribute to their views : those who have nothing to do but to think, take nearly the same interest in the past as in the future. The contemplation of the one is as delightful and real as of the other. The season of hope comes to an end, but the remembrance of it is left. The past still lives in the memory of those who have leisure to look back upon the way that they have trod, and can from it "catch glimpses that may make them less forlorn." The turbulence of action and uneasiness of desire *must* dwell upon the future ; it is only amidst the innocence of shepherds, in the simplicity of the pastoral ages, that a tomb was found with this inscription—" I also was an Arcadian ! "

We feel that some apology is necessary for having thus plunged our readers all at once into the middle of metaphysics. If it should be asked what use such studies are of, we might answer with Hume, *perhaps of none, except that there are certain persons who find more entertainment in them than in any other.* An account of this matter, with which we were amused ourselves, and which may therefore amuse others, we met with some time ago in a metaphysical allegory, which begins in this manner :

"In the depth of a forest, in the kingdom of Indostan, lived a monkey, who, before his last step of transmigration, had occupied a human tenement. He had been a Bramin, skilful in theology, and in all abstruse learning. He was wont to hold in admiration the ways of nature, and delighted to penetrate the mysteries in which she was enrobed ; but in pursuing the footsteps of philosophy, he wandered too far from the abode of the social Virtues. In order to pursue his studies, he had retired to a cave on the banks of the Jumna. There he forgot society, and neglected ablution ; and therefore his soul was degraded to a condition below humanity. So inveterate were the habits which he had contracted in his human state, that his spirit was still influenced by his passion for abstruse study. He sojourned in this wood from youth to age, regardless of everything, *save cocoa-nuts and metaphysics.*" For our own part, we should be content to pass our time much in the same manner as this learned savage, if we could only find a substitute for his cocoa-nuts! We do not, however, wish to recommend the same pursuit to others, nor to dissuade them from it. It has its pleasures and its pains—its successes and its disappointments. It is neither quite so sublime nor quite so uninteresting as it is sometimes represented. The worst is, that much thought on difficult subjects tends, after a certain time, to destroy the natural gaiety and dancing of the spirits ; it deadens the elastic force of the mind, weighs upon the heart, and makes us insensible to the common enjoyments and pursuits of life.

" Sithence no fairy lights, no quick'ning ray,
Nor stir of pulse, nor objects to entice

Abroad the spirits ; but the cloyster'd heart
Sits squat at home, like pagod in a niche
Obscure."

Metaphysical reasoning is also one branch of the tree of the knowledge of good and evil. The study of man, however, does, perhaps, less harm than a knowledge of the world, though it must be owned that the practical knowledge of vice and misery makes a stronger impression on the mind, when it has imbibed a habit of abstract reasoning. Evil thus becomes embodied in a general principle, and shows its harpy form in all things. It is a fatal, inevitable necessity hanging over us. It follows us wherever we go : if we fly into the uttermost parts of the earth, it is there : whether we turn to the right or the left, we cannot escape from it. This, it is true, is the disease of philosophy ; but it is one to which it is liable in minds of a certain cast, after the first ardour of expectation has been disabused by experience, and the finer feelings have received an irrecoverable shock from the jarring of the world.

Happy are they who live in the dream of their own existence, and see all things in the light of their own minds ; who walk by faith and hope ; to whom the guiding star of their youth still shines from afar, and into whom the spirit of the world has not entered ! They have not been " hurt by the archers," nor has the iron entered their souls. They live in the midst of arrows and of death, unconscious of harm. The evil things come not nigh them. The shafts of ridicule pass unheeded by, and malice loses its sting. The example of vice does not rankle in their breasts, like the poisoned shirt of Nessus. Evil impressions fall off from them like drops of water. The yoke of life is to them light and supportable. The world has no hold on them. They are in it, not of it ; and a dream and a glory is ever around them !

1815.

ESSAY VIII.

On Means and Ends.

It is impossible to have things done without doing them. This seems a truism; and yet what is more common than to suppose that we shall find things done, merely by wishing it? To put the will for the deed is as usual in practice as it is contrary to common sense. There is, in fact, no absurdity, no contradiction, of which the will is not capable. This is, I think, more remarkable in the English than in any other people, in whom (to judge by what I discover in myself) the will bears great and disproportioned sway. We will a thing: we contemplate the end intensely, and think it done, neglecting the necessary means to accomplish it. The strong tendency of the mind towards it, the internal effort it makes to give being to the object of its idolatry, seems an adequate cause to produce the effect, and in a manner identified with it. This is more particularly the case in what relates to the *fine arts*, and will account for some phenomena of the national character. The English school is distinguished by what are called *ébauches*, rude, violent attempts at effect, and a total inattention to the details or delicacy of finishing. Now this, I think, proceeds, not exactly from grossness of perception, but from the wilfulness of our character; our desire to have things our own way, without any trouble or distraction of purpose. An object strikes us: we see and feel the whole effect. We wish to produce a likeness of it; but we want to transfer this impression to the canvas as it is conveyed to us, simultaneously and intuitively, that is, to stamp it there at a blow, or otherwise we turn away with impatience and disgust, as if the means were an obstacle to the end, and every attention to the mechanical part of art were a deviation from our original purpose. We thus degenerate, after repeated failures, into a slovenly style of art; and that which was at first an undisciplined and irregular impulse becomes a habit, and then a theory. It seems strange that the love of the end should produce aversion to the means—but so it is; neither is it altogether unnatural. That which we are struck with, which we are enamoured of, is the general appearance and result; and it would certainly be most desirable to produce the effect in the same manner by a mere word or wish, if it were possible, without entering into any mechanical drudgery or minuteness of detail or dexterity of execution, which though they are essential and component parts of the work do not enter into our thoughts, and form no part of our contemplation. We may find it necessary, on a cool calculation to go through and learn these, but in so doing we only submit to necessity, and they are still a diversion to and a suspension of our purpose for the time, at least unless practice gives that facility which almost identifies the two together, or makes the process an unconscious one. The end thus devours up the means, or our eagerness for the one, where it is strong and unchecked, is in proportion to our impatience of the other. We view an object at a distance that excites an inclination to visit it, which we do after many tedious steps and intricate ways; but if we could fly, we should never walk. The mind, however, has wings, though the body has not, and it is this that produces the contradiction in question. The first and strongest impulse of the mind is to produce any work at once and by the most energetic means; but as this cannot always be done, we should not neglect other more mechanical ones, but that delusions of passion overrule the convictions of the understanding, and what we strongly wish we fancy to be possible and true. We are full of the effect we intend to produce, and imagine we have produced it, in spite of the evidence of our senses, and the suggestions of our friends. In fact, after a number of fruitless efforts and

violent throes to produce an effect which wo passionately
long for, it seems an injustice not to have produced it ; if
we have not commanded success, we have done more, we
have deserved it ; we have copied nature or Titian in the
spirit in which they ought to be copied, and we see them
before us in our mind's eye ; there is the look, the expression, the something or other which we chiefly aim at, and
thus we persist and make fifty excuses to deceive ourselves
and confirm our errors ; or if the light breaks upon us
through all the disguises of sophistry and self-love, it is
so painful that we shut our eyes to it; the greater the
mortification the more violent the effort to throw it off;
and thus we stick to our determination, and end where we
began.   What makes me think that this is the process of
our minds, and not merely rusticity or want of apprehension, is, that you will see an English artist admiring
and thrown into raptures by the tucker of Titian's mistress,
made up of an infinite number of little folds, but if he
attempts to copy it, he proceeds to omit all these details,
and dash it off by a single smear of his brush.   This is
not ignorance, or even laziness, but what is called jump-
ing at a conclusion.   It is, in a word, an overweening
purpose.   He sees the details, the varieties, and their
effects, and he admires them ; but he sees them with a glance
of his eye, and as a wilful man must have his way, he
would reproduce them by a single dash of the pencil.
The mixing his colours, the putting in and out, the giving his attention to a minute break, or softening in the
particular lights and shades, is a mechanical and everlasting
operation, very different from the delight he feels in contemplating the effect of all this when properly and finely
done.   Such details are foreign to his refined taste, and
some doubts arise in his mind in the midst of his gratitude
and his raptures, as to how Titian could resolve upon
the drudgery of going through them, and whether it was
not done by extreme facility of hand, and a sort of trick,

abridging the mechanical labour. No one wrote or talked more enthusiastically about Titian's harmony of colouring than the late Mr. Barry, yet his own colouring was dead and dry; and if he had copied a Titian, he would have make it a mere splash, leaving out all that caused his wonder or admiration, after his English, or rather Irish fashion. We not only grudge the labour of beginning, but we give up, for the same reason, when we are near touching the goal of success; and to save a few last touches, leave a work unfinished, and an object unattained. The immediate process, the daily gradual improvement, the completion of parts giving us no pleasure, we strain at the whole result; we wish to have it done, and in our anxiety to have it off our hands, say it will do, and lose the benefit of all our labour by grudging a little pains, and not commanding a little patience. In a day or two, suppose a copy of a fine Titian would be as complete as we could make it: the prospect of this so enchants us that we skip the intermediate days, see no great use in going on with it, fancy that we may spoil it, and in order to have the job done, take it home with us, when we immediately see our error, and spend the rest of our lives in repenting that we did not finish it properly at the time. We see the whole nature of a picture at once; we only do a part: *Hinc illæ lachrymæ.* A French artist, on the contrary, has none of this uneasy, anxious feeling; of this desire to grasp the whole of his subject, and anticipate his good fortune at a blow; of this massing and concentrating principle. He takes the thing more easily and rationally. Suppose he undertakes to copy a picture, he looks at it and copies it bit by bit. He does not set off headlong without knowing where he is going, or plunge into all sorts of difficulties and absurdities, from impatience to begin and thinking that " no sooner said than done ;" but takes time to consider, lays his plans, gets in his outline and his distances, and lays a foundation before he attempts a superstructure

2 A

which he may have to pull to pieces again. He looks
before he leaps, which is contrary to the true blindfold
English principle; and I should think that we had invented this proverb from seeing so many fatal examples of
the neglect of it. He does not make the picture all black
or all white, because one part of it is so, and because he
cannot alter an idea he has once got into his head, and
must always run into extremes, but varies from green to
red, from orange tawney to yellow, from grey to brown,
according as they vary in the original: he sees no inconsistency or forfeiture of a principle in this, but a great
deal of right reason, and indeed an absolute necessity, if he
wishes to succeed in what he is about. This is the last
thing an Englishman thinks of: he only wants to have his
own way, though it ends in defeat and ruin : he sets about
a thing which he had little prospect of accomplishing, and
if he finds he can do it, gives it over and leaves the matter
short of success, which is too agreeable an idea for him to
indulge in. The French artist proceeds bit by bit. He
takes one part, a hand, a piece of drapery, a part of the
back-ground, and finishes it carefully ; then another, and
so on to the end. He does not, from a childish impatience,
when he is near the conclusion, destroy the effect of the
whole by leaving some one part eminently defective, nor
fly from what he is about to something else that catches
his eye, neglecting the one and spoiling the other. He is
constrained by mastery, by the mastery of common sense
and pleasurable feeling. He is in no hurry to finish, for
he has a satisfaction in the work, and touches and retouches,
perhaps a single head, day after day and week after week,
without repining, uneasiness, or apparent progress. The
very lightness and indifference of his feelings renders him
patient and laborious: an Englishman, whatever he is
about or undertakes is as if he was carrying a heavy load
that oppresses both his body and mind, and which he is
anxious to throw down. A Frenchman's hopes or fears

are not excited to that pitch of intolerable agony that com-
pels him, in mere compassion to himself to bring the
question to a speedy issue, even to the loss of his object;
he is calm, easy, and indifferent, and can take his time and
make the most of his advantages with impunity. Pleased
with himself, he is pleased with whatever occupies his
attention nearly alike. It is the same to him whether he
paints an angel or a joint-stool; it is the same to him
whether it is landscape or history; it is he who paints it,
that is sufficient. Nothing puts him out of conceit with
his work, for nothing puts him out of conceit with himself.
This self-complacency produces admirable patience and
docility in certain particulars, besides charity and toleration towards others. I remember a ludicrous instance of
this deliberate process, in a young French artist who was
copying the *Titian's Mistress*, in the Louvre, some
twenty years ago.[1] After getting it in chalk-lines, one
would think he would have been attracted to the face, that
heaven of beauty which makes a sunshine in the shady
place, or to some part of the poetry of the picture; instead
of which he began to finish a square he had marked out
in the right-hand corner of the picture. He set to work
like a cabinet-maker or an engraver, and seemed to have
no sympathy with the soul of the picture. Indeed, to a
Frenchman there is no distinction between the great and
little, the pleasurable and the painful; the utmost he
arrives at a conception of is the indifferent and the light.
Another young man, at the time I speak of, was for eleven
weeks (I think it was) daily employed in making a black-
lead pencil drawing of a small Leonardo; he sat cross-
legged on a rail to do it, kept his hat on, rose up, went to
the fire to warm himself, talked constantly of the excellence
of the different masters—Titian for colour, Raphael for
expression, Poussin for composition—all being alike to
him, provided there was a word to express it, for all he

---

[1] When the author was studying at the Louvre in 1802.—ED.

thought about was his own harangue; and, having consulted some friend on his progress, he returned to
'perfectionate,' as he called it, his copy. This would
drive an Englishman mad or stupid. The perseverance
and the indifference, the labour without impulse, the
attention to the parts in succession, and disregard of the
whole together, are to him absolutely inconceivable. A
Frenchman only exists in his present sensations, and provided he is left free to these as they arise, he cares about
nothing farther, looking neither backward nor forward.
With all this affectation and artifice, there is on this
account a kind of simplicity and nature about them, after
all. They lend themselves to the impression before them
with good humour and good will, making it neither better
nor worse than it is. The English overdo or underdo
everything, and are either drunk or in despair. I do not
speak of all Frenchmen or of all Englishmen, but of the
most characteristic specimens of each class. The extreme
slowness and methodical regularity of the French has
arisen out of this indifference, and even frivolity (their
usually-supposed natural character), for owing to it their
laborious minuteness costs them nothing; they have no
strong impulses or ardent longings that urge them to the
violation of rules, or hurry them away with a subject and
with the interest belonging to it. Everything is matter
of calculation, and measured beforehand, in order to assist
their fluttering and their feebleness. When they get beyond the literal and the formal, and attempt the impressive
and the grand, as in David's and Girardot's pictures, defend
us from sublimity heaped on insipidity and petit-maitreism!
You see a Frenchman in the Louvre copying the finest
pictures, standing on one leg, with his hat on; or after
copying a Raphael, thinking David much finer, more truly
one of themselves, more a combination of the Greek
sculptor and the French posture-master. Even if a French
artist fails, he is not disconcerted; there is something

else he excels in : if he cannot paint, he can dance! If an Englishman, save the mark! fails in anything, he thinks he can do nothing ; enraged at the mention of his ability to do anything else, and at any consolation offered to him, he banishes all other thought but of his disappointment, and discarding hope from his breast, neither eats nor sleeps (it is well if he does not cut his throat),will not attend to any other thing in which he before took an interest and pride, and is in despair till he recovers his good opinion of himself in the point in which he has been disgraced, though, from his very anxiety and disorder of mind, he is incapacitated from applying to the only means of doing so, as much as if he were drunk with liquor, instead of with pride and passion. The character I have here drawn of an Englishman I am clear about, for it is the character of myself, and, I am sorry to add, no exaggerated one. As my object is to paint the varieties of human nature, and as I can have it best from myself, I will confess a weakness. I lately tried to copy a Titian (after many years' want of practice), in order to give a friend in England some idea of the picture. I floundered on for several days, but failed, as might be expected. My sky became overcast. Every thing seemed of the colour of the paint I used. Nature was one great daub. I had no feeling left but a sense of want of power, and of an abortive struggle to do what I could not do. I was ashamed of being seen to look at the picture with admiration, as if I had no right to do so. I was ashamed even to have written or spoken about the picture or about art at all: it seemed a piece of pre-sumption or affectation in me, whose whole notions and refinements on the subject ended in an inexcusable daub. Why did I think of attempting such a thing heedlessly, of exposing my presumption and incapacity? It was blot-ting from my memory, covering with a dark veil, all that I remembered of those pictures formerly, my hopes when young, my regrets since ; it was wresting from me one of

the consolations of my life and of my declining years. I
was even afraid to walk out by the barrier of Neuilly, or
to recall to memory that I had ever seen the picture; all
was turned to bitterness and gall : to feel anything but a
sense of my own helplessness and absurdity seemed a
want of sincerity, a mockery and a piece of injustice.
The only comfort I had was in the excess of pain I felt;
this was at least some distinction : I was not insensible on
that side. No Frenchman, I thought, would regret the not
copying a Titian so much as I did, or so far show the same
value for it. Besides, I had copied this identical picture
very well formerly. If ever I got out of this scrape, I
had received a lesson, at least, not to run the same risk of
gratuitous vexation again, or even to attempt what was uncertain and unnecessary.

It is the same in love and in literature. A man makes
love without thinking of the chances of success, his own
disabilities, or the character of his mistress; that is,
without connecting means with ends, and consulting only
his own will and passion. The author sets about writing
history, with the full intention of rendering all documents,
dates, and facts secondary to his own opinion and will.
In business it is not altogether the same; for interest
acts obviously as a counterpoise to caprice and will, and
is the moving principle; nor is it so in war, for then the
spirit of contradiction does everything, and an Englishman will go to the devil rather than give up to any odds.
Courage is pure will without regard to consequences, and
this the English have in perfection. Again, poetry is our
element, for the essence of poetry is will and passion.
The French poetry is detail and verbiage. I have thus
shown why the English fail, as a people, in the Fine Arts,
namely, because with them the end absorbs the means. I
have mentioned Barry as an individual instance. No man
spoke or wrote with more *gusto* about painting, and yet no
one painted with less. His pictures were dry and coarse,

and wanted all that his description of those of others contained. For instance, he speaks of the dull, dead, watery look in the Medusa's head of Leonardo, which conveys a perfect idea of it : if he had copied it, you would never have suspected anything of the kind. Again, he has, I believe, somewhere spoken of the uneasy effect of the tucker of the *Titian's Mistress*, bursting with the full treasures it contains. What a daub he would have made of it ! He is like a person admiring the grace of a fine rope-dancer ; placed on the rope himself his head turns, and he falls : or like a man admiring fine horse-manship ; set him upon a horse, and he tumbles over on the other side. Why was this ? His mind was essentially ardent and discursive, not sensitive or observing ; and though the immediate object acted as a stimulus to his imagination, it was only as it does to a poet's, that is, as a link in the chain of association, as suggesting other strong feelings and ideas, and not for its intrinsic beauty or hidden details. He had not the painter's eye though he had the painter's knowledge. There is as great a differ-ence in this respect as between the telescope and micro-scope. People in general see objects only to distinguish them in practice and by name ; to know that a hat is a hat, that a chair is not a table, that John is not William ; and there are painters (particularly of history) in England who look no farther. They cannot finish anything, or go over a head twice ; the first view is all they would arrive at ; nor can they reduce their impressions to their component parts without losing the spirit. The effect of this is grossness and want of force ; for in reality the component parts cannot be separated from the whole. Such people have no pleasure in the exercise of their art as such : it is all to astonish or to get money that they follow it ; or if they are thrown out of it, they regret it only as a bankrupt does a business which was a livelihood to him. Barry did not live, like Titian, in the taste of colours; they were not a *pabulum* to his sense; he did not hold green, blue, red, and yellow as the precious darlings of his eye. They did not therefore sink into his mind, or nourish and enrich it with the sense of beauty, though he knew enough of them to furnish hints and topics of discourse. If he had had the most beautiful object in nature before him in his painting-room in the Adelphi, he would have neglected it, after a moment's burst of admiration, to talk of his last composition, or to scrawl some new and vast design. Art was nothing to him, or if anything, merely a stalking-horse to his ambition and display of intellectual power in general; and therefore he neglected it to daub huge allegories, or cabal with the Academy, where the violence of his will or the extent of his views found ample scope. As a painter he was valuable merely as a draughtsman, in that part of the art which may be reduced to lines and precepts, or positive measurement. There is neither colour, nor expression, nor delicacy, nor beauty, in his works.

1827.

ESSAY IX.

Matter and Manner.

NOTHING can frequently be more striking than the difference of style or manner, where the *matter* remains the same, as in paraphrases and translations. The most remarkable example which occurs to us is in the beginning of the *Flower and Leaf*, by Chaucer,[1] and in the modernisation of the same passage by Dryden. We shall give an extract from both, that the reader may judge for himself. The original runs thus:

> "And I that all this pleasaunt sight *ay* sie,
> Thought sodainly I felte so sweet an aire

---

[1] Morris's edit. of Chaucer. The extract has now been given

Con of the eglentere, that certainely
There is no heart, I deme, in such dispaire,
Ne with *no* thoughtes froward and contraire
So overlaid, but it shoulde soone have bote,
If it had ones felt this savour sote.

And as I stood and cast aside mine eie,
I was of ware the fairest medler tree,
That ever yet in all my life I sie,
As full of blossomes as it mighte be;
Therein a goldfinch leaping pretile
Fro bough to bough; and, as him list, *gan* eete
Of buddes here and there and floures sweete.

And to the herber side *ther* was joyninge
This faire tree, of which I have you told;
And at the last the brid began to singe,
When he had eaten what he eate wolde,
So passing sweetly, that by manifolde,
It was more pleasaunt than I coude devise.
And when his song was ended in this wise,

The nightingale with so mery a note
Answered him, that all the woode rong
So sodainly, that, as it were a sote,
I stood astonied; so was I with the song
Thorow ravished, that till late and longe,
Ne wist I in what place I was, ne where;
And ay, me thoughte, she song even by mine ere.

Wherefore about I waited busily,
On every side, if *that* I her mighte see;
And, at the last, I gan full well aspie
Where she sat in a fresh grene laurer tree,
On the further side, even right by me,
That gave so passing a delicious smell,
According to the eglentere full well.

Whereof I hadde so inly great pleasure,
That, as me thought, I surely ravished was
Into Paradice, where *as* my desire
Was for to be, and no ferther to passe

---

from that source. The *Flower and Leaf* is now believed not to be
Chaucer's.—Ed.

> As for that day; and on the sote grasse
> I sat me downe; for, as for mine entent,
> The bird*des* song was more convenient.
>
> And more plea*s*aunt to me by many fold,
> Than meat or drinke, or any other thing.
> Thereto the herber was so fre*s*h and cold,
> The wholesome savours eke so comforting,
> That, as I demede, sith the beginning
> Of th*ilke* world was never seene or than
> So pleasaunt a ground of none earthly man.
>
> And as I sat, the bird*des* harkening thus,
> Me thoughte that I hearde voices sodainly,
> The most sweetest and most delicious
> That ever any wight, I trow truly,
> Heard in *here* life; for *sothe* the armony
> And sweet accord was in so good musike,
> That the voices to angels most was like."

In this passage the poet has let loose the very soul of pleasure. There is a spirit of enjoyment in it, of which there seems no end. It is the intense delight which accompanies the description of every object, the fund of natural sensibility it displays, which constitutes its whole essence and beauty. Now this is shown chiefly in the manner in which the different objects are anticipated, and the eager welcome which is given to them; in his repeating and varying the circumstances with a restless delight; in his quitting the subject for a moment, and then returning to it again, as if he could never have his fill of enjoyment. There is little of this in Dryden's paraphrase. The same ideas are introduced, but not in the same manner, nor with the same spirit. The imagination of the poet is not borne along with the tide of pleasure—the verse is not poured out, like the natural strains it describes, from pure delight, but according to rule and measure. Instead of being absorbed in his subject, he is dissatisfied with it, tries to give an air of dignity to it by factitious ornaments, to amuse the reader

by ingenious allusions, and divert his attention from the
progress of the story by the artifices of the style :

> " The painted birds, companions of the spring,
> Hopping from spray to spray, were heard to sing.
> Both eyes and ears receiv'd a like delight,
> Enchanting music, and a charming sight.
> On Philomel I fix'd my whole desire ;
> And listen'd for the queen of all the quire ;
> Fain would I hear her heavenly voice to sing ;
> And wanted yet an omen to the spring.
>   Thus as I mus'd I cast aside my eye,
> And saw a medlar-tree was planted nigh.
> The spreading branches made a goodly show,
> And full of opening blooms was every bough :
> A goldfinch there I saw with gawdy pride
> Of painted plumes, that hopp'd from side to side,
> Still pecking as she pass'd ; and still she drew
> The sweets from every flower and suck'd the dew :
> Suffic'd at length, she warbled in her throat,
> And tun'd her voice to many a merry note,
> But indistinct, and neither sweet nor clear,
> Yet such as sooth'd my soul, and pleas'd my ear.
>   Her short performance was no sooner tried,
> When she I sought, the nightingale, replied :
> So sweet, so shrill, so variously she sung,
> That the grove echoed, and the valleys rung :
> And I so ravish'd with her heavenly note,
> I stood entranc'd, and had no room for thought.
> But all o'erpower'd with ectasy of bliss,
> Was in a pleasing dream of paradise ;
> At length I wak'd, and looking round the bower,
> Search'd every tree, and pry'd on every flower,
> If any where by chance I might espy
> The rural poet of the melody :
> For still methought she sung not far away :
> At last I found her on a laurel spray.
> Close by my side she sat, and fair in sight,
> Full in a line, against her opposite ;
> Where stood with eglantine the laurel twin'd ;
> And both their native sweets were well conjoin'd.
>   On the green bank I sat, and listen'd long ;
> (Sitting was more convenient for the song ;)

> Nor till her lay was ended could I move,
> But wish'd to dwell for ever in the grove.
> Only methought the time too swiftly pass'd,
> And every note I fear'd would be the last.
> My sight, and smell and hearing were employ'd,
> And all three senses in full gust enjoy'd.
> And what alone did all the rest surpass
> The sweet possession of the fairy place;
> Single, and conscious to myself alone
> Of pleasures to the excluded world unknown:
> Pleasures which no where else were to be found,
> And all Elysium in a spot of ground.
>   Thus while I sat intent to see and hear,
> And drew perfumes of more than vital air,
> All suddenly I heard the approaching sound
> Of vocal music on the enchanted ground:
> A host of saints it seem'd, so full the quire;
> As if the bless'd above did all conspire
> To join their voices, and neglect the lyre."

Compared with Chaucer, Dryden and the rest of that school were merely *verbal poets*. They had a great deal of wit, sense, and fancy; they only wanted truth and depth of feeling. But I shall have to say more on this subject, when I come to consider the old question which I have got marked down in my list, whether Pope was a Poet.

Lord Chesterfield's character of the Duke of Marlborough is a good illustration of his general theory. He says, " Of all the men I ever knew in my life (and I knew him extremely well) the late Duke of Marlborough possessed the graces in the highest degree, not to say engrossed them; for I will venture (contrary to the custom of profound historians, who always assign deep causes for great events) to ascribe the better half of the Duke of Marlborough's greatness and riches to those graces. He was eminently illiterate: wrote bad English, and spelt it worse. He had no share of what is commonly called parts; that is, no brightness, nothing shining in his genius. He had, most undoubtedly, an excellent good plain understanding, with sound judgment. But these alone would probably have raised him but something higher than they found him, which was page to King James II.'s Queen. There the graces protected and promoted him; for while he was Ensign of the Guards, the Duchess of Cleveland, then favourite mistress of Charles II., struck by these very graces, gave him five thousand pounds; with which he immediately bought an annuity of five hundred pounds a year, which was the foundation of his subsequent fortune. His figure was beautiful, but his manner was irresistible by either man or woman. It was by this engaging, graceful manner, that he was enabled during all his wars to connect the various and jarring powers of the grand alliance, and to carry them on to the main object of the war, notwithstanding their private and separate views, jealousies, and wrong-headedness. Whatever court he went to (and he was often obliged to go himself to some resty and refractory ones) he as constantly prevailed, and brought them into his measures."

Grace in women has often more effect than beauty. We sometimes see a certain fine self-possession, an habitual voluptuousness of character, which reposes on its own sensations, and derives pleasure from all around it, that is more irresistible than any other attraction. There is an air of languid enjoyment in such persons, " in their eyes, in their arms, and their hands, and their face," which robs us of ourselves, and draws us by a secret sympathy towards them. Their minds are a shrine where pleasure reposes. Their smile diffuses a sensation like the breath of spring. Petrarch's description of Laura answers exactly to this character, which is indeed the Italian character. Titian's pictures are full of it; they seem sustained by sentiment, or as if the persons whom he painted sat to music. There is one in the Louvre (or there was) which had the most of this expression I ever remember. It did not look downward; " it looked forward beyond this world." It was a look that never passed away, but remained unalterable as the deep sentiment which gave birth to it. It is the same constitutional character (together with infinite activity of mind) which has enabled the greatest man in modern history to bear his reverses of fortune with gay magnanimity, and to submit to the loss of the empire of the world with as little discomposure as if he had been playing a game at chess.

After all, I would not be understood to say that manner is everything.[1] Nor would I put Euclid or Sir Isaac Newton on a level with the first *petit-maître* we might

---

[1] Sheer impudence answers almost the same purpose. "Those impenetrable whiskers have confronted flames." Many persons, by looking big and talking loud, make their way through the world without any one good quality. I have here said nothing of mere personal qualifications, which are another set-off against sterling merit. Fielding was of opinion that "the more solid pretensions of virtue and understanding vanish before perfect beauty." "A certain lady of a manor" (says *Don Quixote* in defence of his attachment to *Dulcinea*, which, however, was quite of the Platonic kind), "had cast the eyes of affection on a certain squat, brawny lay brother of a neighbouring monastery, to whom she was lavish of her favours. The head of the order remonstrated with her on this preference shown to one whom he represented as a very low, ignorant fellow, and set forth the superior pretensions of himself, and his more learned brethren. The lady having heard him to an end, made answer: All that you have said may be very true; but know that in those points which I admire, Brother Chrysostom is as great a philosopher, nay greater, than Aristotle himself!" So the *Wife of Bath*:

> To chirche was myn housbond brought on morwe
> With neighebors that for him made sorwe,
> And Jankyn oure clerk was oon of tho.
> As help me God, whan that I saugh him go
> After the beere, methought he had a paire
> Of legges and of feet so clene and faire,
> That al myn hert I yaf unto his hold.

"All which, though we most potently believe, yet we hold it not honesty to have it thus set down."

happen to meet. I consider *Æsop's Fables* to have been a greater work of genius than Fontaine's translation of them; though I am not sure that I should not prefer Fontaine, for his style only, to Gay, who has shown a great deal of original invention. The elegant manners of people of fashion have been objected to me, to show the frivolity of external accomplishments, and the facility with which they are acquired. As to the last point, I demur. There are no class of people who lead so laborious a life, or who take more pains to cultivate their minds as well as persons, than people of fashion. A young lady of quality who has to devote so many hours a day to music, so many to dancing, so many to drawing so many to French, Italian, &c., certainly does not pass her time in idleness: and these accomplishments are afterwards called into action by every kind of external or mental stimulus, by the excitements of pleasure, vanity, and interest. A Ministerial or Opposition Lord goes through more drudgery than half a dozen literary hacks; nor does a reviewer by profession read half the same number of publications as a modern fine lady is obliged to labour through. I confess, however, I am not a competent judge of the degree of elegance or refinement implied in the general tone of fashionable manners. The successful experiment made by *Peregrine Pickle*, in introducing his strolling mistress into genteel company, does not redound greatly to their credit.

1815.

ESSAY X.

On Consistency of Opinion.

"—— Servetur ad imum
Qualis ab inceptu processerit, et sibi constet."

MANY people boast of being masters in their own house. I pretend to be master of my own mind. I should be sorry to have an ejectment served upon me for any notions I may choose to entertain there. Within that little circle I would fain be an absolute monarch. I do not profess the spirit of martyrdom; I have no ambition to march to the stake, or up to a masked battery, in defence of an hypothesis: I do not court the rack: I do not wish to be flayed alive for affirming that two and two make four, or any other intricate proposition: I am shy of bodily pains and penalties, which some are fond of— imprisonment, fine, banishment, confiscation of goods: but if I do not prefer the independence of my mind to that of my body, I at least prefer it to everything else. I would avoid the arm of power, as I would escape from the fangs of a wild beast: but as to the opinion of the world, I see nothing formidable in it. "It is the eye of childhood that fears a painted devil." I am not to be browbeat or wheedled out of any of my settled convictions. Opinion to opinion, I will face any man. Prejudice, fashion, the cant of the moment, go for nothing; and as for the reason of the thing, it can only be supposed to rest with me or another, in proportion to the pains we have taken to ascertain it. Where the pursuit of truth has been the habitual study of any man's life, the love of truth will be his ruling passion. "Where the treasure is, there the heart is also." Every one is most tenacious of that to which he owes his distinction from others. Kings love power, misers gold, women flattery, poets reputation—and philosophers truth, when they can find it. They are right in cherishing the only privilege they inherit. If "to be wise were to be obstinate," I might set up for as great a philosopher as the best of them; for some of my conclusions are as fixed and as incorrigible to proof as need be. I am attached to them in consequence of the pains, and anxiety, and the waste of time they have cost me. In fact, I should not well know what to do without them at this time of day; nor how to get others to supply their place. I would quarrel with the best friend I have sooner than acknowledge the absolute right of the Bourbons. I see Mr. Northcote seldomer than I did, because I cannot agree with him about the *Catalogue Raisonné*.[1] I remember once saying to this gentleman, a great while ago, that I did not seem to have altered any of my ideas since I was sixteen years old. "Why then," said he, "you are no wiser now than you were then!" I might make the same confession, and the same retort would apply still. Coleridge used to tell me, that this pertinacity was owing to a want of sympathy with others. What he calls *sympathising with others* is their admiring him; and it must be admitted that he varies his battery pretty often, in order to accommodate himself to this sort of mutual understanding. But I do not agree in what he says of me. On the other hand, I think that it is my sympathising *beforehand* with the different views and feelings that may be entertained on a subject, that prevents me retracting my judgment, and flinging myself into the contrary extreme *afterwards*. If you proscribe all opinion opposite to your own, and impertinently exclude all the evidence that does not make for you, it stares you in the face with double force when it breaks in unexpectedly upon you, or if at any subsequent period it happens to suit your interest or convenience to listen to objections which vanity or prudence had hitherto overlooked. But if you are aware from the first suggestion of a subject, either by subtlety, or tact, or close attention, of the full force of what others possibly feel and think of it, you are not exposed to the same vacillation of opinion. The number of grains and scruples, of doubts and difficulties, thrown into the scale while the balance is yet undecided, add to the weight and steadiness of the determination. He who anticipates his opponent's arguments, confirms while he corrects his own reasonings.

[1] See *Memoirs*, i, 211.—ED.

2 B

When a question has been carefully examined in all its bearings, and a principle is once established, it is not liable to be overthrown by any new facts which have been arbitrarily and petulantly set aside, nor by every wind of idle doctrine rushing into the interstices of a hollow speculation, shattering it in pieces, and leaving it a mockery and a bye-word; like those tall, gawky, staring, pyramidal erections which are seen scattered over different parts of the country, and are called the *Follies* of different gentlemen! A man may be confident in maintaining a side, as he has been cautious in choosing it. If after making up his mind strongly in one way, to the best of his capacity and judgment, he feels himself inclined to a very violent revulsion of sentiment, he may generally rest assured that the change is in himself and his motives, not in the reason of things.

I cannot say that, from my own experience, I have found that the persons most remarkable for sudden and violent changes of principle have been cast in the softest or most susceptible mould. All their notions have been exclusive, bigoted, and intolerant. Their want of consistency and moderation has been in exact proportion to their want of candour and comprehensiveness of mind. Instead of being the creatures of sympathy, open to conviction, unwilling to give offence by the smallest difference of sentiment, they have (for the most part) been made up of mere antipathies—a very repulsive sort of personages— at odds with themselves, and with everybody else. The slenderness of their pretensions to philosophical inquiry has been accompanied with the most presumptuous dogmatism. They have been persons of that narrowness of view and headstrong self-sufficiency of purpose, that they could see only one side of a question at a time, and whichever they pleased. There is a story somewhere in *Don Quixote*, of two champions coming to a shield hung up against a tree with an inscription written on each side of it. Each of them maintained, that the words were what was written on the side next him, and never dreamt, till the fray was over, that they might be different on the opposite side of the shield. It would have been a little more extraordinary if the combatants had changed sides in the heat of the scuffle, and stoutly denied that there were any such words on the opposite side as they had before been bent on sacrificing their lives to prove were the only ones it contained. Yet such is the very situation of some of our modern polemics. They have been of all sides of the question, and yet they cannot conceive how an honest man can be of any but one—that which they hold at present. It seems that they are afraid to look their old opinions in the face, lest they should be fascinated by them once more. They banish all doubts of their own sincerity by inveighing against the motives of their antagonists. There is no salvation out of the pale of their strange inconsistency. They reduce common sense and probity to the straitest possible limits—the breasts of themselves and their patrons. They are like people out at sea on a very narrow plank, who try to push everybody else off. Is it that they have so little faith in the course to which they have become such staunch converts, as to suppose that, should they allow a grain of sense to their old allies and new antagonists, they will have more than they? Is it that they have so little consciousness of their own disinterestedness, that they feel, if they allow a particle of honesty to those who now differ with them, they will have more than they? Those opinions must needs be of a very fragile texture which will not stand the shock of the least acknowledged opposition, and which lay claim to respectability by stigmatising all who do not hold them as " sots, and knaves, and cowards." There is a want of well-balanced feeling in every such instance of extravagant versatility ; a something crude, unripe, and harsh, that does not hit a judicious palate, but sets the teeth on edge to think of. "I had rather hear my mother's cat mew, or a wheel grate on the axletree, than one of these same metre-ballad-mongers" chaunt his incondite, retrograde lays, without rhyme and without reason.

The principles and professions change: the man remains the same. There is the same spirit at the bottom of all this pragmatical fickleness and virulence, whether it runs into one extreme or another: to wit, a confinement of view, a jealousy of others, an impatience of contradiction, a want of liberality in construing the motives of others, either from monkish pedantry, or a conceited overweening reference of everything to our own fancies and feelings. There is something to be said, indeed, for the nature of the political machinery, for the whirling motion of the revolutionary wheel which has of late wrenched men's understandings almost asunder, and "amazed the very faculties of eyes and ears;" but still this is hardly a sufficient reason, why the adept in the old as well as the new school should take such a prodigious latitude himself, while at the same time he makes so little allowance for others. His whole creed need not be turned topsy-turvy, from the top to the bottom, even in times like these. He need not, in the rage of party spirit, discard the proper attributes of humanity, the common dictates of reason. He need not outrage every former feeling, nor trample on every customary decency, in his zeal for reform, or in his greater zeal against it. If his mind, like his body, has undergone a total change of essence, and purged off the taint of all its early opinions, he need not carry about with him, or be haunted in the persons of others with, the phantoms of his altered principles to loathe and execrate them. He need not (as it were) pass an act of attainder on all his thoughts, hopes, wishes, from youth upwards, to offer them at the shrine of matured servility: he need not become one vile antithesis, a living and ignominious satire on himself.

A gentleman went to live, some years ago, in a remote part of the country, and as he did not wish to affect singularity, he used to have two candles on his table of an evening. A romantic acquaintance of his in the neighbourhood, smit with the love of simplicity and equality, used to come in, and without ceremony snuff one of them out, saying, it was a shame to indulge in such extravagance, while many poor cottagers had not even a rushlight to see to do their evening's work by. This might be about the year 1802, and was passed over as among the ordinary occurrences of the day. In 1816 (oh! fearful lapse of time, pregnant with strange mutability), the same enthusiastic lover of economy, and hater of luxury, asked his thoughtless friend to dine with him in company with a certain lord, and to lend him his man servant to wait at table ; and just before they were sitting down to dinner, he heard him say to the servant in a sonorous whisper— "and be sure you don't forget to have six candles on the table!" Extremes meet. The event here was as true to itself as the oscillation of the pendulum. My informant, who understands moral equations, had looked for this reaction, and noted it down as characteristic. The impertinence in the first instance was the cue to the ostentatious servility in the second. The one was the fulfilment of the other, like the type and anti-type of a prophecy. No—the keeping of the character at the end of fourteen years was as unique as the keeping of the thought to the end of the fourteen lines of a sonnet! Would it sound strange if I were to whisper it in the reader's ear, that it was the same person who was thus anxious to see six candles on the table to receive a lord, who once (in ages past) said to me, that "he saw nothing to admire in the eloquence of such men as Mansfield and Chatham ; and what did it all end in, but their being made lords?" It is better to be a lord than a lacquey to a lord! So we see that the swelling pride and preposterous self-opinion which exalts itself above the mightiest, looking down upon and braving the boasted pretensions of the highest rank and the most brilliant talents as nothing, compared with its own conscious powers and silent unmoved self-respect, grovels and licks the dust before titled wealth, like a lacquered slave, the moment it can get wages and a livery! Would Milton or Marvel have done this?

Mr. Coleridge, indeed, sets down this outragous want of keeping to an excess of sympathy, and there is, after all, some truth in his suggestion. There is a craving after the approbation and concurrence of others natural to the mind of man. It is difficult to sustain the weight of an opinion singly for any length of way. The intellect languishes without cordial encouragement and support. It exhausts both strength and patience to be always striving against the stream. *Contra audentior ito* is the motto but of few. Public opinion is always pressing upon the mind, and, like the air we breathe, acts unseen, unfelt. It supplies the living current of our thoughts, and infects without our knowledge. It taints the blood, and is taken into the smallest pores. The most sanguine constitutions are, perhaps, the most exposed to its influence. But public opinion has its source in power, in popular prejudice, and is not always in accord with right reason, or a high and abstracted imagination. Which path to follow where the two roads part? The heroic and romantic resolution prevails at first in high and heroic tempers. They think to scale the heights of truth and virtue at once with him " whose genius had angelic wings, and fed on manna,"—but after a time find themselves baffled, toiling on in an uphill road, without friends, in a cold neighbourhood, without aid or prospect of success. The poet

" Like a worm goes by the way."

He hears murmurs loud or suppressed, meets blank looks

or scowling faces, is exposed to the pelting of the pitiless press, and is stunned by the shout of the mob, that gather round him to see what sort of a creature a poet and a philosopher is. What is there to make him proof against all this? A strength of understanding steeled against temptation, and a dear love of truth that smiles opinion to scorn. These he perhaps has not. A lord passes in his coach. Might he not get up, and ride out of the reach of the rabble-rout? He is invited to stop dinner. If he stays he might insinuate some wholesome truths. He drinks in rank poison—flattery! He recites some verses to the ladies, who smile delicious praise, and thank him through their tears. The master of the house suggests a happy allusion in the turn of an expression. "There's sympathy." This is better than the company he lately left. Pictures, statues meet his raptured eye. Our Ulysses finds himself in the gardens of Alcinous: our truant is fairly caught. He wanders through enchanted ground. Groves, classic groves, nod unto him, and he hears "ancestral voices" hailing him as brother bard! He sleeps, dreams, and wakes cured of his thriftless prejudices and morose philanthropy. He likes this courtly and popular sympathy better. "He looks up with awe to kings; with honour to nobility; with reverence to magistrates," &c. He no longer breathes the air of heaven and his own thoughts, but is steeped in that of palaces and courts, and finds it agree better with his constitutional temperament. Oh! how sympathy alters a man from what he was!

> "I've heard of hearts unkind,
>   Kind deeds with cold returning;
> Alas! the gratitude of man
>   Has oftener set me mourning."

A spirit of contradiction, a wish to monopolise all wisdom, will not account for uniform consistency, for it is sure to defeat and turn against itself. It is "everything by turns, and nothing long." It is warped and crooked. It cannot bear the least opposition, and sooner than acquiesce in what others approve it will change sides in a day. It is offended at every resistance to its captious, domineering humour, and will quarrel for straws with its best friends. A person under the guidance of this demon, if every whimsy or occult discovery of his own is not received with acclamation by one party, will wreak his spite by deserting to the other, and carry all his talent for disputation with him, sharpened by rage and disappointment. A man, to be steady in a cause, should be more attached to the truth than to the acquiescence of his fellow citizens.

I can hardly consider Mr. Coleridge a deserter from the cause he first espoused, unless one could tell what cause he ever heartily espoused, or what party he ever belonged to, in downright earnest. He has not been inconsistent with himself at different times, but at all times. He is a sophist, a casuist, a rhetorician, what you please, and might have argued or declaimed to the end of his breath on one side of a question or another, but he never was a pragmatical fellow. He lived in a round of contradictions, and never came to a settled point. His fancy gave the cue to his judgment, and his vanity set his invention afloat in whatever direction he could find most scope for it, or most *sympathy*, that is, admiration. His Life and Opinions might naturally receive the title of one of Hume's Essays—*A Sceptical Solution of Sceptical Doubts.* To be sure, his *Watchman* and his *Friend* breathe a somewhat different tone on subjects of a particular description, both of them apparently pretty high-raised, but whoever will be at the pains to examine them closely, will find them to be *voluntaries*, fugues, solemn capriccios, not set compositions with any malice prepense in them, or much practical meaning. I believe some of his friends, who were indebted to him for the suggestion of plausible reasons for conformity, and an opening to a more qualified view of the letter of their paradoxical principles, have lately disgusted him by the virulence and extravagance to which they have carried hints, of which he never suspected that they would make the least possible use. But if Mr. Coleridge is satisfied with the wandering Moods of his Mind, perhaps this is no reason that others may not reap the solid benefit. He himself is like the idle sea-weed on the ocean, tossed from shore to shore: they are like barnacles fastened to the vessel of state, rotting its goodly timbers!

There are some persons who are of too fastidious a turn of mind to like anything long, or to assent twice to the same opinion. —— always sets himself to prop the falling cause, to nurse the ricketty bantling. He takes the part which he thinks in most need of his support, not so much out of magnanimity, as to prevent too great a degree of presumption or self-complacency on the triumphant side. "Though truth be truth, yet he contrives to throw such changes of vexation on it as it may lose some colour." I have been delighted to hear him expatiate with the most natural and affecting simplicity on a favourite passage or picture, and all the while afraid of agreeing with him, lest he should instantly turn round and unsay all that he had said, for fear of my going away with too good an opinion of my own taste, or too great an admiration of my idol— and his own. I dare not ask his opinion twice, if I have got a favourable sentence once, lest he should belie his own sentiments to stagger mine. I have heard him talk divinely (like one inspired) of Boccaccio, and the story of the Pot of Basil, describing " how it grew, and it grew, and it grew," till you saw it spread its tender leaves in the light of his eye, and wave in the tremulous sound of his voice; and yet if you asked him about it another time, he would, perhaps, affect to think little of it, or to have forgotten the circumstance. His enthusiasm is fickle and treacherous. The instant he finds it shared in common, he backs out of it. His enmity is equally refined, but hardly so unsocial. His exquisitely-turned invectives display all the beauty of scorn, and impart elegance to vulgarity. He sometimes finds out minute excellences, and cries up one thing to put you out of conceit with another. If you want him to praise Sir Joshua *con amore*, in his best manner, you should begin with saying something about Titian—if you seem an idoliser of Sir Joshua, he will immediately turn off the discourse, gliding like the serpent before Eve, wary and beautiful, to the graces of Sir Peter Lely, or ask if you saw a Vandyke the other day, which he does not think Sir Joshua could stand near. But find fault with the Lake Poets, and mention some pretended patron of rising genius, and you need not fear but he will join in with you and go all lengths that you can wish him. You may calculate upon him there. "Pride elevates, and joy brightens his face." And, indeed, so eloquent is he, and so beautiful in his eloquence, that I myself, with all my freedom from gall and bitterness, could listen to him untired, and without knowing how the the time went, losing and neglecting many a meal and hour,

> ———— " From morn to noon,
> From noon to dewy eve, a summer's day."

When I cease to hear him quite, other tongues, turned to what accents they may of praise or blame, would sound dull, ungrateful, out of tune, and harsh, in the comparison.

An overstrained enthusiasm produces a capriciousness in taste, as well as too much indifference. A person who sets no bounds to his admiration takes a surfeit of his favourites. He over-does the thing. He gets sick of his own everlasting praises, and affected ruptures. His preferences are a great deal too violent to last. He wears out an author in a week, that might last him a year, or his life, by the eagerness with which he devours him. Every such favourite is in his turn the greatest writer in the world. Compared with the lord of the ascendent for the time being, Shakspeare is commonplace, and Milton a pedant, a little insipid or so. Some of these prodigies require to be dragged out of their lurking-places, and cried up to the top of the compass; their traits are subtle, and must be violently obtruded on the sight. But the effort of exaggerated praise, though it may stagger others, tires the maker, and we hear of them no more after awhile. Others take their turns, are swallowed whole, undigested, ravenously, and disappear in the same manner. Good authors share the fate of bad, and a library in a few years is nearly dismantled. It is a pity thus to outlive our admiration, and exhaust our relish of what is excellent. Actors and actresses are disposed of in the same conclusive peremptory way: some of them are talked of for months, nay, years; then it is almost an offence to mention them. Friends, acquaintance, go the same road : are now asked to come six days in the week, then warned against coming the seventh. The smallest faults are soon magnified in those we think too highly of: but where shall we find perfection ? If we will put up with nothing short of that, we shall have neither pictures, books, nor friends left— we shall have nothing but our own absurdities to keep company with! "In all things a regular and moderate indulgence is the best security for a lasting enjoyment."

There are numbers who judge by the event, and change with fortune. They extol the hero of the day, and join the prevailing clamour, whatever it is; so that the fluctuating state of public opinion regulates their feverish, restless enthusiasm, like a thermometer. They blow hot or cold, according as the wind sets favourably or otherwise. With such people the only infallible test of merit is success ; and no arguments are true that have not a large or powerful majority on their side. They go by appear-

ances.   Their vanity, not the truth, is their ruling object.
They are not the last to quit a falling cause, and they are
the first to hail the rising sun.   Their minds want
sincerity, modesty, and keeping.   With them—

——— " To have done is to hang   .
 Quite out of fashion, like a rusty mail
In monumental mockery."

They still, " with one consent, praise new-born gauds,"
and Fame, as they construe it, is

——— " Like a fashionable host,
That slightly shakes his parting guest by the hand;
And with his arms outstretch'd, as he would fly,
Grasps the in comer.   Welcome ever smiles,
And Farewell goes out sighing."

Such servile flatterers made an idol of Buonaparte while
fortune smiled upon him, but when it left him, they
removed him from his pedestal in the cabinet of their
vanity, as we take down the picture of a relation that has
died without naming us in his will.   The opinion of such
triflers is worth nothing; it is merely an echo.   We do
not want to be told the event of a question, but the rights
of it.   Truth is in their theory nothing but " noise and
inexplicable dumb show."   They are the heralds, outriders, and trumpeters in the procession of fame; are
more loud and boisterous than the rest, and give themselves great airs, as the avowed patrons and admirers of
genius and merit.   As there are many who change their
sentiments with circumstances (as they decided lawsuits
in Rabelais with the dice), so there are others who change
them with their acquaintance.   " Tell me your company, and
I'll tell you your opinions," might be said to many a man
who piques himself on a select and superior view of things,
distinct from the vulgar.   Individuals of this class are
quick and versatile, but they are not beforehand with
opinion.   They catch it, when it is pointed out to them,

and take it at the rebound, instead of giving the first impulse. Their minds are a light, luxuriant soil, into which thoughts are easily transplanted, and shoot up with uncommon sprightliness and vigour. They wear the dress of other people's minds very gracefully and unconsciously. They tell you your own opinion, or very gravely repeat an observation you have made to them about half a year afterwards. They let you into the delicacies and luxuries of Spenser with great disinterestedness, in return for your having introduced that author to their notice. They prefer West to Raphael, Stothard to Rubens, till they are told better. Still they are acute in the main, and good judges in their way. By trying to improve their tastes, and reform their notions according to an ideal standard, they perhaps spoil and muddle their native faculties, rather than do them any good. Their first manner is their best, because it is the most natural. It is well not to go out of ourselves, and to be contented to take up with what we are, for better for worse. We can neither beg, borrow, nor steal characteristic excellences. Some views and modes of thinking suit certain minds, as certain colours suit certain complexions. We may part with very shining and very useful qualities, without getting better ones to supply them. Mocking is catching, only in regard to defects. Mimicry is always dangerous.

It is not necessary to change our road in order to advance on our journey. We should cultivate the spot of ground we possess to the utmost of our power, though it may be circumscribed and comparatively barren. *A rolling stone gathers no moss.* People may collect all the wisdom they will ever attain, quite as well by staying at home as by travelling abroad. There is no use in shifting from place to place, from side to side, or from subject to subject. You have always to begin again, and never finish any course of study or observation. By adhering to the

same principles you do not become stationary. You
enlarge, correct, and consolidate your reasonings, without
contradicting and shuffling about in your conclusions.
If truth consisted in hasty assumptions and petulant contradictions, there might be some ground for this whiffling
and violent inconsistency. But the face of truth, like that
of nature, is different and the same. The first outline of
an opinion, and the general tone of thinking, may be sound ·
and correct, though we may spend any quantity of time
and pains in working up and uniting the parts at subsequent sittings. If we have misconceived the character
of the countenance altogether at first, no alterations will
bring it right afterwards. Those who mistake white for
black in the first instance, may as well mistake black for
white when they reverse their canvas. I do not see what
security they can have in their present opinions, who
build their pretensions to wisdom on the total folly, rashness, and extravagance (to say no worse) of their former
ones. The perspective may change with years and experience : we may see certain things nearer, and others
more remote; but the great masses and landmarks will
remain, though thrown into shadow and tinged by the
intervening atmosphere : so the laws of the understanding,
the truth of nature, will remain, and cannot be thrown
into utter confusion and perplexity by our blunders or
caprice, like the objects in Hogarth's *Rules of Perspective*, where everything is turned upside down, or thrust
out of its well-known place. I cannot understand how
our political Harlequins feel after all their summersaults
and metamorphoses. They can hardly, I should think,
look at themselves in the glass, or walk across the room
without stumbling. This at least would be the case if
they had the least reflection or self-knowledge. But they
judge from pique and vanity solely. There should be a
certain decorum in life, as in a picture, without which it is
neither useful nor agreeable. If my opinions are not

right, at any rate they are the best I have been able to form, and better than any others I could take up at random, or out of perversity, now. Contrary opinions vitiate one another, and destroy the simplicity and clearness of the mind : nothing is good that has not a beginning, a middle, and an end ; and I would wish my thoughts to be

"Linked each to each by natural piety."

1821.

ESSAY XI.

Project for a New Theory of Civil and Criminal Legislation.

WHEN I was about fourteen (as long ago as the year 1792), in consequence of a dispute, one day after coming out of meeting, between my father and an old lady of the congregation, respecting the repeal of the Corporation and Test Acts and the limits of religious toleration, I set about forming in my head (the first time I ever attempted to think) the following system of political rights and general jurisprudence.

It was this circumstance that decided the fate of my future life; or rather, I would say it was from an original bias or craving to be satisfied of the reason of things, that I seized hold of this accidental opportunity to indulge in its uneasy and unconscious determination. Mr. Currie, my old tutor at Hackney, may still have the rough draught of this speculation, which I gave him with tears in my eyes, and which he good-naturedly accepted in lieu of the customary *themes*, and as a proof that I was no idler, but that my inability to produce a line on the ordinary school topics arose from my being involved in more difficult and abstuse matters. He must smile at the so oft-repeated charge against me of florid flippancy and tinsel. If from those briars I have since plucked roses, what labour has it not cost me ? The Test and Corporation Acts were repealed the other day. How would my father

have rejoiced if this had happened in his time, and in concert with his old friends Dr. Price, Dr. Priestly, and
others! but now that there is no' one to care about it, they
give as a boon to indifference what they so long refused to
justice, and thus ascribed by some to the liberality of the
age! Spirit of contradiction! when wilt thou cease to
rule over sublunary affairs, as the moon governs the tides?
Not till the unexpected stroke of a comet throws up a
new breed of men and animals from the bowels of the
earth; nor then neither, since it is included in the very
idea of all life, power, and motion. *For* and *against* are
inseparable terms. But not to wander any farther from
the point—

I began with trying to define what a *right* meant; and
this I settled with myself was not simply that which is
good or useful in itself, but that which is thought so by
the individual, and which has the sanction of his will as
such. 1. Because the determining what is good in itself
is an endless question. 2. Because one person's having a
right to any good, and another being made the judge of it,
leaves him without any security for its being exercised to
his advantage, whereas self-love is a natural guarantee for
our self-interest. 3. A thing being willed is the most
absolute moral reason for its existence : that a thing is
good in itself is no reason whatever why it should exist,
till the will clothes it with a power to act as a motive;
and there is certainly nothing to prevent this will from
taking effect (no law or admitted plea above it) but another
will opposed to it, and which forms a right on the same
principle. A good is only so far a right, inasmuch as it
virtually determines the will; for a *right* meant that which
contains within itself, and as respects the bosom in which
it is lodged, a cogent and unanswerable reason why it
should exist. Suppose I have a violent aversion to one
thing and as strong an attachment to something else, and
that there is no other being in the world but myself, shall

I not have a self-evident right, full title, liberty, to pursue the one and avoid the other ? That is to say, in other words, there can be no authority to interpose between the strong natural tendency of the will and its desired effect, but the will of another. It may be replied that reason, that affection, may interpose between the will and the act; but there are motives that influence the conduct by first altering the will; and the point at issue is, that these being away, what other principle or lever is there always left to appeal to, before we come to blows ? Now, such a principle is to be found in self-interest; and such a barrier against the violent will is erected by the limits which this principle necessarily sets to itself in the claims of different individuals. Thus, then, a right is not that which is right in itself, or best for the whole, or even for the individual, but that which is good in his own eyes, and according to his own will; and to which, among a number of equally selfish and self-willed beings, he can lay claim, allowing the same latitude and allowance to others. Political justice is that which assigns the limits of these individual rights in society, or it is the adjustment of force against force, of will against will, to prevent worse consequences. In the savage state there is nothing but an appeal to brute force, or the right of the strongest; Politics lays down a rule to curb and measure out the wills of individuals in equal portions; Morals has a higher standard still, and ought never to appeal to force in any case whatever. Hence I always found something wanting in Mr. Godwin's *Enquiry concerning Political Justice* (which I read soon after with great avidity, and hoped, from its title and its vast reputation, to get entire satisfaction from it), for he makes no distinction between political justice, which implies an appeal to force, and moral justice, which implies only an appeal to reason. It is surely a distinct question, what you can persuade people to do by argument and fair discussion, and what you may lawfully compel them to do, when reason and remonstrance fail. But in Mr. Godwin's system the "omnipotence of reason" supersedes the use of law and government, merges the imperfection of the means in the grandeur of the end, and leaves but one class of ideas or motives, the highest and the least attainable possible. So promises and oaths are said to be of no more value than common breath; nor would they, if every word we uttered was infallible and oracular, as if delivered from a Tripod. Bu . this is pragmatical, and putting an imaginary for a real state of things. Again, right and duties, according to Mr. Godwin, are reciprocal. I could not comprehend this without an arbitrary definition that took away the meaning. In my sense, a man might have a right, a discriminating power, to do something, which others could not deprive him of, without a manifest infraction of certain rules laid down for the peace and order of society, but which it might be his duty to waive upon good reasons shown; rights are seconded by force, duties are things of choice. This is the import of the words in common speech : why then pass over this distinction in a work confessedly rhetorical as well as logical, that is, which laid an equal stress on sound and sense ? Right, therefore, has a personal or selfish reference, as it is founded on the law which determines a man's actions in regard to his own being and well-being; and political justice is that which assigns the limits of these individual rights on their compatibility or incompatibility with each other in society. Right, in a word, is the duty which each man owes to himself; or it is that portion of the general good of which (as being principally interested) he is made the special judge, and which is put under his immediate keeping.

The next question I asked myself was, what is law and the real and necessary ground of civil government ? The answer to this is found in the former statement. *Law* is something to abridge, or, more properly speaking, to ascertain, the bounds of the original right, and to coerce the will of individuals in the community. Whence, then, has the community such a right? It can only arise in self-defence, or from the necessity of maintaining the equal rights of every one, and of opposing force to force in case of any violent and unwarrantable infringement of them. Society consists of a given number of individuals; and the aggregate right of government is only the consequence of these inherent rights, balancing and neutralising one another. How those who deny natural rights get at any sort of right, divine or human, I am at a loss to discover; for whatever exists in combination, exists beforehand in an elementary state. The world is composed of atoms, and a machine cannot be made without materials. First, then, it follows that law or government is not the mere creature of a social compact, since each person has a certain right which he is bound to defend against another without asking that other's leave, or else the right would always be at the mercy of whoever chose to invade it. There would be a right to do wrong, but none to resist it. Thus I have a natural right to defend my life against a murderer, without any mutual compact between us; hence society has an aggregate right of the same kind, and to make a law to that effect, forbidding and punishing murder. If there be no such immediate value and attachment to life felt by the individual, and a consequent justifiable determination to defend it, then the formal pretension of society to vindicate a right, which, according to this reasoning, has no existence in itself, must be founded on air, on a word, or a lawyer's *ipse dixit*. Secondly, society, or government, as such, has no right to trench upon the liberty or rights of the individuals its members, except as these last are, as it were, forfeited by interfering with and destroying one another, like opposite mechanical forces or quantities in arithmetic. Put the basis that each man's will is a sovereign law to itself: this can only hold in society as long as he does not meddle with others; but as long as he does not do this, the first principle retains its force, for there is no other principle to impeach or overrule it. The will of society is not a sufficient plea; since this is, or ought to be, made up of the wills or rights of the individuals composing it, which by the supposition remain entire, and consequently without power to act. The good of society is not a sufficient plea, for individuals are only bound (on compulsion) not to do it harm, or to be barely just : benevolence and virtue are voluntary qualities. For instance, if two persons are obliged to do all that is possible for the good of both, this must either be settled voluntarily between them, and then it is friendship, and not force; or if this is not the case, it is plain that one must be the slave, and lie at the caprice and mercy of the other : it will be one will forcibly regulating two bodies. But if each is left master of his own person and actions, with only the implied proviso of not encroaching on those of the other, then both may continue free and independent, and contented in their several spheres. One individual has no right to interfere with the employment of my muscular powers, or to put violence on my person, to force me to contribute to the most laudable undertaking if I do not approve of it, any more than I have to force him to assist me in the direct contrary : if one has not, ten have not, nor a million, any such arbitrary right over me. What one can be *made* to do for a million is very trifling : what a million may do by being left free in all that merely concerns themselves, and not subject to the perpetual caprice and insolence of authority, and pretext of the public good, is a very different calculation. By giving up the principle of political independence, it is not the million that will govern the one, but the one that will in time give law to the million. There are some things that cannot be free in natural society, and against which there is a natural law; for instance, no one can be allowed to knock out another's brains or to fetter his limbs with impunity. And government is bound to prevent the same violations of liberty and justice. The question is, whether it would not be possible for a government to exist, and for a system of laws to be framed, that confined itself to the punishment of such offences, and left all the rest (except the suppression of force by force) optional or matter of mutual compact. What are a man's natural rights? Those, the infringement of which cannot on any supposition go unpunished: by leaving all but cases of necessity to choice and reason, much would be perhaps gained, and nothing lost.

COROLLARY 1. It results from the foregoing statement, that there is nothing naturally to restrain or oppose the will of one man, but the will of another meeting it. Thus, in a desert island, it is evident that my will and rights would be absolute and unlimited, and I might say with Robinson Crusoe, "I am monarch of all I survey."

COROLLARY 2. It is coming into society that circumscribes my will and rights, by establishing equal and mutual rights, instead of the original uncircumscribed ones. They are still "founded as the rock," though not so broad and general as the casing air, for the only thing that limits them is the solidity of another right, no better than my own, and, like stones in a building, or a mosaic pavement, each remains not the less firmly riveted to its place, though it cannot encroach upon the next to it. I do not belong to the state, nor am I a nonentity in it, but I am one part of it, and independent in it, for that very reason that every one in it is independent of me. Equality, instead of being destroyed by society, results from and is improved by it; for in politics, as in physics, the action and reaction are the same: the right of resistance on their part implies the right of self-defence on mine. In a theatre, each person has a right to his own seat, by the supposition that he has no right to intrude into any one else's. They are convertible propositions. Away, then, with the notion that liberty and equality are inconsistent. But here is the artifice : by merging the rights and inde- pendence of the individual in the fictitious order of society, those rights become arbitrary, capricious, equivocal, removable at the pleasure of the state or ruling power ; there is nothing substantial or durable implied in them : if each has no positive claim, naturally, those of all taken together can mount up to nothing ; right and justice are mere blanks to be filled up with arbitrary will, and the people have thenceforward no defence against the govern- ment.   On the other hand, suppose these rights to be not empty names or artificial arrangements, but original and inherent like solid atoms, then it is not in the power of government to annihilate one of them, whatever may be the confusion arising from their struggle for mastery, or before they can settle into order and harmony.   Mr. Burke talks of the reflections and refractions of the rays of light as altering their primary essence and direction. But if there were no original rays of light, there could be neither refraction, nor reflections.   Why, then, does he try by cloudy sophistry to blot the sun out of heaven ?   One body impinges against and impedes another in the fall, but it could not do this, but for the principle of gravity. The author of the *Sublime and Beautiful* would have a single atom outweigh the great globe itself ; or an empty title, a bloated privilege, or a grievous wrong overturn the entire mass of truth and justice.   The question between the author and his opponents appears to be simply this : whether politics, or the general good, is an affair of reason or imagination ! and this seems decided by another con- sideration, viz., that Imagination is the judge of individual things, and Reason of generals. Hence the great importance of the principle of universal suffrage ; for if the vote and choice of a single individual goes for nothing, so, by parity of reasoning, may that of all the rest of the community: but if the choice of every man in the community is held sacred, then what must be the weight and value of the whole.

Many persons object that by this means property is not represented, and so, to avoid that, they would have nothing but property represented, at the same time that they pretend that if the elective franchise were thrown open to the poor, they would be wholly at the command of the rich, to the prejudice and exclusion of the middle and independent classes of society. Property always has a natural influence and authority: it is only people without property that have no natural protection, and require every artificial and legal one.. *Those that have much, shall have none; and those that have little, shall have less.* This proverb is no less true in public than in public life. The *better orders* (as they are called, and who, in virtue of this title, would assume a monopoly in the direction of state affairs) are merely and in plain English those who are *better off* than others; and as they get the wished-for monopoly into their hands, others will uniformly be *worse off*, and will sink lower and lower in the scale; so that it is essentially requisite to extend the elective franchise in order to counteract the excess of the great and increasing goodness of the better orders to themselves. I see no reason to suppose that in any case popular feeling (if free course were given to it) would bear down public opinion. Literature is at present pretty nearly on the footing of universal suffrage, yet the public defer sufficiently to the critics; and when no party bias interferes, and the government do not make a point of running a writer down, the verdict is tolerably fair and just. I do not say that the result might not be equally satisfactory, when literature was patronised more immediately by the great; but then lords and ladies had no interest in praising a bad piece and condemning a good one. If they could have laid a tax on the town for not going to it, they would have run a bad play forty nights together, or the whole year round, without scruple.. As things stand, the worse the law, the better for the lawmakers : it takes everything from others to give to *them*. It is common to insist on universal suffrage and the ballot together. But if the first were allowed, the second would be unnecessary. The ballot is only useful as a screen from arbitrary power. There is nothing manly or independent to recommend it.

COROLLARY 3. If I was out at sea in a boat with a *jure divino* monarch, and he wanted to throw me overboard, I would not let him. No gentleman would ask such a thing, no freeman would submit to it. Has he, then, a right to dispose of the lives and liberties of thirty millions of men ? Or have they more right than I have to resist his demands ? They have thirty millions of times that right, if they had a particle of the same spirit that I have. It is not the individual, then, whom in this case I fear (to me "there's *no* divinity doth hedge a king"), but thirty millions of his subjects that call me to account in his name, and who are of a most approved and indisputable loyalty, and who have both the right and power. The power rests with the multitude, but let them beware how the exercise of it turns against their own rights! It is not the idol but the worshippers that are to be dreaded, and who, by degrading one of their fellows, render themselves liable to be branded with the same indignities.

COROLLARY 4. No one can be born a slave; for my limbs are my own, and the power and the will to use them are anterior to all laws, and independent of the control of every other person. No one acquires a right over another but that other acquires some reciprocal right over him; therefore the relation of master and slave is a contradiction in political logic. Hence, also, it follows that combinations among labourers for the rise of wages are always just and lawful, as much as those among master manufacturers to keep them down. A man's labour is his own, at least as much as another's goods; and he may starve if he pleases, but he may refuse to work except on his own terms. The right of property is reducible to this simple principle, that one man has not a right to the produce of another's labour, but each man has a right to the benefit of his own exertions and the use of his natural and inalienable powers, unless for a supposed equivalent and by mutual consent. Personal liberty and property therefore rest upon the same foundation. I am glad to see that Mr. Macculloch, in his *Essay on Wages*, admits the right of combination among journeymen and others. I laboured this point hard, and, I think, satisfactorily, a good while ago, in my *Reply to Mr. Malthus.* "Throw your bread upon the waters, and after many days you shall find it again."

There are four things that a man may especially call his own. 1. His person. 2. His actions. 3. His property 4. His opinions. Let us see how each of these claims unavoidably circumscribes and modifies those of others, on the principle of abstract equity and necessity and independence above laid down.

FIRST, AS TO THE RIGHTS OF PERSONS. My intention is to show that the right of society to make laws to coerce the will of others, is founded on the necessity of repelling the wanton encroachment of that will on their rights; that is, strictly on the right of self-defence or resistance to aggression. Society comes forward and says, "Let us alone, and we will let you alone, otherwise we must see which is strongest;" its object is not to patronise or advise individuals for their good, and against their will, but to protect itself: meddling with others forcibly on any other plea or for any other purpose is impertinence. But equal rights destroy one another; nor can there be a right to impossible or impracticable things. Let A, B, C, D, &c., be different component parts of any society, each claiming to be the centre and master of a certain sphere of activity and self-determination: as long as each keeps within his own line of demarcation there is no harm done, nor any penalty incurred—it is only the superfluous and overbearing will of particular persons that must be restrained or lopped off by the axe of the law. Let A be the culprit: B, C, D, &c., or the rest of the community, are plaintiffs against A, and wish to prevent his taking any unfair or unwarranted advantage over them. They set up no pretence to dictate or domineer over him, but merely to hinder his dictating to and domineering over them; and in this, having both might and right on their side, they have no difficulty in putting it in execution. Every man's independence and discretionary power over what peculiarly and exclusively concerns himself, is his *castle* (whether round, square, or, according to Mr. Owen's new map of improvements, in the form of a parallelogram). As long as he keeps within this, he is safe—society has no hold of him: it is when he quits it to attack his neighbours that they resort to reprisals, and make short work of the interloper. It is, however, time to endeavour to point out in what this natural division of right, and separate advantage consists. In the first place, A, B, C, D have the common and natural rights of persons, in so far that none of these has a right to offer violence to, or cause bodily pain or injury to any of the others. Sophists laugh at natural rights: they might as well deny that we have natural persons; for while the last distinction holds true and good by the constitution of things, certain consequences must and will follow from it—" while this machine is to us Hamlet," &c. For instance, I should like to know whether Mr. Burke, with his *Sublime and Beautiful* fancies, would deny that each person has a particular body and senses belonging to him, so that he feels a peculiar and natural interest in whatever affects these more than another can, and whether such a peculiar and paramount interest does not imply a direct and unavoidable right in maintaining this circle of individuality inviolate. To argue otherwise is to assert that indifference, or that which does not feel either the good or the ill, is as capable a judge and zealous a discriminator of right and wrong as that which does. The right, then, is coeval and co-extended with the interest, not a product of convention, but inseparable from the order of the universe; the doctrine itself is natural and solid; it is the contrary fallacy that is made of air and words. Mr. Burke, in such a question, was like a man out at sea in a haze, and could never tell the difference between land and clouds. If another break my arm by violence, this will not certainly give him additional health or strength; if he stun me by a blow or inflict torture on my limbs, it is I who feel the pain, and not he; and it is hard if I, who am the sufferer, am not allowed to be the judge. That another should pretend to deprive me of it, or pretend to judge for me, and set up his will against mine, in what concerns this portion of my existence— where I have all at stake and he nothing—is not merely injustice, but impudence. The circle of personal security and right, then, is not an imaginary and arbitrary line fixed by law and the will of the prince, or the scaly finger of Mr. Hobbes's *Leviathan*, but is real and inherent in the nature of things, and itself the foundation of law and justice. "Hands off is fair play"—according to the old adage. One, therefore, has not a right to lay violent hands on another, or to infringe on the sphere of his personal identity; one must not run foul of another, or he is liable to be repelled and punished for the offence. If you meet an Englishman suddenly in the street, he will run up against you sooner than get out of your way, which last he thinks a compromise of his dignity and a relinquishment of his purpose, though he expects ·you to get out of his. A Frenchman in the same circumstances will come up close to you, and try to walk over you, as if there was no one in his way; but if you take no notice of him, he will step on one side, and make you a low bow. The one is a fellow of stubborn will, the other a *petit maître*. An Englishman at a play mounts upon a bench, and refuses to get down at the request of another, who threatens to call him to account the next day. " Yes," is the answer of the first, " if your master will let you!" His abuse of liberty, he thinks, is justified by the other's want of it. All an Englishman's ideas are modifications of his will; which shows, in one way, that right is founded on will, since the English are at once the freest and most wilful of all people. If you meet another on the ridge of a precipice, are you to throw each other down? Certainly not. You are to pass as well as you can. " Give and take," is the rule of natural right, where the right is not all on one side and cannot be claimed entire. Equal weights and scales produce a balance, as much as where the scales are empty : so it does not follow (as our votaries of absolute power would insinuate) that one man's right is nothing because another's is something. But suppose there is not time to pass, and one or other must perish, in the case just mentioned, then each must do the best for himself that he can, and the instinct of self-preservation prevails over everything else. In the streets of London, the passengers take the right hand of one another and the wall alternately; he who should not conform to this rule would be guilty of a breach of the peace. But if a house were falling, or a mad ox driven furiously by, the rule would be, of course, suspended, because the case would be out of the ordinary. Yet I think I can conceive, and have even known, persons capable of carrying the point of gallantry in political right to such a pitch as to refuse to take a precedence which did not belong to them in the most perilous circumstances, just as a soldier may waive a right to quit his post, and takes his turn in battle. The actual collision or case of personal assault and battery, is, then, clearly prohibited, inasmuch as each person's body is clearly defined : but how if A use other means of annoyance against B, such as a sword or poison, or resort to what causes other painful sensations besides tangible ones, for instance, certain disagreeable sounds and smells? Or, if these are included as a violation of personal rights, then how draw the line between them and the employing certain offensive words and gestures or uttering opinions which I disapprove? This is a puzzler for the dogmatic school; but they solve the whole difficulty by an assumption of *utility*, which is as much as to tell a person that the way to any place to which he asks a direction is "to follow his nose." We want to know by given marks and rules what is best and useful; and they assure us very wisely, that this is infallibly and clearly determined by what *is* best and useful. Let us try something else. It seems no less necessary to erect certain little *fortalices*, with palisades and outworks about them, for RIGHT to establish and maintain itself in, than as landmarks to guide us across the wide waste of UTILITY. If a person runs a sword through me, or administers poison, or procures it to be administered, the effect, the pain, disease or death is the same, and I have the same right to prevent it, on the principle that I am the sufferer; that the injury is offered to me, and he is no gainer by it, except for mere malice or caprice, and I therefore remain master and judge of my own remedy, as in the former case; the principle and definition of right being to secure to each individual the determination and protection of that portion of sensation in which he has the greatest, if not a sole interest, and, as it were, identity with it. Again, as to what are called *nuisances*, to wit offensive smells, sounds, &c., it is more difficult to determine on the ground that *one man's meat is another man's poison.* I remember a case occurred in the neighbourhood where I was, and at the time I was trying my best at this question, which puzzled me a good deal. A rector of a little town in Shropshire, who was at variance with all his parishioners, had conceived a particular spite to a lawyer who lived next door to him, and as a means of annoying him, used to get together all sorts of rubbish, weeds, and unsavoury materials, and set them on fire, so that the smoke should blow over into his neighbour's garden; whenever the wind set in that direction, he said, as a signal to his gardener, " It's a fine Wicksteed wind to-day;" and the operation commenced. Was this an action of assault and battery, or not? I think it was, for this reason, that the offence was unequivocal, and that the only motive for the proceeding was the giving this offence. The assailant would not like to be served so himself. Mr. Bentham would say, the malice of the motive was a set-off to the injury. I shall leave that *prima philosophia* consideration out of the question. A man who knocks out another's brains with a bludgeon may say it pleases him to do so; but will it please him to have the compliment returned? If he still persists, in spite of this punishment, there is no preventing him; but if not, then it is a proof that he thinks the pleasure less than the pain to himself, and consequently to another in the scales of justice. The *lex talionis* is an excellent test. Suppose a third person (the physician of the place) had said, " It is a fine Egerton wind to-day," our rector would have been non-plussed; for he would have found that, as he suffered all the hardship, he had the right to complain of and to resist an action of another, the consequences of which affected principally himself. Now mark: if he had himself had any advantage to derive from the action, which he could not obtain in any other way, then he would feel that his neighbour also had the same plea and right to follow his own course (still this might be a doubtful point); but in the other case it would be sheer malice and wanton interference; that is, not the exercise of a right, but the invasion of another's comfort and independence. Has a person, then, a right to play on the horn or on a flute, on the same staircase? I say, yes; because it is for his own improvement and pleasure, and not to annoy another; and because, accordingly, every one in his own case would wish to reserve this or a similar privilege to himself. I do not think a person has a right to beat a drum under one's window, because this is altogether disagreeable, and if there is an extraordinary motive for it, then it is fit that the person should be put to some little inconvenience in removing his sphere of liberty of action to a reasonable distance. A tallow-chandler's shop or a steam-engine is a nuisance in a town, and ought to be removed into the suburbs; but they are to be tolerated where they are least inconvenient, because they are necessary somewhere, and there is no remedying the inconvenience. The right to protest against and to prohibit them rests with the suffering party; but because this point of the greatest interest is less clear in some cases than in others, it does not follow that there is no right or principle of justice in the case. 3. As to matters of contempt and the expression of opinion, I think these do not fall under the head of force, and are not, on that ground, subjects of coercion and law. For example, if a person inflicts a sensation upon me by material means, whether tangible or otherwise, I cannot help that sensation; I am so far the slave of that other, and have no means of resisting him but by force, which I would define to be material agency. But if another proposes an opinion to me, I am not bound to be of this opinion; my judgment and will is left free, and therefore I have no right to resort to force to recover a liberty which I have not lost. If I do this to prevent that other from pressing that opinion, it is I who invade his liberty, without warrant, because without necessity. It may be urged that material agency, or force, is used in the adoption of sounds or letters of the alphabet, which I cannot help seeing or hearing. But the injury is not here, but in the moral and artificial inference, which I am at liberty to admit or reject, according to the evidence. There is no force but argument in the case, and it is reason, not the will of another, that gives the law. Further, the opinion expressed, generally concerns not one individual, but the general interest; and of that my approbation or disapprobation is not a commensurate or the sole judge. I am judge of my own interests, because it is my affair, and no one's else; but by the same rule, I am not judge, nor have I a *veto* on that which appeals to all the world, merely because I have a prejudice or fancy against it. But suppose another expresses by signs or words a contempt for me? *Answer.* I do not know that he is bound to have a respect for me. Opinion is free; for if I wish him to have that respect, then he must be left free to judge for himself, and consequently to arrive at and to express the contrary opinion, or otherwise the verdict and testimony I aim at could not be obtained; just as players must consent to be hissed, if they expect to be applauded. Opinion cannot be forced, for it is not grounded on force, but on evidence and reason, and therefore these last are the proper instruments to control that opinion, and to make it favourable to what we wish, or hostile to what we disapprove. In what relates to action, the will of another is force, or the determining power: in what relates to opinion, the mere will or *ipse dixit* of another is of no avail but as it gains over other opinions to its side, and therefore neither needs nor admits of force as a counteracting means to be used against it. But in the case of calumny or indecency: 1. I would say that it is the suppression of truth that gives falsehood its worst edge. What transpires (however maliciously or secretly) in spite of the law, is taken for gospel, and as it is impossible to prevent calumny, so it is impossible to

counteract it on the present system, or while every attempt
to answer it is attributed to the people's not daring to
speak the truth. If any single fact or accident peeps out,
the whole character, having this legal screen before it, is
supposed to be of a piece; and the world, defrauded of
the means of coming to their own conclusion, naturally
infer the worst. Hence the saying, that reputation once
gone never returns. If, however, we grant the general
licence or liberty of the press, in a scheme where publicity
is the great object, it seems a manifest *contre-sens* that the
author should be the only thing screened or kept a secret:
either, therefore, an anonymous libeller would be heard
with contempt, or if he signed his name thus —, or thus
— —, it would be equivalent to being branded publicly
as a calumniator, or marked with the T. F. (*travail forcé*)
or the broad R. (rogue) on his back. These are thought
sufficient punishments, and yet they rest on opinion without stripes or labour. As to indecency, in proportion as
it is flagrant is the shock and resentment against it; and
as vanity is the source of indecency, so the universal discountenance and shame is its most effectual antidote. If
it is public, it produces immediate reprisals from public
opinion which no brow can stand; and if secret, it had
better be left so. No one can then say it is obtruded on
him; and if he will go in search of it, it seems odd he
should call upon the law to frustrate the object of his
pursuit. Further, at the worst, society has its remedy in
its own hands whenever its moral sense is outraged, that is,
it may send to Coventry, or excommunicate like the church
of old; for though it may have no right to prosecute,
it is not bound to protect or patronise, unless by voluntary
consent of all parties concerned. Secondly, as to rights
of action, or personal liberty. These have no limit but
the rights of persons or property aforesaid, or to be hereafter named. They are the channels in which the others
run without injury and without impediment, as a river

within its banks. Every one has a right to use his natural powers in the way most agreeable to himself, and which he deems most conducive to his own advantage, provided he does not interfere with the corresponding rights and liberties of others. He has no right to coerce them by a decision of his individual will, and as long as he abstains from this he has no right to be coerced by an expression of the aggregate will, that is, by law. The law is he emanation of the aggregate will, and this will receives its warrant to act only from the forcible pressure from without, and its indispensable resistance to it. Let us see how this will operate to the pruning and curtailment of law. The rage of legislation is the first vice of society; it ends by limiting it to as few things as possible. 1. There can, according to the principle here imperfectly sketched, be no laws for the enforcement of morals; because morals have to do with the will and affections, and the law only puts a restraint on these. Every one is politically constituted the judge of what is best for himself; it is only when he encroaches on others that he can be called to account. He has no right to say to others, You shall do as I do: how then should they have a right to say to him, You shall do as we do? Mere numbers do not convey the right, for the law addresses not one, but the whole community. For example, there cannot rightly be a law to set a man in the stocks for getting drunk. It injures his health, you say. That is his concern, and not mine. But it is detrimental to his affairs: if so, he suffers most by it. But it is ruinous to his wife and family: he is their natural and legal guardian. But they are thrown upon the parish: the parish need not take the burden upon itself, unless it chooses or has agreed to do so. If a man is not kind to or fond of his wife I see no law to make him. If he beats her, or threatens her life, she as clearly has a right to call in the aid of a constable or justice of peace. I do not see, in like manner, how there can be law against gambling (against cheating there may), nor against usury. A man gives twenty, forty, a hundred per cent. with his eyes open, but would he do it if strong necessity did not impel him? Certainly no man would give double if he could get the same advantage for half. There are circumstances in which a rope to save me from drowning, or a draught of water, would be worth all I have. In like manner, lotteries are fair things; for the loss is inconsiderable, and the advantage may be incalculable. I do not believe the poor put into them, but the reduced rich, the *shabby-genteel*. Players were formerly prohibited as a nuisance, and fortune-tellers still are liable to the Vagrant Act, which the parson of the parish duly enforces, in his zeal to prevent cheating and imposture, while he himself has his two livings, and carries off a tenth of the produce of the soil. Rape is an offence clearly punishable by law; but I would not say that simple incontinence is so. I will give one more example, which, though quaint, may explain the distinction I aim at. A man may commit suicide if he pleases, without being responsible to any one. He may quit the world as he would quit the country where he was born. But if any person were to fling himself from the gallery into the pit of a playhouse, so as to endanger the lives of others, if he did not succeed in killing himself, he would render himself liable to punishment for the attempt, if it were to be supposed that a person so desperately situated would care about consequences. Duelling is lawful on the same principle, where every precaution is taken to show that the act is voluntary and fair on both sides. I might give other instances, but these will suffice. 2. There should be a perfect toleration in matters of religion. In what relates to the salvation of a man's soul, he is infinitely more concerned than I can be; and to pretend to dictate to him in this particular is an infinite piece of impertinence and presumption. But if a man has no religion at all? That does not hinder me from having any. If he stood at the church door and would not let me enter, I should have a right to push him aside; but if he lets me pass by without interruption, I have no right to turn back and drag him in after me. He might as well force me to have no religion as I force him to have one, or burn me at a stake for believing what he does not. Opinion, "like the wild goose, flies unclaimed of any man:" heaven is like "the marble air, accessible to all;" and therefore there is no occasion to trip up one another's heels on the road, or to erect a turnpike gate to collect large sums from the passengers. How have I a right to make another pay for the saving of my soul, or to assist me in damning his? There should be no secular interference in sacred things; no laws to suppress or establish any church or sect in religion, no religious persecutions, tests, or disqualifications; the different sects should be left to inveigle and hate each other as much as they please; but without the love of exclusive domination and spiritual power there would be little temptation to bigotry and intolerance.

3. As to the Rights of Property. It is of no use a man's being left to enjoy security, or to exercise his freedom of action, unless he has a right to appropriate certain other things necessary to his comfort and subsistence to his own use. In a state of nature, or rather of solitary independence, he has a right to all he can lay his hands on: what then limits this right? Its being inconsistent with the same right in others. This strikes a mathematical or logical balance between two extreme and equal pretensions. As there is not a natural and indissoluble connection between the individual and his property, or those outward objects of which he may have need (they being detached, unlimited, and transferable), as there is between the individual and his person, either as an organ of sensation or action, it is necessary, in order

to prevent endless debate and quarrels, to fix upon some other criterion or common ground of preference. Animals, or savages, have no idea of any other right than that of the strongest, and seize on all they can get by force, without any regard to justice or an equal claim. 1. One mode of settling the point is to divide the spoil. That is allowing an equal advantage to both. Thus boys, when they unexpectedly find anything, are accustomed to cry "*Halves!*" But this is liable to other difficulties, and applies only to the case of joint finding. 2. Priority of possession is a fair way of deciding the right of property; first, on the mere principle of a lottery, or the old saying, "*First come, first served;*" secondly, because the expectation having been excited, and the will more set upon it, this constitutes a powerful reason for not violently forcing it to let go its hold. The greater strength of volition is, we have seen, one foundation of right; for supposing a person to be absolutely indifferent to anything, he could properly set up no claim to it. 3. Labour, or the having produced a thing or fitted it for use by previous exertion, gives this right, chiefly, indeed, for moral and final causes; because if one enjoyed what another had produced, there would be nothing but idleness and rapacity; but also in the sense we are inquiring into, because on a merely selfish ground the labour undergone, or the time lost, is entitled to an equivalent, *cœteris manentibus*. 4. If another, voluntarily, or for a consideration, resigns to me his right in anything, it to all intents and purposes becomes mine. This accounts not only for gifts, the transfer of property by bargains, &c., but for legacies, and the transmission of property in families or otherwise. It is hard to make a law to circumscribe this right of disposing of what we have as we please; yet the boasted law of primogeniture, which is professedly the bulwark and guardian of property, is in direct violation of this principle. 5, and lastly. Where a thing is common, and there is enough for all, and no one contributes to it, as air or water, there can be no property in it. The proximity to a herring-fishery, or the having been the first to establish a particular traffic in such commodities, may perhaps give this right by aggravating our will, as having a nearer or longer power over them; but the rule is the other way. It is on the same principle that poaching is a kind of honest thieving, for that which costs no trouble and is confined to no limits seems to belong to no one exclusively (why else do poachers or country people seize on this kind of property with the least reluctance, but that it is the least like stealing?); and as the game laws and the tenaciousness of the rights to that which has least the character of property, as most a point of honour, produced a revolution in one country, so they are not unlikely to produce it in another. The object and principle of the laws of property, then, is this: 1. To supply individuals and the community with what they need. 2. To secure an equal share to each individual, other circumstances being the same. 3. To keep the peace and promote industry and plenty, by proportioning each man's share to his own exertions, or to the good-will and discretion of others. The intention, then, being that no individual should rob another, or be starved but by his refusing to work (the earth and its produce being the natural estate of the community, subject to these regulations of individual right and public welfare), the question is, whether any individual can have a right to rob or starve the whole community: or if the necessary discretion left in the application of the principle has led to a state of things subversive of the principle itself, and destructive to the welfare and existence of the state, whether the end being defeated, the law does not fall to the ground, or require either a powerful corrective or a total reconstruction. The end is superior to the means, and the use of a thing does not justify its abuse. If a clock is quite out of order and always goes wrong, it is no argument to say it was set right at first and on true mechanical principles, and therefore it must go on as it has done, according to all the rules of art; on the contrary, it is taken to pieces, repaired, and the whole restored to the original state, or, if this is impossible, a new one is made. So society, when out of order, which it is whenever the interests of the many are regularly and outrageously .sacrificed to those of the few, must be repaired, and either a reform or a revolution cleanse its corruptions and renew its elasticity. People talk of the poor laws as a grievance. Either they or a national bankruptcy, or a revolution, are necessary. The labouring population have not doubled in the last forty years; there are still no more than are necessary to do the work in husbandry, &c., that is indispensably required; but the wages of a labouring man are no higher than they were forty years ago, and the price of food and necessaries is at least double what it was then, owing to taxes, grants, monopolies, and immense fortunes gathered during the war by the richer or more prosperous classes, who have not ceased to propagate in the geometrical ratio, though the poor have not done it, and the maintaining of whose younger and increasing.branches in becoming splendour and affluence presses with double weight on the poor and labouring classes. The greater part of a community ought not to be paupers or starving; and when a government by obstinacy and madness has reduced them to that state, it must either take wise and effectual measures to relieve them from it, or pay the forfeit of its own wickedness and folly.

It seems, then, that a system of just and useful laws may be constructed nearly, if not wholly, on the principle of the right of self-defence, or the security for person, liberty, and property. There are exceptions, such, for instance, as in the case of children, idiots, and insane persons. These common-sense dictates for a general principle can only hold good where the general conditions are complied with. There are also mixed cases, partaking of civil and moral justice. Is a man bound to support his children? Not in strict political right; but he may be compelled to forego all the benefits of civil society, if he does not fulfil an engagement which, according to the feelings and principles of that society, he has undertaken. So in respect to marriage. It is a voluntary contract, and the violation of it is punishable on the same plea of sympathy and custom. Government is not necessarily founded on common consent, but on the right which society has to defend itself against all aggression. But am I bound to pay or support the government for defending the society against any violence or injustice? No: but then they may withdraw the protection of the law from me if I refuse, and it is on this ground that the contributions of each individual to the maintenance of the state are demanded. Laws are, or ought to be, founded on the supposed infraction of individual rights. If these rights, and the best means of maintaining them, are always clear, and there could be no injustice or abuse of power on the part of the government, every government might be its own lawgiver: but as neither of these is the case, it is necessary to recur to the general voice for settling the boundaries of right and wrong, and even more for preventing the government, under pretence of the general peace and safety, from subjecting the whole liberties, rights, and resources of the community to its own advantage and sole will.

1828.

ESSAY XII.

On the Character of Burke.[1]

THERE is no single speech of Mr. Burke which can convey a satisfactory idea of his powers of mind: to do him

---

[1] Compare *The Eloquence of the British Senate,* 1807, ii, 206-17, where this paper was originally printed.—ED.

justice, it would be necessary to quote all his works; the only specimen of Burke is, *all that he wrote.* With respect to most other speakers, a specimen is generally enough, or more than enough. When you are acquainted with their manner, and see what proficiency they have made in the mechanical exercise of their profession, with what facility they can borrow a simile, or round a period, how dexterously they can argue, and object, and rejoin, you are satisfied; there is no other difference in their speeches than what arises from the difference of the subjects. But this was not the case with Burke. He brought his subjects along with him; he drew his materials from himself. The only limits which circumscribed his variety were the stores of his own mind. His stock of ideas did not consist of a few meagre facts, meagrely stated, of half a dozen commonplaces tortured into a thousand different ways; but his mine of wealth was a profound understanding, inexhaustible as the human heart, and various as the sources of human nature. He therefore enriched every subject to which he applied himself, and new subjects were only the occasions of calling forth fresh powers of mind which had not been before exerted. It would therefore be in vain to look for the proof of his powers in any one of his speeches or writings: they all contain some additional proof of power. In speaking of Burke, then, I shall speak of the whole compass and circuit of his mind—not of that small part or section of him which I have been able to give: to do otherwise would be like the story of the man who put the brick in his pocket, thinking to show it as the model of a house. I have been able to manage pretty well with respect to all my other speakers, and curtailed them down without remorse. It was easy to reduce them within certain limits, to fix their spirit, and condense their variety; by having a certain quantity given, you might infer all the rest; it was only the same thing over again. But who can bind Proteus, or confine the roving flight of genius ?

Burke's writings are better than his speeches, and indeed his speeches are writings. But he seemed to feel himself more at ease, to have a fuller possession of his faculties in addressing the public, than in addressing the House of Commons. Burke was *raised* into public life ; and he seems to have been prouder of this new dignity than became so great a man. For this reason, most of his speeches have a sort of parliamentary preamble to them : he seems fond of coquetting with the House of Commons, and is perpetually calling the Speaker out to dance a minuet with him before he begins. There is also something like an attempt to stimulate the superficial dulness of his hearers by exciting their surprise, by running into extravagance : and he sometimes demeans himself by condescending to what may be considered as bordering too much upon buffoonery, for the amusement of the company. Those lines of Milton were admirably applied to him by some one—"The elephant to make them sport wreathed his proboscis lithe." The truth is, that he was out of his place in the House of Commons ; he was eminently qualified to shine as a man of genius, as the instructor of mankind, as the brightest luminary of his age ; but he had nothing in common with that motley crew of knights, citizens, and burgesses. He could not be said to be "native and endued unto that element." He was above it ; and never appeared like himself, but when, forgetful of the idle clamours of party, and of the little views of little men, he applied to his country and the enlightened judgment of mankind.

I am not going to make an idle panegyric on Burke (he has no need of it) ; but I cannot help looking upon him as the chief boast and ornament of the English House of Commons. What has been said of him is, I think, strictly true, that " he was the most eloquent man of his time :

his wisdom was greater than his eloquence." The only public man that in my opinion can be put in any competition with him, is Lord Chatham; and he moved in a sphere so very remote, that it is almost impossible to compare them. But though it would perhaps be difficult to determine which of them excelled most in his particular way, there is nothing in the world more easy than to point out in what their peculiar excellences consisted. They were in every respect the reverse of each other. Chatham's eloquence was popular; his wisdom was altogether plain and practical. Burke's eloquence was that of the poet; of the man of high and unbounded fancy: his wisdom was profound and contemplative. Chatham's eloquence was calculated to make men *act:* Burke's was calculated to make them *think.* Chatham could have roused the fury of a multitude, and wielded their physical energy as he pleased: Burke's eloquence carried conviction into the mind of the retired and lonely student, opened the recesses of the human breast, and lighted up the face of nature around him. Chatham supplied his hearers with motives to immediate action: Burke furnished them with *reasons* for action which might have little effect upon them at the time, but for which they would be the wiser and better all their lives after. In research, in originality in variety of knowledge, in richness of invention, in depth and comprehension of mind, Burke had as much the advantage of Lord Chatham as he was excelled by him in plain common sense, in strong feeling, in steadiness of purpose, in vehemence. in warmth, in enthusiasm, and energy of mind. Burke was the man of genius, of fine sense, and subtle reasoning; Chatham was a man of clear understanding, of strong sense, and violent passions. Burke's mind was satisfied with speculation: Chatham's was essentially *active;* it could not rest without an object. The power which governed Burke's mind was his Imagination; that which gave its *impetus* to Chatham was Will.

The one was almost the creature of pure intellect, the other of physical temperament.

There are two very different ends which a man of genius may propose to himself, either in writing or speaking, and which will accordingly give birth to very different styles. He can have but one of these two objects; either to enrich or strengthen the mind; either to furnish us with new ideas, to lead the mind into new trains of thought, to which it was before unused, and which it was incapable of striking out for itself; or else to collect and embody what we already knew, to rivet our old impressions more deeply; to make what was before plain still plainer, and to give to that which was familiar all the effect of novelty. In the one case we receive an accession to the stock of our ideas; in the other, an additional degree of life and energy is infused into them : our thoughts continue to flow in the same channels, but their pulse is quickened and invigorated. I do not know how to distinguish these different styles better than by calling them severally the inventive and refined, or the impressive and vigorous styles. It is only the subject-matter of eloquence, however, which is allowed to be remote or obscure. The things themselves may be subtle and recondite, but they must be dragged out of their obscurity and brought struggling to the light; they must be rendered plain and palpable (as far as it is in the wit of man to do so), or they are no longer eloquence. That which by its natural impenetrability, and in spite of every effort, remains dark and difficult, which is impervious to every ray, on which the imagination can shed no lustre, which can be clothed with no beauty, is not a subject for the orator or poet. At the same time it cannot be expected that abstract truths or profound observations should ever be placed in the same strong and dazzling points of view as natural objects and mere matters of fact. It is enough if they receive a reflex and borrowed lustre, like that which cheers the first dawn of morning, where the effect of surprise and novelty gilds every object, and the joy of beholding another world gradually emerging out of the gloom of night, "a new creation rescued from his reign," fills the mind with a sober rapture. Philosophical eloquence is in writing what *chiaro-scuro* is in painting ; he would be a fool who should object that the colours in the shaded part of a picture were not so bright as those on the opposite side ; the eye of the connoisseur receives an equal delight from both, balancing the want of brilliancy and effect with the greater delicacy of the tints, and difficulty of the execution. In judging of Burke, therefore, we are to consider, first, the style of eloquence which he adopted, and, secondly, the effects which he produced with it. If he did not produce the same effects on vulgar minds as some others have done, it was not for want of power, but from the turn and direction of his mind.[1] It was because his subjects, his ideas, his arguments, were less vulgar. The question is not whether he brought certain truths equally home to us, but how much nearer he brought them than they were before. In my opinion, he united the two extremes of refinement and strength in a higher degree than any other writer whatever.

The subtlety of his mind was undoubtedly that which rendered Burke a less popular writer and speaker than he otherwise would have been. It weakened the impression of his observations upon others, but I cannot admit that it weakened the observations themselves ; that it took anything from their real weight or solidity. Coarse minds think all that is subtle, futile : that because it is not gross and obvious and palpable to the senses, it is therefore light and frivolous, and of no importance in the real affairs of life ; thus making their own confined understandings the measure of truth, and supposing that what-

---

[1] For instance, he produced less effect on the mob that compose the English House of Commons, than Chatham or Fox, or even Pitt.

ever they do not distinctly perceive, is nothing. Seneca, who was not one of the. vulgar, also says, that subtle truths are those which have the least substance in them, and consequently approach nearest to nonentity. But for my own part I cannot help thinking that the most important truths must be the most refined and subtle; for that very reason, that they must comprehend a great number of particulars, and instead of referring to any distinct or positive fact, must point out the combined effects of an extensive chain of causes, operating gradually, remotely, and collectively, and therefore imperceptibly. General principles are not the less true or important because from their nature they elude immediate observation; they are like the air, which is not the less necessary because we neither see nor feel it, or like that secret influence which binds the world together, and holds the planets in their orbits. The very same persons who are the most forward to laugh at all systematic reasoning as idle and impertinent, you will the next moment hear exclaiming bitterly against the baleful effects of new-fangled systems of philosophy, or gravely descanting on the immense importance of instilling sound principles of morality into the mind. It would not be a bold conjecture, but an obvious truism, to say, that all the great changes which have been brought about in the mortal world, either for the better or worse, have been introduced, not by the bare statement of facts, which are things already known, and which must always operate nearly in the same manner, but by the development of certain opinions and abstract principles of reasoning on life and manners, on the origin of society and man's nature in general, which being obscure and uncertain, vary from time to time, and produce corresponding changes in the human mind. They are the wholesome dew and rain, or the mildew and pestilence that silently destroy. To this principle of generalisation all wise law-givers, and the systems of philosophers, owe their influence.

It has always been with me a test of the sense and candour of any one belonging to the opposite party, whether
he allowed Burke to be a great man. Of all the persons
of this description that I have ever known, I never met
with above one or two who would make this concession;
whether it was that party feelings ran too high to admit of
any real candour, or whether it was owing to an essential
vulgarity in their habits of thinking, they all seemed to be
of opinion that he was a wild enthusiast, or a hollow
sophist, who was to be answered by bits of facts, by smart
logic, by shrewd questions, and idle songs. They looked
upon him as a man of disordered intellects, because he
reasoned in a style to which they had not been used, and
which confounded their dim perceptions. If you said that
though you differed with him in sentiment, yet you
thought him an admirable reasoner, and a close observer
of human nature, you were answered with a loud laugh,
and some hackneyed quotation. "Alas! Leviathan was
not so tamed!" They did not know whom they had to
contend with. The corner-stone, which the builders
rejected, became the head-corner, though to the Jews a
stumbling-block, and to the Greeks foolishness; for, indeed,
I cannot discover that he was much better understood by
those of his own party, if we may judge from the little
affinity there is between his mode of reasoning and theirs.
The simple clue to all his reasonings on politics is, I
think, as follows. He did not agree with some writers
that that mode of government is necessarily the best which
is the cheapest. He saw in the construction of society
other principles at work, and other capacities of fulfilling
the desires, and perfecting the nature of man, besides those
of securing the equal enjoyment of the means of animal
life, and doing this at as little expense as possible. He
thought that the wants and happiness of men were not to
be provided for, as we provide for those of a herd of cattle,
merely by attending to their physical necessities. He

thought more nobly of his fellows. He knew that man had affections and passions and powers of imagination, as well as hunger and thirst, and the sense of heat and cold He took his idea of political society from the pattern of private life, wishing, as he himself expresses it, to incorporate the domestic charities with the orders of the state, and to blend them together. He strove to establish an analogy between the compact that binds together the community at large, and that which binds together the several families that compose it. He knew that the rules that form the basis of private morality are not founded in reason, that is, in the abstract properties of those things which are the subjects of them, but in the nature of man, and his capacity of being affected by certain things from habit, from imagination, and sentiment, as well as from reason.

Thus, the reason why a man ought to be attached to his wife and children is not, surely, that they are better than others (for in this case every one else ought to be of the same opinion), but because he must be chiefly interested in those things which are nearest to him, and with which he is best acquainted, since his understanding cannot reach equally to everything; because he must be most attached to those objects which he has known the longest, and which by their situation have actually affected him the most, not those which in themselves are the most affecting whether they have ever made any impression on him or no; that is, because he is by his nature the creature of habit and feeling, and because it is reasonable that he should act in conformity to his nature. Burke was so far right in saying that it is no objection to an institution that it is founded in *prejudice*, but the contrary, if that prejudice is natural and right; that is, if it arises from those circumstances which are properly subjects of feeling and association, not from any defect or perversion of the understanding in those things which fall strictly under its

jurisdiction. On this profound maxim he took his stand.
Thus he contended, that the prejudice in favour of nobility
was natural and proper, and fit to be encouraged by the
positive institutions of society : not on account of the real
or personal merit of the individuals, but because such an
institution has a tendency to enlarge and raise the mind,
to keep alive the memory of past greatness, to connect the
different ages of the world together, to carry back the
imagination over a long tract of time, and feed it with the
contemplation of remote events : because it is natural to .
think highly of that which inspires us with high thoughts,
which has been connected for many generations with
splendour, and affluence, and dignity, and power, and
privilege. He also conceived, that by transferring the
respect from the person to the thing, and thus rendering
it steady and permanent, the mind would be habitually
formed to sentiments of deference, attachment, and fealty,
to whatever else demanded its respect : that it would be
led to fix its view on what was elevated and lofty, and be
weaned from that low and narrow jealousy which never
willingly or heartily admits of any superiority in others,
and is glad of every opportunity to bring down all excellence to a level with its own miserable standard. Nobility
did not, therefore, exist to the prejudice of the other
orders of the state, but by, and for them. The inequality
of the different orders of society did not destroy the unity
and harmony of the whole. The health and well-being of
the moral world was to be promoted by the same means as
the beauty of the natural world ; by contrast, by change,
by light and shade, by variety of parts, by order and
proportion. To think of reducing all mankind to the
same insipid level, seemed to him the same absurdity as to
destroy the inequalities of surface in a country, for the
benefit of agriculture and commerce. In short, he believed
that the interests of men in society should be consulted,
and their several stations and employments assigned, with

2 E

a view to their nature, not as physical, but as moral beings, so as to nourish their hopes, to lift their imagination, to enliven their fancy, to rouse their activity, to strengthen their virtue, and to furnish the greatest number of objects of pursuit and means of enjoyment to beings constituted as man is, consistently with the order and stability of the whole.

The same reasoning might be extended farther. I do not say that his arguments are conclusive : but they are profound and *true*, as far as they go. There may be disadvantages and abuses necessarily interwoven with his scheme, or opposite advantages of infinitely greater value, to be derived from another order of things and state of society. This, however, does not invalidate either the truth or importance of Burke's reasoning ; since the advantages he points out as connected with the mixed form of government are really and necessarily inherent in it : since they are compatible, in the same degree, with no other ; since the principle itself on which he rests his argument (whatever we may think of the application) is of the utmost weight and moment ; and since, on whichever side the truth lies, it is impossible to make a fair decision without having the opposite side of the question clearly and fully stated to us. This Burke has done in a masterly manner. He presents to you one view or face of society. Let him who thinks he can, give the reverse side with equal force, beauty, and clearness. It is said, I know, that truth is *one;* but to this I cannot subscribe, for it appears to me that truth is *many.* There are as many truths as there are things and causes of action and contradictory principles at work in society. In making up the account of good and evil, indeed, the final result must be one way or the other ; but the particulars on which that result depends are infinite and various.

It will be seen from what I have said, that I am very far from agreeing with those who think that Burke was a man without understanding, and a merely florid writer. There are two causes which have given rise to this calumny ; namely, that narrowness of mind which leads men to suppose that the truth lies entirely on the side of their own opinions, and that whatever does not make for them is absurd and irrational; secondly, a trick we have of confounding reason with judgment, and supposing that it is merely the province of the understanding to pronounce sentence, and not to give evidence, or argue the case ; in short, that it is a passive, not an active faculty. Thus there are persons who never run into any extravagance, because they are so buttressed up with the opinions of others on all sides, that they cannot lean much to one side or the other ; they are so little moved with any kind of reasoning, that they remain at an equal distance from every extreme, and are never very far from the truth, because the slowness of their faculties will not suffer them to make much progress in error. These are persons of great judgment. The scales of the mind are pretty sure to remain even, when there is nothing in them. In this sense of the word, Burke must be allowed to have wanted judgment, by all those who think that he was wrong in his conclusions. The accusation of want of judgment, in fact, only means that you yourself are of a different opinion. But if in arriving at one error he discovered a hundred truths, I should consider myself a hundred times more indebted to him than if, stumbling on that which I consider as the right side of the question, he had committed a hundred absurdities in striving to establish his point. I speak of him now merely as an author, or as far as I and other readers are concerned with him ; at the same time, I should not differ from any one who may be disposed to contend that the consequences of his writings as instruments of political power have been tremendous, fatal, such as no exertion of wit or knowledge or genius can ever counteract or atone for.

Burke also gave a hold to his antagonists by mixing up
sentiment and imagery with his reasoning; so that being
unused to such a sight in the region of politics, they were
deceived, and could not discern the fruit from the flowers.
Gravity is the cloak of wisdom; and those who have
nothing else think it an insult to affect the one without
the other, because it destroys the only foundation on
which their pretensions are built. The easiest part of
reason is dulness; the generality of the world are therefore concerned in discouraging any example of unnecessary
brilliancy that might tend to show that the two things
do not always go together. Burke in some measure
dissolved the spell. It was discovered, that his gold was
not the less valuable for being wrought into elegant
shapes, and richly embossed with curious figures; that
the solidity of a building is not destroyed by adding to it
beauty and ornament; and that the strength of a man's
understanding is not always to be estimated in exact
proportion to his want of imagination. His understanding
was not the less real, because it was not the only faculty
he possessed. He justified the description of the poet—

> " How charming is divine philosophy !
> Not harsh and crabbed as dull fools suppose,
> But musical as is Apollo's lute !"

Those who object to this union of grace and beauty with
reason, are in fact weak-sighted people, who cannot distinguish the noble and majestic form of Truth from that
of her sister Folly, if they are dressed both alike! But
there is always a difference even in the adventitious ornaments they wear, which is sufficient to distinguish them.
Burke was so far from being a gaudy or flowery writer,
that he was one of the severest writers we have. His
words are the most like things; his style is the most
strictly suited to the subject. He unites every extreme
and every variety of composition; the lowest and the

meanest words and descriptions with the highest. He exults in the display of power, in showing the extent, the force, and intensity of his ideas; he is led on by the mere impulse and vehemence of his fancy, not by the affectation of dazzling his readers by gaudy conceits or pompous images. He was completely carried away by his subject. He had no other object but to produce the strongest impression on his reader, by giving the truest, the most characteristic, the fullest, and most forcible description of things, trusting to the power of his own mind to mould them into grace and beauty. He did not produce a splendid effect by setting fire to the light vapours that float in the regions of fancy, as the chemists make fine colours with phosphorus, but by the eagerness of his blows struck fire from the flint, and melted the hardest substances in the furnace of his imagination. The wheels of his imagination did not catch fire from the rottenness of the materials, but from the rapidity of their motion. One would suppose, to hear people talk of Burke, that his style was such as would have suited the *Lady's Magazine;* soft, smooth, showy, tender, insipid, full of fine words, without any meaning. The essence of the gaudy or glittering style consists in producing a momentary effect by fine words and images brought together, without order or connection. Burke most frequently produced an effect by the remoteness and novelty of his combinations, by the force of contrast, by the striking manner in which the most opposite and unpromising materials were harmoniously blended together; not by laying his hands on all the fine things he could think of, but by bringing together those things which he knew would blaze out into glorious light by their collision. The florid style is a mixture of affectation and commonplace. Burke's was an union of untameable vigour and originality.

Burke was not a verbose writer. If he sometimes multiplies words, it is not for want of ideas, but because there are no words that fully express his ideas, and he tries to do it as well as he can by different ones. He had nothing of the *set* or formal style, the measured cadence, and stately phraseology of Johnson, and most of our modern writers. This style, which is what we understand by the *artificial*, is all in one key. It selects a certain set of words to represent all ideas whatever, as the most dignified and elegant, and excludes all others as low and vulgar. The words are not fitted to the things, but the things to the words. Everything is seen through a false medium. It is putting a mask on the face of nature, which may indeed hide some specks and blemishes, but takes away all beauty, delicacy, and variety. It destroys all dignity or elevation, because nothing can be raised where all is on a level, and completely destroys all force, expression, truth, and character, by arbitrarily confounding the differences of things, and reducing everything to the same insipid standard. To suppose that this stiff uniformity can add anything to real grace or dignity, is like supposing that the human body, in order to be perfectly graceful, should never deviate from its upright posture. Another mischief of this method is, that it confounds all ranks in literature. Where there is no room for variety, no discrimination, no nicety to be shown in matching the idea with its proper word, there can be no room for taste or elegance. A man must easily learn the art of writing, when every sentence is to be cast in the same mould : where he is only allowed the use of one word he cannot choose wrong, nor will he be in much danger of making himself ridiculous by affectation or false glitter, when, whatever subject he treats of, he must treat of it in the same way. This indeed is to wear golden chains for the sake of ornament.

Burke was altogether free from the pedantry which I have here endeavoured to expose. His style was as original, as expressive, as rich and varied, as it was possible; his combinations were as exquisite, as playful, as happy, as unexpected, as bold and daring, as his fancy. If anything, he ran into the opposite extreme of too great an inequality, if truth and nature could ever be carried to an extreme.

Those who are best acquainted with the writings and speeches of Burke will not think the praise I have here bestowed on them exaggerated. Some proof will be found of this in the following extracts. But the full proof must be sought in his works at large, and particularly in the *Thoughts on the Discontents;* in his *Reflections on the French Revolution;* in his *Letter to the Duke of Bedford;* and in the *Regicide Peace.* The two last of these are perhaps the most remarkable of all his writings, from the contrast they afford to each other. The one is the most delightful exhibition of wild and brilliant fancy that is to be found in English prose, but it is too much like a beautiful picture painted upon gauze; it wants something to support it: the other is without ornament, but it has all the solidity, the weight, the gravity of a judicial record. It seems to have been written with a certain constraint upon himself, and to show those who said he could not *reason*, that his arguments might be stripped of their ornaments without losing anything of their force. It is certainly, of all his works, that in which he has shown most power of logical deduction, and the only one in which he has made any important use of facts. In general he certainly paid little attention to them: they were the playthings of his mind. He saw them as he pleased, not as they were; with the eye of the philosopher or the poet, regarding them only in their general principle, or as they might serve to decorate his subject. This is the natural consequence of much imagination: things that are probable are elevated into the rank of realities. To those who can reason on the essences of things, or who can invent according to nature, the experimental proof is of little value. This was the case with Burke. In the present instance, however, he seems to have forced his mind into the service of facts; and he succeeded completely. His comparison between our connection with France or Algiers, and his account of the conduct of the war, are as clear, as convincing, as forcible examples of this kind of reasoning, as are anywhere to be met with. Indeed I do not think there is anything in Fox (whose mind was purely historical), or in Chatham (who attended to feelings more than facts), that will bear a comparison with them.

Burke has been compared to Cicero—I do not know for what reason. Their excellences are as different, and indeed as opposite, as they can well be. Burke had not the polished elegance, the glossy neatness, the artful regularity, the exquisite modulation of Cicero: he had a thousand times more richness and originality of mind, more strength and pomp of diction.

It has been well observed, that the ancients had no word that properly expresses what we mean by the word *genius*. They perhaps had not the thing. Their minds appear to have been too exact, too retentive, too minute and subtle, too sensible to the external differences of things, too passive under their impressions, to admit of those bold and rapid combinations, those lofty flights of fancy, which, glancing from heaven to earth, unite the most opposite extremes, and draw the happiest illustrations from things the most remote. Their ideas were kept too confined and distinct by the material form or vehicle in which they were conveyed, to unite cordially together, or be melted down in the imagination. Their metaphors are taken from things of the same class, not from things of different classes; the general analogy, not the individual feeling, directs them in their choice. Hence, as Dr. Johnson observed, their similes are either repetitions of the same idea, or so obvious and general as not to lend any additional force to it; as when a huntress is compared to Diana, or a warrior rushing into battle to a lion rushing on his prey. Their *forte* was exquisite art and perfect imitation. Witness their statues and other things of the same kind. But they had not that high and enthusiastic fancy which some of our own writers have shown. For the proof of this, let any one compare Milton and Shakspeare with Homer and Sophocles, or Burke with Cicero.

It may be asked whether Burke was a poet. He was so only in the general vividness of his fancy, and in richness of invention. There may be poetical passages in his works, but I certainly think that his writings in general are quite distinct from poetry; and that for the reason before given, namely, that the subject-matter of them is not poetical. The finest part of them are illustrations or personifications of dry abstract ideas;[1] and the union between the idea and the illustration is not of that perfect and pleasing kind as to constitute poetry, or indeed to be admissible, but for the effect intended to be produced by it; that is, by every means in our power to give animation and attraction to subjects in themselves barren of ornament, but which at the same time are pregnant with the most important consequences, and in which the understanding and the passions are equally interested.

I have heard it remarked by a person, to whose opinion I would sooner submit than to a general council of critics, that the sound of Burke's prose is not musical; that it wants cadence; and that instead of being so lavish of his imagery as is generally supposed, he seemed to him to be rather parsimonious in the use of it, always expanding and making the most of his ideas. This may be true if we compare him with some of our poets, or perhaps with some of our early prose writers, but not if we compare

---

[1] As in the comparison of the British Constitution to the "proud keep of Windsor," &c., the most splendid passage in his works.

him with any of our political writers or parliamentary speakers. There are some very fine things of Lord Bolingbroke's on the same subjects, but not equal to Burke's. As for Junius, he is at the head of his class; but that class is not the highest. He has been said to have more dignity than Burke. Yes—if the stalk of a giant is less dignified than the strut of a *petit-maître*. I do not mean to speak disrespectfully of Junius, but grandeur is not the character of his composition; and if it is not to be found in Burke, it is to be found nowhere.

ESSAY XIII.

On the Character of Fox.[1]

I SHALL begin with observing generally, that Mr. Fox excelled all his contemporaries in the extent of his knowledge, in the clearness and distinctness of his views, in quickness of apprehension, in plain practical common sense, in the full, strong, and absolute possession of his subject. A measure was no sooner proposed than he seemed to have an instantaneous and intuitive perception of its various bearings and consequences; of the manner in which it would operate on the different classes of society, on commerce or agriculture, on our domestic or foreign policy; of the difficulties attending its execution; in a word, of all its practical results, and the comparative advantages to be gained either by adopting or rejecting it. He was intimately acquainted with the interests of the different parts of the community, with the minute and complicated details of political economy, with our external relations, with the views, the resources, and the maxims of other states. He was master of all those facts and circumstances which it was necessary to know in order to

[1] Reprinted from the *Eloquence of the British Senate*, 1807, ii, 466-74.—ED.

judge fairly and determine wisely ; and he knew them not
loosely or lightly, but in number, weight, and measure.
He had also stored his memory by reading and general
study, and improved his understanding by the lamp of
history. He was well acquainted with the opinions and
sentiments of the best authors, with the maxims of the
most profound politicians, with the causes of the rise and
fall of states, with the general passions of men, with the
characters of different nations, and the laws and constitution of his own country. He was a man of large,
capacious, powerful, and highly cultivated intellect. No
man could know more than he knew ; no man's knowledge
could be more sound, more plain and useful ; no man's
knowledge could lie in more connected and tangible
masses ; no man could be more perfectly master of his ideas
could reason upon them more closely, or decide upon
them more impartially. His mind was full, even to overflowing. He was so habitually conversant with the most
intricate and comprehensive trains of thought, or such was
the natural vigour and exuberance of his mind, that he
seemed to re call them without any effort. His ideas
quarrelled for utterance. So far from ever being at a
loss for them, he was obliged rather to repress and rein
them in, lest they should overwhelm and confound, instead
of informing the understandings of his hearers.

If to this we add the ardour and natural impetuosity of
his mind, his quick sensibility, his eagerness in the defence
of truth, and his impatience of everything that looked like
trick or artifice or affectation, we shall be able in some
measure to account for the character of his eloquence.
His thoughts came crowding in too fast for the slow and
mechanical process of speech. What he saw in an instant,
he could only express imperfectly, word by word, and sentence after sentence. He would, if he could, " have bared
his swelling heart," and laid open at once the rich treasures
of knowledge with which his bosom was fraught. It is no

wonder that this difference between the rapidity of his
feelings, and the formal round-about method of communicating them, should produce some disorder in his
frame; that the throng of his ideas should try to overleap
the narrow boundaries which confined them, and tumul-
tuously break down their prison-doors, instead of waiting
to be let out one by one, and following patiently at due
intervals and with mock diginity, like poor dependents,
in the train of words; that he should express himself in
hurried sentences, in involuntary exclamations, by ve-
hement gestures, by sudden starts and bursts of passion.
Everything showed the agitation of his mind. His tongue
faltered, his voice became almost suffocated, and his face
was bathed in tears. He was lost in the magnitude of his
subject. He reeled and staggered under the load of feeling which oppressed him. He rolled like the sea beaten
by a tempest. Whoever, having the feelings of a man,
compared him at these times with his boasted rival
—his stiff, straight, upright figure, his gradual contortions,
turning round as if moved by a pivot, his solemn pauses,
his deep tones, " whose sound reverbed their own hollowness," must have said, This is a man; that is an automaton.
If Fox had needed grace, he would have had it; but it was
not the character of his mind, nor would it have suited
with the style of his eloquence. It was Pitt's object to
smooth over the abruptness and intricacies of his argument
by the gracefulness of his manner, and to fix the attention
of his hearers on the pomp and sound of his words. Lord
Chatham, again, strove to *command* others; he did not try
to convince them, but to overpower their understandings
by the greater strength and vehemence of his own; to awe
them by a sense of personal superiority: and he therefore
was obliged to assume a lofty and dignified manner. It
was to him they bowed, not to truth; and whatever related
to *himself*, must therefore have a tendency to inspire
respect and admiration. Indeed, he would never have at-

tempted to gain that ascendant over men's minds that he did, if either his mind or body had been different from what they were ; if his temper had not urged him to control and command others, or if his personal advantages had not enabled him to secure that kind of authority which he coveted. But it would have been ridiculous in Fox to have affected either the smooth plausibility, the stately gravity of the one, or the proud domineering, imposing dignity of the other ; or even if he could have succeeded, it would only have injured the effect of his speeches.[1] What he had to rely on was the strength, the solidity of his ideas, his complete and thorough knowledge of his subject. It was his business therefore to fix the attention of his hearers, not on himself, but on his subject ; to rivet it there, to hurry it on from words to things :— the only circumstance of which they required to be convinced with respect to himself, was the sincerity of his opinions ; and this would be best done by the earnestness of his manner, by giving a loose to his feelings, and by showing the most perfect forgetfulness of himself, and of what others thought of him. The moment a man shows you either by affected words or looks or gestures, that he is thinking of himself, and you, that he is trying either to please or terrify you into compliance, there is an end at once to that kind of eloquence which owes its effect to the force of truth, and to your confidence in the sincerity of the speaker. It was, however, to the confidence inspired by the earnestness and simplicity of his manner, that

[1] There is an admirable, judicious, and truly useful remark in the preface to Spenser (not by Dr. Johnson, for he left Spenser out of his poets, but by *one* Upton), that the question was not whether a better poem might not have been written on a different plan, but whether Spenser would have written a better one on a different plan. I wish to apply this to Fox's *ungainly* manner. I do not mean to say, that his manner was the best possible (for that would be to say that he was the greatest man conceivable), but that it was the best for him.

Mr. Fox was indebted for more than half the effect of his speeches. Some others might possess nearly as much information, as exact a knowledge of the situation and interests of the country; but they wanted that zeal, that animation, that enthusiasm, that deep sense of the importance of the subject, which removes all doubt or suspicion from the minds of the hearers, and communicates its own warmth to every breast. We may convince by argument alone; but it is by the interest we discover in the success of our reasonings, that we persuade others to feel and act with us. There are two circumstances which Fox's speeches and Lord Chatham's had in common: they are alike distinguished by a kind of plain downright common sense, and by the vehemence of their manner. But still there is a great difference between them, in both these respects. Fox in his opinions was governed by facts—Chatham was more influenced by the feelings of others respecting those facts. Fox endeavoured to find out what the consequences of any measure would be; Chatham attended more to what people would think of it. Fox appealed to the practical reason of mankind; Chatham to popular prejudice. The one repelled the encroachments of power by supplying his hearers with arguments against it; the other by rousing their passions and arming their resentment against those who would rob them of their birthright. Their vehemence and impetuosity arose also from very different feelings. In Chatham it was pride, passion, self-will, impatience of control, a determination to have his own way, to carry everything before him; in Fox it was pure, good nature, a sincere love of truth, an ardent attachment to what he conceived to be right; an anxious concern for the welfare and liberties of mankind. Or if we suppose that ambition had taken a strong hold of both their minds, yet their ambition was of a very different kind: in the one it was the love of power, in the other it was the love of fame. Nothing can be more opposite than these two principles, both in their origin and tendency. The one originates in a selfish, haughty, domineering spirit; the other in a social and generous sensibility, desirous of the love and esteem of others, and anxiously bent upon gaining merited applause. The one grasps at immediate power by any means within its reach ; the other if it does not square its actions by the rules of virtue, at least refers them to a standard which comes the nearest to it—the disinterested applause of our country, and the enlightened judgment of posterity. The love of fame is consistent with the steadiest attachment to principle, and indeed strengthens and supports it; whereas the love of power, where this is the ruling passion, requires the sacrifice of principle, at every turn, and is inconsistent even with the shadow of it. I do not mean to say that Fox had no love of power, or Chatham no love of fame (this would be reversing all we know of human nature), but .that the one principle predominated in the one, and the other in the other. My reader will do me great injustice if he supposes that in attempting to describe the characters of different speakers by contrasting their general qualities, I mean anything beyond the *more* or *less :* but it is necessary to describe those qualities simply and in the abstract, in order to make the distinction intelligible Chatham resented any attack made upon the cause of liberty, of which he was the avowed champion, as an indignity offered to himself. Fox felt it as a stain upon the honour of his country, and as an injury to the rights of his fellow citizens. The one was swayed by his own passions and purposes, with very little regard to the consequences ; the sensibility of the other was roused, and his passions kindled into a generous flame, by a real interest in whatever related to the welfare of mankind and by an intense and earnest contemplation of the consequences of the measures he opposed. It was this union of the zeal of the patriot with the enlightened knowledge of the statesman, that gave to the eloquence of Fox its more than mortal energy; that warmed, expanded, penetrated every bosom. He relied on the force of truth and nature alone; the refinements of philosophy, the pomp and pageantry of the imagination were forgotten, or seemed light and frivolous; the fate of nations, the welfare of millions, hung suspended as he spoke; a torrent of manly eloquence poured from his heart, bore down everything in its course, and surprised into a momentary sense of human feeling the breathing corpses, the wire-moved puppets, the stuffed figures, the flexible machinery, the "deaf and dumb things" of a court.

I find (I do not know how the reader feels) that it is difficult to write a character of Fox without running into insipidity or extravagance. And the reason of this is, there are no splendid contrasts, no striking irregularities, no curious distinctions to work upon; no "jutting frieze, buttress, nor coigne of 'vantage," for the imagination to take hold of. It was a plain marble slab, inscribed in plain legible characters, without either hieroglyphics or carving. There was the same directness and manly simplicity in everything that he did. The whole of his character may indeed be summed up in two words—strength and simplicity. Fox was in the class of common men, but he was the first in that class. Though it is easy to describe the differences of things, nothing is more difficult than to describe their degrees or quantities. In what I am going to say, I hope I shall not be suspected of a design to under-rate his powers of mind, when in fact I am only trying to ascertain their nature and direction. The degree and extent to which he possessed them can only be known by reading, or indeed by having heard his speeches.

His mind, as I have already said, was, I conceive, purely *historical;* and having said this, I have I believe said all. But perhaps it will be necessary to explain a little farther what I mean. I mean, then, that his memory was in an extraordinary degree tenacious of facts; that they were crowded together in his mind without the least perplexity or confusion; that there was no chain of consequences too vast for his powers of comprehension; that the different parts and ramifications of his subject were never so involved and intricate but that they were easily disentangled in the clear prism of his understanding. The basis of his wisdom was experience : he not only knew what had happened, but by an exact knowledge of the real state of things, ho could always tell what in the common course of events would happen in future. The force of his mind was exerted on facts : as long as he could lean directly upon these, as long as he had the actual objects to refer to, to steady himself by, he could analyse, he could combine, he could compare and reason upon them, with the utmost exactness; but he could not reason *out of* them. He was what is understood by a *matter-of-fact* reasoner. He was better acquainted with the concrete masses of things, their substantial forms and practical connections, than with their abstract nature or general definitions. He was a man of extensive information, of sound knowledge, and clear understanding, rather than the acute observer or profound thinker. He was the man of business, the accomplished statesman, rather than the philosopher. His reasonings were, generally speaking, calculations of certain positive results, which, the *data* being given, must follow as matters of course, rather than unexpected and remote truths drawn from a deep insight into human nature, and the subtle application of general principles to particular cases. They consisted chiefly in the detail and combination of a vast number of items in an account, worked by the known rules of political arithmetic; not in the discovery of bold, comprehensive, and original theorems in the science. They were rather acts of memory, of continued attention, of a power of bringing all his ideas to bear at once upon a single point,

than of reason or invention. He was the attentive observer who watches the various effects and successive
movements of a machine already constructed, and can tell
how to manage it while it goes on as it has always done;
but who knows little or nothing of the principles on which
it is constructed, nor how to set it right, if it becomes
disordered, except by the most common and obvious ex-
pedients. Burke was to Fox what the geometrician is
to the mechanic. Much has been said of the "prophetic
mind" of Mr. Fox. The same epithet has been applied
to Mr. Burke, till it has become proverbial. It has, I
think, been applied without much reason to either. Fox
wanted the scientific part. Burke wanted the practical.
Fox had too little imagination, Burke had too much: that
is, he was careless of facts, and was led away by his
passions to look at one side of a question only. He had
not that fine sensibility to outward impressions, that nice
tact of circumstances, which is necessary to the consummate
politician. Indeed, his wisdom was more that of the
legislator than of the active statesman. They both tried
their strength in the Ulysses' bow of politicians, the
French Revolution: and they were both foiled. Fox
indeed foretold the success of the French in combating
with foreign powers. But this was no more than what
every friend of the liberty of France foresaw or foretold as well as he. All those on the same side of the
question were inspired with the same sagacity on the
subject. Burke, on the other hand, seems to have been
beforehand with the public in foreboding the internal
disorders that would attend the Revolution, and its
ultimate failure; but then it is at least a question
whether he did not make good his own predictions: and
certainly he saw into the causes and connection of events
much more clearly after they had happened than before.
He was however undoubtedly a profound commentator on
that apocalyptical chapter in the history of human nature,

which I do not think Fox was. Whether led to it by the
events or not, he saw thoroughly into the principles that
operated to produce them; and he pointed them out to
others in a manner which could not be mistaken. I can
conceive of Burke, as the genius of the storm, perched over
Paris, the centre and focus of anarchy (so he would have
us believe), hovering "with mighty wings outspread over
the abyss, and rendering it pregnant," watching the
passions of men gradually unfolding themselves in new
situations, penetrating those hidden motives which hurried
them from one extreme into another, arranging and analysing the principles that alternately pervaded the vast
chaotic mass, and extracting the elements of order and
the cement of social life from the decomposition of all
society; while Charles Fox in the meantime dogged the
heels of the allies (all the while calling out to them to
stop) with his sutler's bag, his muster roll, and army
estimates at his back. He said, You have only fifty
thousand troops, the enemy have a hundred thousand:
this place is dismantled, it can make no resistance: your
troops were beaten last year, they must therefore be dis-
heartened this. This is excellent sense and sound reasoning, but I do not see what it has to do with philosophy.
But why was it necessary that Fox should be a philosopher? Why, in the first place, Burke was a philosopher,
and Fox, to keep up with him, must be so too. In the
second place, it was necessary in order that his indiscreet
admirers, who have no idea of greatness but as it consists
in certain names and pompous titles, might be able to talk
big about their patron. It is a bad compliment we pay to
our idol when we endeavour to make him out something
different from himself; it shows that we are not satisfied
with what he is. I have heard it said that he had as
much imagination as Burke. To this extravagant assertion I shall make what I conceive to be a very cautious
and moderate answer: that Burke was as superior to Fox

in this respect as Fox perhaps was to the first person you would meet in the street. There is, in fact, hardly an instance of imagination to be met with in any of his speeches; what there is, is of the rhetorical kind. I may, however, be wrong. He might excel as much in profound thought, and richness of fancy, as he did in other things; though I cannot perceive it. However, when any one publishes a book called The Beauties of Fox, containing the original reflections, brilliant passages, lofty metaphors, &c., to be found in his speeches, without the detail or connexion, I shall be very ready to give the point up.

In logic Fox was inferior to Pitt—indeed, in all the formalities of eloquence, in which the latter excelled as much as he was deficient in the soul of substance. When I say that Pitt was superior to Fox in logic, I mean that he excelled him in the formal division of the subject, in always keeping it in view, as far as he chose; in being able to detect any deviation from it in others; in the management of his general topics; in being aware of the mood and figure in which the argument must move, with all its nonessentials, dilemmas, and alternatives; in never committing himself, nor ever suffering his antagonist to occupy an inch of the plainest ground, but under cover of a syllogism. He had more of "the dazzling fence of argument," as it has been called. He was, in short, better at his weapon. But then, unfortunately, it was only a dagger of lath that the wind could turn aside; whereas Fox wore a good trusty blade, of solid metal, and real execution.

I shall not trouble myself to inquire whether Fox was a man of strict virtue and principle; or in other words, how far he was one of those who screw themselves up to a certain pitch of ideal perfection, who, as it were, set themselves in the stocks of morality, and make mouths at their own situation. He was not one of that tribe, and shall not be tried by their self-denying ordinances. But he was endowed with one of the most excellent natures that ever fell to the lot of any of God's creatures. It has been said, that "an honest man's the noblest work of God." There is indeed a purity, a rectitude, an integrity of heart, a freedom from every selfish bias, and sinister motive, a manly simplicity and noble disinterestedness of feeling, which is in my opinion to be preferred before every other gift of nature or art. There is a greatness of soul that is superior to all the brilliancy of the understanding. This strength of moral character, which is not only a more valuable but a rarer quality than strength of understanding (as we are oftener led astray by the narrowness of our feelings, than want of knowledge), Fox possessed in the highest degree. He was superior to every kind of jealousy, of suspicion, of malevolence; to every narrow and sordid motive. He was perfectly above every species of duplicity, of low art and cunning. He judged of everything in the downright sincerity of his nature, without being able to impose upon himself by any hollow disguise, or to lend his support to anything unfair or dishonourable. He had an innate love of truth, of justice, of probity, of whatever was generous or liberal. Neither his education, nor his connections, nor his situation in life, nor the low intrigues and virulence of party, could ever alter the simplicity of his taste, nor the candid openness of his nature. There was an elastic force about his heart, a freshness of social feeling, a warm glowing humanity, which remained unimpaired to the last. He was by nature a gentleman. By this I mean that he felt a certain deference and respect for the person of every man ; he had an unaffected frankness and benignity in his behaviour to others, the utmost liberality in judging of their conduct and motives. A refined humanity constitutes the character of a gentleman. He was the true friend of his country, as far as it is possible for a statesman to be so. But his love of his country did not consist in his hatred of the rest of mankind. I shall conclude this account by repeating what Burke said of him at a time when his testimony was of the most value. " To his great and masterly understanding he joined the utmost possible degree of moderation : he was of the most artless, candid, open, and benevolent disposition ; disinterested in the extreme ; of a temper mild and placable, even to a fault ; and without one drop of gall in his constitution."

ESSAY XIV.

On the Character of Mr. Pitt.[1]

THE character of Mr. Pitt was, perhaps, one of the most singular that ever existed. With few talents, and fewer virtues, he acquired and preserved in one of the most trying situations, and in spite of all opposition, the highest reputation for the possession of every moral excellence, and as having carried the attainments of eloquence and wisdom as far as human abilities could go. This he did (strange as it appears) by a negation (together with the common virtues) of the common vices of human nature, and by the complete negation of every other talent that might interfere with the only one which he possessed in a supreme degree, and which indeed may be made to include the appearance of all others—an artful use of words, and a certain dexterity of logical arrangement. In these alone his power consisted ; and the defect of all other qualities which usually constitute greatness, contributed to the more complete success of these. Having no strong feelings, no distinct perceptions, his mind having no link as it were, to connect it with the world of external nature, every subject presented

[1] Originally printed as part of a pamphlet entitled *Free Thoughts on Public Affairs*, 1806, and republished in the *Eloquence of the British Senate*, 1807, ii. 494, *et seq.*—ED.

to him nothing more than a *tabula rasa*, on which he was at liberty to lay whatever colouring of language he pleased ; having no general principles, no comprehensive views of things, no moral habits of thinking, no system of action, there was nothing to hinder him from pursuing any particular purpose, by any means that offered ; having never any plan, he could not be convicted of inconsistency, and his own pride and obstinacy were the only rules of his conduct.   Having no insight into human nature, no sympathy with the passions of men, or apprehension of their real designs, he seemed perfectly insensible to the consequences of things, and would believe nothing till it actually happened.   The fog and haze in which he saw everything communicated itself to others; and the total indistinctness and uncertainty of his own ideas tended to confound the perceptions of his hearers more effectually than the most ingenious misrepresentation could have done.   Indeed, in defending his conduct he never seemed to consider himself as at all responsible for the success of his measures, or to suppose that future events were in our own power; but that as the best-laid schemes might fail, and there was no providing against all possible contingencies, this was a sufficient excuse for our plunging at once into any dangerous or absurd enterprise, without the least regard to consequences.   His reserved logic confined itself solely to the *possible* and the *impossible ;* and he appeared to regard the *probable* and *improbable*, the only foundation of moral prudence or political wisdom, as beneath the notice of a profound statesman ; as if the pride of the human intellect were concerned in never entrusting itself with subjects, where it may be compelled to acknowledge its weakness.[1]   From

---

[1] One instance may serve as an example for all the rest :—When Mr. Fox last summer (1805) predicted the failure of the new confederacy against France, from a consideration of the circumstances and relative situation of both parties, that is, from an exact know

his manner of reasoning, he seemed not to have believed that the truth of his statements depended on the reality of the facts, but that the things depended on the order in which he arranged them in words : you would not suppose him to be agitating a serious question which had real grounds to go upon, but to be declaiming upon an imaginary thesis, proposed as an exercise in the schools. He never set himself to examine the force of the objections that were brought against his measures, or attempted to establish these upon clear, solid grounds of his own; but constantly contented himself with first gravely stating the logical form, or dilemma, to which the question reduced itself, and then, after having declared his opinion, proceeded to amuse his hearers by a series of rhetorical commonplaces, connected together in grave, sonorous, and elaborately constructed periods, without ever showing

---

ledge of the actual state of things, Mr. Pitt contented himself with answering—and, as in the blindness of his infatuation, he seemed to think quite satisfactorily—"That he could not assent to the honourable gentleman's reasoning, for that it went to this, that we were never to attempt to mend the situation of our affairs, because in so doing we might possibly make them worse." No; it was not on account of this abstract possibility in human affairs, or because we were not absolutely sure of succeeding (for that any child might know), but because it was in the highest degree probable, or *morally* certain, that the scheme would fail, and leave us in a worse situation than we were before, that Mr. Fox disapproved of the attempt. There is in this a degree of weakness and imbecility, a defect of understanding bordering on idiotism, a fundamental ignorance of the first principles of human reason and prudence, that in a great minister is utterly astonishing, and almost incredible. Nothing could ever drive him out of his dull forms, and naked generalities; which, as they are susceptible neither of degree nor variation, are therefore equally applicable to every emergency that can happen: and in the most critical aspect of affairs, he saw nothing but the same flimsy web of remote possibilities and metaphysical uncertainty. In his mind the wholesome pulp of practical wisdom and salutary advice was immediately converted into the dry chaff and husks of a miserable logic.

their real application to the subject in dispute. Thus, if any member of the Opposition disapproved of any measure, and enforced his objections by pointing out the many evils with which it was fraught, or the difficulties attending its execution, his only answer was, " That it was true there might be inconveniences attending the measure proposed, but we were to remember, that every expedient that could be devised might be said to be nothing more than a choice of difficulties, and that all that human prudence could do was to consider on which side the advantages lay ; that for his part, he conceived that the present measure was attended with more advantages and fewer disadvantages than any other that could be adopted ; that if we were diverted from our object by every appearance of difficulty, the wheels of goverment would be clogged by endless delays and imaginary grievances ; that most of the objections made to the measure appeared to him to be trivial, others of them unfounded and improbable ; or that if a scheme free from all these objections could be proposed, it might after all prove inefficient ; while, in the meantime, a material object remained unprovided for, or the opportunity of action was lost." This mode of reasoning is admirably described by Hobbes, in speaking of the writings of some of the Schoolmen, of whom he says, that " They had learned the trick of imposing what they list upon their readers, and declining the force of true reason by verbal forks : that is, distinctions which signify nothing, but serve only to astonish the multitude of ignorant men." That what I have here stated comprehends the whole force of his mind, which consisted solely in this evasive dexterity and perplexing formality, assisted by a copiousness of words and commonplace topics, will, I think, be evident in any one who carefully looks over his speeches, undazzled by the reputation or personal influence of the speaker. It will be in vain to look in them for any of the common proofs of human genius or wisdom. He has not left behind him a single memorable saying—not one profound maxim—one solid observation—one forcible description—one beautiful thought—one humorous picture —one affecting sentiment.[1] He has made no addition whatever to the stock of human knowledge. He did not possess any one of those faculties which contribute to the instruction and delight of mankind—depth of understanding, imagination, sensibility, wit, vivacity, clear and solid judgment. But it may be asked, If these qualities are not to be found in him, where are we to look for them ? And I may be required to point out instances of them. I shall answer, then, that he had none of the profound legislative wisdom, piercing sagacity, or rich, impetuous, high-wrought imagination of Burke; the manly eloquence, strong sense, exact knowledge, vehemence, and natural simplicity of Fox: the ease, brilliancy, and acuteness of Sheridan. It is not merely that he had not all these qualities in the degree that they were severally possessed by his rivals, but he had not any of them in any striking degree. His reasoning is a techinal arrangement of unmeaning commonplaces; his eloquence merely rhetorical; his style monotonous and artificial. If he could pretend to any one excellence in an eminent degree, it was to taste in composition. There is certainly nothing low, nothing puerile, nothing far-fetched or abrupt in his speeches; there is a kind of faultless regularity pervading them throughout; but in the confined, mechanical, passive mode of eloquence which he adopted, it seemed rather more

---

[1] I do remember one passage which has some meaning in it. At the time of the Regency Bill, speaking of the proposal to take the King's servants from him, he says, "What must that great personage feel when he waked from the trance of his faculties, and asked for his attendants, if he were told that his subjects had taken advantage of his momentary absence of mind, and stripped him of the symbols of his personal elevation." There is some grandeur in this. His admirers should have it inscribed in letters of gold; for they will not find another instance of the same kind.

difficult to commit errors than to avoid them. A man who is determined never to move out of the beaten road, cannot lose his way. However, habit, joined to the peculiar mechanical memory which he possessed, carried this correctness to a degree which, in an extemporaneous speaker, was almost miraculous; he perhaps hardly ever uttered a sentence that was not perfectly regular and connected. In this respect he not only had the advantage over his own contemporaries, but perhaps no one that ever lived equalled him in this singular faculty. But for this, he would always have passed for a common man; and to this the constant sameness, and, if I may so say, vulgarity of his ideas, must have contributed not a little, as there was nothing to distract his mind from this one object of his unintermitted attention; and as even in his choice of words he never aimed at anything more than a certain general propriety, and stately uniformity of style. His talents were exactly fitted for the situation in which he was placed; where it was his business, not to overcome others, but to avoid being overcome. He was able to baffle opposition, not from strength or firmness, but from the evasive ambiguity and impalpable nature of his resistance, which gave no hold to the rude grasp of his opponents: no force could bind the loose phantom, and his mind (though " not matchless, and his pride humbled by such rebuke "), soon rose from defeat unhurt,

> " And in its liquid texture mortal wound
> Receiv'd no more than can the fluid air." [1]

---

[1] I will only add, that it is the property of true genius to force the admiration even of enemies. No one was ever hated or envied for his powers of mind, if others were convinced of their real excellence. The jealousy and uneasiness produced in the mind by the display of superior talents almost always arises from a suspicion that there is some trick or deception in the case, and that we are imposed on by an appearance of what is not really there. True warmth and vigour communicate warmth and vigour; and we are no longer inclined to dispute the inspiration of the oracle, when we

ESSAY XV.

On the Character of Lord Chatham.[1]

LORD CHATHAM'S genius burnt brightest at the last. The spark of liberty, which had lain concealed and dormant, buried under the dirt and rubbish of state intrigue and vulgar faction, now met with congenial matter, and kindled up " a flame of sacred vehemence" in his breast. It burst forth with a fury and a splendour that might have awed the world, and made kings tremble. He spoke as a man should speak, because he felt as a man should feel, in such circumstances. He came forward as the advocate of liberty, as the defender of the rights of his fellow-citizens, as the enemy of tyranny, as the friend of his country, and of mankind. He did not stand up to make a vain display of his talents, but to discharge a duty, to maintain that cause which lay nearest to his heart, to preserve the ark of the British constitution from every sacrilegious touch, as the high-priest of his calling, with a pious zeal. The feelings and the rights of Englishmen were enshrined in his heart; and with their united force braced every nerve, possessed every faculty, and communicated warmth and vital energy to every part of his being. The whole man moved under this impulse. He felt the cause of liberty as his own. He resented every injury done to her as an injury to himself, and

---

feel the " *presens Divus*" in our own bosoms. But when, without gaining any new light or heat, we only find our ideas thrown into perplexity and confusion by an art that we cannot comprehend, this is a kind of superiority which must always be painful, and can never be cordially admitted. For this reason the extraordinary talents of Mr. Pitt were always viewed, except by those of his own party, with a sort of jealousy, and *grudgingly* acknowledged; while those of his rivals were admitted by all parties in the most unreserved manner, and carried by acclamation.

[1] *The Eloquence of the British Senate,* 1807, ii. 4–7.—ED.

every attempt to defend it as an insult upon his understanding. He did not stay to dispute about words, about
nice distinctions, about trifling forms. He laughed at the
little attempts of little retailers of logic to entangle him
in senseless argument. He did not come there as to a
debating club, or law court, to start questions and hunt
them down ; to wind and unwind the web of sophistry ; to
pick out the threads, and untie every knot with scrupulous
exactness ; to bandy logic with every pretender to a
paradox ; to examine, to sift evidence ; to dissect a doubt
and halve a scruple ; to weigh folly and knavery in scales
together, and see on which side the balance prepon-
derated ; to prove that liberty, truth, virtue, and justice
were good things, or that slavery and corruption were bad
things. He did not try to prove those truths which did
not require any proof, but to make others feel them with
the same force that he did ; and to tear off the flimsy
disguises with which the sycophants of power attempted
to cover them. The business of an orator is not to convince, but persuade ; not to inform, but to rouse the mind ;
to build upon the habitual prejudices of mankind (for
reason of itself will do nothing), and to add feeling to prejudice, and action to feeling. There is nothing new or
curious or profound in Lord Chatham's speeches. All is
obvious and common ; there is nothing but what we
already knew, or might have found out for ourselves.
We see nothing but the familiar everyday face of nature.
We are always in broad daylight. But then there is the
same difference between our own conceptions of things and
his representation of them, as there is between the same
objects seen on a dull cloudy day or in the blaze of
sunshine. His common sense has the effect of inspiration.
He electrifies his hearers, not by the novelty of his ideas,
but by their force and intensity. He has the same ideas
as other men, but he has them in a thousand times greater
clearness and strength and vividness. Perhaps there is

no man so poorly furnished with thoughts and feelings but that if he could recollect all that he knew, and had all his ideas at perfect command, he would be able to confound the puny arts of the most dexterous sophist that pretended to make a dupe of his understanding. But in the mind of Chatham, the great substantial truths of common sense, the leading maxims of the Constitution, the real interests and general feelings of mankind were in a manner embodied. He comprehended the whole of his subject at a single glance—everything was firmly riveted to its place ; there was no feebleness, no forgetfulness, no pause, no distraction ; the ardour of his mind overcame every obstacle, and he crushed the objections of his adversaries as we crush an insect under our feet. His imagination was of the same character with his understanding, and was under the same guidance. Whenever he gave way to it, it "flew an eagle flight, forth and right on ;" but it did not become enamoured of its own emotion, wantoning in giddy circles, or "sailing with supreme dominion through the azure deep of air." It never forgot its errand, but went straight forward, like an arrow to its mark, with an unerring aim. It was his servant, not his master.

To be a great orator does not require the highest faculties of the human mind, but it requires the highest exertion of the common faculties of our nature. He has no occasion to dive into the depths of science, or to soar aloft on angels' wings. He keeps upon the surface, he stands firm upon the ground, but his form is majestic, and his eye sees far and near : he moves among his fellows, but he moves among them as a giant among common men. He has no need to read the heavens, to unfold the system of the universe, or create new worlds for the delighted fancy to dwell in; it is enough that he see things as they are; that he knows and feels and re-members the common circumstances and daily transactions that are passing in the world around him. He is not raised above others by being superior to the common interests, prejudices, and passions of mankind, but by feeling them in a more intense degree than they do. Force, then, is the sole characteristic excellence of an orator; it is almost the only one that can be of any service to him. Refinement, depth, elevation, delicacy, originality, inge- nuity, invention, are not wanted; he must appeal to the sympathies of human nature, and whatever is not founded in these, is foreign to his purpose. He does not create, he can only imitate or echo back the public sentiment. His object is to call up the feelings of the human breast; but he cannot call up what is not already there. The first duty of an orator is to be understood by every one; but it is evident that what all can understand, is not in itself difficult of comprehension. He cannot add anything to the materials afforded him by the knowledge and expe- rience of others.

Lord Chatham, in his speeches, was neither philosopher nor poet. As to the latter, the difference between poetry and eloquence I take to be this: that the object of the one is to delight the imagination, that of the other to impel the will. The one ought to enrich and feed the mind itself with tenderness and beauty, the other fur- nishes it with motives of action. The one seeks to give immediate pleasure, to make the mind dwell with rapture on its own workings—it is to itself " both end and use :" the other endeavours to call up such images as will produce the strongest effect upon the mind, and makes use of the passions only as instruments to attain a particular purpose. The poet lulls and soothes the mind into a forgetfulness of itself, and " laps it in Elysium :" the orator strives to awaken it to a sense of its real interests, and to make it feel the necessity of taking the most effec- tual means for securing them. The one dwells in an ideal world; the other is only conversant with realities.

Hence poetry must be more ornamented, must be richer and fuller and more delicate, because it is at liberty to select whatever images are naturally most beautiful, and likely to give most pleasure; whereas the orator is confined to particular facts, which he may adorn as well as he can, and make the most of, but which he cannot strain beyond a certain point without running into extravagance and affectation, and losing his end. However, from the very nature of the case, the orator is allowed a greater latitude, and is compelled to make use of harsher and more abrupt combinations in the decoration of his subject; for his art is an attempt to reconcile beauty and deformity together: on the contrary, the materials of poetry, which are chosen at pleasure, are in themselves beautiful, and naturally combine with whatever else is beautiful. Grace and harmony are therefore essential to poetry, because they naturally arise out of the subject; but whatever adds to the effect, whatever tends to strengthen the idea or give energy to the mind, is of the nature of eloquence. The orator is only concerned to give a tone of masculine firmness to the will, to brace the sinews and muscles of the mind; not to delight our nervous sensibilities, or soften the mind into voluptuous indolence. The flowery and sentimental style is of all others the most intolerable in a speaker.—I shall only add on this subject, that modesty, impartiality, and candour, are not the virtues of a public speaker. He must be confident, inflexible, uncontrollable, overcoming all opposition by his ardour and impetuosity. We do not *command* others by sympathy with them, but by power, by passion, by will. Calm inquiry, sober truth, and speculative indifference will never carry any point. The passions are contagious; and we cannot contend against opposite passions with nothing but naked reason. Concessions to an enemy are clear loss; he will take advantage of them, but make us none in return. He will magnify the weak

sides of our argument, but will be blind to whatever
makes against himself. The multitude will always be
inclined to side with that party whose passions are the
most inflamed, and whose prejudices are the most inveterate. Passion should therefore never be sacrificed
to punctilio. It should indeed be governed by prudence, but it should itself govern and lend its impulse
and direction to abstract reason. Fox was a reasoner
Lord Chatham was an orator. Burke was both a reasoner
and a poet; and was therefore still farther removed from
that conformity with the vulgar notions and mechanical
feelings of mankind, which will always be necessary to
give a man the chief sway in a popular assembly.

ESSAY XVI.

Belief, whether Voluntary ? [1]

" Thy wish was father, Harry, to that thought."

IT is an axiom in modern philosophy (among many other
false ones) that belief is absolutely involuntary, since we
draw our inferences from the premises laid before us, and
cannot possibly receive any other impression of things
than that which they naturally make upon us. This
theory, that the understanding is purely passive in the
reception of truth, and that our convictions are not in the
power of our will, was probably first invented or insisted
upon as a screen against religious persecution, and as an
answer to those who imputed bad motives to all who
differed from the established faith, and thought they
could reform heresy and impiety by the application of fire
and the sword. No doubt, that is not the way: for the
will in that case irritates itself and grows refractory
against the doctrines thus absurdly forced upon it ; and as
it has been said, the blood of the martyrs is the seed

[1] First printed in the *Literary Remains*, 1836.—ED.

2 G

of the Church.   But though force and terror may not be
always the surest way to make converts, it does not follow
that there may not be other means of influencing our
opinions, besides the naked and abstract evidence for
any proposition : the sun melts the resolution which the
storm could not shake.   In such points as, whether an
object is black or white or whether two and two make
four,[1] we may not be able to believe as we please or to
deny the evidence of our reason and senses : but in those
points on which mankind differ, or where we can be at all
in suspense as to which side we shall take, the truth is not
quite so plain or palpable ; it admits of a variety of views
and shades of colouring, and it should appear that we can
dwell upon whichever of these we choose, and heighten or
soften the circumstances adduced in proof, according as
passion and inclination throw their casting-weight into the
scale.   Let any one, for instance, have been brought up in
an opinion, let him have remained in it all his life, let him
have attached all his notions of respectability, of the
approbation of his fellow-citizens or his own self-esteem
to it, let him then first hear it called in question, and
a strong and unforeseen objection stated to it, will not
this startle and shock him as if he had seen a spectre,
and will he not struggle to resist the arguments that
would unsettle his habitual convictions, as he would resit
the divorcing of soul and body ? Will he come to the consideration of the question impartially, indifferently, and
without any wrong bias, or give the painful and revolting
truth the same cordial welcome as the long-cherished and
favourite prejudice ?   To say that the truth or falsehood of
a proposition is the only circumstance that gains it admit-
tance into the mind, independently of the pleasure or pain
it affords us, is itself an assertion made in pure caprice or
desperation.   A person may have a profession or employ-

---

[1] Hobbes is of opinion that men would deny this, if they had any
interest in doing so.

ment connected with a certain belief, it may be the means of livelihood to him, and the changing it may require considerable sacrifices, or may leave him almost without resource (to say nothing of mortified pride)—this will not mend the matter. The evidence against his former opinion may be so strong (or may appear so to him) that he may be obliged to give it up, but not without a pang and after having tried every artifice and strained every nerve to give the utmost weight to the arguments favouring his own side, and to make light of and throw those against him into the background. And nine times in ten this bias of the will and tampering with the proofs will prevail. It is only with very vigorous or very candid minds that the understanding exercises its just and boasted prerogative, and induces its votaries to relinquish a profitable delusion and embrace the dowerless truth. Even then they have the sober and discreet part of the world, all the *bons pères de famille*, who look principally to the main chance, against them, and they are regarded as little better than lunatics or profligates to fling up a good salary and a provision for themselves and families for the sake of that foolish thing, a *Conscience!* With the herd, belief on all abstract and disputed topics is voluntary, that is, is determined by considerations of personal ease and convenience, in the teeth of logical analysis and demonstration, which are set aside as mere waste of words. In short, generally speaking, people stick to an opinion that they have long supported and that supports them. How else shall we account for the regular order and progression of society: for the maintenance of certain opinions in particular professions and classes of men, as we keep water in cisterns, till in fact they stagnate and corrupt: and that the world and every individual in it is not " blown about with every wind of doctrine " and whisper of uncertainty? There is some more solid ballast required to keep things in their established order than the restless fluctuation of opinion and "infinite agitation of wit." We find that people in Protestant countries continue Protestants, and in Catholic countries Papists. This, it may be answered, is owing to the ignorance of the great mass of them; but in their faith less bigoted, because it is not founded on a regular investigation of the proofs, and is merely an obstinate determination to believe what they have been told and accustomed to believe? Or is it not the same with the doctors of the church and its most learned champions, who read the same texts, turn over the same authorities, and discuss the same knotty points through their whole lives, only to arrive at opposite conclusions? How few are shaken in their opinions, or have the grace to confess it? Shall we then suppose them all impostors, and that they keep up the farce of a system, of which they do not believe a syllable? Far from it: there may be individual instances, but the generality are not only sincere but bigots. Those who are unbelievers and hypocrites scarcely know it themselves, or if a man is not quite a knave, what pains will he not take to make a fool of his reason, that his opinions may tally with his professions? Is there then a Papist and a Protestant understanding—one prepared to receive the doctrine of transubstantiation and the other to reject it? No such thing: but in either case the ground of reason is pre-occupied by passion, habit, example—*the scales are falsified*. Nothing can therefore be more inconsequential than to bring the authority of great names in favour of opinions long established and universally received. Cicero's being a Pagan was no proof in support of the Heathen mythology, but simply of his being born at Rome before the Christian era; though his lurking scepticism on the subject and sneers at the augurs told against it, for this was an acknowledgment drawn from him in spite of a prevailing prejudice. Sir Isaac Newton and Napier of Murchiston both wrote on the *Apocalypse;* but this is neither a ground for a speedy anticipation of the Millennium, nor does it invalidate the doctrine of the gravitation of the planets or the theory of logarithms. One party would borrow the sanction of these great names in support of their wildest and most mystical opinions; others would arraign them of folly and weakness for having attended to such subjects at all. Neither inference is just. It is a simple question of chronology, or of the time when these celebrated mathematicians lived, and of the studies and pursuits which were then chiefly in vogue. The wisest man is the slave of opinion, except on one or two points on which he strikes out a light for himself and holds a torch to the rest of the world. But we are disposed to make it out that all opinions are the result of reason, because they profess to be so; and when they are *right*, that is, when they agree with ours, that there can be no alloy of human frailty or perversity in them; the very strength of our prejudice making it pass for pure reason, and leading us to attribute any deviation from it to bad faith or some unaccountable singularity or infatuation. *Alas, poor human nature!* Opinion is for the most part only a battle, in which we take part and defend the side we have adopted, in the one case or the other, with a view to share the honour of the spoil. Few will stand up for a losing cause, or have the fortitude to adhere to a proscribed opinion; and when they do, it is not always from superior strength of understanding or a disinterested love of truth, but from obstinacy and sullenness of temper. To affirm that we do not cultivate an acquaintance with truth as she presents herself to us in a more or less pleasing shape, or is shabbily attired or well-dressed, is as much as to say that we do not shut our eyes to the light when it dazzles us, or withdraw our hands from the fire when it scorches us.

> "Masterless passion sways us to the mood
> Of what it likes or loathes."

Are we not averse to believe bad news relating to ourselves
—forward enough if it relates to others ? If something is
said reflecting on the character of an intimate friend or
near relative, how unwilling we are to lend an ear to it,
how we catch at every excuse or palliating circumstance,
and hold out against the clearest proof, while we instantly
believe any idle report against an enemy, magnify the
commonest trifles into crimes, and torture the evidence
against him to our heart's content! Do not we change
our opinion of the same person, and make him out to be
black or *white* according to the terms we happen to be on ?
If we have a favourite author, do we not exaggerate his
beauties and pass over his defects, and *vice versâ ?* The
human mind plays the interested advocate much oftener
than the upright and inflexible judge, in the colouring and
relief it gives to the facts brought before it. We believe
things not more because they are true or probable, than
because we desire, or (if the imagination once takes that
turn) because we dread them. " Fear has more devils
than vast hell can hold." The sanguine always hope, the
gloomy always despond, from temperament and not from
forethought. Do we not disguise the plainest facts from
ourselves if they are disagreeable ? Do we not flatter
ourselves with impossibilities? What girl does not look
in the glass to persuade herself she is handsome ?   What
woman ever believes herself old, or does not hate to be
called so : though she knows the exact year and day of her
age, the more she tries to keep up the appearance of youth
to herself and others ? What lover would ever acknowledge a flaw in the character of his mistress, or would not
construe her turning her back on him into a proof of
attachment ? The story of *January and May* is pat to our
purpose ; for the credulity of mankind as to what touches
our inclinations has been proverbial in all ages : yet we
are told that the mind is passive in making up these wilful
accounts and is guided by nothing but the *pros* and *cons* of

evidence. Even in action and where we may determine by proper precaution the event of things, instead of being compelled to shut our eyes to what we cannot help, we still are the dupes of the feeling of the moment, and prefer amusing ourselves with fair appearances to securing more solid benefits by a sacrifice of Imagination and stubborn Will to Truth. The blindness of passion to the most obvious and well-known consequences is deplorable. There seems to be a particular fatality in this respect. Because a thing is in our power *till* we have committed ourselves, we appear to dally, to trifle with, to make light of it, and to think it will still be in our power *after* we have committed ourselves. Strange perversion of the reasoning faculties, which is little short of madness, and which yet is one of the constant and practical sophisms of human life! It is as if one should say—I am in no danger from a tremendous machine unless I touch such a spring and therefore I will approach it, I will play with the danger, I will laugh at it, and at last in pure sport and wantonness of heart, from my sense of previous security, I *will* touch it—and *there's an end.* While the thing remains in contemplation, we may be said to stand safe and smiling on the brink : as soon as we proceed to action we are drawn into the vortex of passion and hurried to our destruction. A person taken up with some one purpose or passion is intent only upon that : he drives out the thought of everything but its gratification : in the pursuit of that he is blind to consequences : his first object being attained, they all at once, and as if by magic, rush upon his mind. The engine recoils, he is caught in his own snare. A servant girl, for some pique, or for an angry word, determines to poison her mistress. She knows beforehand (just as well as she does afterwards) that it is at least a hundred chances to one she will be hanged if she succeeds, yet this has no more effect upon her than if she had never heard of any such matter. The only idea that occupies her mind and hardens it against every other, is that of the affront she has received, and the desire of revenge ; she broods over it ; she meditates the mode, she is haunted with her scheme night and day ; it works like poison ; it grows into a madness, and she can have no peace till it is accomplished and *off her mind ;* but the moment this is the case, and her passion is assuaged, fear takes place of hatred, the slightest suspicion alarms her with the certainty of her fate, from which she before wilfully averted her thoughts ; she runs wildly from the officers before they know anything of the matter ; the gallows stares her in the face, and if none else accuses her, so full is she of her danger and her guilt, that she probably betrays herself.　She at first would see no consequences to result from her crime but the getting rid of a present uneasiness ; she now sees the very worst　The whole seems to depend on the turn given to the imagination, on our immediate disposition to attend to this or that view of the subject, the evil or the good　As long as our intention is unknown to the world, before it breaks out into action, it seems to be deposited in our own bosoms, to be a mere feverish dream, and to be left with all its consequences under our imaginary control : but no sooner is it realised and known to others, than it appears to have escaped from our reach, we fancy the whole world are up in arms against us, and vengeance is ready to pursue and overtake us.　So in the pursuit of pleasure, we see only that side of the question which we approve ; the disagreeable consequences (which may take place) make no part of our intention or concern, or of the wayward exercise of our will : if they should happen we cannot help it ; they form an ugly and unwished-for contrast to our favourite speculation : we turn our thoughts another way, repeating the adage *Quod sic mihi ostendis incredulus odi.* It is a good remark in *Vivian Grey* that a bankrupt walks the streets the day before his name is in the Gazette

with the same erect and confident brow as ever, and only
feels the mortification of his situation after it becomes
known to others. Such is the force of sympathy, and its
power to take off the edge of internal conviction! As
long as we can impose upon the world, we can impose
upon ourselves, and trust to the flattering appearances,
though we know them to be false. We put off the evil
day as long as we can, make a jest of it as the certainty
becomes more painful, and refuse to acknowledge the
secret to ourselves till it can no longer be kept from all
the world. In short, we believe just as little or as much
as we please of those things in which our will can be supposed to interfere ; and it is only by setting aside our own
interests and inclinations on more general questions that
we stand any chance of arriving at a fair and rational
judgment. Those who have the largest hearts have the
soundest understandings ; and he is the truest philosopher
who can forget himself. This is the reason why philosophers are often said to be mad, for thinking only of the
abstract truth and of none of its worldly adjuncts—it
seems like an absence of mind, or as if the devil had got
into them ! If belief were not in some degree voluntary,
or were grounded entirely on strict evidence and absolute
proof, every one would be a martyr to his opinions, and we
should have no power of evading or glossing over those
matter-of-fact conclusions for which positive vouchers
could be produced, however painful these conclusions
might be to our own feelings, or offensive to the prejudices
of others.

ESSAY XVII.

A Farewell to Essay-writing.[1]

" This life is best, if quiet life is best."

Food, warmth, sleep, and a book; these are all I at present ask—the *ultima Thule* of my wandering desires. Do you not then wish for

> " A friend in your retreat,
> Whom you may whisper, solitude is sweet?"

Expected, well enough :—gone, still better. Such attractions are strengthened by distance. Nor a mistress? " Beautiful mask! I know thee!" When I can judge of the heart from the face, of the thoughts from the lips, I may again trust myself. Instead of these give me the robin red-breast, pecking the crumbs at the door, or warbling on the leafless spray, the same glancing form that has followed me wherever I have been, and " done its spiriting gently ;" or the rich notes of the thrush that startle the ear of winter, and seem to have drunk up the full draught of joy from the very sense of contrast. To these I adhere, and am faithful, for they are true to me ; and, dear in themselves, are dearer for the sake of what is departed, leading me back (by the hand) to that dreaming world, in the innocence of which they sat and made sweet music, waking the promise of future years, and answered by the eager throbbings of my own breast. But now " the credulous hope of mutual minds is o'er," and I turn back from the world that has deceived me, to nature that lent it a false beauty, and that keeps up the illusion of the past. As I quaff my libations of tea in a morning, I love to watch the clouds sailing from the west, and fancy that " the spring comes slowly up this way." In this

---

[1] Written at Winterslow, Feb. 20, 1828. See *Memoirs*, ii. 220, *et seq.*—Ed.

hope, while "fields are dank and ways are mire," I follow
the same direction to a neighbouring wood, where, having
gained the dry, level greensward, I can see my way for a
mile before me, closed in on each side by copse-wood, and
ending in a point of light more or less brilliant, as the
day is bright or cloudy. What a walk is this to me!
I have no need of book or companion—the days, the hours,
the thoughts of my youth are at my side, and blend with
the air that fans my cheek. Here I can saunter for hours,
bending my eye forward, stopping and turning to look
back, thinking to strike off into some less trodden path,
yet hesitating to quit the one I am in, afraid to snap the
brittle threads of memory. I remark the shining trunks
and slender branches of the birch trees, waving in the
idle breeze; or a pheasant springs up on whirring wing;
or I recall the spot where I once found a wood-pigeon at
the foot of a tree, weltering in its gore, and think how
many seasons have flown since "it left its little life in
air." Dates, names, faces come back—to what purpose?
Or why think of them now? Or rather why not think of
them oftener? We walk through life, as through a
narrow path, with a thin curtain drawn around it; behind
are ranged rich portraits, airy harps are strung—yet we
will not stretch forth our hands and lift aside the veil,
to catch glimpses of the one, or sweep the chords of the
other. As in a theatre, when the old-fashioned green
curtain drew up, groups of figures, fantastic dresses,
laughing faces, rich banquets, stately columns, gleaming
vistas appeared beyond; so we have only at any time to
"peep through the blanket of the past," to possess ourselves at once of all that has regaled our senses, that is
stored up in our memory, that has struck our fancy, that
has pierced our hearts :—yet to all this we are indifferent,
insensible, and seem intent only on the present vexation,
the future disappointment. If there is a Titian hanging
up in the room with me, I scarcely regard it : how then

should I be expected to strain the mental eye so far, or to throw down, by the magic spells of the will, the stone-walls that enclose it in the Louvre? There is one head there of which I have often thought, when looking at it, that nothing should ever disturb me again, and I would become the character it represents—such perfect calmness and self-possession reigns in it! Why do I not hang an image of this in some dusky corner of my brain, and turn an eye upon it ever and anon, as I have need of some such talisman to calm my troubled thoughts? The attempt is fruitless, if not natural; or, like that of the French, to hang garlands on the grave, and to conjure back the dead by miniature pictures of them while living! It is only some actual coincidence or local association that tends, without violence, to " open all the cells where memory slept." I can easily, by stooping over the long-sprent grass and clay cold clod, recall the tufts of 'prim-roses, or purple hyacinths, that formerly grew on the same spot, and cover the bushes with leaves and singing-birds, as they were eighteen summers ago ; or prolonging my walk and hearing the sighing gale rustle through a tall, straight wood at the end of it, can fancy that I dis-tinguish the cry of hounds, and the fatal group issuing from it, as in the tale of Theodore and Honoria. A moaning gust of wind aids the belief: I look once more to see whether the trees before me answer to the idea of the horror-stricken grove, and an air-built city towers over their grey tops.

> " Of all the cities in Romanian lands,
> The chief and most renown'd Ravenna stands." [1]

I return home resolved to read the entire poem through, and, after dinner, drawing my chair to the fire, and holding a small print close to my eyes, launch into the full tide of Dryden's couplets (a stream of sound), com-paring his didactic and descriptive pomp with the simple

[1] Dryden's *Theodore and Honoria,* princip.

pathos and picturesque truth of Boccacio's story, and
tasting with a pleasure, which none but an habitual reader
can feel, some quaint examples of pronunciation in this
accomplished versifier.

> "Which when Honoria view'd,
> The fresh *impulse* her former fright renew'd." [1]

> "And made th' *insult*, which in his grief appears,
> The means to mourn thee with my pious tears." [2]

These trifling instances of the wavering and unsettled
state of the language give double effect to the firm and
stately march of the verse, and make me dwell with a sort
of tender interest on the difficulties and doubts of an
earlier period of literature. They pronounced words then
in a manner which we should laugh at now; and they
wrote verse in a manner which we can do anything but
laugh at. The pride of a new acquisition seems to give
fresh confidence to it; to impel the rolling syllables
through the moulds provided for them, and to overflow
the envious bounds of rhyme into time-honoured triplets.

What sometimes surprises me in looking back to the
past, is, with the exception already stated, to find myself
so little changed in the time. The same images and
trains of thought stick by me: I have the same tastes,
likings, sentiments, and wishes that I had then. One
great ground of confidence and support has, indeed, been
struck from under my feet; but I have made it up to
myself by proportionable pertinacity of opinion. The
success of the great cause, to which I had vowed myself,
was to me more than all the world: I had a strength in
its strength, a resource which I knew not of, till it failed
me for the second time.

> "Fall'n was Glenartny's stately tree!
> Oh! ne'er to see Lord Ronald more!"

---

[1] Dryden's *Theodore and Honoria*, princip.
[2] Dryden's *Sigismonda and Guiscardo*.

It was not till I saw the axe laid to the root, that I found the full extent of what I had to lose and suffer. But my conviction of the right was only established by the triumph of the wrong; and my earliest hopes will be my last regrets. One source of this unbendingness (which some may call obstinacy), is that, though living much alone, I have never worshipped the Echo. I see plainly enough that black is not white, that the grass is green, that kings are not their subjects; and, in such self-evident cases, do not think it necessary to collate my opinions with the received prejudices. In subtler questions, and matters that admit of doubt, as I do not impose my opinion on others without a reason, so I will not give up mine to them without a better reason; and a person calling me names, or giving himself airs of authority, does not convince me of his having taken more pains to find out the truth than I have, but the contrary. Mr. Gifford once said, that " while I was sitting over my gin and tobacco-pipes, I fancied myself a Leibnitz." He did not so much as know that I had ever read a metaphysical book:—was I therefore, out of complaisance or deference to him, to forget whether I had or not? Leigh Hunt is puzzled to reconcile the shyness of my pretensions with the inveteracy and sturdiness of my principles. I should have thought they were nearly the same thing. Both from disposition and habit, I can *assume* nothing in word, look, or manner. I cannot steal a march upon public opinion in any way. My standing upright, speaking loud, entering a room gracefully, proves nothing; therefore I neglect these ordinary means of recommending myself to the good graces and admiration of strangers (and, as it appears, even of philosophers and friends). Why? Because I have other resources, or, at least, am absorbed in other studies and pursuits. Suppose this absorption to be extreme, and even morbid—that I have brooded over an idea till it has become a kind of substance in my brain, that I have reasons for a thing which I have found out with much labour and pains, and to which I can scarcely do justice without the utmost violence of exertion (and that only to a few persons)—is this a reason for my playing off my out-of-the-way notions in all companies, wearing a prim and self-complacent air, as if I were "the admired of all observers?" or is it not rather an argument, (together with a want of animal spirits,) why I should retire into myself, and perhaps acquire a nervous and uneasy look, from a consciousness of the disproportion between the interest and conviction I feel on certain subjects, and my ability to communicate what weighs upon my own mind to others? If my ideas, which I do not avouch, but suppose, lie below the surface, why am I to be always attempting to dazzle superficial people with them, or smiling, delighted, at my own want of success?

In matters of taste and feeling, one proof that my conclusions have not been quite shallow or hasty, is the circumstance of their having been lasting. I have the same favourite books, pictures, passages that I ever had : I may therefore presume that they will last me my life— nay, I may indulge a hope that my thoughts will survive me. This continuity of impression is the only thing on which I pride myself. Even Lamb, whose relish of certain things is as keen and earnest as possible, takes a surfeit of admiration, and I should be afraid to ask about his select authors or particular friends, after a lapse of ten years. As to myself, any one knows where to have me. What I have once made up my mind to, I abide by to the end of the chapter. One cause of my independence of opinion is, I believe, the liberty I give to others, or the very diffidence and distrust of making converts. I should be an excellent man on a jury. I might say little, but should starve "the other eleven obstinate fellows" out. I remember Mr. Godwin writing to Mr. Wordsworth, that "his tragedy of *Antonio* could not fail of success." It

was damned past all redemption. I said to Mr. Wordsworth that I thought this a natural consequence ; for how
could any one have a dramatic turn of mind who judged
entirely of others from himself? Mr. Godwin might be
convinced of the excellence of his work; but how could he
know that others would be convinced of it, unless by
supposing that they were as wise as himself, and as
infallible critics of dramatic poetry—so many Aristotles
sitting in judgment on Euripides! This shows why pride
is connected with shyness and reserve; for the really
proud have not so high an opinion of the generality as to
suppose that they can understand them, or that there is
any common measure between them. So Dryden exclaims
of his opponents with bitter disdain—

" Nor can I think what thoughts they can conceive."

I have not sought to make partisans, still less did I dream
of making enemies ; and have therefore kept my opinions
myself, whether they were currently adopted or not.   To
get others to come into our ways of thinking, we must go
over to theirs : and it is necessary to follow, in order to
lead.   At the time I lived here formerly, I had no suspicion that I should ever become a voluminous writer,
yet I had just the same confidence in my feelings before
I had ventured to air them in public as I have now.
Neither the outcry *for* or *against* moves me a jot: I
do not say that the one is not more agreeable than the
other.
   Not far from the spot where I write, I first read
Chaucer's *Flower and Leaf,* and was charmed with that
young beauty, shrouded in her bower, and listening with
ever-fresh delight to the repeated song of the nightingale
close by her—the impression of the scene, the vernal
landscape, the cool of the morning, the gushing notes of
the songstress,

" And ayen methought she sung close by mine ear "

is as vivid as if it had been of yesterday; and nothing can persuade me that that is not a fine poem. I do not find this impression conveyed in Dryden's version, and therefore nothing can persuade me that that is as fine. I used to walk out at this time with Mr. and Miss Lamb[1] of an evening, to look at the Claude Lorraine skies over our heads melting from azure into purple and gold, and to gather mushrooms, that sprung up at our feet, to throw into our hashed mutton at supper. I was at that time an enthusiastic admirer of Claude, and could dwell for ever on one or two of the finest prints from him hung round my little room; the fleecy flocks, the bending trees, the winding streams, the groves, the nodding temples, the air-wove hills, and distant sunny vales; and tried to translate them into their lovely living hues. People then told me that Wilson was much superior to Claude: I did not believe them. Their pictures have since been seen together at the British Institution, and all the world have come into my opinion. I have not, on that account, given it up. I will not compare our hashed mutton with Amelia's; but it put us in mind of it, and led to a discussion, sharply seasoned and well sustained, till midnight, the result of which appeared some years after in the *Edinburgh Review.* Have I a better opinion of those criticisms on that account, or should I therefore maintain them with greater vehemence and tenaciousness? Oh no: Both rather with less, now that they are before the public, and it is for them to make their election.

It is in looking back to such scenes that I draw my best consolation for the future. Later impressions come and go, and serve to fill up the intervals; but these are my standing resource, my true classics. If I have had few real pleasures or advantages, my ideas, from their sinewy texture, have been to me in the nature of realities; and if I should not be able to add to the stock, I can live by

[1] Referring to the year 1809. See *Memoirs,* i. 172-4.—ED.

2 H

husbanding the interest. As to my speculations, there is little to admire in them but my admiration of others; and whether they have an echo in time to come or not, I have learned to set a grateful value on the past, and am content to wind up the account of what is personal only to myself and the immediate circle of objects in which I have moved, with an act of easy oblivion,

" And curtain-close such scene from every future view."

THE END.

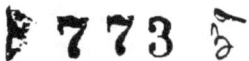

LONDON: PRINTED BY WILLIAM CLOWES AND SONS, STAMFORD STREET AND CHARING CROSS.